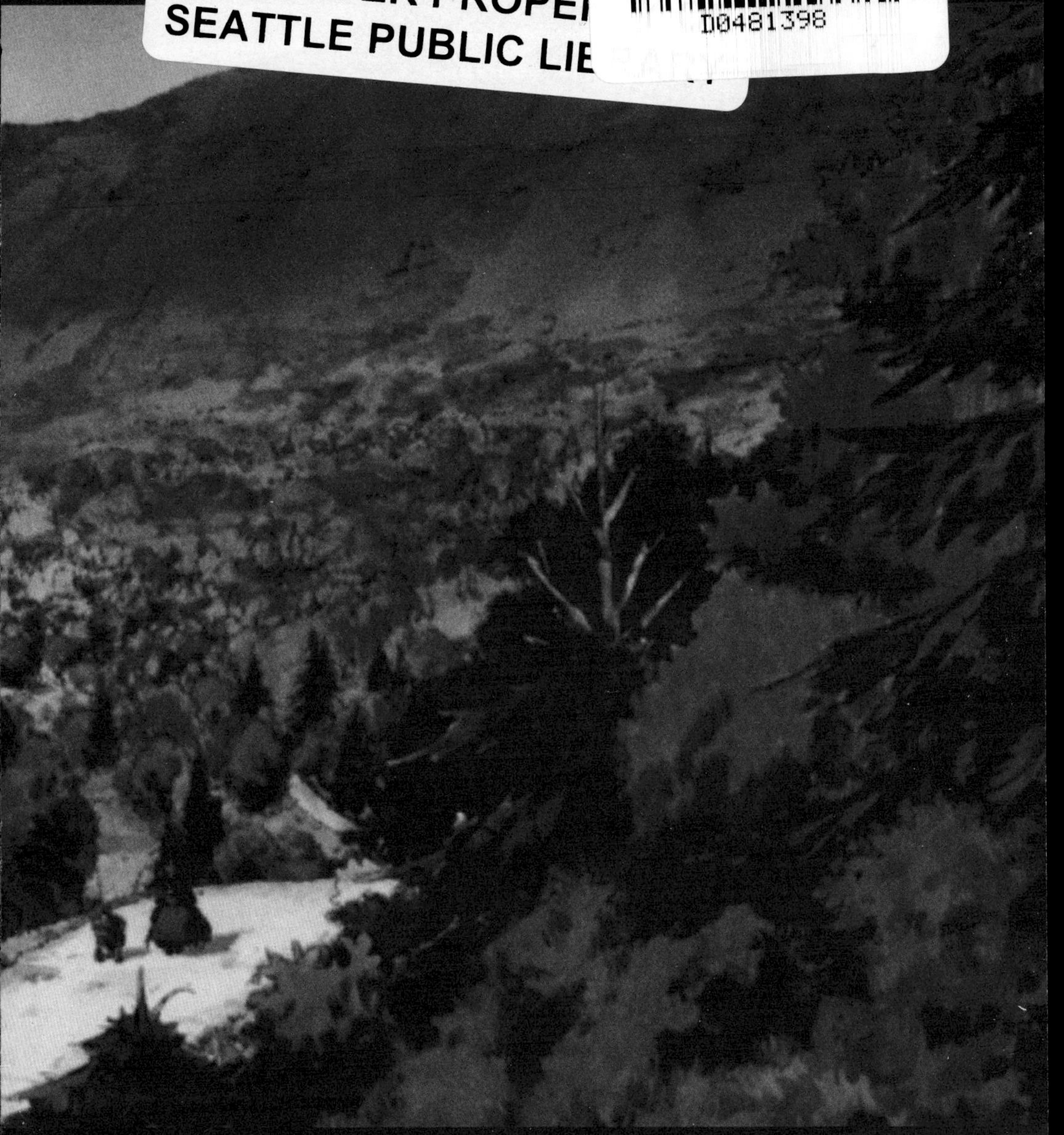

STAR WARS

RONIN

A VISIONS NOVEL

STAR WARS

RONIN

A VISIONS NOVEL

EMMA
MIEKO
CANDON

NEW YORK

Copyright © 2021 by Lucasfilm Ltd. & ®
or ™ where indicated. All rights reserved.

Published in the United States by Del Rey,
an imprint of Random House, a division of
Penguin Random House LLC, New York.

DEL REY is a registered trademark and the CIRCLE colophon
is a trademark of Penguin Random House LLC.

Hardback ISBN 978-0-593-35866-5
International edition ISBN 978-0-593-49697-8
Ebook ISBN 978-0-593-35867-2

Printed in the United States of America on acid-free paper

randomhousebooks.com

2 4 6 8 9 7 5 3 1

First Edition

Book design by Elizabeth A. D. Eno

To every soul who ever hoped to write their heart into the stars

A long time ago in a galaxy far, far away. . . .

At the far edge of the galaxy, a lone wanderer roams the Outer Rim. In defiance of Imperial edict, the RONIN dares to wear a certain blade on his sash. None know his name, nor what he seeks—only that death and disaster follow in his footsteps. No doubt the gods themselves have cursed his forgotten name. . . .

STAR WARS

RONIN

A VISIONS NOVEL

CHAPTER
ONE

TWO MONTHS AFTER the Ronin arrived on the Outer Rim world of Genbara, he ran out of credits. This concerned him less than it did B5-56, who took every opportunity to scold.

"Look at it this way," he told his trundling companion. "No need to worry about where we'll sleep."

A man with no coin had no reason to pace his trek in terms of outposts and inns. He could pay for no bed. Thus, he could wander to his heart's content, and the woodland vistas of Genbara did reward the wandering. Vast stretches of pine were interrupted only by patches of farmland, claimed by settlers rebuilding their lives far from the scars war had left on worlds nearer the galaxy's Core.

The Ronin slept that night under a small lean-to that a local woodcutter had told him of the day before, when he passed the old man's hut on his way into the mountains.

"The mountains, sir? Are you sure?" the woodcutter had said as he sucked his teeth. They sat on the veranda of the man's hut and shared a pot of stale tea. It had been the last in the Ronin's tin, but he offered it freely in exchange for hot water and company. "You'll want to follow this road up, past the ridge. It will take you to a village in the valley. If it's still there."

An ominous thing to say. To the Ronin, it suggested he was on the right course. B5 saw the look in his eye. The droid's own eye flashed from red to blue under his thatched hat as he murmured a warning.

The woodcutter, who had no facility with Binary, mistook the dome-headed astromech's sound for nervousness. He grinned. "There were four villages up there, little droid, when I first built my humble hut. Then there were three, then two—now just the one. Word is they angered a spirit. A spirit that doesn't take kindly to settlers."

Yet he thinks the spirits don't mind him? said a voice in the Ronin's ear.

"Mountains are different," the Ronin said.

The woodcutter, who thought he had been spoken to, nodded sagely. B5 swiveled a baleful eye to fix on the Ronin in what was likely supposed to be a glare. The Ronin pretended not to notice it, but he did remind himself to be careful. On occasion, when in the company of others, his responses to the voice were dismissed. On other occasions, they were not, and this could go quite badly. If the village in the mountains still stood, he would be among new people soon, and they sounded like a superstitious lot.

The following morning, he stretched the cold out of his limbs as he rose and ate half a ration-stick from his pouch, the last remaining. The chewing was slow going, with the ache; he rubbed at the line of old metal that supported his jaw from ear to ear.

B5 grumbled at him all the while, calling him old and simple besides. Surely, the droid said, his master remembered that he had the means to acquire enough credits to fund his fool journey until it killed him—or at least enough to purchase a more up-to-date prosthetic. Yet he hoarded his bounty to the point that some shamefully mundane evil would doubtless get him first. Perhaps the chill, or infection, or worse.

"You know I would be more foolish to try to sell one of these," said the Ronin, patting the treasures hidden in the folds of his robes. "Where would I say I got it?"

Then what do you plan to do with your winnings, other than collect them? the voice asked, rather bitterly at that.

He couldn't give her an answer. Not one she could stand.

Moved by a reflexive guilt, he glanced at the inner lining of the long hooded vest he wore as a cloak. The robe had weighed the same for at least a year now, when he had last added to the collection within. The crystals sewn into the seam glinted as if in greeting, letting off red flickers that illuminated his fingers, elated by the promise of his attention. They wanted him to touch them, to take them and give them use.

He let the robe fall closed, crystals untouched. Here was his reason, even if she didn't care for it: So long as he carried them, they could bring no further harm.

Outside of what harm you commit, she said.

"If you wish me dead," he said as he stepped out onto the needle-strewn path between the pines, "you have only to point the way."

Go on to your little village, then.

Experience told him that she would provide no further advice. After all, she would doubtless prefer that whatever he met in the village be the end of him rather than the other way around.

The chill of the night bled into spring as the sun rose. The Ronin stopped on the ridge overlooking the last village left in the mountains, B5-56 at his side. In the distance, at the far end of a pine-ridden valley, the swooping lines of a crashed ship gleamed whitely. Some sleek, gallant vessel that had met its ignoble end face-first in the sloping mountain-side. Its silver hull shone like a star under the fierce morning light.

Poetic, wouldn't you say? said the voice.

"I would say it's broken," said the Ronin.

B5 whined, disappointed.

"Doing what again? I don't know what you're talking about."

B5 sighed as magnificently as Binary allowed.

Together, they set off down the path to the last village in the mountains. Somewhere within it, they would find the Ronin's quarry—or they would find nothing. A cowardly part of him hoped for the latter. Perhaps it was this part that made him slow as they reached the last rise before the village proper, where a teahouse stood beside an ancient bending pine. A troubling odor wafted out of the structure into the road, and despite B5's scold—didn't they have somewhere to be?—the Ronin let it lure him to the door. He found the shopkeep—a tidy Sullustan fellow whose rounded cheeks had grayed with age—seated on the clean-swept floor, fiddling with a rectangular power droid's wiring and bemoaning its temperamental nature.

The Ronin's shadow startled the shopkeep, who scrambled upright to study the stranger. His wary black eyes flicked up to take in the Ronin's intimidating height, draped in road-stained garb, and down to the two scabbards hung conspicuously at his waist.

You look entirely evil, she said.

The Ronin frowned; the shopkeep flinched. "No, not you," said the Ronin. Then he cursed, which didn't help. "Your power droid. It's leaking. I could smell it from the road. I can fix it for you."

The shopkeep remained wary until B5 peered out from behind the Ronin's cloak. The droid greeted the shopkeep and apologized for his companion's dreadful appearance all in one go. Feed him, said B5, and he'll fix any droid you point him to.

Even ten years ago, the Ronin might have argued for dignity's sake— was he to be some manner of beggar, exchanging menial repairs for menial returns? Now he knew himself with the humility of age. When the shopkeep agreed, he simply asked where the man kept his tools.

The voice said nothing, though her impatience weighed on his mind like the threat of incoming rain. She would have preferred he throw himself boldly into whatever she had lying in wait. He preferred to make himself useful.

The power droid proved an easy enough fix. The Ronin had only to work off the stained front of its chassis and reach around its cabling to identify the leak. His fingers came away silty with exhaust debris that had disrupted the pathway of the power coupling. He asked the shopkeep if there was a sizable transmitter, or perhaps a chronometer he could bear to live without. The shopkeep returned with an ancient holoprojector, which the Ronin deftly dismantled. He found he only needed one of the projector's two safety sealants to properly contain the leak and had the whole thing cleaned and fitted back together within the hour.

"Mortifying, isn't it?" said the shopkeep to B5 as they watched the Ronin work. "I could have repaired an astromech like yourself in my sleep, back during the war. Still could, perhaps. But they never asked the specialists to look after our own power droids, and here I am, utterly helpless when it stops warming my tea."

When the Ronin stood, the shopkeep ushered him out into the shaded seating area just outside the teahouse. He promised to provide a proper pot of his most exquisite blend, which was even now steeping on the humming power droid. "To think I mistook you for a bandit!"

The Ronin merely nodded thanks. From this vantage, he could see the entirety of the village proper. A humble affair, mostly comprising two rows of wooden slat and thatch-roofed houses reinforced with the discarded durasteel remnants of ships that had fallen in the war; these were lined neatly across from each other, aside from the handful of other outlying structures and a pair of simple, unfortified watchtowers. A grand storehouse occupied the center of town, hung with banners and protected by an old ship door. Most of the villagers worked the rice fields that sustained them, while some met in the central square before the storehouse to discuss this or that spot of business, and children ran cackling through the streets. A peaceful tableau. The sort only delicately held, this far into the Outer Rim.

Peace is scarce and dearly bought, she said.

This time, the Ronin managed to hold his tongue, though B5 detected a twitch in his lips; the droid beeped irritably, for which he earned a scold from the shopkeep while the man delivered the tea. B5 primly informed the shopkeep that it was rude to say things others couldn't understand.

"Thank you," the shopkeep chuckled in the Empire's tongue—he thought himself chided. He poured an expertly steeped cup for the Ronin, who accepted the brew and found himself pleased by the local peculiarity of the aroma, faintly sweet with pine.

"How did you come to be traveling the countryside on foot, sir?" asked the shopkeep.

"A certain someone is always after me about exercise," said the Ronin.

B5 whistled hotly.

The shopkeep chuckled. "Of course you're right, he should listen to your sage advice."

The Ronin was inclined to weigh in on B5's smug silence, but his attention twitched away. He let his eyes glide after what had pulled his mind and was drawn toward an oncoming rumble, echoing from the mountains. The source of the sound soon tore down the path the Ronin had walked only an hour before.

An enormously thick and armored vessel, one that had been built for war. It thundered down the mountain path, past the teahouse, toward the village. No branches snapped as it plowed through the trees. It had come this way before. The teahouse trembled in its wake and the shopkeep cursed its passage, as rattled as his teacups.

The sound of the vessel's approach soon reached the town. The figures in the field dropped their tools. Adults grasped at children as they fled toward their homes, sheltering the young with their own bodies.

Scarce peace indeed.

"Bandits—they've been hiding in a deserted village across the mountain," the shopkeep said, low and apologetic as he ducked behind a wall, peeking down at his neighbors below. "Soldiers. Ex-soldiers—or the remnants of Sith troops. We don't know. Does it matter?"

That explained what had happened to the other mountain villages. Angry spirits were, in the Ronin's experience, much harder to come by than bandits.

Will you not go to them? she asked. She meant to tease him. Goad him, more like. It would suit her if he ran toward danger the second impulse told him to. But impulse would so likely see him dead before he accomplished his goal. Moreover, he didn't yet know if this was the sort of bandit who had earned his effort—or if the greater danger yet lay in wait within the village. Soon enough, he would see.

B5 whined lowly, as if his master's thoughts were audible. The Ronin couldn't be certain whether B5 wanted him to go now or if he feared his master going at all. Perhaps he wished for some impossible alternative course of action to present itself. B5 did hate to see the Ronin bleed, and it was all but certain that today, he would.

Below, the armored vessel came to a looming halt in the village square, doubly as tall as any of the houses. There, it opened its doors.

Three slabs of metal broke from its sides and extended forward into ramps, down which the bandits marched. They wore scraps of discarded armor—blaster-scarred white helmets, shoulder plates, greaves—and little else but loincloths, bandannas, and armbands to mark themselves to one another. They fancied themselves mighty for their nakedness.

Such brave men, who stormed down the street to kick open wooden doors and drag out crying villagers.

The voice chuckled. The Ronin gritted his teeth and sipped his tea.

"Sir, it's dangerous—please, wait inside," the shopkeep urged, an arm slung around B5's head, as if in fear the astromech would skid off.

Indeed, two bandits had turned their eyes up toward the teahouse. The Ronin frowned down at them. The distance was too great for them to properly fix on his silhouette, and he had no fear of bandit blasters.

In any case, it was not these bandits who held tight to the edge of his attention, that drove him to study all before him—it was some other presence, a hidden thing, tense and poised to strike. If the Ronin hadn't seen his quarry, he suspected it was because he had not seen them *yet*.

Such was the scene below: The bandits gathered the villagers together in the dusty square. The better to dispose of them, should they so decide. Every last family member was caught, dragged, and made to huddle together in a display of abject helplessness.

"Thank you, thank you for the fine welcome," crowed a bandit wearing the orange pauldron of a commander. "Now it's time to pay up. We've come to collect this year's taxes."

The long-haired bandit beside him leered. "That was an order! Which one of you's the chief?"

A figure emerged from within the crowd, small, lithe, and wild-haired. A child, no older than ten. He walked forward, posture stiff, and in a clear voice declared, "I am the current village chief. And you—you've taken enough."

The commander leaned back, appraising the child. "You? I know you. You're the chief's son." He spat. "Running away and leaving his village to a child. What a coward your father must be."

He broke into laughter, and the other bandits laughed with him.

Up above, the shopkeep whispered to the Ronin, sweat beading his brow. "The village chief is sick," he said, voice tight with anger and with fear. "The boy—he's too brave."

"So valiant!" a bandit howled in the square below.

"'You've taken enough!'" another bandit simpered. "Ahh, you're adorable, kid."

"A brave speech, boy," said the commander, when the laughter had died down. "But a man's word is only as good as his weapon, I'm afraid. Now where's yours? Hmm?"

The boy chief met the commander's leer head-on. That alone nearly made the Ronin stir from his seat.

Then the boy chief's arm shot straight into the air.

As it flew up, two shots fired, one from either side of the village. The Ronin tracked the trajectory of each bolt.

One had come from a rooftop near the square, another from one of the watchtowers overlooking the village. On the rooftop stood a three-eyed Gran in light armor, carrying a rifle with a bayonet blade, flat teeth bared. Up in the tower, a well-wrapped Tusken, already taking their next aim with a long sniper rifle. Gran and Tusken each fired another bolt, and another, rapid and precise. With each blast, a bandit fell.

"Well done, guards—I leave the rest to you!" the boy chief cried, and he dashed out of the square, leading the villagers in a herd. Not a single straggler was left behind. They had practiced this evacuation.

What a clever bunch of mice, trapping the cats, the voice said.

"Don't be rude," said the Ronin.

The shopkeep was too nervously enthralled by the violence to mind his guest's muttering.

Below, more hired bodyguards burst out of their hiding places—bounty hunters, by the look of their sturdy, mismatched gear.

A bug-eyed silver protocol droid with a blaster-blackened chassis stalked out of an alley, their rotary blaster cannon mowing down the bandits in the square.

A lean, scaled Trandoshan hurtled down the main drag, taking advantage of his long arms and long weapons—a blade and a naginata—to carve through any bandit who dared cross his path.

A floating dome of a cockpit exploded out from a pile of crates, piloted by a dextrous Dug crouched in its center. A blade hung from each of the five insectile legs sprouting from the drone's underbelly, and it whirled in a storm of slashes as its pilot howled a battle cry.

A stray bolt lanced up from the fight and caught a support beam of the teahouse; the shopkeep gasped, appalled in the midst of victory.

The Ronin, meanwhile, could only frown. Something on the wind kept his attention squared not on the bodyguards, nor the bandits desperately ducking for cover, but on the bandits' massive vessel. He felt the voice's attention settle there too.

For all the violence the bodyguards had unleashed, that lurking tension remained. It bled into the Ronin's limbs, winding ever tighter in each of them as a hatch on the bandit vessel's flat roof slid open.

From that hatch rose a figure, carried by a lift. Her dark cloak and veil hid her from the glaring sun as she stood atop the vessel, a short staff held loosely in her grasp. The Ronin shivered at the sight of her.

Well, said the voice. *Run along now.*

The tea tasted sour at the back of his throat. His fingers tightened minutely on the teacup. He had no reason to doubt what he saw.

Yet something held him still. Perhaps that it had been a good year, at least, since he last faced one of his quarry. Perhaps that he did not yet have *proof* of what he faced. After all, he didn't recognize the veiled figure's stance. He felt that he should have.

As if I've ever lied to you. What else do you think she could be?

He didn't know. Yet neither did he move. The world turned without him.

The Trandoshan now stood in the square amidst a scattering of bodies, his blade and naginata at the ready, as he turned his sharp-toothed maw to face the bandits' vessel. "Surrender," he called to the bandit standing over them all. "Do so, and we might just spare your life."

The bandit raised her staff to her shoulder. The sneer carried in her snarl. "You're confused."

"What?" the Trandoshan growled.

"*You'll* surrender." Her head tilted back. "Although I'll kill you anyway."

The bandit had barely finished when the protocol droid at the edge of the square let loose a stream of blasterfire from its rotary cannon alongside a string of curses. In the blink of an eye, the bandit unfurled her weapon.

From the end of her staff, six red blades of light extended outward in a deadly flower. When she spun the staff, it formed a white-red shield of light that deflected every last one of the blasts.

"Red lightsabers—she's one of the Sith!" the protocol droid shouted.

More than anything, it was a warning.

The bodyguards' following cascade of blasterfire had an air of panic. They no longer fought to win, but to survive, no doubt driven by memories of the war and the fiendish devastation that followed each Sith warrior.

The bandit deflected every bolt, her lightsaber parasol a whirl of color. One shot ricocheted off her shield and screeched through the sky, straight into the teahouse.

The Ronin moved at a speed he hadn't asked from himself in years. In the blink of an eye, he no longer sat before a low table but stood beside the curved pine in front of the teahouse. When he glanced behind him, he saw smoke and rubble. The blast had carved a hole straight through the teahouse wall. The shopkeep had fallen back and, thankfully, the Ronin did not smell singed flesh.

The scorch of metal, now. That was a different matter.

Beside the shopkeep lay B5-56, twitching on the floor, hat knocked askew. Blue shivers of electricity washed over the droid's surfaces. An old heat crept up from the Ronin's gut to his head, matched only by an accompanying chill.

He had delayed too long.

I told you, didn't I? she whispered, although there was a bite to it. Whatever she felt toward him, B5 was another matter.

"S-sir, what should we . . ." the shopkeep stammered, too shocked to hide behind his remaining walls, let alone flee into the mountains.

"Shopkeep," said the Ronin, "do you think you can repair him?" He picked up the teakettle from where it had fallen on the floor as the shop-keep nodded uncertainly. "Make sure my partner is fully operational by the time this water boils."

The shopkeep looked from the Ronin to B5, large eyes unblinking. He nodded once, then again. "Yes—yes, of course!"

A bit of the commander in you yet, I see, she said as the Ronin turned to leave the teahouse. He found he lacked the stomach to reply.

CHAPTER TWO

"KEEP FIRING! DON'T give her a chance to strike!" the Trandoshan called to his fellows.

They panicked so quickly, these rats. The bandit—the Sith—smirked behind her half-mask, a piece of lacquered armor wrought in the long-toothed grin of a proper demon. It had been so long since she was last correctly named. The people of these mountains called her all manner of superstitious things—an evil spirit, a devil witch, a god of foul luck—or they called her bandit, thief, and villain. But Sith? They were too eager to believe the Sith extinct.

So, she would relish the opportunity to recall her truest self.

The bounty hunters—for that was what they were—fired upon her in a frantic wave. The Sith flourished her lightsaber forward, letting it bloom. The auxiliary fit onto the hilt channeled the power of the kyber crystal straight, then outward into six blades that, when she spun the weapon, resembled a parasol. It was, more important, a conveniently deadly shield.

For now, manipulating the physical lift caused by the parasol's spin let her leap up, carried skyward. The shots drew up short. Fear. It throbbed in time with her eager heart.

"No good!" the Trandoshan howled to his underlings. "Fall back! Don't let her engage in close combat! Hrk—"

The Sith had landed before him. As she stood, her hand swept up, and with the black current of the Force, the bandit grasped the Trandoshan by the scaled throat as effortlessly as if she had taken it with her own fingers. She squeezed until his eyes bulged, pleased by the flow of her power. Living things outside of her own body rarely moved so lithely with her intent. Something in the air today had sharpened her.

"What were you saying about close combat?" she asked.

The bounty hunters cried out, fearful for one of their fellows. The Sith paid them no mind. Blasterfire sounded behind her again. Her men had risen, invigorated by her turn on the field. They knew they couldn't lose whenever she deigned to join them.

The Trandoshan gargled, feet kicking at the air. His eyes darted from side to side, to where his men were now hunted by hers. Her own gaze never strayed. She heard screams. Thuds. He gasped. She suspected he had just seen someone die.

Some part of the Sith sympathized, even understood. But she had no true feeling for men who lived for the vainglory of credits.

"Did you really think you could stand a chance against a Dark Lord?" she mused.

The bounty hunter struggled to speak, words barely able to escape his mouth with her hold on his throat. "R-run! We can't hope to—"

No last words for men without creed. She dropped the Trandoshan. He fell toward the ground, and in the same moment she thrust with her sword arm. Her six short blades speared him through, unfurling on the opposite side of his corpse in a burst of red light.

On the far side of the square, the protocol droid shuddered. Cursed. Opened fire with its rotary cannon.

The Sith flung the body off her saber and lunged toward the droid. Its circuitry couldn't hope to keep up with her as she was, a living torrent bright with the white flare of the Force. She struck the droid down with a swift bisection—and halted.

As it clattered to the sand at her feet, she inhaled smoke. Blasterfire thickened the air with its searing heat, and on the ash she tasted some new shadow.

The Sith straightened and turned just so to glance over her shoulder. There, in the mouth of the village's lone cross street that led to the square, stood a darkness of a man. Tall and tattered at his edges, though his broad frame and steady step brought to mind the inexorable chill of a glacier.

Smoke roiled between them. She realized abruptly the wrongness of him: Bright power seethed within a murky shell.

"You're no villager," she said. "Who dares face me?"

"A simple wanderer," he said, and his voice curled at the edge of her memory like parchment set alight.

Her lip twisted behind her mask. She knew a threat when she met it. Fire called to fire, no matter how—or for what mad reason—it tried to douse itself.

She shucked the lightsaber's parasol auxiliary and tossed the slender contraption forward. Her blood told her to meet the man with her blade. The auxiliary landed tip-first on the gravel of the village square. Tottered.

The Sith flew. She leapt up through the air, saber raised, and brought it crackling down upon the man's skull.

Until she—it—the world stopped. She shuddered in midair, muscles trembling with kinetic energy suddenly seized. Her body would not move. Neither would her lightsaber. It hovered, centimeters from the man's impassive face, caught with his naked palms.

No—between. A sliver of space sheathed his hands from her sizzling blade, a fraction pulsating with the feverish pressure of white flare shot through with black current. The Force.

"You. You're a Jedi," she snarled.

The very word disgusted her. She so rarely had reason to even think it, here on the edge of civilization. She would have to now. For what reason would a Jedi, vaunted protector of the Empire, have to go slumming in the Outer Rim? None but her, the lone surviving Sith in this half-forgotten sector of the galaxy. This man thought he could kill her.

Let him try.

The man—the Jedi—shoved her away explosively, rejecting every last one of her molecules in a raging white burst. She flew back, her body a puppet. Instinct brought her limbs back in sync. It was as if for a furious moment her body had been so much nothing. She twisted in the air and landed hard on her heels.

Blade out, she faced the man, eyes wide as she tracked his every breath. His hand rested by his hip, by one of the hilts at his belt. Two scabbards. Not just a Jedi—a *knight*, deemed by his masters to be worthy of a blade.

So much the better. She would enjoy wrenching it from his dying grasp.

"It's been a long time since I killed a Jedi." She remembered her last. She, a whip of a girl. He, a grimacing tower of a man. He had split as cleanly as the protocol droid now sparking on the far side of the square.

She came for the Jedi again. No man died simply because she wished it.

And again, her blade met a jarring stop. This one was more honest and true, a twinned flare of light. Another lightsaber clashed against her own—crimson.

No Jedi would carry such a color. Unless—to mock her? No.

The Sith dodged back, lightsaber held up to ward off the other. "You . . ."

The man's hand moved by his waist. She tensed to meet whatever blow he would bring to her next. Instead a whistling screech came from behind. She whipped around.

The protocol droid's severed torso hurtled toward her through the air, sailing on the black current. She sliced through it and spun back to face her opponent—the man had already lunged with blinding speed, his blade up.

"Coward," she hissed, dodging back again.

"It's a shame I'm not a Jedi," the man said when he landed, head tilted as if in apology. "You might have had a chance."

The Sith bared her teeth behind her mask. She straightened and flung off her cloak, revealing her billowing white hair, matched by the white mark on her brow. She wished to face him unimpeded.

No Jedi indeed. And indeed, a shame as well. A Jedi, she might have understood. This man, however . . . All she knew for certain was that she could not afford to second-guess one of her own.

The bandits have killed another of those guards, the voice said in his ear.

The Ronin's jaw twitched. He wished she wouldn't interrupt his focus. Then again, she wanted to see him dead at the Sith bandit's feet.

I'm sorry, is this distracting?

"Is it?" he muttered under his breath.

"Talking to yourself, old man?" taunted the bandit as she advanced on him, her white hair a blaze.

He had managed to draw her out of the village, across the fields, toward the river that coursed down the center of the valley. He had seen the rapids glinting between the trees when he stopped on the ridge from which he first saw the village. He couldn't spare a glance as they neared it, but the rush of water filled his ears. The current was fast. If he could shove the bandit in—

The bandit's next lunge drove him to hop onto the skewed trunk of an ancient tree that jutted over the river, out of her reach. She leapt after him. Her blade flashed behind her, severing the trunk.

All of them splashed into the river, and the Ronin's balance wavered as he steadied himself on the now floating tree.

The bandit took the moment of his imbalance to throw herself forward again, straight down the length of deadwood. He dodged around her and unleashed an upward cut as he went. The slash halved her mask and sent it flying into the air. She rounded on him in the next second, as if she had not just lost a vital piece of armor.

Someone had trained her, years ago. She wielded her lightsaber with a direct intensity, aiming always to kill—the sort of bladework he associated with battlefield instruction. But the next dodge, which brought her out of range, that one had the fluidity of forms practiced on a training mat.

Now they've rounded up the last of the villagers, the voice said. *Right on schedule, I suppose.*

The Ronin couldn't respond before the bandit brought her lightsaber down on his, again and again. The pure physical power of her blows made their log bob in the raging waters. He could only weave around her after each strike, which seemed to infuriate him.

Let her kill you or take care of her already, she said. *This is getting cruel.*

Such confidence. He needed to borrow some for himself. He felt the slowness of his muscles, the lag in his bones. Age, perhaps. An absence of proper practice, more likely. Sensitivity to the Force faded in those who neglected to cultivate it, and he had spent too long only searching. This bandit, conversely, had fed her strength until it roared like a deadly inferno.

He did need to end this soon. The water eddied ever faster under the surface, and he heard, not far, the roar of a cascade. A waterfall. A theatrical sort of interruption, and not one he cared to navigate.

A new voice called to them then. A man raced up the crest of a hill overlooking the river—a surviving bandit carrying a banner. "Boss! Bounty hunters taken care of—and we've got the village chief kid!"

The Sith bandit's mouth twisted into a toothy grin as she glared at the Ronin. "There. We don't fight fair either. Drop your weapon."

The Ronin squared his jaw; how long had it been since he left the teahouse?

Long enough, she promised, as if she stood just behind his ear. He couldn't trust her with his life, but he could trust her not to lie. She didn't like to, and she never did what she didn't like.

He sheathed the lightsaber in its scabbard, wrapped snug in his sash beside its companion, though his sword hand hovered there. His other hand hung naturally beside it. There was a narrow band on this wrist, simple and black. It remained inert.

"I told you to throw down your weapon, not sheathe it," the bandit snapped. She sneered. "Or do you not mind who dies for you?"

No faith to spare? she asked. *You trust him or you don't.*

His thumb brushed the interior of the cuff—the fraction that faced his torso. A pale circle the size of his knuckle lit up on it and blinked red, red, blue.

* * *

This is how the voice laid it out for him, later:

B5-56 shivered to life under the shopkeep's hands. The shopkeep had worked with frenetic obsession, ever on the verge of petrified terror. He had kept his attention fixed on the astromech, feverishly ignoring the screams and wails of his neighbors in the square below. He only ever paused to stare, momentarily, at the water simmering in the kettle.

It was, indeed, poetic, the synchronization of the kettle's screech with B5's revival. The Sullustan shopkeep barely threw himself out of the way as the droid tore out of the remains of the teahouse, snapping free of power cables.

B5 skidded toward the rise and down the hill, then launched forward into the air with his thrusters—an improbable missile darting at sudden degrees. Years of his master's devoted attention to his hydraulics lent him odd agility, and B5 careened through the village streets with a quickness. As he barreled down the main drag toward the square, a rectangular hatch on his front chassis slid open. Out from it, a box emerged, lined with orderly cartridges. In a blink, they lit and burst into the air.

Ribbons of light danced up from the box, twisting like fish into the sky. They dived like shrieking raptors.

Each missile hit with firework impact. The first slammed square into the chest of one bandit, then another into the next and the next. When the smoke cleared, not a single bandit had been left standing. Only the villagers, their chief, and the single surviving hired guard remained.

The Sith bandit learned the price her men had paid when the last one met a missile to the back. He fell with a gurgle, off the hill where he had called to her, and tumbled to the shore. The river current tugged at his limp legs.

The last shot came for her. It screeched through clear sky, arching over trees and river toward her skull. She knocked it from its path with her saber. She never let her eyes stray from her opponent.

On the other side of the bobbing log, the old man held his left hand up, palm turned toward her. The circle on his wrist cuff blinked blue and blue.

Was he gloating? The monster.

She didn't need to see what had happened in the village to know what he had done. He was Sith, like her, which meant he was without mercy for those he deemed his enemy. He wanted to kill her; he would think nothing of killing every last one of those who had pledged themselves to her service.

The old man didn't care to know what made a man a bandit—or what had made her into herself. In all likelihood, he cared nothing about banditry at all. Had she been anything but Sith, he would have passed through this village as indifferently as a cold wind.

But she *was* Sith, and so was he, and he had decided that meant he had the right to kill her. Inspired by the traitor's madness, then, that cur who had ended the rebellion with his faithless blade. She bared her teeth, the white flare of the Force rising in her like a bonfire.

Their log careened down the river, toward a thunderous waterfall she well remembered. It was an end as punctuated as any other. She would not give him a chance to escape, even if it meant losing hers.

She came for him again, then, knowing the cost and not caring. She was alone now, but so was he. They plunged together toward the drop. The white flare surged through her. She struck the man's lightsaber, barely unsheathed, as hard as she had ever struck anything.

The power of her blow sent him sailing off the log, through the air— over the end of the waterfall.

She cursed herself as he plummeted out of sight into the mist. She didn't regret her violence; she never did. But the white flare that blazed so bright within her could at times steal her focus. The advantage had been hers—the old man's blade still caught in that strange scabbard, hers at the ready to cleave him through. Now here he was gone, and she could not be certain she had killed him.

She maintained her posture on the log and seized the trunk in place at the very edge of the cascade—half to prove to herself she could still summon the black current of the Force, the cool intent that allowed her to manipulate her world as easily as her own fingers—and she walked to the end to stare down into the roiling pool at the bottom.

No matter how she searched, she saw no body.

The Sith cursed herself again as she hopped off the log, down past the roaring water, toward a mossy boulder that jutted up from the pool below. She landed atop it, feather-light.

From there she could see that a paved path bordered one side of the pool at the base of the falls. A narrow trail led down to it from the cliffs above; both it and the path had been hidden from bird's-eye view by a bulging, spray-dampened overhang. The path curved around the pool to an entrance that had been carved into the cliffside beside the falls—a squared-off doorway. It led, she suspected, to a temple, or a shrine, or some other forgotten thing; the whole affair was dusty with neglect.

Faint footsteps with a staggered gait trailed through the dust and past the doorway. That explained the lack of a body.

There, behind the curtain of water, the Sith spied her prey. A red length of light glinted behind the thundering falls. She swiped forward—her blade touched only water. He had hidden farther in.

She smirked. Let the old man sneak, dodge, and hide. He was tired, and injured, and she had a need to make him pay.

She raised her hand and guided the log at the top of the falls forward. The torrent broke around its sides, parting the veil of the flood—clearing a path.

She didn't wait to lock eyes with her opponent. She threw herself forward, a streaking blaze of white Force, and she cut him down before he had the chance to block, let alone to swing.

It was as his top half toppled over that she realized her error. The hands holding the red lightsaber behind the falls were lifeless, cold, and metal. The bisected statue thudded to the stone temple floor.

Simultaneously, another red blade lit the damp dark—a third lightsaber. The end of it stuck out of her midsection, and she found that it was hot, but cold, and that most of all, she hated it.

The third red blade disappeared. The Sith bandit fell forward, as still as the statue, and as the man who had killed her.

*   *   *

The Ronin retracted the blade of the scabbard auxiliary he usually kept at his waist, then reattached it to his sash. The unlovely length of dura-steel and component parts looked nothing like the handsome hilt of the lightsaber he more usually wielded. That was its strength. Not even the opponents who should have known better suspected that he carried more than one red blade.

He frowned as he considered the old Jedi statue, desecrated, beside the body of the young Sith warrior, quite dead.

You're right, the voice said, thoughtful. *Now* this *is poetry.*

If she was disappointed that the bandit had failed to kill him, she hid it well.

He offered her no answer but for a brief, silent prayer before the remains of both statue and woman. Then he gathered the dead bandit's lightsaber from her limp hand and his own blade from the statue's. The latter was still humming, endlessly red. He slid the humming length back into its scabbard.

When are you going to fix that dreadful thing? she asked. *It was so nearly the death of you today.*

He said nothing to this as well; she understood why he hadn't or she didn't, and either way, he would never discuss it, not with her.

The walk to the village took rather more time than he might have wished, thanks to the aches and pains of his fall, as well as the rigors of bladework. He thought himself lucky to have survived. By the time he returned to the village, his cloak was nearly dry, and the sun had arced past its zenith.

B5-56 spied him at the end of the main road before the rest and blatted out a scolding chime as he raced up, dragging the bandit's parasol auxiliary through the dirt behind him. The Ronin put up a pacifying hand in apology. The villagers, meanwhile, regarded his approach in a nervous awe that he didn't like to see.

The shopkeep came running down the road from the opposite direction, his power droid bouncing in his wake. "Master Ronin!" he cried, and doubled over, wheezing. "Y-you were incredible, sir."

However, the Ronin found his gaze drifting up, toward the smoking shell of the bombarded teahouse. Such a structure took time, diligence, and no small amount of resources to construct, here on the edge of colonized space. "I've troubled you," he said.

The shopkeep snorted but was too short of breath to protest. Convenient, as it meant the Ronin was free to take the bandit's auxiliary from B5 and hand it to him. "Here. A tip for the additional service."

The shopkeep received the auxiliary with a fascinated mumble, too tired to refuse the gift. He held the device with light, practiced hands. He had confessed himself a mechanic, at one time, before he took himself to this far-flung reach of the Outer Rim. In any case, even if he had not personally witnessed other Sith iterations on lightsaber technology, he clearly recognized the auxiliary for what it was: a clever, specialized contraption that could fetch him an enviable price from the right buyer.

Before the shopkeep could ask any undesirable questions, the boy chief stepped forward to face the Ronin. He held himself as straight as he had when he'd ordered his bounty hunters to kill, and he stood square when he declared, "Our village owes you a debt."

"Think nothing of it," said the Ronin.

"Such humility. Surely you must be a Jedi knight," said the boy. "Please, I must know our savior's name."

The Ronin squared his jaw shut.

Oh? Why not? she said.

The Ronin turned aside. He withdrew the bandit's lightsaber from the folds of his cloak and dropped it to the ground. The boy chief watched, puzzled, until the Ronin withdrew his blade from its scabbard and the boy's face froze, illuminated by the length of red light.

Gasps flooded the square. The only surviving guard, the Gran who had fired from the rooftop, tensed where he stood a few meters away. He no longer held a weapon, but his hands clearly wanted one.

B5 trilled a low warning: No theatrics.

The tip of the Ronin's lightsaber punctured the hilt of the bandit's. He didn't need to think of where best to break it; the black current of the Force guided him to its shatter point with the ease of familiarity. The durasteel shell broke, and the end of his saber met the whispering kyber shard that had powered the bandit's blade.

He leaned down and retrieved the crystal amidst the villagers' hushed whispers, tucking the shard away to join its brethren in the inner lining of his robe. More than a year since it had last received an addition. It always managed to weigh so much heavier on his shoulders than it should.

"You . . . who even are you?" the shopkeep gasped. At the Ronin's glance, the shopkeep, who had thrown himself into the demanding work of fixing an astromech as finicky as B5 while his village was under siege, quailed behind the boy chief.

Well. Everyone had a limit.

The boy chief, though, moved not at all. He stared up at the Ronin with hard eyes, his mouth determinedly expressionless. What was it the shopkeep had said? Too brave.

How familiar, she said. *Where have I seen that face before?*

The Ronin clenched his molars, just once, as if biting through a thin bone. The face of a child too ready to become old, that would become the face of a man too ready to die. What could possibly protect a boy who expected to meet his own death from rushing toward it with all speed? Nothing the Ronin could provide.

Instead, he reached into the folds of his robe and retrieved the kyber crystal he had just tucked away. The boy thought nothing of putting his hand out to meet his, though he took the bleeding crystal with a hint of surprise; it weighed little.

"It will ward off evil spirits," said the Ronin. "Take great care of it."

Then he turned from the boy as, within him, she cackled.

The Ronin left the village by way of the valley, walking toward the crashed silver ship at the other end of the mountains. At first B5-56 urged him to turn back—to claim food, or shelter, or credits. When the Ronin continued to walk, undeterred by his droid's scolds, B5 opted instead to complain.

What could have possessed him to leave a kyber crystal with hapless villagers? How could they expect to protect such a treasure against the Empire's agents? Did his master not realize he had left them defenseless with contraband of the highest order?

The Ronin snorted at this last. He was no protector, and B5 knew better. "It was all I had to offer for the tea," he said. "Would you have preferred I give them you?"

B5 chirred, somewhere between miffed and outraged, but resigned himself to muttering.

The Ronin took the scold closer to heart than he admitted. The part of him that thought in logical bursts regretted leaving the crystal. It would be hard for the village to sell, if they decided to—if they recognized its worth. Those who bought kyber were either enemies of the Empire or its most ardent servants. Both would want to know where the crystal had come from. The truth would bring trouble for the village before it caught up to him.

He prayed the villagers understood. That they realized it was in their best interest to keep the thing. Kyber thrived when nurtured. It desired people and wanted to give of itself. Properly homed, it could promise the village generations of health and vigor. A better spirit by far than what had haunted them before—the ghosts of war that should have passed on long ago.

When the Ronin and B5 stopped to rest that night—in the lee of a low hill, having found no other shelter—they saw in the distance the billowing smoke of a funeral pyre rising from the direction of the village.

"Ah, I should have told them to check the temple," he said.

You have time yet to turn back and tell them, said the voice, which suggested to him that he was better off doing nothing of the sort.

"Is there anything left for me here?" he asked her instead. "Or is it on to the next road?"

She was silent for a time, and he chewed through his last half of a ration-stick, watching the smoke spiral into the star-specked violet of late evening.

When at last she spoke, it caught him by surprise: *You're not as alone as you think.*

She said nothing else that night, and it took him some time to find his rest. A chill had settled into his bones.

CHAPTER THREE

*D*ON'T YOU HAVE *work to do?*

On the damp stone floor of the temple behind the waterfall, a body stirred. Its second movement was greater and more abrupt. She lurched upright from the ground, gasping. The world addled her with its light-lessness. Her palm skidded over her pounding forehead. Her other hand fell to her stomach.

There was a hole in her chest armor, blackened around the edges, where the old man's lightsaber had run her through. She remembered the white heat and red flare of the blade protruding from her stomach. Yet the ache she felt when she pressed her palm to her gut was only re-membered. Her unblemished skin didn't look as though it had earned any pain at all.

It made no *sense.* She knew in her blood and bones what had happened—their duel, her death—and even if she doubted herself, she could rely on the evidence. The shorn Jedi statue, her own victim, loomed over her. The statue's other half lay abandoned on the floor, the lightsaber it had held no longer anywhere to be seen. Her weapon was also gone. She had only herself, but that was mystery enough.

Mountains. She remembered something about mountains, from

some long-ago lesson. Mountains are strange, her master had said. Gods live within them, and spirits, and the things that you can't rightly call either. She wished to scoff at this. In all her time in the mountains of Genbara, she'd never met anything greater and more frightening than herself.

Except, now, for the man who had just killed her.

And, except for whatever it was that had just undone his work.

She had died, yes? She stared hard at the hole in her armor. More, she remembered—hot, cold, and nothing. And yet.

Yet here she breathed, here she ached—she, bandit, Sith, *Kouru,* she was called Kouru—whatever she was, dead couldn't be it.

"What the hell?" Kouru groaned. She sat hard on the halved statue's dais and stared at the torrent of the waterfall, through which an evening orange filtered. She found herself thinking, rather petulantly, that the swine had taken her lightsaber.

So? Take one of his.

Kouru's lip twisted. "I want both."

That's all?

No. Kouru wanted him dead. He was her unfinished work, this man. She wouldn't rest until she had stricken him from the living world. She knew this with a clarity she had rarely felt outside of the rare moments when the black current freely opened itself to her.

Yes. Focus. You'll need it. Now run along. He had a head start.

It would take Kouru some time yet to think on the coaxing murmur in the hearing part of her soul—the whisper that urged fury, blood, and vengeance. By then, she would believe it a part of herself and give it no second thought at all.

CHAPTER
FOUR

WITH NOWHERE TO sleep but for under the stars, the Ronin did so, and he woke up damp. When he did, B5-56 reported that he had prayed for his good master's sanity to return, but as his master was continuing on the road away from the village, B5 wouldn't hold out hope.

"And here you're always after me to be some sort of vigilante," the Ronin said under the drying heat of midmorning. "You understand that's a charitable sort of endeavor, yes?"

B5 whistled something the Ronin wouldn't have repeated to a child.

"Not very pious of you."

They repeated some iteration of this argument every few months. It had a seasonal feel that the Ronin appreciated, because it let him mark time as they moved from sector to sector, moon to planet to moon.

The road today was wide and clear. It had broadened the farther they got from the village, and now that they neared the crashed silver ship at the end of the valley, the Ronin spied a crossroads where their road met an even wider track. This occurred beside a copse of pink-blossomed trees, which surrounded the buried nose of the silver vessel.

From within the flowered shade, a melody played. A flute of some sort. A musical phrase flourished, paused, and repeated with new form. The player was practicing.

The Ronin slowed his step as they neared. A figure came into view among the trees, seated on a rock, working through the song in stretches as they sorted through the proper movements of mouth and fingers. The snatches of melody were at times familiar, at times not.

I think you like this better than a true performance, the voice mused.

"I think they're a little sharp," he said.

"Oh, I'd say flat," said the musician. They raised their head, and though their tone smiled, their face was largely concealed by a mask—a white vulpine shape with slashes of red at the mouth and brows. Their simple garb, kimono over trousers, was morbidly white as well, though it had the faded look of bones left to dry in the sun. It might once have held color. It was now as pale as their hair, knotted at the back of their skull. "Don't look so abashed," they cajoled. Unlike their dress, their voice was all light and life, with the fluid cant of a born storyteller. "I'd rather know my flaws now than when I'm trying to earn dinner. Are you headed to the spaceport?"

"If that's where this road leads," said the Ronin.

"Then let's share it."

B5 chirred as the musician got up to join them, flute tucked away into the wrap thrown over their shoulder before they hopped down off the rock.

"Did he now?" said the musician to B5. "My apologies. I could play while we go, but not well."

"My partner is greedy," said the Ronin over B5's affronted squawk.

"He knows my value. Here, I'll tell a story. What sort do you prefer? Though I'm afraid most trend depressing, what with a war behind and a war ahead."

"You think I'd like to hear of war?"

The musician glanced meaningfully at the scabbards affixed to the Ronin's waist. "You have the look. It's not often you see a man styling himself such a warrior wandering the back roads of the Outer Rim. Two blades! It's nigh old-fashioned, sir . . ."

They wanted his name. The Ronin offered none. The musician neglected to take the cue and turned to B5.

B5, little traitor, trilled a suggestion.

"Oh, really? Master Ronin, then." The musician bowed their head in thought. "Fine. You may call me the Traveler. We'll match."

"Why would I want that?" the Ronin asked. He meant: Why would *you*?

"Camaraderie," said the Traveler, as if it had been decided.

The Traveler continued with them, matching the Ronin's pace and chatting with B5 until their newfound party of three reached the crossroads. There, the Traveler turned in the direction that led to the spaceport—as did B5, who paused only to swivel his head and chirp chidingly at the Ronin, whose step had slowed.

The Ronin had not intended to head for the port when he woke. Nevertheless, he found himself following droid and Traveler both, though he kept a step behind. Under other circumstances, he would at this moment have been planning to lose this inquisitive satellite sooner rather than later, likely in the first crowd the spaceport mustered. Now he wondered.

Not as alone as you think, she'd said.

She hadn't clarified because there was no need to. She only ever directed him toward one sort of being—those whom he and she had once called brethren, and whom she hoped would soon run him through. They were an increasingly rare breed, the Sith, never so common as the Jedi whom they had betrayed, and made rarer every year by the Ronin's own hunt. Was this "Traveler" his next mark? He couldn't yet be sure.

Inwardly, he cursed his negligence again; he had for so many months allowed himself to lie fallow, and now when it came to the pulse and flow of the Force, he was as intuitive as a brick. Admittedly, even in his prime he had run into no small amount of difficulty differentiating a being sensitive to the manipulation of the white flare and black current from a being merely saturated with it. The latter applied to all life, to a degree. The finer points of philosophy lay beyond the Ronin's ability to describe. He only knew that it was terribly common for any honest artist to shimmer with white flare and course with black current, and this musician was no exception.

In the Traveler's favor, he didn't recognize them, and they seemed old enough that he would have expected to. At one time, he had known every warrior who called themselves Sith—nearly every one. Not the bandit.

She would have been quite young when the war ended.

He stretched the arm he had bruised on his topple off the waterfall and strove to phase out the Traveler's banter with his droid. "No hints?" he asked under his breath.

"What was that?" said the Traveler.

B5 swept in with an excuse, calling his master senile and eccentric besides. The Traveler looked, if anything, more intrigued. The Ronin was compelled to shrug in vague agreement. He had been called worse.

Unsociable, she said, which was not the hint he had asked for.

He wanted to remind her: I killed a woman yesterday. Instead, he called B5 a gossip and resolved himself to listen. It was as yet entirely possible that he would part ways with this musician without either of them trying to murder the other.

The road to Osou spaceport, the main point of interplanetary departure on all of Genbara, thickened with traffic over time. By the afternoon, they had joined an impromptu caravan of treaded wagons, landspeeders, and other travelers on foot. Most had come from the outlying farm villages that sold goods at Osou's central market, which unfortunately made the Ronin and his companions all the more unusual.

The Traveler did nothing to dissuade the attention, telling tales as they walked in a bright, compelling voice that faltered far less often than their flute. To the children riding on their mother's wagon, drawn by a massive scaled boar, they told fairy tales; to the sisters carting a haul of fresh red fruits, the latest gossip from the Core; to the elderly uncle driving the sputtering landspeeder that brought up the rear, a ghost story. The Ronin preferred eavesdropping on these accounts to the news about which most of the adults wished to speak.

"Oh, yes, Imperial unification, what a wonderful thing," said an aunty toting baskets of rice on a pole slung over her shoulder. "Twenty years of peace! Tell that to my cousin. He got the hot end of a bandit's blaster bolt just last year. We could barely afford the bacta treatment. How's that for peace?"

"I'm telling you, it's going to get worse," said the uncle beside her, herding his sturdy beast of burden, a shaggy, antlered creature taller at the shoulder than the hip that towered well enough to provide shade to everyone nearby. "The Emperor didn't fight with his siblings about who got to sit on the throne because it didn't matter when his Empire belonged to the lords. The princes, though, now that their father's on his deathbed, they think they have something to fight for."

"Well, let them squabble." The aunty sniffed, shifting her load. "Out here, we'll be fending off the same old pirates."

An aunty toting an apothecary chest on her back sucked her teeth. "And who'll do the fending, if they're taking our kids for their fights? They're recruiting at the port. You'll see the posters."

There was a degree of discontented murmuring about this. The Ronin found he agreed. He did not, however, voice this agreement. Already the others were eyeing him, as if the opinion of the tall, blade-carrying stranger could assuage their fears of future violence—or at least give them something more concrete to worry at. He suspected they had only accepted his presence in their midst because while traveling in the company of a performing musician, he seemed less a threat than a curiosity. That would have changed if they realized he carried something other than metal in his scabbards.

"They're always recruiting," said a frail old voice. "That's not what you should be looking for." It was the uncle on the landspeeder who liked ghost stories. The Traveler, riding beside him, tilted their head with interest. "It's the bodies. They're going missing again."

A ripple of discomfort washed over the caravan. Anxious gossip begot more of the same. When nervous about the future, people liked to know they weren't nervous alone. But this declaration spread a worse and more cloying air than the possibility of drought or an unreasonable new governor, and the company's faces grew taut with a feeling far more difficult to exorcise: fear.

"Don't," said someone. "Let's not—"

They were drowned out by the aunty with the apothecary chest. "I heard so too." She raised her chin at those who glared at her to hush. "A village on the little red moon over Buna. They had pirates. The local lord sent some of his most trusted Jedi, but the reports stopped. He sent more Jedi, and they found no one left. No pirates, no Jedi, no villagers. Nothing at all."

"Oh, that's hearsay."

"It isn't, I heard on the HoloNet. They had to apologize to the families. Couldn't send the bone shards home."

"Of course not! Jedi don't leave bones. Not the good ones. The spirits take them."

"The Force, Aunty."

"Same same! Don't say such things. It's gruesome. Unlucky, probably."

"Luck," grunted the rice-carrying aunty. Her hands, hooked on either end of the pole across her back, had faint burn scars at the knuckles and peeking from beneath her palms. The sort of scar a person got from handling the heat of large cannons on the ramshackle vessels at the front. "You talk like it's a story. It isn't. I remember. Every battlefield left bodies—until that Sith witch came through."

Beside the Ronin, B5-56 trilled a low cautionary note. An uncle mistook it for fearful and placed a warm hand on the droid's hat. Feeling himself patronized, B5 warbled. Someone laughed, halfhearted, but they laughed alone.

Everyone knew the stories. The unholy sorcery of the Sith. The dark lord and his witch, he who killed and she who resurrected, stealing the dead from their right to join the Force—or the spirits, or the sublimity beyond the galactic order, depending on who you asked. No matter what anyone believed, the stolen ghosts were blasphemy of an order beyond reckoning. The witch's demon army had been fearsome as much for the unceasing devotion with which they pursued the Sith's ends as for the threat they posed to every facet of natural order.

That was why, in all likelihood, the company's eyes traveled slowly, inevitably, toward the Traveler. Who but a storyteller could hope to make sense of the wrongest thing in the world? The Ronin intended to keep his eyes forward, yet they drifted toward the Traveler as well. The way they spoke of the Sith would prove informative.

For their part, the Traveler had at some point exited the uncle's landspeeder to walk more closely to the center of the group. They held a hand to their chin in thought, and though their fox-masked head was bowed, when they spoke, it was clear they realized they would be listened to.

"I've seen some things," they said, "and I've heard some others. Ghosts, demons. Spirits and gods. Each use broadens the words—and deepens them. I count myself lucky to hear the words you choose, Aunty. You've seen the things you tell us of, and you're willing to do that telling. We ought to listen, and learn, and remember, I think, that stories about the dead often say true things, even if not quite the truth. Does that sound right to you?"

The aunty with scarred hands grunted and turned away.

The Ronin frowned. The answer pleased some, but he found it less telling than he might have desired.

The caravan remained quiet after that. It drifted into parts and pieces down the road as friends and neighbors paired off, whispering together. Some managed to laugh. The imposing white plaster walls of Osou spaceport were in sight, and the sun was setting. They would get to rest in the warmth and light of civilization, and no one needed to fear a ghost unless they particularly wanted to.

Except for you, she said.

She could be a bit of an ass.

A cloud front had haunted the caravan for the past few kilometers, and just as Osou's gates came into view, it broke into a sudden, drenching rain. Most of the remaining caravan took off at a run. B5-56 elected to retreat beneath the drooping limbs of an expansive tree beside the road; he did hate to get his hat wet. The Ronin joined him, half to see what the Traveler would do.

It was not, by this point, a question of whether they would stay but how they would justify doing so. The answer: They did not. They simply lingered, observing the rain with a curious air until they dug into the bag thrown over their shoulder and extracted a small pouch. This, they offered to the Ronin. It contained a selection of speckled red fruits.

"Not in my diet, I'm afraid," they said.

"Are they in mine?" asked the Ronin.

"If you're asking whether they're poisoned, you'll have to take your inquiry to those sweet young ladies carrying their wares to market— you rude, rude man."

The Ronin took the fruits, which were more tart than sweet, but kind on his jaw, which had developed an ache in the returning damp. Not that the Traveler could have possibly known about this particular pain, unless they knew far more about him than they were willing to confess.

"You're put out." The Traveler sighed after a length of quiet. They crossed their arms, contemplative. "My apologies. Was I insufficiently dramatic for your tastes?"

"My life is dramatic enough already."

The Traveler clucked their tongue in sympathy. "Oh, the woes of an old warrior boldly flaunting at least one remarkably illegal weapon."

They glanced knowingly at the hilt of his lightsaber, and at the scabbard into which it fit. The Ronin frowned, which the Traveler waved off.

"I never saw a thing, Master Ronin. I only say it at all because our friends aren't wrong about the posters, and the princes have sent more than that to every spaceport in the galaxy, even to this little world. If you're as tired of drama as you claim, you'll want to be a touch more careful once this rain lets up and we reach port."

B5 sang a thank-you because the Ronin remained thoughtfully silent. It was difficult to believe this person was one he needed to be warned of, and indeed it was entirely possible that the voice had meant to warn him of someone else.

But a Sith warrior was nothing if not clever.

It would be better, he decided, to take his leave. If the Traveler wanted more than his friendship and stories, they would pursue, and if they did so with a blade of their own, the Ronin would do what was required of him. If they wanted only those stories, well, it would still be better to leave them unsatisfied. Either way, he would have his answer.

In the end, they weren't difficult to shake. The rain let up soon after, but the trio didn't reach the market until after dark. There, the Traveler found both the local teahouse and the cantina vying for their services. As they negotiated, the Ronin and B5 continued on into the unnamed alleys of Osou, in search of someone willing to trade a meal for a vaga-bond's skilled repair.

As the caravan gossip suggested, the Ronin found there were indeed posters. He stood before the plastered walls of a communal storehouse that was covered with them. Some of the posters advertised holodra-mas, while others proclaimed the glory of the Genbara system's lord or his favored prince. More advertised the honor (and compensation) of applying to the armed forces of this or that prince, while a smattering posted the dates for the annual exams required of all the Emperor's citizen officials.

The freshest poster, still crisp at the corners, depicted a glowering, scarred face—a man wanted for banditry, extortion, and disturbance of the peace in the countryside, who had long plagued a mountain village only two days' walk from Osou. The bounty was considerable, the like-ness unflattering.

B5-56 squawked, indignant.

"You're just mad they didn't mention you," said the Ronin.

B5 opened a flap on his side and stuck out an articulated metal digit that sparked. Whether he was attempting to be rude or violent, he was interrupted.

"My, that's troublesome," said the Traveler. They stood beside the Ronin, and their frown was just visible beneath the curve of their mask. "Quite the character, aren't you?"

There was no one else on this street, which wasn't far from the dock-yard that made up the majority of the spaceport. It was an industrial sort of avenue that saw its fair share of foot traffic during the day, but on a quiet world like Genbara, most people let their lives be ruled by the orbit of the sun rather than by chronometer. It being dark enough for the river frogs to sing, the Ronin had expected himself to be quite alone but for B5. It was troublesome indeed, then, to find the Traveler had insisted on tracking them down.

"Now this seems like a bit of exaggeration," they went on, "but I thought you should know that there was a Gran at the cantina making all manner of wild claims. Something about dark warriors—Sith, if you'll believe it—descending on a poor farming village in the mountains just south of here. I told him that I peddled in the fantastic, but his story was simply absurd. I'd just met a man coming from that direction, after all, and he surely would have mentioned an event as remarkable as the return of the Empire's most hated foes."

"Is that a warning?" asked the Ronin.

"I suppose it would be, if you had reason to need one."

It came a bit late. Another voice called from down the street. "You— Sith scum."

The Ronin glanced toward the voice. On one end of the street, at an intersection with the main avenue where the central market spread, stood not one but a multitude of beings, all plainly armed and armored. Among them, the Ronin recognized the Gran bounty hunter from the village in the mountains, the one whose companions had been slaughtered by the bandits.

B5 crooned uneasily. The Ronin glanced in the opposite direction. Another group approached from that end of the street, far enough away that they were as yet concealed by the shadows of the darkened town. They carried themselves with an ambitious air, expecting a fight.

Talk about trouble, the voice mused. *And just when you'd found a friend.*

The Ronin snorted. The voice saw no reason to clarify her meaning, but he expected nothing and so couldn't be disappointed. He wasn't about to befriend anyone, least of all the sort of person who would tell a cantina full of bounty hunters that they had just entered town with the sector's most profitable target.

He still sensed no particular enmity in the Traveler. This disconcerted, somewhat, given how many gruesome tales they surely knew of the Sith rebellion. He would have expected revulsion, or at the very least trepidation, but he detected only a trace of curiosity and a concerning degree of focus. Even if they weren't the sort of trouble he most feared, he could now be certain that, at best, they had a distasteful interest in brewing the sort of trouble that was. That was exceptionally irritating, but it didn't necessarily warrant murder.

In any case, he could linger no longer. The Ronin sighed as he lowered himself to speak to B5. "Keep an eye on them."

Then he leapt straight up and swung himself cleanly onto the tiled
roof of the storehouse plastered with posters. Below, B5 cursed at him
in Binary while the bounty hunters cursed at him in a handful of lan-
guages and the quickest let loose the first wave of blasterfire.

He sent no backward look to see who followed, but the memory of
the Traveler's interest flickered all through the chase, an unnerving
tickle at the back of his mind.

CHAPTER
FIVE

ALARM BELLS CLANGED. Lights flared haphazardly across the town. Splatters of blasterfire sprayed upward at shadows that proved to be nothing—an open window, a futon hung out to dry. More troublingly, illumination spilled from within homes and outside businesses as the people of Osou woke to the clamor.

The local Imperial troops had also been roused. The Ronin saw them here and there, smartly clad in their burnished red-and-black armor. Only a handful thus far, and he suspected they were alone, led by no Jedi. Otherwise, he would already have been found.

The Ronin nevertheless understood this was a bad assumption. Thus he kept to as-yet-shadowed roofs as he ran, feet swift and soundless even over the clay tiles. When he came to a fully lit intersection, a flick of his hand made the bright glare of the comm tower in the center of the square falter. In a sputter of dark, he leapt over the street from one slanted roof to the next and ran farther.

His pursuers were more coordinated than he liked. They had left some half dozen of their own at strategic intersections. These bounty hunters held amplified lanterns, which they swung to illuminate every moving darkness at street level and overhead. Small flying recon droids swooped past one another over the roofs, spotlights clashing as they vied to catch their bounty.

One such droid, a narrow, palm-sized disk with two thin articulated arms and a staring white eye in its middle, zipped past the Ronin where he crouched in the lee of a balcony. It slowed for a moment, swiveling its eye in his direction. The Ronin made a shooing motion with his hand. On the opposite side of the street, a loose tile skidded halfway down the roof. The little droid's eye light flared as it dived across the way toward the disturbance.

The Ronin exhaled relief and took the moment to check his wrist cuff. It remained dark. B5-56 had made no effort to contact him. So much the better; it meant the droid had no reason to. The Ronin had set no rendezvous point, but they would find each other in the end. They always did.

Cautiously, the Ronin stepped just out of the shadow, the better to judge his course.

This would be so much easier if you took it seriously, she said.

"What do you mean by that?" he muttered, though he knew.

You know who you are—what you are. This filth should be nothing to you. Why persist in pretending they deserve your caution?

He felt a tug at his waist, as if she had placed a hand on his lightsaber. He tightened his mouth against a frown. She knew better. He wouldn't turn such a weapon on anyone but those who could properly defend themselves from it.

You have alternatives, she said.

His fingers rested briefly on the second hilt.

No. He could do without.

That said, tonight he regretted himself a bit more pettily than he usually did. It had been a long time since he found himself hunted—since he had shown the world the kind of man he truly was.

You think you're hiding? she asked.

"I thought that was obvious," he said, because he knew it would annoy her. She didn't mean his skulking about in the dark of a nothing town. She meant his weapons, and that they lay in plain view at his waist, just as the Traveler had criticized. But these, too, he didn't ever intend to hide, no matter how illegal any of them had become, nor that he would only be mistaken for a Jedi by those who had never met one. Every being he met deserved a warning before they faced him.

Though some apparently took his gear as some kind of invitation instead.

They really are haunting you, aren't they? she said. *You don't think that little fox is only after your story?*

The Ronin scowled at her openly now, as if she were at his shoulder. But he was alone at the end of this dark stretch of tiled roof, which ended just before the massive main entrance to Osou's dockyard. "Even if a story's all they want—that would be bad enough."

She knew it too. He couldn't afford a companion. Even a trustworthy friend was obligation and liability. What was she playing at?

A sudden light burst down the street toward the entrance of the dockyard, the beam broad and sharp. A landspeeder. It had rounded the corner and was coming his way. Two bounty hunters sat in it, one to drive and the other to hold a lantern on a pole that shone so bright it illuminated every corner of the street.

The Ronin threw himself forward, off the ledge of the roof that faced the dockyard. He clung to the eave with his fingers, the balls of his feet pushed against the wall to keep himself in the shadows. Then the light faltered—swerved—and he was obliged to haul himself back up onto the roof because his arms were shaking with fatigue.

There, at the far end of the avenue, the landspeeder spun in a tight circle. The bounty hunters who had been in it were still in evidence, but they clearly were no longer in control.

The speeder spun higher and higher over the avenue, and it did so upside down. Its driver clung to the headrest of their seat, their feet kicking five meters above the ground. Their passenger struggled to clamber onto the skyward-facing bottom of the speeder, but the repulsorlifts threatened to jettison them off.

Abruptly, the upside-down speeder fell toward the street. The bounty hunters screamed as it swooped at an angle. The whole thing collided with a gang of their compatriots dashing onto the avenue, and it bowled over the lot like an infuriated, feral wall.

Don't gawk, she hissed. *Go.*

The Ronin was already moving. Not back down the street—light filled every crevice of the ongoing disaster behind him—but forward. He dropped off the roof into the alley beside the dockyard and ducked through the darkly yawning entrance.

Though he slid into the shadows cast by dimmed ships, his ear strained to hear more of whatever the hell was happening outside. Blasterfire—of course. Screaming—yes, yes. The ceaseless mechanical cries of a machine compelled to function outside the physical rules of its being—there, that was the problem.

No landspeeder flew *upside down.* The fundamental tenet of its gravitational system forbade it. Only one power in the galaxy could so defy the laws of the universe. Someone, the Force coursing through them, had seized the speeder with a focus and intent the Ronin had not seen in decades. A flagrant display of obscene control. And for what? To distract his pursuers?

To herd you, she said.

Yes. Every act of great power came from great need. Whoever had turned the black current against the bounty hunters wanted more than a distraction. They wanted him funneled away from the town and among the ships.

Now here he was, slipping between and beneath the hulls of battered scout vessels, transports, and freighters. She watched him sneak, offering neither agreement nor warning, merely waiting to see what came of him next. Whatever lurked, she had already warned him of it. He couldn't yet say what shape it would take. He had lit too many small fires to easily identify the one that had caught best and brightest.

All he knew was that he had flaunted himself most carelessly in the mountains. He had also managed to spend months missing news of galactic unrest, a political shift so dire that it had apparently agitated Imperial agents—and all this did concern him, though it wasn't his business. There was, on top of all this, the matter of the bounty hunters.

Even if it was the Traveler's fault that he was presently being pursued, they couldn't feasibly have summoned such a sizable collection of bounty hunters to remote Genbara within the few hours they were apart. Nor could they have put up those unbecoming posters of the Ronin's unsmiling face—not while walking beside him on a country road. No, the Traveler was but fractionally culpable. Someone else had put a price on his head. Perhaps the same someone who had tossed the speeder through the air like a plaything.

Jedi, he thought—an old reflex that burned in his chest and head. The possibility, the threat, it dizzied him like river rapids. Yet even as he feared the thought, he doubted it nearly as soon as he had it. What manner of Jedi resorted to trickery and deceit? What Jedi lured their prey into the still dark of an empty dockyard?

One he could not afford to underestimate. He sensed their next trick already. One ship, a sharp-nosed light freighter with broad, curved wings at its base, hummed nigh inaudibly. Its lights were yet dark, intentionally so, and no internal system that generated an excess of sound had been activated. But there was someone waiting within—someones, perhaps.

The black current of the Force had always guided him first to the intricacy of electric mechanism. He could more intuitively grasp the minute capacity for malfunction within a passing droid than he could the complexity of a living being that stood directly before him. Regardless, the people in the freighter didn't want anyone to know they were bringing it to life. It was to his advantage that he did.

What did they intend? To fire on him? They had to know the futility of such an assault, if they knew him for a Sith. Perhaps they thought to catch him in the full brunt of their engines bursting viciously to life. That, he would want to avoid.

Or was he nothing to them? Would they even know to fear him?

The Ronin's fingers shook, slightly so. His chest shivered in sympathy, and he clenched his fist to ward off his frailty. He needed calm. Direction. A way out of this port and off Genbara before—

The jerk at his waist was quite slight. He might not have noticed it, were he not assiduously searching for some sign, any sign, of danger. The possibility that he would not otherwise have noticed . . . It disturbed him powerfully, when he saw what had been taken.

The telltale thrum of a lightsaber made him turn, his hand falling to his waist. His fingers found only one hilt. The other was gone—taken—

and the blade flaring in the dark not three meters away was a distinctly familiar red. It illuminated the face of the Sith bandit, grinning, her teeth made scarlet by the light of the blade she had stolen from his waist.

He understood her presence in his bones before he registered her in his brain. His blood ran cold and his heart beat in a great empty lack. He had not seen one of her kind in so very long. He was so sure he should hear a voice laughing in his ears, but there was only his breathing, low and shuddering—and the bandit, her focus entirely upon him.

No further pause. The bandit came for him. The Ronin sprang back, skidding over the dust of the dockyard floor and having immediately to leap up to avoid a tangle of power cables. The bandit followed, lightsaber a furious whirlwind of movement. Everywhere he leapt, she was on him in an instant, gouging through durasteel with her blade and leaving a trail of sparks.

He spun out his scabbard auxiliary, readying himself to block her—he could trust no other weapon to do so—but his body, mind, *soul* wouldn't let him stand and engage. He could only think with the frenetic need of a drowning man that he had to get away, to find high ground. He feared, clinically, that he had begun to panic. In another lifetime, this would have shamed him. It didn't now because he understood with horrible clarity the danger of what he beheld.

A fallen warrior no longer dead. A living curse. A demon, they'd called her kind during the war. The bandit would from now on pursue him with relentless need. She would never stop, not until she had him skewered on the length of his own blade and had carved his remains to her satisfaction. Or the satisfaction of her master.

And he was still tired, and old, and shaken. He felt his infirmity in the way he missed a jump by half a meter and had to scrabble up onto the jagged hull of a transport, and in how, when she whipped a reinforced cargo crate at his head, he ignited the scabbard auxiliary to cut it down when it would have been so much cleaner, *smarter* to simply dodge—

And he felt it when the bandit, stalking across the pitted hull of an ancient transport, lashed out with her arm and a wave of pure black current threatened to throw him off his feet. He kept himself upright with a ferocious desire, his robes whipping in the burst of her fury.

The bandit never slowed. She flew forward, lightsaber a red wound in the night. He hadn't fully recovered his footing from the onslaught of her attempt to throw him from the hull, and he was forced to finally catch her blade with his. Their lightsabers hissed and crackled as they ground against each other. For a second, he met her eyes.

Fire and amber, pupils blown, incandescent with her need to unmake him. He knew then with the pulsing core of him: He would have to kill her again or she would never fall.

A blaster bolt cut through their clash. It lanced between the cross of their sabers, and where the bandit snarled over her shoulder, the Ronin once more leapt back, flourishing his lightsaber off and melting into the shadows beneath the nearest scout ship.

The bounty hunters had found them, attracted by the unmistakable sounds of their fight. More of them fired toward the bandit. She deflected each bolt, then gestured roughly upward with her free hand.

The Ronin had only seconds to understand what was happening before a bounty hunter—that poor foolish Gran from the village—came hurtling through the dark, limbs flailing, straight toward him.

This time, he dodged. At the frayed edge of his conscience, it was all he could think to do. By some luck, the Gran flew past him and into a canopy of cargo netting—netting that he could have sworn was too far away, just a moment before. Either way, the bounty hunter tumbled into it with relative softness.

Lucky, was it? she asked.

"Not the time," he snapped.

The bandit was coming for him again, bounding off the transport and lunging into his hiding spot. The Ronin dashed off under a hull, sprinting back toward the entrance. He now had a sense of what had happened. The bandit had cornered him in the dockyard to make it her death trap. Therefore, it was time to leave.

As if in perfect time with that thought, his wrist cuff buzzed. A glance at his wrist showed the blue circle of light below his palm blinking a message.

"Up," said B5, and that was all.

Indeed, the Ronin heard the creak of docking bay doors opening overhead. A blanket of moonlight spilled over the vessels.

Up. Yes, that would do.

The Ronin gathered white flare in his legs, crouched, and jumped up onto the nearest hull—a scouting vessel—then up again to the next, the laser-scarred shielding of an off-model freighter. He leapt again and again, making his way toward a pyramid of cargo crates beside loading machinery and a web of maintenance walkways. Between these, he would be able to clamber his way to a position that would let him make a final jump to the dockyard roof.

He felt the bandit's pursuit not via the Force but through instinct and understanding. He didn't look or listen for her; it was unnecessary. She followed him as surely as a tide followed a moon.

She gained on him steadily. *This* he felt in the shiver of the white flare and black current. She nipped at his heels, a white-spiked fury boiling in black surf. She was a vision of a warrior. What a Sith she would have been.

Weakness made him stop a second too long. He dared to turn and see her. They stood across from each other in pale light, he on top of the pulley rigging that let crews load their ships, she crouched on a mainte- nance walkway, pulsing lightsaber held low and at the ready. They were separated only by empty space and many meters of distance, so much farther apart than they had been on the log as they rushed down a rag- ing river. Yet it felt like she was on the verge of sinking her teeth into his throat.

"Stop running," she spat, and her voice was so very much the same as it had been the last time she demanded he kill or be killed. "This doesn't end until you face me."

He knew it to be true. Yet end it did, prematurely, when a light freighter's engines roared. It was the long, sharp-nosed ship that he had seen readying its systems when he first entered the dockyard. It surged up from the floor, broad, scarred wings extending as it scattered the bounty hunters surrounding it, and it came to a skillful halt between the Ronin and the bandit. The stenciled writing on its side called it the POOR CROW, and its lower hatch hung open from its bottom, the walk- way extended toward him. Through it he saw B5, who shrilled at him to jump.

"Quite the executive decision," muttered the Ronin.

They could argue about it later. For the last time, he leapt. He flew through the air, grasping toward the *Crow*'s walkway.

But he had miscalculated. The bandit leapt too.

He saw what would come next in the fragment of his mind's eye where he at times beheld such things, a flash colored by the visceral shades of shifting possibility.

The bandit would grasp him either by his limb or by his robe, and it didn't matter, because either way, she would knock him askew, and with that he would lose his chance. They would fall to the ground, and even if B5 and the *Crow* returned, it would be too late, because she would have had the upper hand for too long, and he would already be dead.

Yet the moment he grasped the inevitability of his fate, it broke.

The bandit's body jerked mid-flight, struck in the torso from the side by no visible power. She flew back through the night air and collided with a cargo tower, her lightsaber slicing through the crates she fell past. The Ronin saw this from the *Crow*'s walkway, onto which he had landed safely and scrambled up as he stared down.

The bandit had not merely fallen, she had been *pushed*—and not by an assaulting wave of black current, such as she had thrown at him mere minutes before, but a powerful, targeted blow of that same power. And, whether she had been too wholly focused on the Ronin to withstand it or because the push itself had been so eerily precise, she fell.

He was free.

Free to run, in any case, which he had long since learned was not much freedom at all.

CHAPTER
SIX

THE RONIN STOOD as the *Poor Crow* roared out of the docking bay, into the night sky. The walkway closed as he moved up into the
ship. Inside, B5-56 rocked side-to-side and trilled in that fretful tone
between anxious and infuriated. Beside him crouched the Traveler.
They stood as the Ronin neared, wiping their palms on their wide white
trousers, and tilted their head, smile just visible beneath the curve of
their stylized mask.

"You seemed in need of an exit strategy," they said.

"So I was," said the Ronin. "I suppose you're the better liar between
us."

"A convenient one, though." The Traveler turned their back to the
Ronin, as if they had nothing to fear, and beckoned him down a well-lit
corridor. "I've helped you leave, which I think we should consider a
public service. That Sith warrior down there seems quite set on hunting
you down, which I suspect means she'll stop pestering those poor folks
planetside in favor of chasing after us. What a favor we've done them."

The Ronin followed the Traveler, hands in his sleeves. B5 trailed at
his heels, muttering placations. The signals the droid sent to his cuff
told rather a different story: a warning in a pattern of blue flashes.

Play along, why don't you? coaxed the voice. *When's the last time someone who knew you for a Sith didn't try to stick a blade between your ribs?*

Her encouragement left him all the warier. She had directed him to the Traveler, after all. Just what did she hope to see them do?

The *Crow* was tidy and well kept, though spare and visibly cobbled together in places. He heard no other passengers, though someone had to have prepared it for launch in the docking bay, and someone had to be flying the thing. It relieved him, somewhat, to know there were so few to concern himself with. The corridor opened up into a wider stretch broken by sliding panels that had now been folded into the walls. This made for a modest gathering space and galley, though it also was empty. As the Traveler stepped into it, the sound of the ship changed, as did the feel of it under the Ronin's feet. The *Crow* had begun its ascent through Genbara's atmosphere, into the black of space.

The Ronin was by this point ragged and well aware of it. His options were limited. He did not trust the Traveler, nor this rescue, and neither did B5. Thus, it was with a kind of exhaustion that he sighed and unsheathed the second weapon that hung at his waist.

The blaster had an unusual elegance because it was old and because it was more often maintained than it was used. In the same motion he withdrew the weapon, the Ronin fired it at a panel in the hallway, in front of which B5 had strategically lingered. The panel fell away, smoking, revealing a mess of piping, wires, and other circuitry.

The Ronin had a certain technical expertise, yes, but the *Crow*'s innards proved to be as much of a collage as its hull. He was very possibly about to regret this. He expected that he would more likely regret it if he let the Traveler stop him. They had turned in shock at the sound of the blast, and he had less than seconds to act.

So, the Ronin flicked his wrist, and with the black current, he tore the first wire he saw from its mooring and prayed.

Gravity faltered. How fortunate.

The Traveler let out an "oh" of surprise as their feet left the floor, and another grunt as the Ronin grasped the back of their neck via the black current. It wasn't a choking hold, but it pacified, and it made clear the holder's intent. With that mask, he still couldn't quite see their expression, but they didn't seem to be in a panic, which was either admirable or quite foolish.

"I would have you explain yourself," said the Ronin, his feet incongruously anchored, though everything else within the ship had begun to bob up into the air—except for B5, who had engaged the magnetic clamps retrofitted into his treads to remain stuck on the floor. "For every lie, another system goes dark."

"So dramatic," said the Traveler, very nearly enthused. A man less experienced in interrogation might have missed the tension in the back of their tone. "Ask away! I do hope to keep the air around."

"You knocked down the bandit."

"Yes."

"You upended the speeder."

"Yes. I'm sorry—I thought you had questions?"

The Ronin waited a silent second. The Traveler raised their hands.

"You were looking for me, weren't you?" he said. "On the road to Osou. Why?"

"Oh, now that's simple, I—"

Before the Traveler could answer, a white flash exploded through the hall, followed by a roar of static—some manner of grenade, the Ronin thought, just before the next staggering sensation hit. The end of a staff collided with the soft flesh under his sternum. An electric charge followed, surging through the metal into his body.

The Ronin crumpled and lost his hold on the Traveler. For a moment, they tried to brace themself in thin air—then some unseen crew member re-engaged gravity. Everyone who had not already been on the deck thudded onto it: the Traveler, and their rescuer.

This latter was a wizened old woman in a whirl of dark robes, who sprang up as nimbly as a grasshopper, staff twirling in her hand. It whistled through the air, aimed at the Ronin's skull. If it made contact, it would drive his nose into the metal plating of the deck with breaking force.

B5 didn't care to let it. He let out a screech and charged the woman's knees, half a dozen hatches flying open on his sides to reveal sparking, spinning, slicing tools meant for cutting and welding durasteel—excellently suited to wrecking flesh.

The Traveler, still on the floor, threw out a groggy hand. Another of their characteristically precise manipulations of the black current shoved B5 off course, to the droid's shrill protest.

This placed the lot of them at four separate corners of the galley hall. They faced one another with battlefield readiness, each weighing the direction they should first strike—

"No! No, no, no! How many times do I have to say it? No Force nonsense on my ship!"

The shouting came from over the comm. It was young and feminine, for all it snarled.

"It's not the Force, Ekiya, dear," said the old woman. Her eyes never strayed from the Ronin. One hand shifted to adjust her hold on her electrostaff, the other went to her belt and sash, heavy with pouches that were no doubt full of other disorienting tricks. "It's just good preparation."

"It's a mistake, is what I think it is." The Traveler declared this while staggering upright, hands up toward all three others. "We were only better defining the situation, Aunty, no one—"

"I understand the situation," the Ronin replied.

You understand nothing, she snapped.

The Ronin balked at the strangeness of her tone, sharp with something he might have called fear, had he not known her better.

No. She needed him off guard. There could be no other explanation. She wanted his death, and he would, as ever, refuse to oblige.

The Ronin's hand fell to his sash. He missed his proper lightsaber, but he still carried the scabbard auxiliary, and that was all he needed—it would be far less precise to shred into the *Crow*'s gut with than his blade, but he had lost the luxury of time the moment he lost the element of surprise. So, he would do what he needed to, even if it required breaking the ship in its entirety.

It was a clean thought, practical and direct. Beneath it slithered something cruelly cold and unexpected. He found his palm was sweating. His breath was rank in his throat.

He had broken ships before. It was brutal, and he regretted it—but it was also necessity.

Necessity? This time, her snarl came with a barrage of colors spun from a hundred lives, tessellated upon one another into a single dense and vibrant image: her face, locked in an expression of furious grief. *You think you ever knew the word?*

The accusation stole his voice from his throat and the will from his fingers.

He expected, in the far-off fog of his thinking mind, that he would soon be dead. She had succeeded. He was too caught by the reflection of her grief to defend himself.

The violence did not come. To his right, he saw the Traveler raise a low, cautious hand at the old woman, who reluctantly lowered her staff.

The Ronin let out a slow, slow breath. He took his hand from the remaining weapon at his waist and held it to his forehead. B5 whined, tools still out and whirring with sparks. The Ronin shook his head. "What do you want?" he asked, harsh with fatigue.

"Well," said the Traveler to the growing silence of the room, "what we really wanted was your help."

"You must be wondering why we'd go to such trouble to rescue an errant Sith warrior," said the Traveler as they poured tea into unpretentious ceramic cups. These sat upon the low wooden table that had unfolded from the *Poor Crow*'s galley deck at the press of a button. The wood was dinged and scratched, but it was real. The Ronin caught himself wondering where it had come from. He suspected he had not earned an answer.

He sat on one side of the table, alone but for B5-56. The Traveler had taken a seat on the other side next to the old woman, called Chie, who accepted her cup with idle calm that belied the intensity with which she maintained her focus on the Ronin. She masked her attention well. She had fought Sith before.

"What part of your rescue involved pointing me out to the local bounty hunters?" asked the Ronin as he accepted his own cup.

"Now, now, that was all you," said the Traveler. "We had nothing to do with the wanted posters either, thank you very much. That's just what you get for waving your lightsaber around when the local authorities are already on edge. There *is* a war waiting in the wings, you know."

B5 hummed an accusatory scold.

The Traveler waved a hand to concede their point. "I suppose I did use all that to herd you onto our ship—but that was just very expedient of me."

"*My* ship, Fox. And for the record, not feeling so hot about you dragging this walking grudge against gravity generators onto it." This came from the far side of the galley. The *Poor Crow*'s pilot was a round-faced young woman with a muss of thick black hair. An impressive array of tattoos, floral and colored, spun down her muscled arms. She sat cross-legged away from the table, not deigning to share it with the rest. She had preoccupied herself with cleaning the panel the Ronin had shot from the wall because it seemed she found looking at the Ronin ruinously irritating. "Would you tell him that the next time he throws a tantrum on the *Crow*, I'm throwing him out the air lock?"

B5 warbled indignation.

"Let's be fair, Ekiya," said the Traveler. "It was less a tantrum than a strategically calculated threat to commit multiple homicide. But to the point—I feel obligated to explain our interests, Master Ronin, although I'm afraid it requires revisiting a subject you were somewhat reluctant to hear anything about."

"I would rather you tell it than force me to ask any more leading questions," said the Ronin.

"I'll spare you the theatrics, at least."

And though the Ronin didn't wish to hear the story told at all, he appreciated this.

Popularly, it begins with that fellow they called the dark lord. They say he was a Jedi, first—a knight, of course, because how else would he have come to wield a lightsaber? But he was ill suited to the role. Temperamental, arrogant, and hungry for power. Small wonder he turned on his fellow knights, and with such ambition! He rebelled against the clans—against the Empire itself!—and recruited droves of ignoble warriors to his cause.

Together, their army came to be known as the Sith, after that legendary demon host. They cut down Jedi by every dishonorable trick imaginable, stealing their lightsabers and their kyber. They desecrated the once-sacred crystals until the kyber bled, and refashioned them into all manner of unbecoming shapes, perverting the law of the sword, etcetera, etcetera—I'm sorry, I told you no theatrics, but here I am, letting my opinion out.

To the point, off they go, that dark army, conquering planets left and right, turning the hallowed Force upon the very populace they were meant to protect. Such wicked folk, don't you think? Especially when they targeted the temple-strewn peaks of old Rei'izu. The sacred heart of the Empire, its ancient home! What monsters.

It was a maddening blow, to see Rei'izu taken by those who bore so little respect for its heritage. Although, well, you would have to be a bit of an academic to put it like this, but one could say that until that day, the Empire wasn't really *the* Empire. It surely had once been, centuries ago, but all it had known for generations was the feuds of lordlings vying for control over this or that stretch of space. But this bit of Sith sacrilege, well, it gave those lords a reason to unite.

Not that, ultimately, this alliance had anything much to do with winning the war. Within days of Rei'izu's subjugation, the Sith fractured, fell to infighting—took one another clean out. Who can say why? Perhaps they were possessed by angry gods, spirits, so forth. Perhaps Rei'izu itself cursed them. Perhaps they sullied what they shouldn't have—all manner of artifacts were kept in Rei'izu's esteemed temples, some well known to be spiteful when ill used. The storied kyber mirror of Shinsui Temple, for example. But that's another sort of tale.

Whatever the case, when the Sith fell, they took Rei'izu with them. It vanished. Where it had been there was but space, an emptiness, a nothing. It pained the Empire to see its homeworld taken, disappeared without a trace. But, oh, in the same breath, the Empire was so very relieved to see that, conveniently, evil had proven the seed of its own destruction.

Indeed, the Empire has enjoyed these twenty long years of peace ever since, all that lordly bickering done away with, thanks to the accidentally civic-minded Sith.

Here the Traveler paused, sipping their tea. They spoke with a lilting cadence, their rests as intentional as their words. This quiet lingered.

If they were waiting for the Ronin to speak, well, he was waiting too, though he did so unconsciously at first. As the silence dragged on, he realized what he wanted to hear was also what he was being denied: the voice. She said nothing.

Was she still angry with him? She had every right to be.

But then, she had urged him toward this Traveler—as well as to listen to them. What did she wish for him here, if not death? He was afraid to ask; more than an answer, he feared she wouldn't respond.

The Traveler offered mercy. "The thing is," they said, placing their cup back down on the table, "we have reason to suspect the Sith might not be as disappeared as people like to think. That warrior you were tussling with, for example. She seemed a bit off to me. What about you?"

"Well," said the Ronin, "I did kill her a few days ago."

This made the old woman's gaze sharpen fractionally. The pilot, meanwhile, had given up pretending to care about the panel in her lap. She stared hard at the Ronin, simmering with distrust.

"Yet she didn't look particularly dead," said the Traveler, easy as ever. "Which is disconcerting, given the implication. It's been ever so long since the galaxy saw such vigorous ghosts. Although if we believe the gossip on the road, perhaps we've only just noticed it's happening. The disappearing dead—do you recall? I suppose now we've seen what happens when those expired Jedi wander off. Although I'm not about to claim they've *all* been remade as demons, bent on pursuing you . . . What do you make of it all?"

"Are you asking me if any other Sith got up after I killed them?" asked the Ronin.

"Did they? No? Then that just goes to show it *is* a new and pressing concern. We're after the reason underlying these resurrections, you see.

That infamous witch, as they called her. She seems less vanished than we thought. Not that we've had any idea where to find her."

"What would you do, if you did?"

The Ronin willed his face impassive as he asked. B5, beside him, remained unusually silent. The old woman and the pilot had both gone still, but the Traveler bowed their head, a kind of apology.

"What would you?" they asked. "We don't like to presume. But for all you carry the mark of a Sith, you don't seem too fond of them. You proved as much when you tried to kill that woman who's hunting you down. Well, when you *did* kill her. And the others before her—oh, yes, we know your credentials. How did you imagine we tracked you down? In any case, we find ourselves in need of someone who might have a better sense of where to look for that clever old witch—and seeing as you've such a sterling record of hunting down others of your ilk . . . we did hope you might lend us your expertise."

A tension built within the galley hall, winding all its occupants into tighter and tighter knots. The old woman and the pilot stared with equal reservation, though the old woman hid it better. The Traveler also coiled, even beneath their fluid demeanor.

The Ronin wished fervently that the voice would tell him what to think. But she maintained her silence. Even if she spoke, he knew she wouldn't answer the questions he now needed to ask.

What had changed? He didn't imagine she had ever liked to see him kill Sith, but she had always permitted him those victories. If he could no longer properly fulfill the hunt—his last obligation—then he had two choices. He could surrender, or . . .

No. He would not choose. Not yet. Not until he better understood just what had happened to the witch. He owed her that much, at least.

"Rei'izu," he said. "The witch took it, and she's kept it for her own. We'll need to find a way back."

His acquiescence evidently shocked his new comrades. The old woman's eyebrows shot up, and the pilot's eyes widened.

The Traveler, meanwhile, recovered their calm as nimbly as they hid their anxiety; a hint of a smile curled from beneath their mask. "Where do you suppose we ought to begin our search, Master Ronin?"

The Ronin stood. Tension returned to the old woman's frame, and the pilot's hand strayed unconsciously to her side, where she kept a blaster. The Traveler showed no sign of fear whatsoever. The Ronin wanted to call them a fool, but he had learned better.

"Set a course for Dekien," the Ronin said to the pilot. "We'll find a relic there, sacred to the Sith. It will guide our path."

The little crew exchanged odd, uneasy looks. But the pilot seemed to like what she saw in the Traveler's posture. She nodded and got up also, heading for the cockpit. The old woman remained in her seat to finish her tea, and she placed a subtle hand on the Traveler's wrist. This was no doubt to stop them from following the Ronin, who had turned on his heel.

B5 lingered behind, sensing the Ronin wished to be alone. At least, the Ronin wanted to believe that was the reason. He knew the droid hadn't much cared for how he conducted himself in those long-ago days they had both just been reminded of.

CHAPTER
SEVEN

Kouru drifted in space, hating it. She was a deadened thing, out here—more so even than she had been in that derelict temple behind the waterfall. It had always been this way for her. From her first journey into the black, when the Jedi came to claim her for a distant clan, the stars had never been anything but a hungry, taking light.

That she willingly subjected herself to them now was testament to her need. She sat hunched over before the controls of the scout vessel she had hijacked, her eyes on the screen tracking the *Poor Crow*.

Damnably, her attention was of needs divided. The lightsaber Kouru had stolen sang to her with an insistence she'd never felt before.

What do you make of it?

Kouru half-thought she heard a voice. She didn't bother looking for it; she had done so the first few times the whisper cloyed in her ear. It had made her feel foolish to find no source, which she loathed. So, she wouldn't look. Already, she could barely remember the nothing-words she hadn't thought.

She returned her attention to her stolen prize. Her *broken* prize.

Kouru had encountered the flaw after she stole the scout ship and was alone inside it: No matter how she manipulated the hilt, the red length of the old man's lightsaber would not retract. While this explained, in part, his need for that dreadful scabbard, she had no similar recourse other than to stick the thing into the hull.

Therefore, she broke it further—disassembled the entirety into its component parts. Kouru couldn't quite explain how she'd done it so deftly. Old instinct, perhaps—or need?

Regardless, she was lucky to have the components largely intact. They lay before her on the console, waiting to be reconfigured. It would be no mean feat. Kouru had constructed her own lightsaber, and her auxiliary, but she was no technician.

You have my aid, where you need it.

Kouru's hand fisted over the dismantled parts, and she shook her head free of murmurs. Focus. She required focus.

Looking over the lot, she encountered two oddities.

First, the components. Kouru examined each in turn, yet for the life of her, she could find no obvious imperfections, nor anything missing that she expected to need. The cycling field energizer showed unusual signs of wear, as was to be expected; the blade had been caught in a perpetual loop. Had that been by design?

Yet as Kouru rebuilt the lightsaber, she couldn't discern what mechanism might have triggered such a loop. Broken after all, then? But if that was the case, it couldn't have been broken so terribly, or she couldn't have solved the problem so easily: Once reassembled, the hilt in Kouru's palm remained inert; it would not emit a blade until she told it to.

And here was the second strangeness—the ornamentation. The lightsaber *looked* old, the oldest it was possible for such things to be. It looked, in short, like an heirloom blade, the sort the scion of a Jedi clan would wield. Kouru turned the reconstructed hilt over in her hands, running her thumbs over the worn leather strips wound around fingernails of shiny metal, and across the curve of the plain guard at its end.

As a weapon, it was beautiful. As a weapon of the Sith, it made no sense. Kouru ignited the lightsaber, as if she needed to be sure of its color, even though she had only just laid eyes on the kyber from which the weapon drew its hue. The red blade sprang forth, and the kyber crystal within seemed to murmur against her palm.

It reminded her, faintly, of her own blade, now gone. Her lightsaber had always seemed somehow to be fighting her. She had pieced it together in the shadow of a battlefield, the kyber crystal freshly stolen from the lightsaber of a Jedi her master had watched her fell mere hours before.

"It seems a waste to destroy a weapon already forged," Kouru had said.

"Better to make it your own," her master had responded. "Don't whine. You have the blueprint. And tell me if you're troubled. I didn't like making mine either. But we help each other, Kouru. All right?"

This was how the Sith had fashioned their sabers, built to the order of the holographic blueprints shared from cell to cell. There was a man who'd drawn them, Kouru knew, another Sith, whose instinct lay in mechanical spark and pathway. He'd sent the auxiliary plans soon after Kouru finished her blade. She had seen the promise of his offering when her master's saber was reforged as a shining red fan.

Kouru's lightsaber had never whispered as sweetly as this scion's blade. It had bucked, snarled at her. She had relished the struggle to properly wield her weapon; it had kept her focused and determined. Now she felt the difference. The stolen lightsaber in her hand, for all it had been strangely askew within itself, was an extension of her flesh. A master-piece. It unsettled her, in part because she hated any intimacy with this emblem of the Jedi, and in part because it simply couldn't exist.

No Jedi heirs had ever joined the Sith. They wouldn't have. As the legacy of the clans' inherent cruelties made flesh, the scions had been the Sith's most hated foe.

How else to explain it?

The question came in earnest—even if she couldn't precisely deter-mine where it had come from—and thus it demanded an answer. Kouru thought, to her creeping horror, that she could provide one.

She raised her eyes over the red glow of the lightsaber to where the *Poor Crow* lurked in the dark of space. A man waited for her upon it. She wanted, first and foremost, to be angry with him. For killing her. For—

Her breath hitched. No matter how she gritted her teeth, it was fear that slicked through her veins.

There was one among the Sith who had chosen a strange shape for his lightsaber. No clever auxiliary for him, no. Instead, he had styled his hilt after a scion's inheritance, a bloodline blade. It had been a declara-tion: I am my own blood, and these are my own people. Never again do I serve the Jedi. Never again do I yield to their lords.

At the thought of that man, Kouru's mind was hazed by the pressure of space, cluttered by memory. She drew into herself in the scout vessel's cockpit and breathed, though not as deeply as she should have. Despite her efforts, the recollection seeped forward and suffused her mind.

Yes, Kouru. Fear. Fear comes first. Feed it. Nurture it. Do this, and you'll have your fury when you need it.

Mere days after their victory on Rei'izu, word came: The Empire had rallied, and the lords had forged new alliances. There would be no more room to breathe, heal, and mourn the lost. A great fleet was gathering under the Emperor's banner, and the Sith would defend the world they had claimed for their own, or they would die.

Kouru and her master were called to the flagship, the dark lord's own vessel. She had gazed up at the great pitted hull with such young-hearted pride. It was a hideous beast, and it had survived many horrors. She thought it a powerful thing. She was pleased to serve it and her lord—the lord she had chosen.

She never did see the man, before the end. It was known that he was angry. That he had quarreled with the witch. Kouru thought little of this. She quarreled with her master all the time, and what did that matter? They loved each other still, and they would serve each other until they died. That was the promise of the Sith rebellion. The lord and the witch had declared it so. Kouru knew it was true, because for that promise, they had sworn to take Rei'izu, and had Rei'izu not fallen? It had seemed so simple, at the time.

The end began as they came upon an arm of the Imperial fleet, one composed of medical freighters and transports. They meant to claim the freighters for their own—they had lost so many supplies on Rei'izu. It would be grueling, Kouru knew. She was tired. They all were. But they had just shown the galaxy what they could do when they did it for each other. They could burn any world they chose.

Not a shot was fired before the dark lord's flagship began to break around them. Kouru remembered the dim dark of every corridor interrupted by flashing lights. The screech and buckle of a ripping hull. The roiling sparks and choking smoke.

They thought it a Jedi attack, or some other Imperial terror. An infiltration, someone swore—there was a point in the belly of the flagship where it had all begun to shatter. Kouru said: "Then let's find them." Her master said: "Yes."

She was lying, Kouru learned. She followed her master thoughtlessly, led by trust, and only realized her error when she had been shut into an escape pod—alone.

The last thing Kouru saw through the viewport . . . she came to think it a dream. A nightmare. But for those first years she swore to herself that she saw her master unfurl the graceful fan of her saber as if her blade was more than light sans substance. As if a weapon built to cut through flesh could do anything to mend a ship torn full asunder. As if in the smoke of that collapsing ship, she had some enemy to meet. A murderer. One who thought gutting a ship wasn't enough if he could have no blood with it. A man who closed in on her, holding a long red blade fitted to an old and beautiful hilt.

Then there was nothing but Kouru, left to drift long hours in space, not dead, not alive, but screeching. She had wanted to cut through the walls of her pod and sink her blade into deserving flesh. To rend something, anything with her nails and teeth.

But space and propulsion separated her from any possibility of satisfaction. She screamed her rage at that, too, until her throat was bloody and soundless when she landed on the muddy ground of a backwater Outer Rim planet and its shanty distilleries.

It was days before she reached a proper spaceport and got word of the galaxy beyond that murky pit of a world. The war, over. The Sith, dead. Dead, because they had killed themselves taking Rei'izu. Or because they had killed one another. Or because the ghosts the witch had stolen had at last turned on their cruel mistress and—

But that wasn't the truth, was it? You knew better.

Kouru clutched the hilt of her stolen blade, exquisite and *familiar*, and stared fixedly at the ragged transport hanging in the black. The *Crow.* Her quarry.

The Sith hadn't died on one another's blades—they had died on only one. He had killed her, too, in the end.

And would you call yourself dead, Kouru?

What *could* she call herself, other than hateful?

Kouru's thumb trembled on the lightsaber's control. She turned it off, the blade withdrew, and she let out a shaking breath.

Whatever was wrong with the old man that had made him unable—or unwilling—to fix his blade, Kouru had done it where he failed. Now it was hers to wield. Hers to control.

She snorted and loosened her limbs. The panic had receded and she could think again, enough to wonder at herself. She had spent so many years playing lord of the muck in the dust of the Outer Rim, carving a niche out of insignificance just to know herself alive.

All that playacting, when she could have been hunting *him*. The man who had taken her reason to live when he took the lives of all the others. The man who had only days ago killed her with the lightsaber she now held. Just as he had killed her master.

The traitor had been no delusion, she now realized. She, grieving girl, had not concocted him in her desperation to blame *someone* for the terrors she had endured. He was as real as the relentless blade she had wrested from his waist. He—

Pay attention.

Kouru's eyes flicked up to the screen tracking the *Poor Crow* just as it jumped to hyperspace. She scanned the calculations assessing its trajectory and keyed commands into the scout vessel as she did so.

Never once did she question her familiarity with the scout ship's systems, or where she had learned to manipulate them. Her bright fixation blinded her to the oddity of her newfound conviction: She was going to kill the old man. She knew this and had known it for days now. What lit her up anew was the understanding of *why*.

It would mean something, for him to die. It would make room for something new to live—to be reborn. The flame of the rebellion he had extinguished would find fuel in the blaze of his demise. Kouru would make it so.

CHAPTER
EIGHT

ONE FACE, STRICKEN with horror, mouth elongated with death, became another. This one, slack in shock. The next, twisted and rageful. More and more, eyes wide and darkly shining, then dull and unfocused. One death upon more. The stench of burning cloth and metal and flesh so deeply saturated in his nose that for weeks and months every time he inhaled, the singe tickled his throat.

Her face, last and most striking. The length of her black hair undone, wild with the throes of her fury and resignation. Her grief. The long croak pouring out of her throat. The wordless wail that became a curse.

He wished to kneel before her, hands on his knees, to lay his neck out for her sentence. Instead his hands gripped the hilt of his red blade as he lifted it up and—

The Ronin jolted upright. He had been prodded, a finger to his cheek.

He came to himself where he had sat, cross-legged on the ground. He had chosen an out-of-the-way offshoot of the main corridor near to the back end of the *Poor Crow,* just by the point where he had entered through the lower hatch. The offshoot led to the storage area where one might keep gear for less hospitable climes and little else. He had thought it the most unobtrusive place to simply be, and he had rested his back against the hull to think. Now every muscle he was aware of ached.

The Traveler was crouched in front of him, hand hovering in front of them, finger still outstretched. From this angle, the Ronin couldn't make out their face behind the fox mask, but he expected they were smiling, and smugly at that.

"You really are in terrible shape," they said. "You didn't even hear me."

"You aren't a danger," the Ronin said. He meant: I would have known if you meant to kill me.

"Flatterer." The Traveler stood and nodded him upward as well. "Come on, now. This is the most depressing place imaginable for anyone to fall asleep."

"I was meditating."

"Then meditate in a bunk."

It would take a few days to reach Dekien, the Traveler explained as they led him down the main corridor of the *Poor Crow.* There were few established hyperlanes here in the Outer Rim, and furthermore, they wished to take a circuitous route to avoid detection. Whose detection, they didn't specify.

"I don't suppose you're hiding an instinct for this sort of navigation?" they asked over their shoulder. "No? What about some manner of concealment? Not that either? Just the unsparing instinct for sophisticated mechanical sabotage, then. Ah, well."

"You're nosy," said the Ronin.

"Sociable." The Traveler paused before a door that swished open to a spare cell of a bunk. There was no lock on it. Within: a bed, a table, a lantern, empty shelves. "Listen," they said, "you're underslept, underfed, and embarrassingly rusty."

The Ronin agreed with all three but frowned for dignity's sake.

"No need to sulk. I say it because we want you in top form by the time we're chasing after your ominous relic. Now it's going to take us a few hours to clear sparring space, so you have at least that long to sleep like a person and eat like one too. And if you'd like to do something about the truly tremendous amount of grime on your person, I suggest a visit to the tidy little room over yonder. It's called a—"

"I know what it's called. You, though . . ."

The Traveler put a hand to their chest. "What about me?"

"Traveler, Fox. What do I call you?"

There was a silence. "Whatever you like, I suppose."

"That's a lot of freedom."

"Then I'll trust you to exercise it wisely."

They left him there. He found he was still frowning. Something of their indifference struck him as true, and some other part of it resonated in the hollow of his heart.

He didn't like to think of why he recognized the feeling, so he glanced at his wrist. The cuff was dark. He had seen no trace of B5-56 since he woke. He pushed down a second shallow pang.

Someone had left a tray of foodstuffs on the low table beside the bunk. Not rations, either. Rice steamed in a bowl alongside stewed vegetables and an unidentifiable, toothsome protein. On the whole, better fare than he could often expect.

It left him rather unable to sleep.

Yet sleep he did, somehow, after what felt like hours lying on his back with his eyes closed, unbearably aware of the vessel thrumming beneath him and of the absence of the voice within.

He was woken a mere few hours later. "A bit of practice," said the Traveler as they led him down to the cargo hold in the belly of the *Crow*. "If we don't clean that rust off you, you're going to be gored by a demon before you ever get us to Rei'izu."

Now the Ronin stood in a cleared section of the long hold. Cargo containers had been shoved about to make rudimentary obstacles, or arranged in the loading zone just outside.

Though fed and slept, the Ronin itched with an odd loneliness. B5 had passed them on the way down and chosen to say little more than a cursory greeting before returning to assist the pilot's debate with the navicomputer. The voice had not spoken at all. Perhaps this was why he relished the opportunity to face his opponent.

The Traveler sat on a low stack of containers at the far end of the cargo hold, observing the Ronin. Weighing their opponent, as the

Ronin intended to weigh them. He had seen their skill, in a manner of speaking. Their precision, and the extravagance of it. They had not yet moved against him body-to-body; he hadn't even seen them run.

More than that, he wished to *see* them. Though he had from the start been aware of their natural presence in the Force, it stubbornly eluded his ability to make sense of it. Where the bandit had shone radiant and boiled dark all at once, the Traveler was a shadow in an ill-lit pool. The Ronin wondered how they would shine when they faced him, uncloaked.

At the same time, his limbs buzzed with apprehension. It had been decades since he last fought anyone he didn't intend to wound. The notion sent a thrill through his blood. Therefore, it concerned.

But it was the old woman, Chie, who stepped out onto the scraped floor, electrostaff held loose at her side. She read the hesitation in his posture.

"Really?" she snorted. "I near brained you mere hours ago."

So she had, although she misread the reason for his stall. Either way, it wouldn't do to disrespect her, so he inclined his head to agree.

They slid into position across from each other. The Traveler watched intently from their perch. "Well?" they said. "Have at it."

Chie came at the Ronin with liquid speed, then dodged low and around him. He moved not at all, sensing her feint. The electrostaff stabbed so near his face that had he inhaled, the tip of his nose might have skimmed its sizzling end.

Out of the corner of his eye, he saw Chie's mouth tighten. Irritation or satisfaction? She remained difficult to read, and she had only grown more careful since he last saw her. She was most clearly legible through the Force, an uncommon experience for him. There, she was all black current run through with a bright line of white fire—the singular intent with which she pursued him.

He tracked the line of her to follow her strike. The next one was true, a spin that seemed to lift her off the ground, the staff twisting over her shoulders to carry momentum before it swung down with whistling speed.

The Ronin slid to the side, then back to dodge her swift backward kick.

She clucked her tongue. "You're not here to run from me."

The scold hit him squarely where nothing else yet had. "I'd rather not be shocked," he said from the other side of a short pyramid of cargo containers.

"Then block."

He raised a brow.

She smiled, more a baring of teeth. "Is it because I'm not a Jedi?"

"You aren't."

"Neither are you." She leapt up onto the crates and sprang forward in one lithe movement, electrostaff crackling toward his head. "You haven't ever been, I wager."

This he deflected with the unignited length of his scabbard auxiliary, and her grin met his glower.

"Now, don't take me for a purist," she said, bounding back and up the tower again. "I'm not sure I'd call any of your lot 'Jedi' these days, least of all the clan bloodlines. Tell me, did they teach you what you were? Or was it just blood and blades from the day they named you one of their own?"

The Ronin hefted his scabbard and eyed Chie as she paced the top container. He, the wolf on the ground. She, the falcon above. "The masters, they told us stories," he said. "Our proud heritage. The lineage we now shared with the clan, bound by the Force. They thought it a good way to tell children who they should die for."

"You disagreed."

It wasn't a question but another feint. The Ronin let Chie corner him this time. She wanted the measure of his reflexes, and to his surprise, he wanted this too. They found a rhythm readily, her strikes, his deflections. This carried them so ferociously across the cargo hold that the Traveler was forced to flee their spot on the containers near the entrance.

"I understood the seed of your rebellion." Chie's voice remained as level as the Traveler's in the middle of a story, even as she swung, testing the Ronin's instincts, urging him always to return her strikes. "The Jedi weren't worth serving. Not as a shadow of what they should be—what they once were."

The Ronin scoffed. She nearly took him out at the knee.

"Healers," she said, "artisans, defenders. Monks! Servants of the weak and of the gods. Then they pledged themselves to their lords instead of to the people, and look what's become of them. Sword this, sword that. And they're not even as good as they think."

Chie's hand slipped into her robes—this he saw. He expected a knife, not the blaster.

Two shots, lightning-fast, and the second singed the edge of his sandal because she predicted the angle of his flight. The bolts scarred the wall and a container. A third seemed on the way until the Traveler flung out their arm and stole the blaster from Chie's hand with an expert whip of black current.

"Aunty, please!" They clutched the weapon with the desperation of distaste. "I told Ekiya we'd behave—and that does, I think, include not murdering one another."

"Tell him to try harder."

The Ronin said nothing in order to catch his breath. He *was* trying, and that amazed him to realize. Chie inhabited the fullness of her body to an extent he had rarely encountered, even among the most martially gifted Jedi—or Sith. He expected she'd give any of them trouble, even ones more willing to draw their blades.

"There's no point to this until you meet me as you truly are," said Chie. Now she stood below and he above. She waited for him to return to her level, balancing on her staff. "Here, Sith."

He remained above. "You say you understood our resistance. Yet I think you scorn me as well."

"You were such children about it."

Her contempt pricked his nerves.

"Angry children," she went on. "The worst the Jedi had to offer. Conquering planets under the banner of liberation. Taking their young people to be your foot soldiers, just like you had been taken. You can't really be defending that. Then again, we don't know when you turned on the Sith, do we?"

The Ronin moved before he thought to, willing himself calm but unable to find serenity in stillness. So, he leapt. He descended on Chie in a billow of cloak—and lunged past her. She swept her staff to trip him. He hopped over it, his eye on the shift of her feet and hands.

His silence and flight only fanned the flames of Chie's disdain. "Tell me," she said, "did you follow in the footsteps of other betrayers, or were you one of the first to turn your blade on your own? When you murdered your first Sith, did they still think you a companion?"

The Ronin's head roared, a blazing fire. Soot in his nose, ash in his mouth.

Chie had him in a corner now, and her staff thrust toward him again. She expected him to go up, perhaps, or to the right. So when he seized the end of her staff just under the shrieking electric head and yanked down and to his side, it broke her grasp.

Chie let go rather than let herself be dragged forward. Instinct made her hop back out of his reach, but she was smiling with some kind of true delight. "There you are."

The Ronin felt—nothing. Nothing, because he could not abide the alternative. His grip on the staff tightened. His body yearned for the follow-through. The lunge, the snap. He held himself violently still.

Chie would come for him again, he knew. Prodding, cutting, a knife seeking blood. She wouldn't stop until he did worse than take her weapon. She had not yet gotten what she wanted, so she couldn't surrender, no matter what she lost, or what he did to make her, *break her*—

"Well! That looks exhausting. Why don't you put those down before you throw out your back?"

The Ronin inhaled. A series of thuds brought him back to the cargo hold. All about him, cargo containers toppled from their towers and to the floor from where they had been floating, rising into the air and vibrating with tension.

The Traveler's doing? No. They stood at the ready by the entrance, hands out to seize the black current of the Force should they need it. They hadn't, yet.

Chie, meanwhile, stood unmoving in the middle of the hold, gazing at her opponent. Her stare was piercing and her mouth chillingly even; an accusation sans malice. She simply found him wanting.

He was. He knew it. Had known since the day he killed his first Sith. That had not stopped him yet. It made him a damnable thing.

"I think we're done for today." The Traveler's hands lowered and they stepped toward him. The Ronin gripped Chie's staff more tightly, and they balked.

"Yes, I think we are," said Chie.

She intercepted the Traveler and directed them out of the hold with her. Less courtesy than scorn. Her murmur on the way out the door left no room for doubt.

"I know you want to trust him, dear," she said to the Traveler. "That's why I can't. I believe you've now seen at least one reason why you shouldn't."

The Traveler's response was too distant to make out; not that the Ronin could hear much of anything over the remembered din of roaring flame and screeching metal collecting in his ears.

For hours, they left him there, alone. He soon lost track of the time because he gave himself a purpose that drank up his sense of it.

The scabbard auxiliary lay before him in its multitude of component pieces. Emitter matrix, focusing lens, field energizer, flux aperture, stabilizing ring, so on, so forth; he lingered on the kyber shard. It was one of many he now possessed, but it had been with him longest of those that remained in his keeping. He had not touched it or any other one of the components for some time now. He didn't yet know what to do with the lot.

He had known since the bandit stole his proper blade that he would want to remodel the scabbard. Idly, he wondered whether she had managed to contain it. Likely so. The flaw in the blade was more in its old wielder than its construction.

The same was true of his scabbard. It had a use—more than one. He had made it as a prison and as a trick. But its shape was impractical for regular use, though he might have grown accustomed to it, given time. Having a lack of that, he would be best served by fashioning himself a replacement to mimic the weapon he had lost.

He had components enough to do more than that. His younger self would have been lost for days in the possibility of so much kyber. The man he was now festered with doubt. He needed a blade. He trusted himself with it, mostly. He did not want himself to have it on this ship.

Footsteps approached the hold, carelessly heavy. Not Chie or the Traveler, then. The pilot. What had they called her? Ekiya.

The footsteps stopped at the entrance. Out of the corner of his eye, he saw their owner steel herself. Her fists clenched. Ekiya had avoided him thus far, preferring the company of her crew and B5-56. Now she entered boldly. She was afraid but unwilling to let it stop her.

"Bee says you're sulking," she said to announce her presence. "Which, fine, I guess I'd sulk too if everyone in the galaxy had a good reason to hate my guts."

The Ronin had nothing reasonable to say to this. He returned to the contemplation of his components. Ekiya seemed content to ignore him. She cared more for her cargo than for him. But as she began to right the crates he had thrown into disarray, he realized he couldn't leave her to it.

He wrapped the components in the cloth upon which he'd laid them and went to offer his labor. Ekiya eyed him skeptically, then directed him to place the crate he was presently touching off to the side.

As he followed suit with others, she broke the seal of one that had toppled off the largest makeshift pyramid. She wanted to inspect the contents—to ensure they remained unharmed.

The Ronin didn't know what to make of what she uncovered from the layers of soft packing material. Packages of varying size and shape. She scanned every one with a datapad to assess its condition. It had never occurred to him to wonder about the *Crow*'s cargo.

Once satisfied with the contents of one container, Ekiya repacked it and moved on to the next. By then, the Ronin had returned as much of the cargo hold to its natural state as he could, with the exception of the space Ekiya took up to run her assessment.

"If you still want to help, lay out everything in those two over there," said Ekiya without looking up. She indicated the containers she meant with a nod. "And be careful, would you?"

So, he unpacked. Packages varied by weight and shape, and every so often, they spoke to him. One that weighed heavily and had to be carried in two hands was some manner of archaic timepiece, as was another, palm-sized and circular. Another shimmered like light under his palm—a lantern, by his guess. Artifacts? He couldn't say.

The next package he lifted tinkled in his hands, a broken sound. It fit entirely within one palm and he winced as he laid it down. Something about it pulsed into his fingers, curiously familiar. Ekiya came over without his having to ask. She grimaced as she crouched and scanned the package before setting both pad and scanner down to painstakingly unwrap it.

With every layer she peeled back, the prickling sensation in the Ronin's fingers increased. Unconsciously, his hand drifted to the concealed lining of his cloak, and only when she finished did he understand why.

Ekiya had uncovered a yellowed ivory carving, barely the size of his thumb. It had once been circular, with curling branches and two small birds seated amidst rounded flowers. Now a crack ran down the middle, and it threatened to fall apart at Ekiya's nervous touch.

Within the crack, something glimmered. A faint light, fragile like dust in sunlight, but the Ronin recognized its character, crystalline and alive. Kyber.

Ekiya caught him staring. She sighed heavily. "No hiding this one, huh?"

It wasn't really a question. "No. I felt it the moment I touched it . . . Although it was undetectable while still in the crate."

Ekiya frowned at the carving, contemplative. "I guess if a Jedi's close enough to the cargo hold that they're in my crates, we're screwed anyway."

Just how much kyber did she have stowed on the *Crow*? The Ronin suspected he understood how she'd managed to hide the shards. A deft piece of craftsmanship resonated in the Force—like a masterfully designed garden evoked the world, or a priest in prayer evoked a god. Kyber always shivered with its own power, obvious and eager, but if incorporated into a masterwork, its presence might feasibly be missed.

It begged the question: What did Ekiya mean to do with it all? He hadn't seen such a kyber trove outside Jedi keeping but for the one he carried in the seam of his clothing. Ekiya was no Jedi. No Sith. She had far less presence in the Force than either the Traveler or Chie; she was alive, but she made no eddies. It was not hers to command.

What reason did she have to hoard the shards?

Ekiya saw the question in his frown. "I'm taking them home," she said, and she did not elaborate.

She turned back to the broken carving before her, still frowning, now scrolling through her datapad. He moved to the next crate, but she stopped him with her next question.

"Why'd you do it? Turn on the Jedi, I mean." Her eyes remained on her datapad. "And don't give me the party line. Why did *you*?"

No one had ever asked the Ronin this before. Largely, this was a co-incidence of his anonymity, and of everyone who could have known to ask being dead. Yet it shocked him, in the way of an elbow unexpectedly jolted. He couldn't answer, not quickly.

"You're not my first Sith, you know," she said. "I'm not afraid of you."

"Clearly."

She shot him a sour look and went back to the work. "I saw you—all of you—the day you came to Rei'izu."

Abruptly the Ronin both understood a great deal about Ekiya and did not at all know how he should speak to her. He stood there, silent, hands useless by his sides as she went on.

"Guess I looked strong enough to fight and smart enough to know I couldn't fight you. You rounded me up with the first troopers you shipped offworld."

By "you," she meant the Sith. The Ronin would not have met her. Those first days on Rei'izu, he had been otherwise preoccupied. He was nonetheless culpable. He knew this as keenly as Chie did.

"And wouldn't you know it, we're a week offworld and what've you done? Who knows! But Rei'izu's not there anymore. So it's just me and a bunch of other terrified kids at the front line of some nothing moon, facing down the Jedi and the Empire while our Sith commander loses his mind. Real fun, let me tell you. Especially when he got all 'well, it's time to make a last stand' about it." Ekiya wrinkled her nose. "Don't get me wrong. The Jedi weren't any help either. We had to take care of the guy ourselves. And he—it got messy."

The Ronin was positive he should say something. He could not imagine anything he said would be worth hearing.

Ekiya snorted. "They didn't even know what to do with us, after. Bunch of freaked-out kids with no home to go to. I mean, they tried. I guess. Whatever. We had one another. That was *all* we had—oh, forget it. Look, what I mean is, I deserve an answer. Don't I?"

She did. Of this he was certain. Silence would have served him better, but that wasn't his right here, now was it? "What do you want to hear?" he asked.

"I mean, an apology would be nice." She scoffed. "Who am I kidding, no it wouldn't. I just want to *know*. What was so bad about the Jedi that you didn't think anything of hurting us?"

The Ronin had no answer; there wasn't one. No justification, only the truth. He still felt, viscerally, that he owed it to her. He touched the aching metal on his jaw and said, slowly, choosing careful words to find his point, "My lord told me to kill someone . . . and I didn't. Wouldn't. At the time, I knew it was a no. I didn't realize it was also a yes. I didn't understand what we would become. And I can't . . ."

Ekiya's focus remained on her datapad at first, her brightly painted fingernails hard at its sides. When the Ronin trailed off, struggling for words to satisfy her, she threw him another look over her shoulder. Her mouth had a rueful twist; she accepted his shortcoming, even as she recognized it for the lack it was. It said volumes about what she understood that he couldn't.

"Go get some rest," she said, and returned to her work.

He ceded the cargo hold to her, grateful for the reprieve.

Simultaneously, he clung to that sense of wrongdoing—that guilt. This, more so than his reflexes or his command of the Force, was what he needed to learn to reckon with. Until now, he had largely done so by not thinking about it. But Chie had only needed the slightest push to unseat him. The witch would no doubt need far less.

He could avoid his sins no longer. Of course he couldn't. They had at last begun to hunt him in turn.

CHAPTER
NINE

THE RONIN REFASHIONED the auxiliary in the privacy of his bunk. The next time he faced Chie in the cargo hold, he met her with the red blade she expected. She expressed her pleasure by doing her damnedest to brain him with her staff. When they had nearly wrung themselves out, he sprang his surprise. The blade retracted and the hilt extended until it matched the length of her own staff. She allowed him this alternative, though she criticized his form at every opportunity—and always, always: "You should be eating more."

Meals on the *Poor Crow* were a company affair, taken around the table in the galley. Ekiya had equipped the ship to do far better than warm spacefaring rations. There was rice at every meal, fresh protein, and vegetables both raw and pickled. After the first, he asked Ekiya in low tones whether any of her broken artifacts were mechanical in nature. He had an expertise, he said. He could help. She balked a moment, then B5-56, lingering at her side, hummed confirmation. Ekiya, brow furrowed, said she would sleep on it.

She didn't give him permission, in the end, though she offered him analgesics when she caught him rubbing his jaw.

"What for?" he asked.

B5 whined at Ekiya, who squinted at the Ronin, unimpressed. "You weren't kidding, Bee. He must be insufferable when he's got a cold."

Even without analgesics, the Ronin slept deeply—until, abruptly, he woke. The dreams never flared so sharply as they had the first time he drifted off in the *Crow*'s hatchway, but they persisted. He hadn't been given to any dreams at all for much of the last few years. The ones he suffered now would have troubled him under any circumstances. He nevertheless took them as an opportunity. He sat with them, thought on them, and didn't push them away, no matter that he wanted to. They hurt to examine no matter what facet he viewed them through, but he was determined. More than once, in the deep of a rest cycle, he was awake, still weary, and acutely alone.

The Traveler noticed. They took to passing by his bunk at ever so convenient times. They always happened to have some tea to offer, and they would invite him to play a round of shogi.

"That sounds a bit much for a man half asleep," he said the first time.

"I know," they said, conspiratorial, "I expect it means I'll win."

The Ronin had learned shogi as an apprentice. In his youth, it had been fashionable for a Jedi master to use the game to train their most promising apprentices how to manage a battlefield. He hadn't cared for it then. Later, when he was no longer a Jedi, he had found a different and more intimate appreciation for the game. It had nevertheless been years since he last played it.

Presumably, the Traveler's familiarity with the game stemmed from a similar history. There was still little the Ronin could say about them with any certainty. They avoided disclosure at every opportunity.

They did not, however, condemn him to silence, for which he was grateful. Quietude could too easily be filled by his own thoughts, which were at these late hours always unkind.

Instead, the Traveler supplied stories. Folktales, ghost stories, parables, and gossip from every planet from the Core to the Outer Rim. Histories, too—ancient tales, and more recent ones.

Those of his new companions, for example.

* * *

Chie, now, she's an idealist, you know. A bounty hunter by trade, to hear her tell it. A specialist. Only takes jobs that end in her nearly beating the life out of a Jedi knight. That's how we met.

Oh, I see that look. What an accusation! A Jedi, me! No, I was but an observer. A little moon on the Outer Rim was suffering for its lord's desires. The lord had a new mine in a neighboring system and found himself in want of labor. He sent his Jedi to round up volunteers. Their recruitment methods left something to be desired.

Chie challenged them to a duel, of course—it's what they prefer, these Jedi, and they accepted all too readily. I did warn them, or I tried, but they could not fathom why they should heed the concerns of a mere storyteller. I was too mortified to insist. To think Jedi knights would fail to see what was so clear to me!

Ah, well. They earned their end. I watched on—from a polite distance, mind you—and to my disconcertion, Chie turned to me upon her victory. I believe she thought she might have to kill me next. Fortunately, I was able to convince her that I knew of a more pressing problem. Sith this, Sith that. My fortune soon doubled; it wasn't Jedi in particular she so loathed, but any being who dared to abuse the Force for their own selfish ends. She signed right on.

I did wonder what convinced her so swiftly. It wasn't trust—I still doubt she trusts me entirely—but she *believed.* I suspect it comes down to her training. She must have had some sort of it. Perhaps with one of those orders the Empire tried so very hard to stamp out after the clans swore fealty—the ones who saw the Force in ways the Empire prefers we not think it should be seen.

You should listen to the way she speaks of gods. It's the same way she speaks of ghosts, and of the Force. She certainly thinks both Jedi and Sith go about things entirely the wrong way around. Then again, she's an aunty, and they do tend to feel the rest of us are idiots about nigh on everything we do.

The Ronin coughed at this. He had not been young for quite some time, but Chie certainly had him by an order of decades, and he was given to respect his elders, even when—perhaps especially when—they wished to stave his head in.

The Traveler laughed and sighed and agreed, though in a conspiratorial fashion. The Ronin laughed in turn, unprompted, though he stifled the sound with his tea. The Traveler seemed to think they had won.

He thought: I shouldn't encourage this.

Yet when they spoke, he continued to listen.

Oh, Ekiya. I fear we're a terrible influence on her. Before she got mixed up in our delusions of grandeur, she was doing her best to fix what we old fools had broken.

We were in the market for a pilot, Chie and I. Ekiya is that, obviously, though I wouldn't quite say it's her calling. We'd gone looking for anyone who might know a thing or two about navigating Rei'izu—yes, yes, we did suspect that was our ultimate goal, even before you lumbered along. You can thank my marvelous intuition.

To the point, we searched out Rei'izu's refugees, and we stumbled on Ekiya and her crew in a neighborhood of just such folk on a trade station in the Mid Rim.

Ah, yes, her crew—the survivors. Those children who outlived the Sith who commanded them. She's still quite close with them, you know. I fear most of her fellows think her fairly mad for joining us. Perhaps she is.

Her friends do rather more concrete goods, you see. In this case, helping their brethren refugees conceal some rather illicit material from an Imperial investigator. Yes, the same sort in the hold, the ones in which they embed kyber shards—ah, perhaps that's not mine to explain. Suffice to say that they're rather personal works, and they're terribly important. But you know how the Empire is about kyber.

So, we helped. I did some lying, Chie did some hitting. I admit that at one point I encouraged the investigator's Jedi escort that he ought to lock himself in an escape pod and refuse to come out—it was just more convenient, you know?

Perhaps that was what convinced Ekiya to forsake her more tangible work for our foolish crusade. I don't presume to know. I do hope she gets something out of it, of course. She deserves whatever satisfaction the universe is willing to yield her.

The Ronin agreed with this sentiment. It was no hardship to wish he had done better than he had, or to want the ruins he had left in his wake to flourish. What was hard was to face them, to speak with them, to be in some way party to that recovery he so hoped for. It was not his right.

The Ronin suspected—hoped?—it would be easier to hear the Traveler's own tale. They continued, as the nights went on, not to offer it. He was compelled instead to study them.

First, he knew them for a Jedi—probably. They had been trained by one, at least. However, he could say the same for himself, and he wouldn't have claimed the title even before Chie had lectured him against it. Yet the Traveler's training was as evident in their skills as it was in his own. If there was another way to become so sharpened in the Force outside the Jedi clans, the Ronin didn't know of it.

Second, he expected a Jedi with such useful martial skills to carry a lightsaber. The Traveler's waist was conspicuously free of any such thing. They had that mask, that flute and their mediocre skill with it, and their hands, ever moving in concert with their voice. The Ronin suspected they didn't care to be violent. To an extent, he understood. But only to an extent.

Third, they had spoken on the Sith's predilection for honing skills outside the martial with an interest that bordered on delight, if not envy. It couldn't be either. They had come to him because they meant to end a threat that could only have started with the Sith themselves. This begged a question: Why? And another: Who, or what, had set them on this path? And why would they not say?

Fourth, they were a shameless cheat.

Their shogi board was plain and wooden, and the black paint daubed on the calligraphic characters identifying each piece had chipped near entirely away from a dozen of them. The Traveler always behaved for the first few turns as they laid out their pieces and determined who had the initiative. The game continued on in this sedate way for a time, as they each advanced and retreated across the board, capturing and redeploying each other's pieces.

But sooner or later, the pieces began to subtly shift from one square to the next whenever the Ronin sipped his tea, or when he looked away because B5 had something especially quarrelsome to say about his strategy. The droid had grown tired of distance on the third night and now accompanied him more often. Neither of them commented on the end of their estrangement, as they both preferred.

B5 said nothing about the Traveler's cheating either, though the droid surely noticed it. To be fair, the Ronin also said nothing. He had decided he would only bring it up once he caught the Traveler in the act. It made the game a test of some of those skills the Traveler had so sorely criticized.

It's remarkably tolerant of you, the voice said on the fourth night.

The Ronin grunted, his hand to his chin as he examined the board. The Traveler had just slid one of their silver generals into the promotion zone—an audacious maneuver, yet he still hadn't seen them do it.

The pressure of her amused silence forced him to acknowledge something he might have preferred to ignore: The Traveler's sustained interest, and their desire to speak with him and to him, had served him well. They created time and space in which his mind could consider the size and severity of the little wounds he kept being reminded of. They had become, in themself, an anchor.

Careful . . . Wouldn't want to grow careless. She had a mocking tone, and yet . . .

The Ronin's hand fell from his mouth as his chest stirred. She had been gone for days, and her absence had hurt; her return hurt also, especially as her presence felt as natural as air in his lungs.

It haunted as well. None of this made *sense.* The voice had only ever directed him toward Sith warriors who would have gladly murdered him if he hadn't murdered them first. The sole exception to the pattern sat across from him, head tilted at his continued silence.

She had, certainly, directed him toward the Traveler. But they were not Sith—the Ronin assumed—and neither did they seem to harbor violent intent. At least, not toward him. If they did, they surely would have struck by now. The only violence they vocally entertained was the kind they hoped to commit upon the witch, and to this end, they desired the Ronin's assistance.

Why, then, had she brought them together? What did she *want*?

The Traveler continued to study him, their chin resting on their palm. The Ronin worried in a cold, slick part of his gut that he owed them an explanation. He feared anything he said would lose him whatever confidence he had been afforded. He feared more than anything that he owed them some manner of truth.

Just as the Ronin's mouth opened, the Traveler reached across the table to offer him a ration-stick. "I know," they said, "*revolting.* But I'm afraid it's all I can manage until Ekiya wakes up."

"I've eaten enough in the last four days to kill a bantha," said the Ronin.

"Well, you were either asking for nutrients like some sort of adorable baby bird, or you wanted to say something."

The Ronin didn't glower, because that would have been peevish. Worse, he felt himself soften.

"Oh, look." The Traveler smiled at the board. "I've won."

They had, but only on account of sliding their chariot when he wasn't looking. The game could continue for a few more rounds, but their victory was assured.

The Ronin snorted. "You should teach me how to do that."

"And lose my advantage?"

He caught himself before he asked for another round. He was enjoying himself. That should have concerned him more than it did. An echo of the voice's warning, playful and inscrutable, rang in his ears: *Careful, careful, careful.*

He couldn't trust the Traveler. He shouldn't have wanted to. And yet.

"If you won't teach me a trick, teach me something else," he said. "Something of yourself."

The Traveler tensed ever so slightly, though they maintained their feckless air. "There's less to know than you imagine."

The Ronin held his tongue. He had come to suspect that they abhorred silence; if faced with it, they quickly filled the gap.

They sighed theatrically and shrugged even more so. "Oh, you know.

Suffice to say that I was once someone else, and I'm glad I no longer am—but who's to say whether who I am now is entirely better? I'm sure you understand."

This admission felt more akin to a victory than he might have imagined. It also revealed a danger, and he let himself smile, private and bitter, as they mutually cleared the board to reset it.

He wasn't about to forget who he was, so long as the voice lingered to remind him. This crew knew him as well, but only to an extent. There would come a time, he was sure, when that changed, and they learned the full truth of the man they had invited onto their ship.

Perhaps it would have been more just or kind to tell them now and spare them later grief. But it would not be wise. He needed these allies now, as much as—if not more than—they needed him. He could not afford to drive them away. Not yet. Not until he understood just what had become of the witch. Not until he knew whether he would be required to kill her.

The voice laughed at him then, and she chuckled to herself all through the next game.

CHAPTER
TEN

THE APPRENTICE HAD come to his study to be scolded. The wood-and-paper door slid open to emit a stiff-backed Twi'lek boy in tidy robes. He emanated a rigidity born of fear as he knelt on the woven floor and bowed his pale-blue head. He made for a striking contrast with the fat old tooka-cat lounging on the sill of the curved window facing east, through which the rich yellow sunlight of Watoru's two suns spilled.

"I'm told they found you in my library," Hanrai said from behind his low wooden desk.

The apprentice didn't speak. Hanrai suspected the boy had been instructed not to. The shouts and grunts of the other apprentices practicing their forms echoed up from the courtyard below. The cat yawned and turned over, limbs stretched. Hanrai sighed. This made the apprentice's forehead pinch, though the boy hurriedly smoothed the frown away.

"My *private* library," Hanrai went on. "At night. Hours after curfew . . . But I haven't said anything you don't already know, so I suppose there's no point repeating it to you, is there, Yuehiro?"

The boy raised his head at that, eyes bright with piercing interest. "You know my name."

"I do. I know the name of every Jedi apprentice in my clan. Shouldn't I? I've adopted you all."

Yuehiro frowned, doubtful. Hanrai acknowledged that he deserved this. They had never once spoken to each other. To the apprentices, the Jedi lord who was in every legal respect their father was but a looming presence in distant windows, passing down halls with his aides and guests, rarely if ever seen sparring with his knights.

Yuehiro in particular had cycled through three names since his arrival four short years ago. The apprentices were always allowed to choose a new one upon adoption. Some clans encouraged it. Yuehiro's new names were more personally motivated and had come with a change in terms of address in addition to a move into the boys' dormitory. He had likely assumed this beneath Hanrai's notice as well. It seemed to concern the boy that it was not.

"Why should you know?" Yuehiro asked. "You don't ever come to see us. You don't teach us either, not anymore . . . my lord."

Yuehiro bowed his head again at the end, but lifted it when Hanrai sighed. Curiosity flickered across the boy's face as he studied his lord anew. Hanrai knew what he saw: an old knight past his prime, though power lingered in his thick waist and broad shoulders. A statesman with the shadow of a warrior. Yuehiro frowned because he searched for some other facet, not the Jedi or the lord, but the humor.

"As it turns out, being a lord comes with a troublesome amount of very tiresome responsibilities," said Hanrai. "I'm often much busier than I'd like, and with matters I don't entirely care for."

"Then why did you accept the lordship?" Yuehiro asked. "You could have remained a knight. Most of the Jedi did."

Hanrai held up a hand. "I've answered a few of your questions—first, answer a few of mine."

Yuehiro quieted, mouth shut with wary precision. This gave Hanrai pause. Yuehiro had been reprimanded for his questions, and harshly. That much was more than evident.

"What did you think to find in my library that you couldn't find elsewhere?" Hanrai asked. "That you didn't want anyone to see you looking at?"

Yuehiro clenched his fists over his knees. "The bodies, my lord."

"Ah." Hanrai sank back on his heels. He undid his seat to be cross-legged and let out a longer sigh. "Ah, yes, I suppose you've all been talk-ing."

Yuehiro frowned at Hanrai openly, as confused as he was intrigued. Either way, he couldn't help himself from speaking. Ah, youth! "Yes," Yuehiro said. "Of course we have. Well—not everyone believes it, yet. But they will. Because of Master Numoda. He's gone, isn't he? Dead, I mean."

"What makes you think that?"

"You sent him to the Engai system weeks ago, to root out smugglers. Then we heard there was a complication. Then we heard nothing. None of the masters will say. But Master Numoda's bones didn't come back— and they should have, for your shrine. So I . . . I wanted to read the rec-ords on the Sith rebellion. About the witch."

Hanrai nodded along with the boy's explanation. By the end of it, that rigid fear had returned to temper Yuehiro's enthusiasm. Hanrai let him be silent awhile before he spoke. "Do you understand why those records are private?"

"No." Yuehiro said it with such certainty. "We're to be Jedi, aren't we? We should know what we might face. How are we to protect against what we can't recognize?"

Hanrai smiled then, a genuine smile of real pleasure. He did miss this sort of pupil, and never as keenly as when he got to engage them. "I don't believe you're wrong, Yuehiro. However, I don't believe you've considered your teachers' concerns either, or their responsibilities. Do you not trust them to tell you when it is time for you to know an impor-tant thing?"

Yuehiro's forehead creased. He didn't trust them, and it shamed him too much to admit. He didn't need to; Hanrai could read the consterna-tion easily enough.

"All right, then," Hanrai said, straightening. He opened a drawer on his desk and retrieved a small green stone stick with a seal carved onto the end. This he handed to Yuehiro. "This seal will grant you entry to my library," he said. "But only during the hours before curfew."

Yuehiro took the seal like a fragile thing. "Why are you giving this to me?"

"Because you don't trust your other masters," he said. "Because it seems you might learn to trust me, and you certainly trust yourself. And because I want you to become a Jedi, Yuehiro. So I don't want to hear any more about you skipping on sleep or drills either, am I understood?"

Yuehiro gripped the seal, head bowed once more—less for politeness's sake, or gratitude's, Hanrai thought, than to let himself think. "You're . . . I think you'd be a good teacher, my lord. Why did you stop?"

Hanrai knew his smile then was a little tight. He would have wished it less so. It disappointed him to realize the memory still felt like a failure. Dwelling on such things did little for anyone, least of all those who had been failed. It was instead his responsibility to accept his mistake and to act on it with the wisdom earned from error.

He wouldn't distress a child with these reflections. For all Yuehiro was bound to learn in Hanrai's library, this matter would be best left for a time when the boy was older, wiser, and more able to hold his tongue.

"I'm afraid the galaxy had another use for me," he said. "But you've let me revisit that old calling, and for that I'm grateful."

He dismissed Yuehiro then, just as his aide, Masamu, came in. Masamu had clearly been waiting on the other side of the door, distressed by the amount of time Hanrai was wasting on a student that he could have spent reading one of no doubt several missives or directing multiple conniving political actions.

"You are being indulgent, my lord," Masamu said as he took his seat across the desk.

"Am I?" asked Hanrai, reaching to the windowsill, where he ran his fingers through the stomach fluff of the basking tooka. "I think I've done a fairly good job of ensuring we know when Yuehiro will be in my files—not to mention what he'll have his nose in."

Far better also that the boy not feel compelled to be secretive about it. Hanrai needed to cultivate trust. He had made that mistake before.

Masamu sighed through his nose. "The princes each demand a response, my lord. If I may, I do not think they will permit you to remain neutral much longer. Each fears that if you ally with his brother, he is in danger of losing the loyalty of his Jedi."

"You've told them this is preposterous, yes? That no true Jedi would ever betray their sworn lord."

"My lord . . ." Masamu winced.

Hanrai chuckled. "I know. Do they truly think so little of us now? That we hold our bonds with one another over our bonds to our masters?" He sighed. "Of course. Well, you tell them I'll suffer no Sith heresies in the clans and *then* tell them where they can artfully shove their—"

A flashing light caught Hanrai's eye, small and discreet. It came from the datapad he kept on the lower right of his desk, always within reach. This pad served only one purpose, and he never let it out of his sight.

Masamu's eyes also fixed on it, pupils blown wide.

Hanrai scooped up the datapad and scrolled through the message he had just received. It was brief and to the point, as these reports always were, and for once, it made him smile.

"Well," he said to Masamu, who had turned to him in a cold sweat, "now you can tell those faithless princes that I've been called away. And that perhaps I'll have an answer for them when I return."

"My lord—" Masamu stammered as Hanrai stood, "if they ask where you've gone—"

Hanrai grinned. "Why, to Dekien. Let them think I'm having myself a vacation. Perhaps that will put things in perspective."

CHAPTER
ELEVEN

THE THING ABOUT having a giant scowl of a Sith warrior on
your ship was that you couldn't really sleep, not deeply. By the fourth
night, Ekiya was seriously considering drugging herself and only didn't
because it seemed like a waste of perfectly good narcotics.

Consequently, she burned her palm on the teakettle before she
dragged herself into the cockpit to see if her contacts had gotten back to
her about the gear she'd requested for their trek into Dekien. Chie was
already in there, fiddling with the communications console and seeming concerned by it.

It wasn't the first time Ekiya had caught Chie in the middle of wrestling with the *Crow*'s hodgepodge assemblage of a comm system. Chie
had people, ones she talked to in layers of code and encryption. So
what? Ekiya did too. Either way, she wasn't one to pry. Fox was, but
lucky for Chie, they were an absolute dunce with any tech more complicated than a glow rod. Chie nevertheless made a point of never sending
her communiqués when they were around. Their Fox was an inveterate
snoop. If you didn't want them asking questions, you made sure they
didn't know there were questions to ask.

The thought made Ekiya's nose wrinkle as she slumped into her seat.

She choked it all down with her next yawn. "Aunty, you know I can send things for you."

Chie tutted as she toggled a switch. "I wouldn't want to trouble you."

"You're not trouble."

Chie studied her. "You're troubled, all the same."

"You aren't?" Ekiya scanned the rest of the *Crow*'s lights and so forth; at a glance, it looked okay, but she knew herself. She'd be running maintenance checks again by the end of the day. Just in case. Who knew when that big grimace of a Sith might pull another round of Force whatever and upset the *Crow*'s stomach? Ekiya winced. "I mean, I trust Fox."

"You'd have to, to have followed them this far," Chie said, like a hypocrite, given that she'd done the same thing.

"Counterpoint—maybe I'm desperate."

Chie raised her brows as if to say, Aren't we all? For the moment, she gave up on whatever she had been trying to send and leaned back in her seat to observe the running river of light outside the cockpit. "Well, at the moment, you don't sound particularly trusting."

"Maybe it just doesn't feel fair. I mean, you've heard them, right? At night, in the galley . . . Fox told him about *us*."

"Yet still they say nothing of themself."

"Right. Yeah. That." Ekiya knuckled her forehead. "I don't know. Obviously they used to be some kind of Jedi—or Sith, I guess."

"Or something else entirely."

"What are the odds of that?"

"Given the Empire's penchant for hunting down alternative schools of thought on the nature of the Force, admittedly slim."

Although again, counterpoint—both Chie and Ekiya nurtured just such heretical beliefs. Ekiya had her relics. Chie had her . . . whatever it was that made her so inviolably tranquil as she observed the liquid light of hyperspace.

There was a power in Chie. A steadiness. Ekiya relied on it, even when it unnerved her. She knew her way around violence, sure. Had to, piloting the *Crow* on her own. She knew her fists and feet and teeth, and a blaster when she really needed to get mean. But Chie could talk about killing like a soldier did, or a Jedi, and it always left Ekiya squeamish. No one's fault but her own. At the end of the day, they both had things worth making people bleed for. Chie was just better at finishing the job.

Chie met her gaze. With anyone else, Ekiya would probably have felt scrutinized. From Chie, it just felt like being seen and seeing in turn. Chie smiled wryly. "For what it's worth, my credits are still on the Jedi."

"Oh, yeah? When was the last time you bet on anything?"

"Let me rephrase. I'm sure of it." Chie's head bent in contemplation—or hesitation. It left Ekiya unexpectedly fretful. "I've made some inquiries. I was told of a certain Jedi clan, which is in the process of being absorbed into another. Their lord passed recently, and his designated heir has been missing for some time."

"What makes you think that has something to do with Fox?"

Chie's look chided. "They were the subject of my question. That was the answer."

"But who *gave* the answer?"

"I don't know that you'd care for them."

It wasn't a scold, per se, nor was it denial. Chie simply preferred not to say. If Ekiya pressed, well—Chie probably still wouldn't say. She just didn't want to be forced to withhold the information. Ekiya was inclined to respect the unspoken request. Chie knew what she was about. The secrets she chose to keep felt categorically different from the ones Fox did.

Was *that* fair? It didn't feel fair.

The problem was that it felt bad when Fox kept secrets, but it also felt bad to pry. On one hand, prying confirmed just how *many* secrets Fox was sitting on, but on the other, surely they'd share anything truly important. But if that was true—and Ekiya had to believe it was, or what was she even doing here—then Chie was invading Fox's privacy purely because she thought she had a right to do so. Which, hell, maybe she did. Fox demanded a lot of trust. Thus far, Ekiya had been content to blithely afford them a lot of it.

Something about having that Sith on board just made it much, much harder.

"Do you think I should be looking into things too?" Ekiya asked. "I know some folks—"

"You needn't look for things I've already found," said Chie. She meant: No need to get your hands dirty when I already have.

"Well. If there's anything you think I should know . . ."

"I'd tell you. I don't pretend to imagine I can wrangle a Jedi entirely on my own—let alone a Jedi *and* a Sith. I rely on you."

"Thanks," Ekiya mumbled. It felt better than she wanted to admit.

"Mind you, I don't want you to think I'm angry with them. Or that I no longer believe what they say. You get as old as I am, you learn to recognize when someone sounds strange because they think gods speak through them and when someone sounds strange because the gods actually do. I've always known they'd lead us to *something*."

"You really think we're going, then. To Rei'izu." Ekiya could barely say the name; it flustered her.

Chie looked as curious as she was baffled. "You don't?"

"Kind of have to, don't I?" Ekiya mumbled, busying herself with the maintenance checks she'd promised herself she wouldn't run again. But she needed something to occupy her hands and mind so she wouldn't circle back to the crates of relics filling her cargo hold—every one of them handed to her in exchange for a promise: *I can bring them home.*

It still felt a little like a lie every time she said it.

Ekiya was reasonably sure that most of the Rei'izu refugees who'd surrendered their relics to her over the years had seen the exchange through the lens of piety and ritual. Give the kyber lantern you made when Grandma died to the nice young Rei'izu woman. She says she'll take it where ghosts ought to go. Send the lady back off into the space between worlds not because you trust her word, per se, but because it feels more right for the relic to leave. No one's supposed to keep the dead. Not like that. The bones come home, but the kyber—the ghost, soul, whatever—that's for the temple.

What were any of them supposed to do with all those relics and all that kyber if the temple was gone because Rei'izu was gone because the Sith had swooped in and torn the whole thing apart? Collect ghosts, more or less. And cross their fingers that their dead figured out they were supposed to leave, eventually.

Of the relics in the cargo hold, four were Ekiya's—hers and her crew's, the one she'd left behind because Fox had the gall to give her reason to believe she could maybe do something for the unquiet dead.

Not that Ekiya could say exactly *why* she'd believed them when they said where they were going. Definitely wasn't the Force stuff. She'd learned to steer well clear of that, after the Sith. Wasn't the way Fox talked, either, like some kind of charlatan street magician aiming to part her from her last credit.

Maybe it came down to how they handled kids. Or aunties and uncles. Or the way they knew how to tell a quiet story when you couldn't stand to hear a loud one.

They made it so easy to hope. Hope that the tangible, grimy real could become luminous, if only you looked at it just so.

Ekiya did believe Fox. She had to. Otherwise, she wouldn't still be asking every displaced Rei'izu soul she met to please hand over their ghosts. Either she was a magnificent liar playing her own people for a profit she'd never acquire—because like hell she'd get away with selling all that kyber—or she really, truly, sincerely believed that by following Fox to their witch, she could bring all those ghosts home. She must have come by that faith pretty easily, too, because she'd done all that without blinking for going on two years now.

That was what made the Big Grimace such a problem. Something about his mere presence flung open the door to doubt. Was she too afraid of the Sith at large to be able to reconcile with working with one of them? Or was her problem that the flesh-and-blood palpability of him made their impossible aim seem a little too terrifyingly real?

"Still troubled, I see," said Chie, because even if she was neither Jedi nor Sith, she was an aunty, and aunties just knew these things.

"I think I'm right to be more than a little leery of a Sith."

"I won't disagree."

"But you won't agree either?"

Chie gazed out the window just as they dropped into the sharp black of real space. "I agree that we ought to be wary."

It was easiest to be wary when Ekiya didn't have to look at the man. He frightened her, as an idea. But face-to-face . . . He brooded on his own, like some kind of giant depressed mynock, and he got wry with

B5, and Chie, and Fox—and he'd been so careful with the relics. She'd found herself almost wanting to tell him they were ghosts. Then she'd remembered he was the reason the ghosts had so far to go before they found home.

Maybe it was right that he would help them get there. But she couldn't really trust him to do it. Certainly not on his own.

She told herself that was why she wanted to help. Why she pinged her contact again to ask for an additional piece of new gear. It probably wouldn't be ready by the time they arrived in the Dekien system, but maybe, with a little luck, it would be by the time they left.

Later, when they got the original gear shipment from her contact, Ekiya handed the Sith—Grimace?—Grim, she decided—his package in the galley with something nearing aplomb. His brow creased as he sorted through the contents of the bundle in his lap. "This seems inappropriate to the task."

He had likely expected some manner of spelunking gadgetry. He obviously didn't know what had become of Dekien. That was what he got for spending all his time traipsing around the boonies, menacing the locals with his laser sword.

"The alternative is getting incredibly arrested," Ekiya said. "And that's if the Empire gets you before the bounty hunters."

Having taken a less circuitous route than the *Poor Crow,* Grim's likeness from the Genbara wanted posters had made its way to the Dekien system days ago. Not everybody believed a Sith warrior was on the loose, but enough people had their eye out that Grim needed to keep his head down if he didn't want to lose it.

Grim frowned further as he looked over the pass folded in among his gear. "I suppose I'd simply prefer a subtler approach."

"Look, just let Fox do the talking." Ekiya patted him on the shoulder. "Or signal me and Chie to come stage a daring rescue. And if anyone gets up in your business, just make the face."

Grim inclined his head, but a note of anxiety lingered in his otherwise stoic expression.

"Yeah, that's the one."

The look left Ekiya antsy too, both because she couldn't quite believe she'd just tried to soothe a Sith warrior the size of oh, two, two and a half standard-sized beings strapped together under a traveling cloak and because she rather hated to imagine what could be waiting for them on Dekien that could have the man so unnerved.

CHAPTER TWELVE

THE FIGURE IN the holo wore a modest yellow kimono delicately flourished with white, blue, and orange blossoms. With an upraised palm and a pleasant smile, she guided the audience's eye to the images of natural splendor that unfurled around her.

Dekien, the unpolished gem of the Outer Rim. Here, nature flourished. Pink-leafed jewel trees towered over narrow valleys cut from stone the hue of dawn and twilight. Flowers bloomed in every season. White in spring, yellow in summer, blue in autumn, and lilac in winter. The rivers ran clear as glass, and the sea shone in every color known to living eyes. Truly, it was the pinnacle of untouched beauty . . .

Now the world of Dekien has been refashioned for your every pleasure. Visit the multi-tiered teahouses overlooking exquisitely preserved vistas of mountains, forests, and deserts. Enjoy breathtaking theatrical performances held on mobile lotus stages that manipulate the land itself. Partake of the galaxy's finest liquors as you cruise in a state-of-the-art pleasure barge that enables you to enjoy the night sky from every angle across the globe!

And while I have you, may I be the first to say: On behalf of
Eternity Enterprises, welcome to Dekien.

Here, the holo repeated. The Ronin stared blankly through it toward
the device from which it played, a projector on the ceiling of the pleasure barge's main deck. The multi-story vessel was as impressively large
as most things on Dekien, with billowing gold sails akin to a carp's fins,
its sides painted fancifully to evoke grandly white and crimson scales.
The guests were gathered on the top deck lounge, which was surrounded
on all sides by a facsimile of open air—screens that projected the view
from outside, and an internal system that blew meticulously controlled
breezes over the platters of delicately carved fruits.

They had only just left port, so through the screens the Ronin could
see quite a few of the attractions the tour company holo advertised.
Towering gilt pagodas, extravagantly painted theaters and outdoor
stages, teahouses, casinos, cantinas, and every imaginable sort of distraction, separated by a glittering feast of artificial waterways and connected by a never-ending web of red-lacquered bridges.

"Is it really all like this?" he muttered.

"You mean the entire planet?" asked the Traveler, gazing out a screen
with a contemplative air. "More or less."

"In twenty years?" the Ronin asked. When he had last seen Dekien, it
had been a fairly attractive rock.

"Well, an empire always likes you to know it's very impressive. And
ours had just run out of war to demonstrate its impressiveness with. So:
a celebration of its glory in peace. Of sorts."

The Ronin grimaced and the Traveler laughed, and as the pleasure
barge at last peeled away from Dekien's capital city of Dazenma, out
onto the open sea, a new segment of the holo began to play.

Welcome, dear guests. You have now embarked on the journey
of a lifetime. Before you await the heavenly Seikara Caverns,
where inspiration is sure to strike.

This gorgeous cave system stretches ten kilometers through
cathedrals of solemn bloomstone and subterranean valleys of

lush bioluminescent foliage. Eternity Enterprises's artisanal re-
pulsor bridges allow guests to explore the entire length of the
cave, and they have been strategically positioned so that no
matter where you stop, you are sure to behold magnificence.

In the name of preserving Seikara's charms, our highly se-
lective system permits only a handful of guest passes each
month. You have each been granted one such pass, and with it
you will walk paths few beings have ever had the privilege of
venturing down.

Whatever it is you seek in Seikara, know the Eternity Enterprises barge is fully equipped to enable your pursuit of epiphany. Whether you wish to consult with a priest or indulge your
artistic insights, allow us to foster your dream in the making.

Few of the other guests paid the holo much mind. They had no doubt
waited months, if not years, for their visit to Seikara, and so they had
nothing to learn from it. Given the dress and carriage of these guests—
uniformly sumptuous and confident in their leisure—the Ronin was
once more struck by how swiftly his crew had earned passage. Ekiya's
contact was to thank for that.

Beside him, B5-56 expressed his opinion on the average fashion
sense, even as the droid sported a rather more intricately woven hat
than he had before.

"If they hear you, they're going to throw you off the ship," said the
Ronin. "Hypocrite."

Now, now. Don't lash out, said the voice.

"I look like an ass."

A black cloak upon black robes, and more black up to and including
his boots. Worst of all, a half-mask fixed over his lower face, stylized in
a gruesome, long-toothed scowl—all to conceal his prosthetic, lest it
prove too distinctive. He had only been allowed to keep his kyber, which
he had rescued from the lining of his vest into a pouch now secured to
the inside of his robes.

They had received the wardrobe from the same contact who provided their passes, after the *Poor Crow* touched down in Dazenma. A

lean young man who shared Ekiya's intent stare came aboard, hauling a crate of supplies. He'd left near as soon as he'd arrived, though not before giving their crew an amused once-over.

"Be grateful," Ekiya said when the Ronin had first had to face down his reflection. "We're getting a discount. Shogo said he hadn't laughed so hard in years."

"What am I supposed to be?" he asked.

"An *artiste*."

The Traveler hadn't suffered nearly so much. But then, they had dressed a bit like a jackass to begin with. Their mask remained, but their hair had been more elaborately bound up, and their pale robes were cleaner and brighter, though not so luxurious and patterned as those worn by Eternity's other clientele. Now they spoke in low tones to a woman weighted down by multiple layers of silk who kept sending the Ronin intrigued glances—but not low enough to go unheard by likewise fascinated eavesdroppers.

"Most sought-after theatrical leading man in the Akeno sector, you know," the Traveler said. "But he has abjectly refused, point blank, again and again, to have anything to do with a holoperformance. I know! The thing is, this role, well, it's terribly compelling. Never before been performed. A dramatization of a historical piece, you see—recent history, at that—and I think he finds it satisfactorily *challenging*. Even so, he's said he'll only consider the role if—*if*—he receives due inspiration from the spirit of Seikara."

"And you imagine he will?" the woman whispered, delighted to have a secret.

"I wouldn't be here if I didn't—I don't get paid if he doesn't accept!"

"They are having entirely too much fun," the Ronin muttered.

"You could stand to lighten up." Ekiya strolled up beside him, carrying a platter of improbably colored bites of foodstuff and dressed head-to-toe in the understated uniform of a barge employee. Her slicer friend had provided only two passes, and the rest of the crew had been compelled to find other ways aboard. "Eat your woes away?"

"Oh, no, he'll break the spell." Chie came up beside Ekiya, similarly dressed. "He needs to maintain that hearty villainous glower."

She nevertheless gave him a nod of sympathy before she and Ekiya melted back to make way for the cluster of approaching guests.

"Is it true?" a willowy Kaminoan man in diaphanous robes separated from the herd to ask. His narrow fingers pressed together as his slender neck bent with interest. Unfortunately, he could not feasibly be speaking to anyone but for the Ronin—or B5, though the likelihood of that was depressingly slim. "Are you playing *him*?"

"Who?" asked the Ronin.

"The *dark lord*," the Kaminoan enthused.

For a stretch, the only thing the Ronin could hear was the voice in his head laughing herself breathless.

"Oh, don't tell me you're getting excited about a propaganda piece," the Kaminoan's companion—an aristocratic Mon Calamari in resplendent geometric patterns—sniffed, her nostrils flaring.

"I am not. Propaganda? It's historical. Romantic. The dark lord and his witch—"

"Yes, so romantic, the way they killed all those Jedi." The Mon Calamari turned her baleful bulging eye to the Ronin. "Tell me. Who's funding the piece, hm?"

"Don't be gauche," said the Kaminoan.

"It isn't gauche, it's the point—come now, which prince thinks he wins the next war by telling us how his father won the last one?"

This rapidly descended into what could diplomatically be called heated philosophical debate. Each artist vied to outdo their fellows for depth and acuity of insight. They argued for the moral character of one prince or the academic credentials of the other. Some offered this or that popular lord as a more viable substitute. Or what of the Jedi? The ones elevated to lordship were a splendid example of moral fortitude without being nearly as preachy as they once had been.

They're all very certain that one *prince should win,* the voice said in that light way she did when she wanted very much to see someone swallow their own swill.

"But what do we make of the missing Jedi?" asked the Kaminoan with some concern.

"The what?" the Ronin asked, despite himself.

"If you're going to entertain conspiracy, then I'm going to need more wine," said the Mon Calamari.

"I only mean to say that it's concerning, isn't it?" The Kaminoan turned to the Ronin, presumably for support. "I was certain you must have heard, sir. They say there are reports of Jedi fallen in the line of duty, but their bones have yet to be returned to their clans. And they say, well, they say it's like when the witch stole the dead to make them into her demons. I don't believe that's truly what's happened, of course, but it's strange, don't you think?"

"It's politics at best, mysticism at worst," the Mon Calamari insisted. "No one's truly missing. Mark my words, those Jedi bones will turn up in some prince's ancestral shrine within a matter of a months. Either way, he'll claim it signifies the will of the Heavens—and grants him divine right to inheritance."

"Why can't it be the witch?" the Ronin heard himself ask.

He was stared at. He had earned this, and for the sake of their clandestine pursuit, he should have shied away. Yet he stared back, arms folded, waiting.

"It can't be the witch because the witch is dead," said the Mon Calamari.

"You're eager to believe she is," said the Ronin.

"I hope you're joking." The Mon Calamari gave him a disdainful look; she preferred to think him mad than to entertain the possibility that he spoke any amount of truth. The Kaminoan likewise winced. "I'm half-convinced this witch never lived. I hardly care either way. We give her far too much credit when we pretend to be frightened of her, when all she did was kill Jedi. Any worthy warrior could do the same. She, the Sith, they were nothing to the Empire. It endures now as it did before, impervious to petty conspiracy."

Anger stirred under the Ronin's sternum; he recognized it, now, when he might not have a week before. He had buried it so deep, and now he was all fissures through which it seeped, a dark, relentless fire. He needed to master himself, or he would do worse than upend cargo. He needed not to speak again.

Yet he did. "The Sith killed and died. You call that petty? What do you call yourself?"

The Mon Calamari held her ground, nostrils flared. She thought his ego bruised. If only.

"We are artists, sir." This came from a Pantoran woman dressed in rosy sunset hues that contrasted with her blue skin; she had been quiet thus far, but she spoke with demure confidence. "It isn't for us to determine the fate of Jedi or galaxy. We only mean to bear witness and to speak of it to those who come after. That is our role. To relay visions and instill them in the people. Is that not why you pursue the spirit of Seikara? What vision do you seek?"

The Ronin didn't wish to answer. More pressingly, it occurred to him that he might not be able to. His throat had closed. The Pantoran woman lowered her gaze, as if shy—she meant to deflect his anger. It still roiled within him, and he realized with dawning frustration that it needed some outlet lest he burst.

Abruptly, the Traveler slid between the Ronin and the woman, their tone conciliatory as they exclaimed, "Oh, no—no, no, no—do excuse me, miss, but I fear we are all very much in danger of disrupting the master's *process*."

With that, they smoothly shepherded the lot away, singing apologies and looking over their shoulder only to nod even more apologies in the Ronin's direction. "Please, if you have any questions, you *must* direct them to me—I can't guarantee an answer—oh, no, miss, of course not! Although . . ."

The Ronin heard little of what came after this. He had already turned on his heel. B5 chirred in his wake and followed him out of the main lounge, into a hall. The droid offered violence or other distractions if his master should be foolish enough to get himself cornered again. This was a joke, probably. The Ronin wanted too much to take him up on it to answer.

A vision, was it? If he was very lucky, he would never see such a thing again. He had left the relic on Dekien for that very reason.

Ekiya found him first. She still had that platter of delicacies, and she joined him at the rail at the back of the barge, where they were somewhat shielded from view by the vessel's voluminous golden sail fins. The barge skated over the sea, the repulsorlifts making riotous white waves below. Ekiya offered him a bite; he declined; she tipped the whole thing over the edge. By reflex, he caught the platter, though the food was lost.

"Would've been more worth it to save the food," she said.

"You threw it away."

"I mean, all of it was the worst." Ekiya shrugged. "You've seen the people who order this crap. You think they taste anything but credits?"

The Ronin didn't have much of an opinion on taste. Long ago, he had been considered a bit of a dullard on that count by his peers. He would have argued that he was the one who gave the Sith the ability to refashion their lightsabers howsoever they pleased, and was that not a feat of aesthetic indulgence? They would have said it didn't count because the most interesting thing he had done with his own lightsaber had been unconscionably pretentious.

Years later, when he was alone, he had at last used his designs to make himself a proper auxiliary. He suspected his comrades would have found plenty to criticize in that too. After all, he had built it first and foremost not as a declaration but to serve a need.

To this day he couldn't say what had first damaged his now stolen blade. A fight. A curse. His own unsettled feeling and the ill will of the Force. Regardless: It had burned and burned, and he had, in the end, been less willing to douse the fire than to forge himself the scabbard, built of components scavenged from the blades of the recently dead.

The scabbard had proved its use time and again—it had concealed what it needed to and enabled his cunning—but it had always been rather ugly.

I would argue that the one you built first indicates a sense of the theatric, the voice said, which was not in fact a compliment, all things given.

"No point listening to those people anyway." Ekiya took the platter back from him and eyed the lounge suspiciously. "I mean, they care. Some of them. But if that's how they talk about the dead, why do we want to hear them talk about anything else?"

When he said nothing, she sighed and leaned on the railing. "I get it, you're sad or something. Who isn't? I just want to know what's up with those caverns. Is Seikara really blessed? And if it is, won't you, I don't know, burst into flames if you try to enter them?"

"That's not how any of this works," he said.

Oh, what do you know? she said.

"Is it haunted, then? Or, what, possessed?" Ekiya pressed on, dissatisfied with his vague shrug. "Oh, come on. You're a—whatever you are. The Force listens to you. Spirits, gods, aren't you lot supposed to be all in touch with that sort of thing?"

Chie laughed as she joined them, hands tucked neatly at the small of her back. "They say the spirits were closer to all of us, once."

"Aren't you supposed to be working?" the Ronin asked. B5 prodded his knee: Behave.

"Have you no insights to share?" Chie asked, head canted. The Ronin bent his head to acquiesce. She patted his elbow. "Now, I haven't met a spirit, much less a god, but I'm given to suspect that they were less than pleased when the Jedi turned from them in favor of the Empire. Although I suppose you could say that most of us have forgotten how to treat them properly. They wouldn't mind talking, but we don't remember their language."

"I pray," said Ekiya, somewhat belligerently.

"I do as well," said the Ronin, which earned him Ekiya's grudgingly approving side eye.

"And I know about ghosts." Ekiya plucked at the hem of her sleeves. "Proper ones, I mean. Not whatever's going on with that lady who was chasing Grim on Genbara."

"A ghost out of place. A ghost compelled, you might say," said the Traveler, unusually somber as they approached also—fortunately with no more wealthy visionaries in tow. The Ronin made room for them at the railing and they nodded in a sort of thanks, though they kept their hands folded in their sleeves. "There's a reason they took to calling her ilk 'demon' during the war."

"You know a story?" prompted Chie.

The Traveler was silent a moment, then a moment more, a singular contrast with the music spilling out from the main lounge behind them. The Ronin had until then been acutely aware of the Dekien system sun. A fulsome diamond thing, it beat down on his nape from Dekien's cerulean sky and spiked back into his eyes through the barge's fluttering sails and again from Dekien's piercingly radiant waters. It was made all the worse by the absurd amount of black he had been stuffed into, and the snarling mask that condensed and heated his every breath. Yet for a moment, he thought of none of these things, waiting only for the Traveler to speak.

The voice was also silent, but he felt her curiosity, fixed and intent. She wanted to know what the Traveler had to say, perhaps even more keenly than he did. He had never known her to take such an interest in a person other than himself.

"We've all heard of these demons," said the Traveler at last. "Leashed ghosts, wielded against their will. But there are other tales. Ghosts anchored by their own unmet wants. Or ghosts summoned and kept by the needs of others. A knight who let his brother strike him down—who returned to guide the child who would at last bring his brother peace. An old master, passing to the demands of time in a fraught age—who remained to urge her pupils to restore tranquility." They hesitated, head bowed. The corner of a sardonic smile peeked from below their mask. "One wonders if we live in such a time, when ghosts might linger until they rise to shape the world—to become more than they were as the sediment of flesh. I might wish for it, myself."

The Ronin, bemused, realized that his heart yearned for something similar. He expected it was on account of how many ghosts he had made in his time, and that he would selfishly prefer they find something other to do than haunt him.

Or perhaps it was that he felt himself as good as dead anyway, and that he would have liked a better explanation for why he stubbornly remained in the world.

You're nothing like them, she hissed. Her tone stung his ear, and he grimaced unconsciously.

"In any case," said the Traveler, more buoyant and like themself than at any time since the crew had left the *Crow.* "I suspect that whatever has been granting visions to Seikara's visitors has more to do with that spooky Sith relic you expect to find there than some great spirit of ages past."

"Lucky us," said Ekiya.

Luck? No. The Ronin doubted it had anything to do with that.

CHAPTER
THIRTEEN

DEKIEN REEKED. THERE was no better word for the stench of excess that drowned every street corner and stained the very atmosphere. Kouru had not felt such an unwelcome slick on her skin in over a decade.

Simultaneously, it relieved her to have her feet on solid ground. The white flare and black current of the Force pulsed through her in equal measure, flowing from every vital thing on the world and into her, through her. She was connected again—*herself* again—and grateful for it.

The trouble was her quarry. With all swiftness, the old man and his crew had taken themselves from the Dazenma spaceport where their freighter landed to a harbor for local travel. There, they boarded a pleasure barge that departed from a gilt pagoda owned by Eternity Enterprises—a stylistic affair decorated with flairs reminiscent of Dekien's unique flora. Fanciful illustrations of their destination were emblazoned on a board outside the departure hall: the Seikara Caverns.

Kouru wouldn't have thought much of flying her stolen scout vessel straight to the caverns and ambushing the old man there, but she knew wealth when she saw it, and this cavern operation dripped with credits.

The caves would be as jealously guarded as the Emperor's trove. It would do her no favors to be brazen on this leg of her hunt.

Her options were thus: lie in wait or pursue.

Kouru knew which hangar the old man's freighter hid in, and she had no doubt she could get into it. Once inside, she would only have to bide her time until his return. But she remembered the moment she had nearly caught him on Genbara, before he leapt onto the freighter's ramp, and the precision of the black current strike that had thrown her back down into the dockyard.

When the old man had fought her in the mountain village and shoved her back in that dingy square, it had been with a full explosion of white flare, a blast entirely unlike the current-driven arrow of black Force power that had later felled her.

To wit: He was not alone. And though Kouru knew herself strong, she also knew that the old man had killed her once—and that with an ally, he might kill her again, and more easily. She therefore didn't like to think of cornering him in such an enclosed space as the *Poor Crow*, where she could so handily be flanked.

Hence, a pursuit. To her advantage, if she caught him in these distant caves, far from the vessel he had flown in on, he would have nowhere to flee that she could not run him down with her own legs. If she had her druthers, he would bleed out on Dekien, and then when she was once more compelled to go into space—

Run—don't be seen.

Kouru was momentarily unsettled by another sourceless murmur, but in the same moment, she melted into the boldly colored crowd milling down the street, unsure of why but knowing she *needed* to. She soon realized—hoped?—that it was the wise black current of the Force that had coaxed her into this narrow alley across from the tour company's departure hall.

The crowd drew back with haste and delighted whispers as a lord's retinue passed, the lord's varnished palanquin hovering in their midst. Kouru had seen more palanquins than she liked floating down Dekien's lanes, but this one announced itself like no other—not with grandeur, but with the character of its attendants. Jedi.

Kouru's gut flared at the sight of the brown Jedi cloaks and white robes, the lightsabers hung proudly at the sash of each one who had been granted the title of knight. She bared her teeth in shadow as the lord exited his palanquin. His robe, his sash, his cloak—the expense of' the fabric spoke to a man of his station, but he carried himself just like his retainers, and he wore a hilt at his waist too.

A Jedi *and* a lord. She had heard some knights were elevated to the role in the wake of the Sith rebellion. Kouru held as little love for the Empire as she did for the Jedi clans—hungry hypocrites, the lot of them. She shouldn't have been caught off guard to see the two mingle so thoroughly within a single man. Perhaps she wasn't uneasy. Perhaps this was merely disgust.

She watched with narrowed eyes as the Jedi lord led his entourage into the Eternity Enterprises pagoda, the company's employees rushing to keep up with him.

Here, this is your chance.

Kouru's lip curled in irritation as she glanced over her shoulder—she still couldn't say what at.

It was no terrible bother to keep herself slight and unobtrusive in Jedi eyes. She had never found Jedi to be particularly observant in the ways that mattered. They cared most about those who held weapons, and those who walked with intent to wield them. It had behooved Kouru and her fellow apprentices—those who had been considered unreliable, many of whom had one day become Sith—to learn to make themselves seem small and vulnerable. Though it chafed Kouru to adopt the pose, she had a graver need than dignity.

Milling through the Eternity pagoda with a gaggle of tourists, she overheard what she needed:

Said an attendant, "I'm afraid this month's barge to Seikara left just two hours ago, my lord—"

Said the lord, "It's no trouble. We'll take a faster vessel. If you would just lend us one of your navigators."

Kouru grimaced as she listened, scanning through the offerings projected at a kiosk. The Jedi lord arranged his journey with the casual tone of a man who expected obedience on account of his warmth. Merely listening made her want to punch his ear. Even so, she wondered: Just what did this lord think to find in these caverns? She doubted it was the enlightenment the tour company advertised—not because she thought a Jedi above seeking truth with credits, but because she knew better than to trust coincidence.

If this Jedi lord was after her prey, she would have to beat him to it—or kill him, should he get in her way.

Don't get distracted.

No, of course not. But . . .

Out of the corner of her eye, Kouru followed a pair of young Jedi. Not knights—they carried no lightsabers—but the lower caste of graduated apprentices that the clans called guardians. Those not deemed worthy of a blade, but trusted to run patrols for their masters as they walked through the crowd outside the departure hall.

Simultaneously, she heard the Jedi lord direct his retainers, determining who would ride with him on the commandeered vessel and who would take the smaller scouting skiffs ahead to observe and guard. There was no question where these young Jedi—these young, weak, foolish guardians—would be assigned.

A shallow pang of recognition, akin to sympathy, tugged at Kouru's chest. If she had been so unlucky as to be left with the Jedi, she might well have been left to this meager fate. She remembered well what it was to be used, to be molded, directed, made an extension of another's wants with no regard for her own.

Something of the thought gave her pause. She half-expected someone to speak.

When no one did, she inhaled slowly to recognize the pain, then exhaled out the whole.

Perhaps these guardians did not deserve to die. But every worthy fight came with sacrifice.

Later, she stood over two young Jedi guardian bodies on the scout skiff where she had hidden herself since their departure from Dazenma's harbor. They had died swiftly, at least, and one of them had not even had the chance to be afraid before she cut them down. Now she only had to get the skiff up and running before the Jedi lord's vessel caught up to her and sensed something amiss.

She readied herself to tip the bodies into the sea.

No. They have a use yet. Didn't you?

Ah. There it was.

Kouru did not turn to the voice, but she *recognized* it, and with that recognition, she brought to bear her attention. "A use?" she said. "Be clear or be silent."

There was the hum of the skiff. The crush of the waves. The ringing in Kouru's ears.

Then: *Well, Kouru. This will go better if you let me take care of you.*

Then: nothing. A silence so full that she could only call it a warning. It left Kouru shivering under all the heat of sun and sea. Yet in the silence, there was freedom, and Kouru was determined to savor it.

She nevertheless pulled the bodies back into the shadow of the skiff interior, where they were sheltered from the sun. She told herself she chose to. It was better to believe it so.

CHAPTER
FOURTEEN

"THAT'S A LOT of Jedi. There's like a whole herd of them down there." Ekiya broke off and turned to Chie. "A pack? A gang?"

"A pride," Chie said sagely, glancing at the Traveler.

The Traveler, however, sighed under their breath, then cursed with a word that made even the Ronin stare. "A headache," they proposed. "We can't be seen."

The Jedi had arrived before the Eternity Enterprises barge—special dispensation, a commandeered vessel, a mysterious certainty on the part of the lord, and a strained air among his subordinates. Ekiya relayed this from staff gossip. She had mingled while the rest of the crew hung back in one of the barge's private suites.

Now her nose wrinkled at the Ronin. "I guess Grim's probably killed a bunch of their buddies, huh? Can't we just say he got cast for his looks?"

"Well," said the Traveler, "perhaps we could, but when I said 'we' can't be seen, I meant me too."

That earned them another look from the crew.

"As if I'm not the most suspicious person you know," said the Traveler. "But I am serious. This could go quite poorly."

Chie came away from the curved window through which she had been observing the situation on the dock. Her gaze held a mild scold that made the Traveler raise their hands in surrender. She touched their shoulder. "I assume you know this lord. What would bring him here?"

The Traveler pressed their hands together in front of their mouth in a gesture of deep thought. "Lord Hanrai . . . has a curiosity. He could conceivably be after an encounter with whatever grants the visions of Seikara."

"You think he believes in that?" Ekiya asked.

"I think he'd know better than to assume it's nothing." The Traveler's fingertips had whitened with pressure. This Hanrai concerned them. "We may be better off just assuming he's after this relic of yours, Master Ronin."

Either way, they couldn't wait. The Ronin laid a hand on B5-56's head. The droid warbled confirmation; he had successfully acquired and modified a map of the Seikara Caverns from the pleasure barge's database, and he projected it into the center of the room for the crew to see. The fully colored version of the map for visitors had been reduced to blue lines, allowing them to better chart a course through the caverns' interior architecture.

The narrow beach at which the pleasure barge was docked quickly gave way to a steep incline layered in thick tropical vegetation. Eternity Enterprises had cleared a winding path through the foliage to the mouth of the caverns, all of which could be seen from any point on the beach.

"We have two immediate choices," the Ronin said. "Through the front, or . . ." At his gesture, B5 swiveled and panned the holo to look down on the caves from overhead. "We enter from above."

"It's a cave, Grim," said Ekiya. "You know, so called because it's a dark place underground? 'Above' is where the rock is. Unless you're saying you want to blast a hole in the mountains."

The Ronin held up a hand. "There's already a hole."

From the entrance overlooking the beach, the Seikara cave system extended some ten kilometers into the planet before it became largely untraversable to those without special equipment, due to its intersection with an underground river. The Ronin indicated a point about three kilometers from the entrance where the cave temporarily widened into a tremendous basin, then traced his finger up from the basin to a gap in the mountains overhead. B5 highlighted the breach in the cave ceiling that had collapsed.

"We reach this point and go down," said the Ronin.

"Oh, sure," said Ekiya. "Just sprint three klicks uphill through jungle and throw yourself down a lightless sinkhole—and hope you outpace the Jedi below."

"Yes, you're right. We'll want to delay the Jedi as much as possible," said Chie as Ekiya threw her an incredulous look. Chie turned to the Traveler. "I'll insert myself with the attendants seeing to the lord's entourage. Keep an eye on their progress and ensure they're slowed to our liking."

"Aunty, what if one of them recognizes *you*?" Ekiya protested. "If this Hanrai guy's so 'curious,' he might know your face too."

At this, the Traveler's mouth nigh imperceptibly tightened. They seemed about to voice an objection when Chie clucked her tongue.

"The Jedi don't all hate me, you know," she scolded. "Some of them like that I've rid them of their rivals. If Hanrai takes issue, well. Trouble is trouble. I'll manage. But at least you'll have forewarning." She paused only to quirk a smile at the Traveler. "Ah, don't look so anxious. You think I've anything to fear from a Jedi with the arrogance to call himself a lord?"

The Traveler's fingers grazed Chie's wrist. "Don't underestimate him. He's a clever old man."

"And I'm a clever old woman. Now be clever yourself, why don't you?"

Ekiya groaned. "Guess I'll steal us a way out. Might as well have a way to bolt on the off chance we don't all die. You with me, Bee?"

B5 warbled agreement and let the holo fade out, at which point the Ronin found himself facing the Traveler.

"I'm with you, then. I daresay we have the easy part," they said, and though their tone was light, they said nothing else for a good long while.

* * *

In their favor, the guests that disembarked from the pleasure barge thrilled at the sight of a Jedi lord. It was no excessive trick for the Ronin and the Traveler to slip off the end of the barge, to the dock, and swiftly into the thick of the forested slope that bordered the entrance to the Seikara Caverns. Subtropical foliage bloomed lushly up from the black-sand beach, dense with a dozen shades of green and leaves wider than the Ronin was tall.

The path to the cave mouth had, to the Ronin's vague irritation, been lined with shrine gates, painted freshly red. The Traveler clicked their tongue at his hesitation and hurried him forward into the shadows of the undergrowth. So long as they lingered at the coast, they risked being seen not only by Jedi, but by Eternity security droids.

The Ronin had journeyed this way before—though the last time he had moved through the cavern, not over it. But he generally recalled the direction of the cavern collapse that had created the tremendous doline. From there, they would descend and go as fast as possible to the end of the cavern, where the relic waited.

"Don't suppose *you* have any useful skills here?" the Ronin asked. They had lowered themselves into the yellow-flowered brush as a many-legged drone cruised over the canopy. "Say, camouflage."

"I'm doing my best," said the Traveler. "Let's just be subtle, yes?"

That hardly sounds like a real answer, said the voice.

The Ronin had to hide his relief. He had feared her angry on the barge, with all that talk of ghosts and demons. That she was still with him even as he made his way to the relic gave him some unearned sense of security.

By contrast, the Traveler left the Ronin ill at ease. As they slipped together through undergrowth and between spindly trees with gossamer branches, the Traveler said little or they said nothing. It shouldn't have set his teeth on edge—their sneaking was better served by silence—but he had realized two things. First, that this was the first time he had been truly alone with them, and that he was expected to rely on a person who had not seen fit to be honest about their skills. Second, that he had never imagined them capable of such quiet.

If you want so terribly to talk, she said, *why not ask what they did to ensure the Jedi hate them as terribly as a Sith?*

The Ronin brushed a stinging insect from his face and glowered in the direction he felt her in. She was always most palpable at her most prickly.

Shouldn't you? she asked. *Don't you have the right?*

Again, two items. First: Should he? Yes, in all likelihood. It would certainly benefit him to know just what manner of being he had agreed to partner with. But the right? Here he couldn't agree. Perhaps his answer would have been different if the Traveler had seen fit to ask him for stories of his rebellion days. They hadn't. Therefore, what could he ask them in turn?

And yet.

And yet . . . she murmured.

And yet they had found him. He, who had spent two decades roaming the fringe of civilization, losing himself to the seasons of distant worlds. He had been content to blame their meeting on his confrontation with the bandit, in the fight where they had both made public fools of themselves as they sought to kill each other in the way only Sith could. Of course those in the market for a Sith would swiftly make their way to such an ill-advised explosion.

And *yet* the Traveler had found him so immediately. Not a day after he left the village, he had met a musician on the road, waiting.

The Traveler caught his gaze. "You're staring."

The Ronin frowned. "I'm concerned."

"About me? Or perhaps for me?" The Traveler touched their chest. "How sweet."

"I know very little about you."

"That's intentional."

"What if I wanted to know more?"

"Then you should ask." Their teasing tone suggested he was unlikely to be rewarded for his efforts.

They were again forced to wait. A pair of drones had descended to scan the clearing ahead. The Traveler touched his shoulder and pointed upward, into a tangle of interwoven branches above—the abandoned nest of some massive flying creature. The bower proved large enough to hide them both.

As they lingered, the Ronin took it upon himself to shed that infernal mask that had completed his costume. The humidity of the jungle had left him nearly choking on his own breath. He massaged the jaw as he did; the underlying scar ached with the extra weight he'd asked it to bear.

The Traveler relaxed against the woven wall of the bower, watching him. Wary. Or curious.

The Ronin thumbed the edge of his prosthetic. "I'll tell you how I got it."

"Do you expect I'll be impressed?"

"As a trade," he finished.

"Eager, aren't you." The Traveler spread their hands. "What do you want that I haven't offered?"

He nearly laughed. As if they'd offered anything! "I won't be choosy."

The Traveler placed their chin in their palm and adopted the attitude of scholarly attention. As they did, the Ronin realized that he had just promised to explain himself. It would be difficult, as he was neither in the habit of telling his own stories nor even of recollecting them.

But the sight of the Jedi lord on the beach had driven a spike into his heart, and those stories were bleeding to the surface of his mind whether he tried to recall them or not. He remembered, with a keen and throbbing darkness that echoed with each pulse of ache in his jaw, the last time he had faced a lord. That lord had not been a Jedi, but he had been a master of them. Or he had been, until he died.

"A foolish moment," the Ronin said at last, quiet under the creak of the trees and the distant hum of the drones. "I let a man strike me and didn't respond in kind."

The Traveler seemed somehow to see past him, through him. Their focus peeled away the prosthetic to reveal the length of knotted skin and malformed jaw that was the left edge of the Ronin's face; they seemed even to see the blackened wound it had originally been—a scorch mark left by a blaster bolt barely dodged.

"It must have been a terrible strike, to leave a scar like that," they said.

"He was very afraid."

"Is that why you spared him?"

"He was dead anyway." And the Ronin had taken the man's blaster, to ensure it wouldn't happen again. That weapon now hung at his waist beside his lightsaber. An ornamental piece of frippery modified to more practical use.

The Traveler sighed. "I have a feeling you've left out all the interesting bits."

To be fair, he had. "You're the storyteller. What am I missing?"

"Motive, for one."

"Betrayal."

"Your own?"

He waved a hand in acquiescence.

"Ah, see, now you've told me *his* motive. A wounded heart! But what drove you to wound him? Why turn your back without defending yourself? It's an enticing little puzzle."

"So I *have* won your interest."

The Traveler tilted their head to acknowledge the loss. Then they raised it and stood. "Ah, I believe the way is clear. Let's be quick, lest we're caught again and compelled to share more dreadful secrets."

The Ronin had hoped to push, but indeed, the drones had left, and they weren't far from their goal. At the other edge of the clearing yawned a gully. Within it lay more forest, half a kilometer down.

"Quite the cave you have here," said the Traveler at the edge.

"It isn't mine." The Ronin pointed to the far end of the doline, which was now bordered with another of those red-painted shrine gates. Fanciful bridges and wooden walkways floated across the gulley in a meandering fashion and extended through the gate, into the caverns that loomed darkly beyond. "That way."

"It does occur to me to wonder . . ." said the Traveler as they studied the doline, determining how best to get down. "Is it possible that with all the fussing they've done with the local landscape, our acquaintances at Eternity might already have found this relic of yours?"

The Ronin frowned. "If the visitors are still suffering visions . . ."

"Oh, you can come down with a vision for one of any number of reasons, and most of them have nothing to do with the Force. The power of suggestion, for example."

The Ronin frowned more deeply. "You speak as though you suspect it's gone."

The Traveler straightened a bit, seeming taken aback by their own suggestion. "I . . . well. Maybe I'm looking for reasons not to throw myself down a very large hole in the middle of—"

They caught themselves at the end. They and the Ronin both stilled as the sound of voices echoed down lengths of stone, coming from below their feet, through the caves that led back, toward the coast.

More guests. Whether they were Jedi or not remained to be seen. It would be wiser to get so far ahead that they wouldn't be able to tell who was nipping at their heels.

By unspoken agreement, the Ronin and Traveler both hopped over the edge of the hole, into the forest below, down and down—and forward.

Ekiya waited until the majority of the Jedi had followed after their lord into the caverns to begin vetting the skiffs in earnest. She had kept careful watch on all of them—with B5-56's help—as those poor guardian grunts who constituted the lesser Jedi were assigned their shifts.

The lord's entourage had brought four skiffs, all of them armored affairs with actual cannons mounted on the front. Overkill, really. Any one of those Jedi could break a civilian's neck as soon as look at them, yet they swarmed around their lord like he needed protection from a murder—gaggle?—of teething rancors.

One of the skiffs remained oddly untouched. Ekiya thought it likely that she'd missed the scouts who originally got out of it—or that she'd been the victim of some casual Jedi mind nonsense. Either way, that lone skiff made the most appealing first target. So, once the rest of the pleasure barge's guests had swanned off into the caverns, she moseyed into the kitchen. She got another platter of food from the contact who'd sneaked her and Chie onto the staff roster and signaled B5 to be at the ready.

Only a few Jedi remained on the beach. Two on the deck of the vessel they'd commandeered—a sleek white thing sculpted to evoke a fisher bird—and another couple standing watch on the path that led up to the entrance to the cavern. Couldn't be too good at their jobs, though, seeing as they hadn't yet caught Fox or Grim. Ekiya got to sashay down the dock to the abandoned skiff with nary a side glance from any of them.

First she knocked on the gleaming side panel of the skiff. Nothing. She knocked again and called out in her politest tone: "Food?" Nothing again.

Well, then.

Ekiya tapped the comlink she shared with B5, who proceeded to trundle down the pleasure barge's gangway bearing a platter with tea and tea set. She took the droid's tray once he caught up to her and proceeded to wait under the relentlessly sweaty heat of Dekien's meridian sun as B5 sliced the door open.

Nothing continued to happen as this occurred. Set her teeth on edge. If no one was in the skiff, fine. That meant Ekiya really had missed them getting out. But if someone *was,* then they sure as hell knew she and B5 were trying to get in, and they were just . . . waiting.

The door slid open. The smell of death rolled out. Ekiya coughed and nearly dropped her platters.

One moment, two choices: Yell for help, because someone had definitely died in one of the Jedi skiffs—and possibly screw every chance her crew had of getting out of this alive. Or deal with whatever the hell had died—been killed?—on a Jedi scout skiff herself.

Ekiya gritted her teeth. She tipped the food and tea set into the water just as she had off the deck of the barge and, armed with dual metal platters, readied herself to smack the hell out of whatever moved.

Beside her, B5 chirred.

"Yeah," she muttered, "you give 'em whatever you've got, bud."

They stepped in together.

The skiff was darker than the outdoors because the lights weren't on, though the harsh sun still spilled in through the wide one-way windows.

She saw the bodies first. They hadn't even been hidden. Two young folks—maybe her age, if that—laid out on the ground, dressed like Jedi, glaze-eyed and slack-jawed in death.

She saw their killer next. B5 snarled an electronic warning. Ekiya whipped around as the door slid shut to meet two fire-and-amber eyes in a grimacing face. The Sith demon's hand snapped toward her throat, and Ekiya swung the platters with all her might—

Hanrai slowed his step and turned to glance back over his shoulder. All around, the Seikara Caverns sang—the black current of the Force flowing in perfect harmony with the shimmering white flare. Through all that, he felt with acute certainty that something, somewhere, had knotted, condensed, and burst, and it had done so not ahead, but behind.

His quarry lay before him. He knew this without doubt, as he felt that too. Hence his retainers, knights and guardians, with whom he walked down the lattice of Eternity's bridges toward the end of the caverns.

Yet something behind him also boiled—or had, as now it quieted.

"Something troubling you, my lord?" asked the tidy older woman who'd claimed the role of attendant to his party.

"Not at all, Chie," Hanrai said, and he once more turned forward. "Nothing you and I can't take care of on the way back."

CHAPTER
FIFTEEN

No MATTER HOW far they flew from the doline, the caverns never darkened. The light came first and foremost from the walkways, the wooden bridges and lanterned paths Eternity Enterprises had installed for their guests. A pale-gold line led them through colossal cathedrals of stone no sunlight had ever touched. It glimmered over the coursing underground river that cut down the center of the cavern, and it reached up the walls as far as it could go until the natural dark consumed the ceiling. Here and there, the ceiling also glittered. Colonies of bioluminescent bacteria made constellations in stalactites or flowered in the crevices of the phytokarst left by generations of their lichenous predecessors.

The Ronin remembered his first journey down this path more faintly than he liked. The memory was obscured both by the veil of time and by a second, less kindly curtain—that of the drunken state that had led him to this deep hole of the world in the first place.

The Traveler seized him by the elbow. The Ronin jerked back from where he had just meant to leap. The platform ahead floated on repulsorlifts over the river, and beneath it, a massive scaly back, rippled with dark spines, breached the surface of the rapids in an ill-lit curve. The

creature it belonged to was doubtless wider than the platform and longer than ten of them strung together. After an eon of a minute, its barbed
tail slithered back under the surface, and only then did the Traveler release the Ronin's sleeve.

"You seem distracted," they said in the cheerful tone of a scold.

"I'm focused."

But he let them stick closer from then on. The Traveler's instinct for
the presence of life exceeded his own, and he would have been a fool to
ignore it.

The cavern sloped deeper and deeper into the planet's crust, and the
farther they went, the faster the water ran. The texture of the air changed,
condensing. Some familiar yet unnamable desire coaxed the Ronin ever
faster.

A final shrine gate awaited them at the crest of a darkly yawning cavern over a titanic black lake. The wooden walkways extended out to the
sides of the open space, lining the warp and weft of the walls. They led
to a platform at the far side, which had space enough for guests to sit
and meditate upon the magnitude of the wild splendor. Unlike much of
the walkways, the platform was built into a stone ledge that jutted from
the natural wall. At this juncture was a shrine, pleasingly austere: a
waist-height carved stone pillar and a tiled roof to protect the home of
the spirit within.

The Ronin frowned as he approached the pillar.

"Desecrating shrines now, are we?" said the Traveler. "I suppose I
can't be shocked."

"No. This is new."

There had been no shrine gates the last time he came to the cavern,
to say nothing of the shrine itself. It nevertheless struck him as appro-
priate. He had not been the first to follow a call into this dark heart of
Dekien.

"All right then, what *are* we looking for?" asked the Traveler, though
they were cut off when the Ronin seized their collar and leapt from the
platform.

He had caught, at the edge of his attention, an encroaching presence.
It puzzled him slightly that the Traveler had not, given their prior sen-

sitivities, though perhaps that could be blamed on their usual feckless approach. No time for that now.

They plunged into the penetrating cold of the watery abyss. Training and the black current of the Force kept them from breaking any bones, but the full shock of the temperature shift made the Ronin shiver. Simultaneously, that odd yearning that had grown in him since they entered the cavern bloomed through his chest and limbs and drew him down, forward and down.

The currents below the lake proved hungry. Great shadows undulated just out of clear view. The Ronin pushed himself, tracing that old, increasingly visceral recollection. The Traveler kept up with him—he thought—but the murk of the water made it difficult to keep track of them. So did the call in his head, his heart, his entirety, which wanted him to dive and dive—to a crevice in the wall that lay directly below the platform above.

The closer he swam, the more apparent it became that the crevice was smoothed, both by time and by sentient intent. He dived toward it and through it, into an entirely black passage. His lungs burned as he dragged himself forward, his limbs growing sluggish with their own weight. Still, he pushed—called by that other need. He wanted dearly to answer. He *remembered.*

Light reached for him from above, pallid in the gloom. He pursued it upward. His legs kicked, arms reached, and when he emerged again into the world above, he gasped with a chest that ached to have air in it again. For a long moment he treaded there, body desperate to sink back into the water, but his eyes too entranced by what he saw to let it.

The spell broke only when the Traveler burst out of the water, too, heaving and hacking. They dragged themself bodily to the shore—the cave floor sloped gradually out of the pool they had emerged into—and after coughing up some gouts of water, fell on their back to wheeze.

"You are a jackass," they declared when the Ronin joined them. "And I do not like you anymore."

The Ronin was momentarily tempted to tip them back into the water. Then they removed their mask to better glare, and he balked.

Their face wasn't especially visible now, without the industrial lights provided by the walkways, but they had entered a space not entirely without its own illumination. Stalks of some tall, bioluminescent grass blanketed the hill around which the dark pool ran. More of the constellation lichen bloomed over slender stone plinths lining the slope. And from somewhere, faint fist-sized globules of gaseous light floated, never reaching far above the plinths before they winked out into the dark.

So, in a way, he could see the Traveler more clearly than he ever had before. They were not human. He had suspected this; he had never seen them eat, nor sleep, only drink an idle cup of tea now and again. Their eyes were as thoroughly white as their hair, and though the Ronin couldn't name their species, if the faint lines on their face indicated age in the way they did for humans, they were long past youth. Younger than Chie, almost certainly. Old enough to know they were.

But there were no particular distinguishing marks upon that face. No telltale scars or otherwise remarkable features. Attractive, by the Ronin's standards, but he was given to think such things about a variety of folk. More than anything, they looked tired. This he understood and all too well.

The Traveler frowned, then sighed and held up the red-marked mask. "No," they said, "I'm afraid this *isn't* my face."

"Why the mask?"

"Why not?" The Traveler sat up, the fox countenance cradled in their palms. "I've been flippant. But I think you understand. If you didn't, you'd use your own name."

The Ronin allowed them the grace of turning his back so they could wipe their face and fit the mask back onto it.

When they stood, they joined him and took in the hill at his side as they retied their hair. "Quite the graveyard."

"Yes." The wanting pull in the Ronin's chest had quieted until the Traveler correctly named the grotto for what it was: a place for the dead, and for the living to recognize them. Now the wanting called him forward again, and he stepped over ancient soil, up the hill. The plinths he passed flickered in his wake; the lichen had burrowed most deeply in the grooves of the old characters carved into them.

"I suppose it makes sense . . ." the Traveler mused as they followed behind him, those light globules tagging at their heels. "The Empire classified Dekien as an uncivilized world—wild, ripe for the taking. But you can't live in this galaxy long without realizing how ill fitting such words are. Every day, we walk over the monuments of what came before us. We see where people used to live and no longer do, for one reason or another. Because they left, or were made to. Or they died, or we killed them."

"They drew me here, the first time. The dead," said the Ronin. "I wanted silence. Something like it. Whatever I could get."

As he spoke, the Ronin realized he wouldn't have admitted as much a day ago—perhaps not even an hour, or a minute. But now he had seen the Traveler's face, and together they had come to a haunted place he remembered through an unseemly haze. He couldn't put a simple name to it: not grief, not rage, not despair. A hot and hateful desolation that had threatened to burn him to nothing, and that he had prayed the dark would extinguish.

He had returned from these graves alive. Cursed, he thought, as cursed as this whole galaxy, which couldn't properly end a single thing. However dead the people who had left these graves, they had risen to call him. And in answering them, he had failed to die. No end, no reprieve. Just life, persisting terribly.

"This relic we're after . . ." said the Traveler. "It's here because you left it."

"Yes. It was what remained of a choice. One I . . . wished to forget." The Ronin paused to turn and look at the Traveler where they stood, inspecting a particularly well-preserved plinth. The mobile lights seemed oddly attracted to them, bobbing by their ankles and past the folds of their sodden sleeves. The sight of it stirred something in the Ronin's chest. The ancient ghosts who loved this grotto had once called the Ronin to their home, but the lights had never attended to him so closely.

The Traveler smiled when they noticed his attention. "You *are* worried about me. Well, you don't know anything about me, really. You might as well be worried over nothing."

"I am aware of what I don't know. Have I not been asking?"

That smile melted away. They stood stiffly now, a strange mirror to the plinth that so interested them. "I . . ."

"I've gone twice now, you know."

"I'm trying," the Traveler said, riddled with more heat than it seemed either of them expected. They straightened and turned away, gazing down the hill toward the pool from which they had emerged. "I— perhaps when the situation is somewhat less dire. I understand it's not liable to grow *much* less so while we're hunting a Sith witch with the power to resurrect the dead—but—that is to say, maybe when the Jedi aren't breathing *right* down our necks—"

"When we get back to the *Crow*, then," said the Ronin.

"Right then?" said the Traveler, who had some sort of constitutional objection to not being an equivocating cheat. "We don't know what's—"

The Ronin's fixed stare stopped the words in their throat. "I've followed you until now," he said. "I've been patient. I believe you owe me this."

"Fine!" The Traveler threw up their hands. "I owe you, o magnanimous one. Now where's this thing you left?"

"I can't believe this. I literally can't believe this!" Ekiya knew she was complaining. That didn't stop her. "What did I want to do this morning? Oh, nothing fun, no—gonna go make nice faces at rich jerks so we can go traipse around a spooky cave and get our grabby little hands on a haunted Sith relic—but no! It can't even be that simple! It has to get worse!"

"Yes," intoned her terrible new companion, "worse."

Ekiya scowled over her shoulder at the Sith woman, who raised an arch eyebrow. This accented her freshly blackened eye, which was the only thing Ekiya liked about her. Ekiya nevertheless got the message; the Sith never let her hand stray far from the hilt at her waist. She'd already proven herself willing to turn the awful thing on.

"*The* worst." Ekiya returned to the controls, keeping the scout skiff skimming over the trees that topped the length of the Seikara Caverns. "You know when I wanted to get kidnapped by a homicidal Sith lady to pilot her stolen ship laden down with two dead Jedi? I'll tell you when! Never!"

"You haven't been kidnapped," said the homicidal Sith lady. "We're collaborating."

"Oh, sure, that's what I call it when someone menaces me with a laser sword."

"You struck first."

And Ekiya had been an idiot to think two serving platters would take down the vengeful ghost of a Sith warrior. Or, she'd known it wouldn't do her any good, but she'd figured it preferable to go down swinging. She could only call herself lucky that the Sith demon was so shy of Jedi attention—as shy of it as Ekiya. The Sith couldn't twist Ekiya up in the Force with so many Jedi on hand to sniff her out, and Ekiya couldn't scream for Jedi rescue if she wanted her crew to have a chance of escaping.

Why the Sith hadn't just killed her like she'd killed the Jedi—that she didn't yet know. The demon had apparently driven herself out here. What did she want with a pilot?

Either way, here they were, screeching through the sky together, hoping desperately that they'd get to the end of the cave before the Jedi squad got there first.

And then what?

"What happens when we land?" Ekiya asked mutinously. "When you don't need me anymore? Am I getting choked, bisected, or plain old stabbed?"

"I'll do nothing you don't make me," said the Sith, like a liar.

Ekiya's lip curled. "Sure."

The trick would be getting the drop on her again. It was possible. Ekiya had done it, once, when she was years younger and more foolish—and desperate, and had help. When it was her and the other conscripts huddled in that frigid cave figuring out which of them would poison their Sith commander, and which of them would have blasters, and which of them would have knives. Ten tried it, six made it. This time, it was just Ekiya and B5-56.

"I'm not going to kill you," the Sith said—and with an odd determination. She sat cross-legged in the seat beside Ekiya's and looked for all the world like she believed herself. Or like she wanted to.

"Right," said Ekiya. And though she knew she shouldn't push, she asked, "Why?"

"I've made my choice," the Sith ground out. She knuckled her temple and sent Ekiya a narrowed amber glare. "I'm Kouru."

Ekiya had no idea what to do with that. But, as Kouru was definitely having some manner of Sith demon crisis, and as Ekiya had glaringly few alternatives other than figuring out how to remain not-killed by the aforementioned crisis-having Sith demon, she said, "Great," and, "I'm Ekiya."

Kouru grunted. Then she pressed the full heel of her palm to her forehead, squinted, and indicated a point on the map projected on the navigation console. "Go there."

"What's there?"

"Do you want to reach your friends or not?" Kouru snapped.

"If it's Force stuff, you just have to say," Ekiya muttered.

Kouru looked strangely offended at the prospect.

Terrible.

Kouru was terrible—as terrible as every Sith before her and just about every Jedi Ekiya had ever met to boot. Not Fox, granted. But only because Ekiya was soft, chronically, irrevocably, and she liked that Fox was foremost gentle, and she liked that they cared, sincerely, about everybody they met, even the ones they only knew for a minute. She liked, a bit shamefully, that *they* didn't like the part of themselves that was some kind of Jedi.

Despite herself, she liked Grim too. Parts of him, anyway. The part that got confused when someone did him a basic favor. The part where he was gracious, and that he prayed. The part that Fox liked—and that B5-56 apparently adored.

She liked B5 fine. A lot, even. The droid was earnest, and he apologized, and she'd never met a droid so willing to sit and teach her about what wild, clever thing he was doing when he did it. So if B5 cared about Grim, she did too.

Which didn't make it easy to see the little astromech, flickering in the far corner of the scout ship, just on the other side of the two dead Jedi.

His lights blinked off and on; he rocked; he stilled. He'd been trying to get in touch with Grim since their skiff peeled out of the Seikara harbor. No word yet.

Ekiya glanced at her own comlink. Still dark. No word from Chie, let alone Fox. Something didn't want their signals getting through. Maybe they could blame the caverns themselves. Perhaps shortsightedly, Ekiya wanted it to be so—because it was one thing if the riled ghosts of a creepy Sith-haunted cave wanted to keep them apart, and another thing entirely if the Jedi were running interference. So what if Ekiya didn't know how to kill a woman who'd already died? A Sith, she knew how to fight. A Jedi . . .

She gripped the controls. If her luck turned, maybe she'd get to land on one.

CHAPTER
SIXTEEN

At the top of the grotto hill stood a collection of cracked and eroded stones. They had once served as something like a shrine, or whatever the people who came before would have called it. On the Ronin's first visit, he had left the relic on a flat stretch of rock in the center of them. He crouched to better examine this section. It was empty.

"Well, what am I looking for?" asked the Traveler over his shoulder.

"A shard of kyber." The Ronin held up his fingers to indicate the approximate size—quite small, about the dimensions of what one would fit into a lightsaber. "It . . . came from the Shinsui Temple mirror. On Rei'izu."

"Did it, now?" The Traveler wanted either to laugh or to wail. "That explains Seikara's reputation for visions, then."

The Ronin grunted agreement. "It would. If it were here."

The Traveler had let one of the gaseous lights play over their hand and rest in their palm. They froze as he said this. "You think it isn't?"

The Ronin waved his hand over the empty stone before him. It seemed there was a disturbance in the lichen where he had originally placed the shard, but that was all the evidence it had ever been there.

The Traveler dropped their hand. The light that had hovered over their palm wavered and blinked out as they crouched beside him. "Oh."

Their small dismay was worse than any curse. It left them both suspended in the dread of realization. Their prize was gone.

Had it been taken? The Ronin laid his hand flat on the stone, searching for any sign of what could have done so. Some intelligence. Something possessed of purpose and desire. Life saturated these caverns—the lichen in every crevice, the massive serpents in the lake. Death flourished, too—the ghosts he had followed into this dark hole of the galaxy. They lingered; he felt them.

His jaw clenched, a nerve in his teeth panging sharp and bright. Were those same ghosts his thieves? Had they only ever led him here, to their forgotten rot, to steal his shard for themselves?

"Careful," said the Traveler.

The Ronin looked over his shoulder; the stone shivered under his hand, then cracked. "You . . . Before we entered, you wondered if it might already be gone. What made you think it was?"

The Traveler held as still as the cave and as absence. Then they settled their hand on his arm. Their fingers were chilled from the water, the hem of their sleeve soaked through. The Ronin was no warmer, nor drier, yet through their cool touch he realized what a terrible fire he had become. He was all anger, fear, and worse. He shook.

The Traveler's tone was soft and sure. They meant to offer him an anchor. "I did wonder whether our entrepreneurial acquaintances at Eternity Enterprises might have stumbled across the relic, but that was before I knew about this peculiar little garden. I think we can say with certainty that they haven't the slightest idea this place exists. If they had, can you imagine what they would have done to it?"

The Ronin bared his teeth for the punchline; it was the most he could offer in turn. He had diminished, and he was grateful. It allowed him to confess, "I don't know what to do."

The Traveler stood, and he saw that under their mask, their mouth was tight with stress. Yet when they spoke, they were determined. "We find another way."

You ought to leave, the voice said.

The Ronin startled, and visibly, for the Traveler frowned. He hadn't realized the voice had gone silent—it was as if her attention was divided, distracted by something other than him. That deepened the Ronin's concern, but not more so than her warning. She had spent all this time urging him forward. Now she wanted him to leave? Just what did she want from him?

But he was not in the habit of discounting her warnings. They were few and far between, and though always selfishly motivated, she did not lie. Thus, he stood as well. "It won't do us favors to stay."

His new surety gave the Traveler pause, but they agreed. "I think you're right. But I'm not going out the way we came in."

"What makes you think we have an option?"

"We must! Obviously, we must." Their sweeping gesture encompassed the entirety of the grotto graveyard. "Someone erected these graves. Someone tended them—for a time. And you can't expect *everyone* to ritualistically hurl themselves into a watery abyss brimming with giant serpents just to pay their respects. Can you imagine a better way to prematurely bloat your graveyard's occupancy rate? No. There's another exit."

The Ronin conceded this, as well as their follow-up argument: "That breeze is coming from *somewhere*."

This search proved more fruitful and took far less time than he expected it to. It mortified him, a little, to realize it had been there all along—a narrow path carved into the rock face surrounding the grotto that wound around the circumference, where it ended on a ledge over the pool they had surfaced in.

"How did you get out the first time?" the Traveler asked as they stepped onto the path, testing its solidity. "Don't tell me you swam against the current."

"I was younger," said the Ronin. "Hurry up."

The little gaseous lights trailed after the Traveler for a time even as they reached the section of the path that exceeded the height of the grave hill, as if reluctant to see them leave. The Traveler hesitated for a moment. Did they mean to pray? But they pressed forward, and the Ronin thought himself grateful for that. The call of the dead that had lured him in grew fainter as he followed the Traveler up the path; what ghosts remained were confident in their ability to endure, to summon him again whensoever they wished. He could run, but never far enough to escape them.

The ledge overlooking the grotto opened up into a hewn tunnel that in turn led back to the lake cavern. The tunnel was broader than the underwater passage through which they had gained entrance to the graveyard, so they moved through it side by side until they reached the other end. Here, another ledge loomed some twenty meters above Eternity Enterprises's circle of golden bridges, themselves floating another thirty-some meters over the grand black lake below.

The path from their high shelf continued in the form of a carved stone bridge that arched improbably through the air from one side of the cavern to the other. They hadn't seen it when they first came upon the lake; the structure was somewhat concealed by the shadows cast by the natural undulations of the ceiling. It seemed to the Ronin that those who had hewn the bridge from the original rock had wanted it to *feel* separate, like a path from one world to the next.

It did, most conveniently, feel separate enough that it did not at all occur to the cave's other visitors to look up. Eternity's guests had at last reached the great lake chamber, accompanied by Jedi in their more dour colors. The guests milled along the circle of bridges, appreciating the lake or seeking a moment with the shrine. The hushed, delighted murmur of their awe traveled up to where the Ronin and the Traveler crouched at the end of the tunnel, eyeing the Jedi and weighing whether it was safe to step out onto the bridge.

The Traveler nodded forward. The Ronin couldn't disagree. Careful, then. They walked one after the other, not for fear of the bridge's width, but to better avoid being seen by those gathered beneath. The Ronin took the lead; the shadows that hid the bridge also obscured what lay at its opposite end, and old habit wanted him to be first to meet whatever dangers might lurk ahead.

As such, he was first to see what awaited them—another ledge, which led to a darkened chamber very slightly illuminated. Natural light crept down from an upward-curving tunnel just beyond. The Ronin couldn't see as much of it as he wanted to, as a man stood in the way, at the lip of the entrance to the chamber.

A Jedi, certainly. The very lord the Jedi below had come to escort, in all likelihood, given the richness of his clothes. A lord who nevertheless held himself like a proper old knight.

The lord—Hanrai, the Traveler had called him—was abruptly far more *present* as he stepped from ledge onto bridge, a steady beacon of white flare near perfectly buoyed on a steady, churning pool of black current. Hanrai approached with a steady, unhurried pace.

The Ronin's foot shifted back, his hand falling to the lightsaber hilt at his waist. His fingers twitched over the grip of his blaster next. Instinct wanted him ready to meet Hanrai's blade with his own, but he needed to weigh every option at his disposal. Not that he expected a bolt to get far past a Jedi knight's bladework.

As Hanrai neared, it became apparent that he was smiling. When he spoke, he did so with the warmth of familiarity. "There you are. I didn't expect you to take the hard way down. But I see you remembered the way out eventually."

The Ronin racked his memory for the old Jedi's face. There had been a number of them, when he was younger. Knights who saw a driven youth as one of their own—as a man who would one day succeed them, if he could only bring himself to heel.

No. He did not know this man. He understood this to be true because it was the Traveler who inhaled behind him, soft and sharp. "Don't draw," they said, only for his ears. "Hanrai, he—this isn't a fight we win."

The Ronin's gaze flicked to the cuff at his wrist, still dark. B5-56 had sent no warning. Neither had the voice, outside her first. This moment was his own to escape. His and the Traveler's.

"Do we have a choice?" he asked them, hand never straying from where it waited.

"A choice? I think you made it a while ago," said Hanrai. When he spoke next, it was louder, and this declaration echoed all through the lake cavern to the crowd below. "A duel, then. A straightforward affair. The victor leaves as he likes."

"Don't," the Traveler insisted.

Hanrai countered their protest by igniting his lightsaber. It shone blue as water through glass, and as Hanrai lunged, it cut the air with the smooth certainty of a crashing wave.

The Sith bandit had been all scathing intensity, untempered because she was untested. None had truly challenged her when she reigned as the greatest power on little Genbara. Hanrai, on the other hand, was a hardened knight of the Empire, and he moved with all the wisdom and conviction of a man honed by years of bloody service. There would be no catching his blade, not with hands and not with the Force.

The Ronin met Hanrai's strike with the red shock of his own blade. The power behind Hanrai's blow sent him skidding back. The tactician within him wanted to dodge the next thrust, to let the Jedi's own blows carry him astray—but that sort of maneuver only worked when one had no need to worry about who one might leave unguarded. The Ronin would have to keep Hanrai on the opposite end of the bridge. Preferably, he would have the Jedi off the bridge entirely.

As the Ronin judged Hanrai, he knew himself judged in turn. They each measured the risk of every lunge, the cost of every hesitation. When the next strike came, it was impossible to say which man moved first—who swung, who countered.

More troubling: No matter how he tested Hanrai's defenses in jabs and sparks of white flare and black current, he found no vulnerability to exploit. Hanrai guarded his stance, his grip, his lightsaber—here was a man who remembered the Sith predilection for tricks. He deftly leapt over the Ronin's attempt to knock him off his feet with a sudden extension of the staff he had built into his auxiliary, and he dodged under the following attempt to run him through with the ignited end.

Here also was a man who hadn't missed a day of training since the end of the war. Hanrai's focus never wavered, and though the pulse of his white flare made the Ronin suspect he was enjoying himself, his gaze remained stern.

For his own part, he felt sure and sleek, far more so than he had when he faced the bandit or Chie—perhaps more so than he had since the days before he first brought that cursed kyber shard into the gullet of these caverns. Days of honing himself with sparring matches and clever games, of eating and sleeping, of allowing himself the creature comfort of camaraderie, had done him well. He fought with purpose and belief.

In the end, that was his weakness.

No more than a minute had passed of this wariness, these blows exchanged and countered. The Ronin had just begun to think there might be an opportunity—if he could maneuver the Lord Hanrai just so, he might leave the Jedi open to the Traveler's particular gift for precise strikes from a distance.

But when he allowed himself a backward glance, he saw his error. The Traveler no longer stood alone at the graveyard end of the bridge.

Chie had joined them, though how and from where, the Ronin had not the time to wonder. For an instant, Chie's hand hung at the Traveler's elbow like a comfort, keeping them back from a fight they clearly lacked the will to face. Then she stepped to the side, off the ledge, and pulled the Traveler down with her.

Both plunged. The Ronin threw out a hand in desperate reflex to temper the terrible physics of their fall down to the lake—and was interrupted by another of Lord Hanrai's wave-strong strikes.

This time, their lightsabers ground together. "Leave my itinerant student to Chie," said Hanrai, as if suggesting where they should each sit at a shared meal. "They'll manage each other. I want the measure of you, Sith. Meet me as you are. No distractions."

The Ronin bared his teeth. No distractions? What a fool this Jedi was—as all his kind had proved to be. No matter how the fight turned from here, the Ronin would never be able to banish the fear.

But he would beg it to make him stronger.

At the sight of her companions falling off the stone ledge toward the lake, Ekiya exclaimed some vile curse. Kouru clapped a hand over her mouth and was bitten for her trouble. She growled at the woman, voice low: "If you want them back alive, you'll be quiet."

They crouched beside each other in the mural-carved stone chamber the Jedi lord had left, B5-56 hovering just behind them. Opposite their own shelf, on the far side of the cavern, the old man and his fox-masked companion had emerged from a tunnel only to be greeted by the Jedi lord—the Jedi who had stolen Kouru's prey.

Yes. Now's your chance. Strike while he's vulnerable.

Kouru shook her head, wanting to dislodge the mounting pressure between her eyes. She heard it clearly every time now, that whispering want that sought to control her. The clouding need that had first murmured to her as she rose in the desolate Genbara temple, the itch that dogged her like a hunger, a ghost behind her mind. Though what manner of ghost haunted the already dead . . .

Not a ghost. Kouru had a name for a power that ensnared the dead and rewove them into weapons—into demons. *Witch.* But that thought invited more implications than Kouru had the power or patience to conceive. As Ekiya had flown them into the jungle, Kouru had tried to understand what it meant for the witch to be alive. If she was. Kouru wasn't. That had not yet impeded her, outside of how her death rendered her vulnerable to the witch's demands.

It was too much. The only thing Kouru could know and hold as a truth was that the witch wanted her to kill the old man. She thought: I am content with that. If he was the betrayer she thought him to be—and the blade she had stolen from him left her all but certain that he was—then she did want him to bleed, and to be dead, and most preferably by her own hand.

But she wanted, vitally, to choose how it was done.

You needn't resist so, Kouru. I want only to help.

Kouru gritted her teeth. She had conceded to the witch's guidance already. Had directed Ekiya to a dewy glade on a hill in the midst of the wet mountain jungle. Had led the way out of the skiff to a veil of tangled vines draped over the hillside and cut these away with her lightsaber. Had found a short, stone-hewn passage waiting on the other side, which opened into a chamber lined with carved murals, which led to a narrow bridge arching over the lake cavern. And there, ahead, she saw her quarry.

Her need for the old man's death spiked again within her as she tried to focus on him defending against the Jedi lord. She wanted ravenously to throw herself at their duel, to seize her revenge while he was distracted.

The impulse ran up against unexpected resistance from within; a clear-cut memory of what had happened each time she faced the old man thus far. He fought with the determined cunning of a warrior who cared not at all for the dignity of his name because he instead cared to *win*. Kouru wouldn't overcome him until she played his game better than he did—

You have the advantage now . . . Really, Kouru, it will go better for you once you let go.

Kouru's fist clenched. She railed instinctively against compliance, even as she yearned for what it drove her toward. It was a miserable, tangled way to be, but she clung so to it. No matter how deliciously distilled she had been in her obedience to the witch, now she saw submission for what it was, and it soured her soul. She pinched her forehead with ferocity, her nails threatening to puncture her skin—

"Hey." Ekiya tapped her arm lightly, as if daring to prod an unstable chemical. "Hey—what's up?"

Kouru bared her teeth. "Nothing."

"Looked like something." Ekiya raised her hands at the ensuing glare. "Whatever—Force stuff. I don't care. I just want—"

Ekiya evidently didn't know what she wanted. Her eyes flicked between the arch above and the bridges below, unable to settle. Of the two, she hated the latter more.

Down in the cavern, on the golden bridges encircling the lake, pampered socialites swarmed, herded by Jedi. Within that swarm was the one Ekiya called Fox—the half-Jedi not-Jedi, whom Kouru suspected had dealt her that decisive blow in the dockyard on Genbara.

Fox had landed on the main platform on the far side of the cavern from the ledge on which she and Ekiya crouched. Their fall from the stone bridge had been slowed and softened. This Kouru knew because Fox was not a smeared heap of no-longer-white robes. Some of that redirection had been the application of Fox's own power—they were nearly all black current—but no small number of the lord's Jedi retainers had also thrown out their hands to guide their plummet.

The way the collected Jedi maneuvered around the edges of the lake cavern spoke to their true intent. Some guided the socialites toward the red shrine gate that led back to the cavern entrance; others moved in the opposite direction to take positions that blocked any avenues of escape. They wanted Fox cornered, but alive.

"What's she doing?" Ekiya hissed, gripping a comlink. Her eyes were fixed on Fox as well, and on the old woman facing them. This one Ekiya called Chie, and it was Chie who had given Ekiya greatest cause to be upset; she clearly still wanted to trust the old woman, no matter that her eyes told her she could not afford to.

Chie, already on her feet, stood across the shrine platform from Fox, who had only just begun to drag themself to their knees.

"They're going to fight," said Kouru. This was obvious, but Ekiya needed to hear and accept it, or she would soon become vexing.

"No—why?" Ekiya's jaw squared. "This doesn't make *sense*—"

"No whys." Kouru grasped the other woman's white-knuckled hand. "No reasons. You decide what you want and you pursue it. Questions come later. If you still care to ask them."

Ekiya glared, but she didn't ask anything else. No why are you still helping me or why should I listen to you. She was focused. Pragmatic, despite her whining. Kouru had instantly liked this about her. It was why she had decided, despite the witch's urging, that she would prefer, in the end, not to have to kill her. Practical souls did the galaxy good, and Ekiya was every sort of practical.

Instead, Ekiya said, "You said 'alive.'"

"What?"

"My people—'if you want them back alive.' You're not here to kill them? Looked like it on Genbara."

Kouru opened her mouth to say: Just one. Then shut it, teeth clenched against the witch's *push*, which drove down on her like a nail into a tree—

LET GO

"Shut up," Kouru snarled. "Not you," she growled at Ekiya's offended face. At last she ground out, "What's . . . what's victory worth if it's half won by another?"

It didn't feel entirely correct even as she said it. Yet it made sense, didn't it? How could she have her revenge without the dignity of taking it herself?

The pressure within her sat dangerously askew.

To Kouru's mild disconcertion, Ekiya nodded, eyeing her with a look that wasn't respect, though neither was it contempt. Understanding? Perish the thought. Kouru barely understood what she herself felt or thought—let alone said or did.

At least now there was a goal, something Kouru could pursue until her mind righted itself.

She looked down again—at the main platform on the opposite side of the cavern, then at the bridge directly ahead. At each point, a pair of opponents squared off. She lacked the power to stop the duel in front of her, and she wouldn't reach the other in time to make a difference un-less . . . Her gaze tracked up to the cavern ceiling above.

Now you want my help? Well, then. It's all I've ever asked for, Kouru.

Kouru knuckled her forehead but decided to, for the time being, ac-cept that the witch wasn't purely a problem.

Directly above the cavern, in the density of the forest above, awaited their scout skiff— and the promise that lay within.

Didn't I tell you they had a purpose? Unleash them. They are yours to command.

Two dead Jedi who had not yet run out of use.

CHAPTER
SEVENTEEN

I T WOULD BE fast and sudden or it would be nothing. So many Jedi in so small a place—"You call this small?" Ekiya gestured at the cavern, hundreds of meters in length—would be the death of them.

Kouru sent Ekiya away, up to the skiff, and stationed the old man's droid where she needed him—safe in the entry chamber, with a good view of a specific section of the lake cavern ceiling. Then she jumped.

She skated, skidded down the cavern wall, pushing and pulling the gravitational streak of her fall with the black current of the Force. When she slammed into the bridge directly beneath her, she came down with the pressure of the white flare, hard enough to rock the repulsor-lifts. The socialites upon the bridge scattered to its golden edges, shriek-ing. They shrieked again when the red flash of Kouru's lightsaber bisected the bridge and sent them all tumbling to the lake below.

Kouru leapt off the debris onto the next floating walkway. There she met a pair of Jedi guardians. They dodged past her, toward the slick cavern walls. They would climb and slide down to the lakeside shore to rescue those helpless citizens who had fallen. This was their prerogative—just as it was Kouru's to cut down the walkway they threw themselves from as she sprung off it herself. The halved walkway careened in their wake. She would make them as busy as she could.

She met her first knight on the next bridge. A hulking black-hoofed being, he made himself a wall with his swooping black horns and bristling white mane, emerald blade ignited as a warning. A shame she didn't have time to enjoy him.

On the arch overhead, the clash between two old men hungry to die continued, ever more fervent. Before her on the shrine platform lay her goal, a frenetic dance between the betrayer and betrayed. Neither fight would wait for Kouru to tease this Jedi.

The knight charged with his behemoth entirety, a man accustomed to the intimidating weight of himself doing half the work of a duel. Kouru slid sideways, flipped over the edge of the railing, and caught herself on the underside of the walkway.

Kouru had acted more on impulse than plan and was briefly startled to find she *knew* exactly what she needed to do. Liquid-quick, she ripped open a particular panel beneath the walkway and plunged her hand into the innards to wrench out a precise piece of hardware. She couldn't even name the object as she let it drop. The walkway began to drop with it—no time to question. She propelled upward as the whole thing began to tilt until it floated perpendicular to how it had—and she launched herself toward the next bridge.

Her fingers latched onto its foot and she flipped up onto it. There she stopped, purposefully, no matter that the pressure urged her forward, forward—"Don't do that again," she snarled, hand fisted against her chest. "I won't be puppeted."

Oh, Kouru. It would be so much easier if you just—

Kouru clenched her teeth as if against searing pain. As if to echo her frustration, the cavern shook. Voices cried out in shock and panic—the socialites who had been rescued onto the shore of the dark lake, which was now further darkened. They shrieked in terror because one of the dripping black coils in the water had lurched up onto the beach.

A long neck, resplendent with spines and shining black scales, led to a maw lined with needle-sharp teeth, revealed in silver threat as the frilled serpent let out a piercing screech.

The cavern shook again. Another serpent roiled in the churn at the opposite end of the lake. It threw itself against the wall as its barbed tail lashed up toward the walkways hovering above it.

It was almost as if the serpents were meant to help her—though Kouru had no facility for calling living creatures.

Consider them a gesture of goodwill. I have more than one way to help you, Kouru.

Kouru's skin still crawled. The witch working through a demon under her control was one thing, but this, manipulating the world outside of—no. She had to focus.

The Jedi knights Kouru would have faced next threw themselves past her as they hurtled off the remaining walkways down to the beach, or in the opposite direction toward those trapped on the other side of the cavern. They dodged around her, like they thought she would try to stop them. Of course not—she merely needed them out of her way.

Don't waste my gift—hurry along.

Kouru shook her head clear. Yes, the way was open. No more wasted time. She would deal with the witch later.

On the platform by the shrine, Fox danced out of Chie's reach. A part of Kouru was infuriated to see it, imagining having to face such a farce of an opponent. At least the old man had seen fit to meet her blade when he dodged and wove. Fox was as yet empty-handed. She couldn't even say if they carried a lightsaber.

Chie seemed to share none of Kouru's irritation, and for all her opponent tried to escape, she never let them. She was as constant as the current itself, though Kouru sensed no particular openness in her to suggest sensitivity to the Force. That brightened Kouru's interest—she had always admired those warriors who made themselves deadly without the ability to manipulate current and flare.

There was a pattern to the fight, if you could call it that. Chie lunged, Fox slipped away, and Chie said something. Fox faltered, recovered, dodged. With every second, Fox's movements became more rigid, Chie's more fluid, and she never paused even when speaking.

Kouru heard "traitor," "lost," and "fondly"—then "gentle soul" and "favored pupil." Every word left Fox more frightened than the last, especially: "He wants you to come home."

Of course he does. Old fool.

"Quiet—you told me to focus," snapped Kouru.

Chie had backed Fox to the wall by the small shrine. To Kouru, they looked as though they had been speared. It made her underestimate the ferocity of what came next.

Fox drew from their sleeve a hilt, and they slashed forward with a blade. A lightsaber, searingly pale as a white winter sky, and burning like unto the flare in the Force itself. It blistered through Chie's staff and sent the shorn half flying.

Chie leapt back out of reach; Fox didn't move, only stood there, shoulders heaving, saber ignited and shivering. Its light seemed almost to pulse and sputter. An unstable build, thought Kouru. A flaw in the crystal—or in the wielder. Kouru had seen the like just days ago, when she dismantled the old man's blade. But Fox did have a lightsaber. That answered one question: Whether they were a true Jedi. Or whether they *had* been.

Chie adjusted her stance as she studied Fox. She neither raised the remaining half of her staff nor advanced, only opened her mouth to speak. She had never been more dangerous.

So, Kouru threw her off.

An inelegant launch, she would readily admit, but as effective as it needed to be. She swept her hand out as she landed on the final plat-form, and with a hurtling wave of black current shoved Chie to the edge and over the brink.

Fox sprang to action a second too late. They lunged forward, scrab-bling across the platform to catch Chie with some no doubt far more masterful manipulation of the Force. Whatever they managed to do in those first few seconds was interrupted when Kouru grabbed them by the arm and hauled them upright.

Just in time, too. She heard the shriek and echo of B5's blasterfire overhead—the rumble and crack of rock at last giving way—and the thunderous roar of the scout skiff's engines with Ekiya at the controls—as the cavern ceiling collapsed upon them all.

Hanrai could not rightly remember his last experience of honest shock. It was, as such, something of a delight when the cavern ceiling caved in.

The totality of the scenario rushed into his awareness as he reflexively broadened himself to become far more than the honed point he had made himself for the duel.

His opponent had demanded the fullness of his attention. The Sith was more pure, refined power than Hanrai had allowed himself to dream of. Trust his old student to exhume more than he imagined possible; they'd always had a knack for exceeding expectations.

But this explosion of rock and schism of stone, this he couldn't blame on them. *This* he had to pin on the stolen scout skiff screeching down through the shower of destruction, and on the two figures still on the surface, standing at the edge of the collapse and gazing slack-faced at the aftermath.

Hanrai realized with a sharp sorrow that he recognized both of them. These two individuals who had, through ruthless application of black current spiked with white flare, torn the cavern itself apart. Young Jedi guardians. Part of his retinue.

Or they had been, before they were killed. The puppets overhead, silhouetted by the sun as they stared down on the damage they had wrought, were no longer Jedi of Hanrai's clan. He could only pray that he would one day recover their bones.

After all, they hadn't been moved by their *own* astounding disregard for what their actions might do to Seikara, to the people within, or to the fragile histories that would be shattered and buried—no, that indifference lay squarely on the power who had already stolen so many of Hanrai's dead.

His attention lanced down—past the little astromech withdrawing into the chamber on the far end of the bridge—to the carnage below.

There in the mess of bodies and stone by the lakeside he identified Chie—fallen, but alive. Others—many injured, many grievously. His Jedi had done well to protect those they had, compelled to give up every other pursuit in the name of shielding themselves and the helpless innocents they defended. Some would soon be dead regardless.

One of those below was dead already, though this hadn't stopped her. A furious Sith demon with a blaze of white hair. She had caught Hanrai's old student—also alive, thankfully—and was dragging them aboard the waiting scout skiff.

The skiff's pilot meant to return for the Sith. Hanrai knew this like he knew suns set. He could not afford to let this one run its course.

He had kept himself poised to counter the Sith even as he stretched his awareness to make sense of the world. The man had proved a shrewd swordsman, driven by chasmic reservoirs of edged feeling. He moved only when he needed to, and then with terrible clarity of purpose. Now he moved not at all, and Hanrai expected the next strike to come would be swift and merciless. He needed to remain on guard.

But the blow did not come, and the Sith was a remarkable stillness. Even as the scout skiff streaked up toward the stone arch, he didn't move. His eyes remained fixed on the point above the cavern where Hanrai's attention had first turned—on the two young once-were-Jedi who stared back down at him, unblinking, motionless, their deed now done. They were as mirrors, this Sith and those demons. Empty and unheeding.

How fortunate. Chie had warned him of the man's frailties—had described them to Hanrai in terms of instability and danger. She had not imagined they might present an opportunity. At least, for these precious seconds, Hanrai could have confidence that the man would be unable to interfere.

The scout skiff screeched nearer and nearer. Hanrai let his eyes flutter closed. He extended his intent—made contact.

He got no further. His student wouldn't allow it. They recoiled from his attempt. Whatever they did next within the skiff forced the entire vessel to shift course and career up and out of the cavern, abandoning the Sith in their wake.

Hanrai let his eyes open and gazed up after the fleeing vessel. It was as he had feared, but also as he expected. To say the least, his student didn't think him an ally.

"More's the pity," he said, though the Sith was still too undone by his own fractured mind to respond. Just as well. They would have time to speak soon enough.

CHAPTER
EIGHTEEN

THEY LEFT THE Seikara Caverns in a frenzied mechanical shriek. Ekiya had steeled herself against going back for Chie, who'd just thrown herself and Fox off a bridge. But B5-56, Grim—them, she hadn't meant to abandon. Except Fox, dragged into the skiff by Kouru, had taken one look out the cockpit window, spied that old Jedi lord, and lost their idiot mind.

Granted, it was creepy as hell how Lord Hanrai had seemed to look straight into the cockpit and right at them, like he could lock eyes with any being in a vessel moving that quickly amidst all that debris. That didn't excuse Fox throwing a Force-based trauma fit to the tune of hurtling the skiff upward and forward at speeds that exceeded any kind of parameter built into the poor thing's framework.

They rocketed out of the collapsed cavern. Ekiya about lost her lunch on the controls. By the time she had full control of the skiff, the only reason she could have had to turn back around would have been to get caught. While she lacked what she would have called full control of her mental faculties, she knew enough not to want *that*.

So off they flew, the scout skiff careening through the jungle, dodging trees and survey droids, until it skipped out onto the piercing white-blue of the Dekien sea.

They had pursuit, for a while. But Ekiya knew all about evading Jedi, and Kouru did her part to guide Ekiya as she had on their journey into the jungle. She sat cross-legged in the copilot's seat to Ekiya's right, eyes closed, brow creased, intermittently offering direction. Soon, all sign of pursuit disappeared from the skiff's sensors. It was just them and the scintillating waters straight on to the horizon.

In her gut, Ekiya wanted to turn back. The professional in her bones kept her on track. Focused. Forward.

If only Kouru had shared similar instincts. Instead, she started turning over her shoulder to glower at Fox, seated on the floor around where the two dead Jedi had been sprawled. To be fair, it frightened Ekiya to see them like that. She'd seen Fox be a lot of things, even quiet, but never *listless*.

"Get up," Kouru snarled at them.

"Lay off," Ekiya hissed.

Kouru's lip curled. "Waste your sympathy elsewhere." Her hand stretched out, and for an awful gut-wrench of a moment, Ekiya thought the Sith was going to do something truly evil with it.

Instead, Fox shifted a bit, glancing down at their torso. From the folds of their damp white robe, they drew a slender shape, which vibrated slightly—until it flew out of their grasp and into Kouru's. Up close, Ekiya recognized it as something like the hilt of a lightsaber. More beautiful, though. Elegantly bound in thin strips of black-dyed leather and ornamented with shards of bright silvered metal.

"An heirloom," snorted Kouru. "The kind of lightsaber only wielded by a bloodline heir. No good person carries a blade like this."

Fox hadn't grabbed after the stolen hilt. This was weird, Ekiya realized, because she'd seen how effortlessly they could manipulate the physical world with the Force. Now they just sat there, chin balanced on their fingers as if in thought. "Good people, was it?" they asked. "Are we talking about good people, Ms. Bandit?"

Kouru sneered.

"Wait, *bandit*?" snapped Ekiya.

Kouru had the gall to look at her with some kind of patronizing pity—like she was a fool for not knowing. Ekiya about bit her. Again. For some reason, that made Kouru look like Ekiya *had* bitten her, and like she was genuinely offended by it. She rose, and Ekiya realized with flaring dread that she'd just seriously pissed off an undead Sith warrior—

A Sith warrior who was suddenly still standing, but croaking, chin arched up. Her arm twitched as if she meant to move it, but it remained rigid by her side. Ekiya stared over her shoulder at Fox, who had not moved. But the direction of their masked gaze remained fixed on Kouru, who shivered in the hold of some kind of terrifying full-body Force prison.

Ekiya hated it.

Fox's head canted toward her. Ekiya felt her fear and hatred *seen*— and hated that even more—but in the next second, Fox looked away. Kouru gasped and her hand whipped up to her throat.

"I'm not saying I don't understand why you got into the business, Ms. Bandit," Fox said lightly. "Your rebellion had been crushed. Of course you sought salve for the wound—a means to feel powerful again. And what better way to feel strong than to hunt prey who can't fight back?"

"Trying to get moral with me, bloodline scum?" Kouru rasped, winded but undaunted. "Your kind took me from my home. Tried to make me a puppet for your power. I don't know what makes you so afraid of Jedi, but you're just as deluded. If you gave half a damn about my 'prey,' you'd do something other than—whatever this is. Chasing Sith across the Outer Rim and delving into tourist traps."

Ekiya needed to keep her eye on the controls. This was very difficult to do while terrified the two Force-sensitive wackos on her skiff might at any second come to otherworldly blows.

Then Fox laughed, and it wasn't wholly the laugh Ekiya knew. It rang far more sharply in her ears. Kouru grimaced, and Ekiya feared *she* would start biting people next.

"Please!" Ekiya begged. "I am trying to drive, you jerks!"

Kouru rounded on Ekiya, who now expected she was about to take the brunt of the biting—but something made the Sith demon stop, and it wasn't Fox. Kouru almost softened. Her mouth opened, as if to—who knew what. Who cared!

"Nope," said Ekiya. "Shut up. I'm getting us to port, and then we're getting the *Crow,* and *then* we can figure out what the hell we're doing about—everything. But until then, I don't want to hear another word out of either of you."

It was a long, silent trip back.

To wit, Ekiya wanted nothing more than to get back on her ship. The *Poor Crow* was security, freedom, and the comfort of worthwhile tea and an actual bed. If she had the *Crow,* she could get over the frustrated grief of never having really known Chie, the guilt of abandoning B5-56, and whatever the hell it was she felt about Grim.

She would have her relics—all the ghosts kept safe in her hold. She was always better when she had something to take care of.

So, of course, because the galaxy was nothing if not reliably spiteful, the *Crow* was no longer in the hangar where Ekiya had left it.

Kouru was not annoyed. That would have been childish. Fox was merely meditating, their posture wholly tranquil in the center of the scout skiff's floor. Yet that tranquility was so undeserved that Kouru desperately wanted to cut a hole in the hull around their seat to drown them in the oil-slicked sea.

They had been left together in the scout skiff at Dazenma's main harbor as Ekiya went to secure her ship. The dockworkers studiously ignored their vessel—a stroke of luck for which Kouru grudgingly had to credit Fox. She certainly wasn't doing anything to facilitate it.

Not on purpose, at least. It was possible the witch had once more offered unasked-for assistance.

Kouru frowned at the thought and rubbed her forehead again. The witch's foreign pressure . . . She seemed oddly reticent in this moment, as if Fox's presence had somehow made her shy.

"If you think I haven't noticed you, you're quite wrong," said Fox, though their masked face didn't turn in her direction.

"What are you talking about?" said Kouru.

"Your friend, Ms. Bandit."

"It's not my friend."

Kouru surprised herself with her vehemence. Fox's head tilted, and she could almost feel their confusion, as if she'd spoken a language they didn't.

"You really don't know what we're after, do you?" they murmured.

"And I don't care," Kouru snapped. This was a lie, but she would rather have cut out her own tongue than let this cretin hold anything else over her.

The moment dissipated as Kouru raised her head. Nigh simultaneously, Fox did as well. They both sensed the presence beyond the door. Not a dockworker. Ekiya. Upset.

Before the skiff's door slid open, Fox spoke. "If I ever again suspect you intend to strike her," they said, light as air, "I'll put the offending limb somewhere you'd never imagine it would fit."

Kouru stared at them as Ekiya stepped through the door. Kouru was shaken, but not by Fox's threat. She was concerned she might learn to like them.

Ekiya took precedence. She refused to speak until the door had shut behind her. Then she pointed at both of them in turn, arm sweeping. "No," she said, though neither had moved. "Still no talking. I've heard way more from either of you than I ever want to hear again."

She cursed her way over to the back of the scout skiff, toward the planetary navicomputer display. Kouru and Fox followed her with their attention; neither trusted the other enough to move, as it would have required getting dangerously close to each other. Ekiya ignored both of them, calling up a map of Dazenma and zeroing in on the section of the port where she had, presumably, just been.

"Somebody took the *Crow*," she said. "I want it back. *I*, not *we*. 'We' don't need my ship so 'we' can do whatever—hell, this isn't about me either. It's about what's on that ship that doesn't belong to any of us, least of all the *Jedi*."

She said the last word like a curse.

"What's so valuable that you left it unguarded on a rust bucket like that?" asked Kouru.

She expected Ekiya to round on her with a fury. When all she got was a back still staunchly turned, her mouth tightened.

"Things. Just things," said Ekiya, newly old with frustration. "It doesn't matter. Not to you. But I need them back, and you're going to help me because—"

"I owe you," said Fox from the floor.

Ekiya broke off, pointing at them. She said nothing as she shut her mouth, offering them a gracious chance to not stick their foot in theirs.

Fox stood, stretching. "I imagine it's more that *we* owe you." They glanced toward Kouru. "But don't let me speak for you, Ms. Bandit."

Kouru suppressed the urge to sneer. "I owe you too," she said to Ekiya. She did. The woman could easily have ended Kouru's hunt by crying for Jedi rescue at the beach before Seikara, and she hadn't. Moreover, she'd provided Kouru respite, however unintentionally—space enough to more fully understand that her mind was no longer wholly her own. Kouru knew when to recognize the value of other people. She knew when to recognize the trouble of them, too, which was why she said to Fox, "You 'Ms. Bandit' me again, and you're the one who'll be finding new ways to affix their limbs to their body. I've a name. You'll use it."

If nothing else, Kouru still had their lightsaber. They were going to have to behave, if they ever wanted it back.

Ekiya exited the scout skiff into reality. It was beautifully grimy and smelled of engine grease. Vermin's Reach was the seedy part of jeweled Dazenma—as in, not the district where tourists went for the dangerous vibe, where they expected to get pickpocketed for the thrill of it, but the district where tourists got politely escorted back home. The cantankerous tourists who refused to leave—and you'd get those now and again—didn't make it home at all.

This particular port within the larger district lived inside a converted warehouse made of haphazard leftover building materials from Dekien's grander projects. It was a nexus through which more illicit pleasures cycled before they found their way to the pretty people in moneyed climes, and where people like Ekiya came to roost when they had stuff to hide. Most of the ships were nondescript enough, fishing vessels and cargo tugs, and their stolen scout skiff fit right in—aside from the fact that its cannon was more obvious than was typical.

The people looked refreshingly real too. Every species Ekiya recognized and some she didn't, wearing clothes they lived in and talking about real things, like whether it was lunch yet and where they hoped to find it.

The aunty who ran the dockyard was an old Hutt who was as much muscle as fat and who wore her bulk with the grace of experience. She was talking to a skinny young man in front of her office. When the manager raised her head to squint at Ekiya's approach, the man turned too. He scratched the back of his head, bowed thanks to the aunty, and sauntered over to Ekiya with a lackadaisical grin.

"Kiya, long time no see. Still chasing pipe dreams, huh?"

She plucked at his trim beard. "Wasn't I doing that before? I need clothes, Shogo—and info."

Something in her tone gave her away. Shogo led her off with a hand on her shoulder, his grin just a hair too wide to be sincere.

They went together down the pier to the low-slung houseboat Shogo operated out of. On one hand, she didn't love leaving her scout skiff so far behind. On the other, what was she going to do if a bloodthirsty ex-Sith (ex as in dead) and an emotionally volatile ex-Jedi (ex as in what was even going on over there?) went for each other's throats? Yell about it? Right, sure. She was better off hoping they exhausted each other.

Shogo's slicing setup hadn't changed much since Ekiya last saw it, but then he'd always preferred running clean. A few datapads and other such lay stacked on a counter alongside the unobtrusive gear he strapped on for outdoor work. He took advantage of all that plus his unremarkable face to get in, get out, and get the job done.

Ekiya had met more ambitious slicers, sure—but they were the ones that went big and got caught. Shogo worked on the same job for years at a stretch in a hundred quiet ways until a planet-wide banking system fell, or a Jedi fleet went dark, or some other wild bit of hell. He had no business calling her new crew any kind of dreamers.

Maybe. Sort of.

"It's the *Crow*," she said as he handed her new clothes. "It's gone."

He winced as if he'd suspected as much and went to haul out a communications deck while she changed. She didn't bother finding a back room to pull it all on—trousers, kimono, and a work vest, all clean but stained with the strain of actual labor. She and Shogo had seen too much of each other bleeding out over the years to care much about things like being naked. And right now, she needed the familiarity.

Shogo gossiped while he worked, catching her up on the rest of their old trooper crew. Sae and Haba were off in the Outer Rim helping to set up an independent comm network—and they were in bed together again, but that wouldn't last any longer than it ever did. Kabeji was off in the middle of the Core working on wiping those exploitative loans off the map by way of disappearing this or that banker—she'd sent Shogo some fantastic rice candy, if Ekiya wanted to try some, they were in the corner over there. He hadn't heard from Unsuke in months, but that was how it went, and soon enough the guy would turn up with a new lead on Sith auxiliaries or some other bounty to dump on Shogo's lap for want of a buyer.

Then Shogo winced even more acutely, eyes on his deck. "Hell, Kiya. Don't tell me those relics were on the *Crow*."

She asked, too tightly, "Where else do you think I'd be keeping them, Sho?"

He showed her the report. Requisitions. Imperial. Ekiya sat down on the floor of his little houseboat and thought, at first, that she'd have to try very hard not to scream. Instead, she felt empty. It couldn't be the haze of shock. She'd expected this, after all, even as she'd hoped that it was some other unforeseen complication that had whisked the *Crow* away. So why did seeing for certain just who had taken her ship make her feel so empty?

Shogo sighed and let himself slowly down onto the floor as well. His knee still bothered him. It'd never been the same after their commander had shattered it, that first awful mission away from home. By the time the rest of them had been able to afford a transplant, he'd been too nervous about proprietary parts to want anyone else's tech in his body. His brace was his own bespoke creation.

That was why she'd commissioned him for a new prosthetic, when they were still on their way. She could see the thing waiting for her on his worktable. Sleek and durable. Homemade. Perfect for a certain dour jawline. Assuming Grim wasn't dead by the time she got it to him.

Ekiya groaned into her palms. "You doing your exercises?"

"Still can't think about yourself, huh?" Shogo handed her the bag of fancy rice candy. Ekiya took one out because it was expected of her, but she couldn't bring herself to fiddle with the bright-colored wrapper.

Shogo had the awkward look of a man who didn't know what to do with someone else's feelings. Frankly, Ekiya didn't either, so she couldn't fault him for how long it took him to speak again.

"You're not going to want to hear this," he said, "but you have to. This mission of yours—Rei'izu, the relics, that mystic, whatever you were doing here with that big guy you picked up on Genbara—it's a lost cause. It was lost even before those Imps took the *Crow*. You get that, right?" He leaned in, searching for something in her face. "Come on, Kiya—you're the one who always kept us fed. Watered. Everything we needed to be alive first so we could dream later. What is it about this that you can't let go of? How do I bring you back?"

Ekiya had a dozen different ways to finish that argument for him. Words about making home and finding peace where you ended up, not in far-gone fantasies—or helping the people in front of you, not the ghosts you'd already lost. So why couldn't she get any of that out of her mouth?

"I don't know," she said dully. "Can't justify it. Just got under my skin."

Maybe it was Fox who had made her want Rei'izu in the first place, but any faith she'd been storing in them had crumbled at the same time they fell apart in Seikara. Ekiya hated to think of how quickly Fox had turned their power on Kouru. No matter that Kouru was a bandit, or a Sith, or whatever—it didn't sit right with her. So it wasn't Fox who made Ekiya want Rei'izu now.

Because she did still want it.

Ekiya flopped backward to lie flat on the floor. "What else am I going to do?" she asked the unlit ceiling. "I can't just let it go. Not if there's a chance."

The Sith witch's demons weren't the only restless lost. The ghosts nestled in the lanterns and mirrors and other lovely relics within which those kyber shards were embedded—they needed Rei'izu. Needed home. If Ekiya could get it back for *them,* for the dead and for the living who'd entrusted them to her, then that made all the horrid and the hurt and the heartbreak worth it. She'd fight to reclaim Rei'izu until it killed her because Rei'izu mattered to someone, even if it didn't always matter to her.

Shogo nudged her boot with his own and sighed. "Something needs to be yours, Kiya . . . Guess it might as well be this." He tossed her a datacard. "That'll get you through the front gate of the high lords' ship-yard. You're going to want to get to the *Crow* before they ship it out of atmo. Everything after that is up to you."

Ekiya held the card up in thanks. It was all she could ask of Shogo. For the rest, she'd have to trust Fox. And she did. Mostly she was just starting to worry that trust would kill her first.

CHAPTER
NINETEEN

THE HANGARS OF Dazenma soared skyward in varnished and lacquered pagodas. Multicolored banners hung from the lip of their roofs in stately array. Every craft ascended and descended in strict tapestry, coordinated by Dekien's exacting municipal flight directors. On landing, the *Poor Crow* had been relegated to the low-tiered, humble hangars on the fringe of Vermin's Reach. Now it waited for them at the topmost tower of an egregiously palatial monstrosity.

Kouru couldn't hide her distaste.

Ekiya elbowed her side. "Make that face in front of a Jedi and they'll cut it off."

"Not if I cut theirs off first," Kouru muttered.

But that would be *obvious,* and they had just been thoroughly lectured on how much they needed subtlety.

Mid-lecture, Kouru had treated Fox to her most dismissive glare. "Won't your mask stick out?" she asked.

"Oh, don't you worry about me," they said. "I'm much better at this than you are."

Irritatingly, they were. When Fox sauntered through the ornate wooden gates to the high lords' hangars, not a soul glanced their way.

As Kouru and Ekiya nipped at their heels, no one paid them much mind either. They drew quizzical looks at first, but in moments this attention inevitably strayed elsewhere.

Even as they crossed the rolling stone courtyard that separated the main gate from the first tier of hangars, no one looked. They passed more checkpoints, obvious and otherwise. Neither stern-faced guards in dark uniform, nor beautiful attendants in sweeping patterned kimono, nor even Jedi, who walked the premises in watchful pairs, looked at them for more than a handful of seconds. Each and every one was steadfastly inattentive to the three infiltrators.

It galled. This was no show of Imperial incompetence; it was a single master flaunting their control. Fox strolled unheeded into the heart of Jedi power and never flinched.

Once they reached the hangar, Fox ushered them to a guest lift—carved entirely of fragrant wood—and shooed away the wealthily clad couple who tried to join them. Only once they had keyed in the desired floor did they turn to their companions. "You'd be doing me a tremendous favor if you relaxed."

"I'll keep that in mind," said Ekiya, arms crossed. Her eyes remained fixed on the courtyard vanishing below, visible through the latticework of the lift walls.

Fox turned to Kouru.

Kouru bared her teeth. "I'm relaxed."

"I'm aware. Could you rein it in? Even a little?"

Kouru bristled. She wouldn't ask what they meant. That much was obvious. Where Fox slid through the world as if they themself were a whorl of the black current, manipulating minds as proficiently as they manipulated landspeeders, Kouru seared through, a never-doused core of white flare. She threatened Fox's work simply by existing in proximity to it.

Frankly, she liked to know she could disrupt such a skilled master with so little effort. In any case, the time for subtlety would soon pass. Kouru carried two lightsabers now, the one she had taken from the old man, the other from Fox. Once they reached the tier where the *Poor Crow* had been docked—

Don't be an idiot. Play along.

Kouru scowled and turned away. She yearned to snap at the witch, but the idea of doing so in Fox's presence—it struck her as foolish, perhaps even dangerous. Their attention remained trained on her, as did their expectation. She prickled under it. But she couldn't give them what they wanted. She didn't know *how*.

Your education was tragically stunted. Here, then.

Kouru frowned more deeply. She flexed her hands open and closed, and with each flex felt an unusual palpability to what she could only call herself. It was as if she had all at once become aware of another dimension to her being. When she clenched her palm, her light folded in on itself—no longer fractured and diffuse, but collected and intense.

Fox leaned ever so slightly forward, seemingly astonished. "Well. You could have done that sooner."

Kouru knew she couldn't have—not without the witch's assistance, no matter that she didn't want it. Worse, Fox continued to watch her as the lift rose, as if they doubted she'd done it . . . or that she'd done it on her own. She hadn't, and she hated that, but more than that, she hated *Fox*. That was far easier, in any case, than hating something she couldn't even punch. "Aren't you supposed to be concentrating?" she bit out.

Fox clasped their hands behind their back and turned benevolently forward. Kouru wanted dearly to kick them off at the next tier. Ekiya muttered a halfhearted scold. The three of them spent the rest of the ride in congealing silence.

Kouru realized that she needed these people to be, if not happy, then content with her presence. Without them, she would be hard-pressed to reach the old man with any alacrity. If she had to trouble herself with rescuing Ekiya's ship and cargo first, so be it. She even treasured the act as one she performed more for her own need than for—

She pushed the thought aside. Suffice to say that she lacked the hubris to imagine she was, at present, better off alone. Even so, she was beginning to wonder whether trusting Fox was possible, let alone worth it.

They radiated threat. If they could smudge interest from a mind as soon as they looked at the being the mind belonged to, who knew what they could do with sustained focus?

Case in point, as they exited the lift, Fox strode forward, buoyed by perfect confidence in their own ability. Ekiya kept close and Kouru trailed after, grimacing at every face who turned toward them, then away.

Dozens of faces. The topmost tier of the grand pagoda housed the *Poor Crow*—the central attraction, surrounded by technicians—and a full half squadron of fighters. More crew tended these vessels, droids and mechanics, and the suited-up Jedi who would pilot each ship. Ekiya's freighter would leave with an escort.

As they reached the ramp leading up into the *Crow,* a Jedi coming down it stopped short and glanced a second longer at Fox than anyone had before. He was a knight, human, tidily put together and weathered by experience, and as the seconds drew on, he frowned. Fox clucked their tongue, made a shooing motion with their hand, and the Jedi shook his head. He proceeded off into the hangar with sharp purpose in his stride.

"Creepy," said Ekiya.

"Very," said Kouru.

"An old friend," said Fox, with a dismissive tone that suggested they considered "friends" as engaging as common lint. "Don't dawdle."

Ekiya and Kouru exchanged a look; Ekiya's meant concern, and Kouru's did too, after a fashion. Ekiya cared about Fox, and probably to an extent about the Jedi. Kouru cared that as far as she could tell, Fox was the least trustworthy variety of Jedi she knew.

Kouru understood her distaste for the black current came in some part from its resistance to her control. She also understood that every time she saw it slide through a being's brain and reroute their intent, her teeth chilled as if against ice. The thought of such control turned on her—it sickened. She'd rather be a truly dead thing. No. She'd rather kill what dared touch her that way.

She had a memory, one she rarely allowed herself to recollect. She had been young, freshly taken by the Jedi and always agitated. Crying, or screaming, or fighting. A master had often come to her then, grasped her hands in theirs, and lulled her into quiescence. She remembered neither their name nor their face, only the murmur, and the subtle pulse of the black current as she was submerged within it.

Only once she had been rescued by the Sith had she at last been allowed to scream.

Kouru touched the back of her head, brow creased. She expected a weight. A voice. She was met with silence.

Beside her, Ekiya's discomfort lost to her urgency. Once on the *Crow*, she pushed her way in front of Fox even as Kouru said, "Now what?"

Fox gestured Kouru's hand away from the lightsaber hilt she had grasped. "We get what we came for."

Did that not mean the ship? Kouru frowned as they passed one, two, three crew members still on the freighter. A pair of technicians by the engine room. A Jedi guardian in the galley hall. Ekiya dismissed all this on the way to the cargo hold, in the belly of the ship.

The doors hung open—they could see this from the ladder they dropped down into the loading zone. The first one down, Ekiya slowed as she approached, though Kouru couldn't immediately make sense of why.

The hold was strikingly empty.

Ekiya couldn't speak. Kouru saw devastation in her stillness, anger in the cut of her shoulders. Kouru rapidly realized that the problem lay in what the *Crow* no longer held.

Fox dared to touch Ekiya, a hand to her arm, and the woman was too furious to shrug them off. "They'll have taken it all to Hanrai's Imperial Dreadnought. Classified the lot as recovered valuables, I expect. Now bound for a museum, or—"

"Or stowed to be returned as *gifts* to show people who they belong to." Ekiya cursed and covered her mouth. "I know. I *know*. I hate them."

"We'll get them back," said Fox.

"Oh? From a Jedi lord's *Imperial Dreadnought*?"

"As luck would have it, the *Crow* is already headed there. We only need allow ourselves to go with it."

Kouru scoffed. "Really? We're just going to sail into the belly of that beast?"

"Would you rather be flicked out of the sky like an inconvenient insect?" Fox asked. "Or are you perhaps hiding some other special Sith talent?"

Kouru glowered; Fox tilted their head.

Ekiya groaned and pushed one hand into either of their faces. "For the love of everything, just get us there."

They hid in plain sight. Ekiya skulked neurotically in the cargo hold and Fox stood idle guard by the ladder that led to it while the *Crow* was in flight. Kouru took herself to the gunner pit in the *Crow*'s left wing. She imagined any more time spent having to be stared at by Fox would end in her attempting to remove their mask and then their eyes.

This allowed Kouru to watch as the *Poor Crow* departed the grand pagoda in the escort of six fighters. The Dekien air traffic conductors sent them in time with another squadron on the opposite side of Dazenma, and they looped past each other as they sailed out of the atmosphere. Kouru imagined, for her own amusement, the ships all crashing into each other and raining fire down upon Dazenma's pleasure quarters.

No such luck. The *Crow* and its Jedi escort danced out into the black, leaving behind one perfectly unmarred temple to Imperial decadence only to head toward another.

Someone had dared to call the Dreadnought the *Reverent*, and it ate up a devastating slash of sky, all white expanse flourished with gold and green. Red pillars accented its command deck, an allusion to the Imperial seat the immense vessel represented. Gilt and grandeur. An Empire that thought itself untouchably vast. Indeed, Kouru's eyes couldn't capture the *Reverent*'s entirety. It hollowed her gut to think that she might never truly wound the giant. How could she? Her nails, clutched around her wrist, dug minute crescents into her flesh.

You're expanding. Dim yourself.

"I know what I'm doing," Kouru growled and clenched her fists, eyes shut tight. The cuts in her wrist throbbed as she drew the white flare back into herself. Control. More *control*. She breathed in through her mouth, out through her nose, and opened her eyes to fix on the reality before her—what she could reasonably grasp and therefore contain.

The *Crow* had shifted course in the time since she closed her eyes. She saw neither Dekien nor the *Reverent*. Fine. She liked seeing neither.

Instead, she only had to behold the hungry black and winking glimmer of space and space and space.

Kouru's gut reflexively twisted. Yet as she breathed again, she felt . . . nothing. No terror, no rage. No shameful panic. Only the black and her body, an intensity of white Force condensed into her sole self. She was alive—or something close to it. She was not afraid.

Really?

Kouru knit her brow and, hands open on her knees, searched the newly realized dimension of her self for a trace of that old instinct. She knew she hated space—the enormity of it, the loneliness and threat— yet that fear seemed somehow beyond her, locked in a box she could just barely imagine yet couldn't seem to *find*—

What good has fear ever done you? I told you, didn't I? Let go.

Kouru rubbed the back of her neck, hard. As if that would help. She needed—to be elsewhere. With people. The witch grew reticent around them, and Kouru desired that very much, even if it meant facing more of Ekiya's upset or Fox's insipid jibes.

She clambered up out of the gunner pit only to find a person in the corridor. Not one of the crew they were meant to be hiding from, which was good. Just Fox, which was distasteful, to say the least.

Fox didn't so much as offer Kouru a hand as she hauled herself up the ladder. Not that she would have accepted it if they had. But the way they stared at her—and she could tell they were staring, even with that idiot mask—made her feel like a subject of study, examined under a lens.

"You seem distracted," said Fox.

"Only because *you* keep being distracted by *me*," she snapped.

"You're rather insistently distracting." Fox looked down for a moment. In this narrow corridor of light freighter, they had nothing of interest to see but their sandals. "I don't suppose you asked for this."

Kouru, who had been flirting with the idea of tipping Fox into the gunner pit, froze. "I don't know what you're talking about."

"Oh, you know. Resurrection. Being leashed to the witch and all."

Kouru flinched back and hated herself for it. She knew. She *knew*. But admitting it—hearing it—acknowledging the witch was too much. Too dangerous. Too—

"It's only, well. In my experience, her demons haven't generally been so . . . self-possessed."

There it was. The dreadful thought she had not allowed herself to have. Kouru had seen the witch raise her demons before—during that final great muster when the Sith took Rei'izu. They didn't last. They weren't meant to. And they had never been much more than shades, coalesced into purity of purpose.

What, then, was Kouru? She didn't dare ask, for fear of what she might lose if she did.

Let go, she heard, not as a murmur but worse, as a memory. Let go, let go.

"Shut up," Kouru snarled, hand braced at the back of her neck.

Fox stiffened, withdrawing a hairsbreadth. Kouru relished their wariness, this precipitate to fear, though she couldn't say whether she meant the snarl for them or for the thing welling inside her. Fox was afraid, and Kouru liked it as much as she hated it, because if they were to be fearful, Kouru wanted them quailing from *her*.

And she didn't want to be shivering herself.

Kouru lurched forward; Fox stepped back. The sound of approaching footsteps brought them both up short.

A Jedi rounded the corner of the corridor—the knight whose friendship Fox had dismissed in the hangar not an hour before. Fox and Kouru drew instinctively apart; Fox had brushed off the suggestion that knocking elbows with the crew would endanger their control, but Kouru doubted it would help.

The knight slowed as he neared, angled himself to walk between them, and slowed further. Brow knit, his gaze drifted sideways. Toward Fox. "Wait . . ."

Fox backed up another step, restive. The Jedi's attention remained trained on them. Kouru waited a cold second for Fox to do something. Anything. To upend the Jedi's brain with the black current—or to push *him* into the gunner pit—but they didn't move.

So Kouru threw a punch, sharp and direct, into the Jedi's jaw. He dropped like a stone.

Fox lunged forward to catch the Jedi. They didn't manage to grab him before he knocked his head on the edge of the gunner pit, though they did stop him from toppling headfirst down the shaft. When they looked up, cradling the sagging body, Kouru stood over them.

"Wonderful," Fox intoned. "You're lucky you didn't kill him."

"I wasn't trying to." Kouru nodded at the pit.

Reluctantly, Fox let her help them lower the Jedi down into it, until he had been settled limply in the gunner seat. They closed the pit hatch after him, and Kouru welded the hatch shut with the flaring tip of the old man's lightsaber. When Fox frowned, she stabbed through the hatch to make a single hot, glowing hole. "There," she said. "Now it's ventilated."

Fox shook their head as if annoyed. But when they spoke, it was evident they were more annoyed with themself. "I've been unfair to you. Expressed some of my own frustrations as if they were your fault."

Kouru scowled to hide her confusion. "Don't think an apology gives you the moral high ground."

"As if you care anything about—" Fox inhaled, stood, and fixed their hair. "What's happened to you—it's profound. And as you might have guessed, I have some familiarity with the phenomenon."

"Are you offering me help, Jedi?"

They didn't like to be called that. Their glower peeked from behind their mask. "If you would humble yourself to accept it."

A scoff rose in Kouru's throat, and she caught it there. Something else pulsed within her, under her skin. She was infested. She almost wished she could forget she knew that she was. The thought sickened her like week-old meat.

If you fear their intentions, you shouldn't, said the witch. *They don't hate you.*

Kouru stared over her shoulder. The *Crow* hummed around her, Fox breathed in front of her, and cooling metal popped below. "Don't do that again," she said to the witch, a threat. It brought her no comfort to realize that, in the case of future transgressions, she knew not where to direct retaliation.

"You do hear her, then. Clearly, I mean."

Kouru couldn't bring herself to look right at Fox. No matter that the witch held her tongue, the longer Kouru was aware of the weight of her

attention, the heavier it grew. Like a pebble held until it became an anchor.

"She's the reason we're cavorting around these 'tourist traps,' you
know," said Fox. "We'd very much like to find her. So on one hand, I
encourage you to consider joining us to ask her a few pertinent questions."

Kouru scowled because she didn't know what else to do. She wished
Fox silent. They were as insensitive to others' desires as usual.

"On the other hand, you ought to know that our conversation is unlikely to be the friendly sort. Either way . . ." They bowed their head in
thought. "I certainly don't blame you for your grudge against our large,
brooding friend. But I encourage you to consider who you might be
outside his influence. I don't mean who you are unto yourself. That's no
sort of question for a dead woman to ask, if she wants to be more than
dead. Just tell me, Kouru, for your own sake—what exactly do you think
you're doing? Who is it you're trying to be? And who for?"

"Who are you?" she spat back, knowing herself petulant.

To her surprise, Fox pondered the retort. "I can tell you who I think
I am—who I'd like to be. Someone who corrects their mistakes. Who
ensures the world won't suffer overmuch for what they've already done
wrong." Then, smilingly, "Now you."

"That's none of your concern."

"I rather think it is, given how intent you are on gutting my companions."

"Just one of them—and you," Kouru snapped. Then she fell silent. To
her own incredulity, she found herself honestly ruminating. She had no
immediate answer to offer. But she wanted one.

Irritatingly, Fox nodded, thoughtful. "Well, think on it, why don't
you? I suspect that at the very least it will be more satisfying to murder
someone because you wanted to rather than because someone told you
it was a good idea."

Kouru eyed them suspiciously. "You're the worst Jedi I've ever met."

They put a gracious hand to their chest, taking it for the compliment
it was.

CHAPTER
TWENTY

THE RONIN KNEW it impossible, yet he couldn't banish the cloying scent of autumn from his nose. Space smelled nothing of autumn. It was monumental absence, an obliterating thing. He often wished he could find solace in it, but he was inevitably distracted by whatever mechanism had ferried him into the dark.

This time: a Jedi Dreadnought called *Reverent*. A palace in the shape of a knife, regally white and flecked with gold. He couldn't help but admire the pristine intricacies of its interior workings, though he knew all too well the cost of maintaining a vessel of such devastating size. It took people. It took planets. Lives and homes, reshaped in service to Empire.

The *Reverent*'s trappings were no less impressive. The Ronin's knees pressed into a woven mat, and he faced a sliding lattice door. Outside, he heard voices shouting not with panic but exercise, as well as, if he was not mistaken, running water. Most strangely, that incorrigible scent—osmanthus, interwoven with other vegetal fragrances. The lord of this ship was an excessive sort.

Also a cautious one, though it might not have seemed so to the casual observer. The Ronin had been left conscious and unbound, and he had been permitted the dignity of retaining both weapons, though they had taken his pouch of kyber. It seemed a contradiction for the Jedi to allow him the transgression of his lightsaber, especially as it was the more dangerous of his possessions. They had also left him his wrist cuff, though it was dark and had remained so. He didn't know what had become of B5-56.

In any case, a sane man in his position could hope for neither rescue nor self-liberation. The Ronin was acutely aware that at least one guard always knelt outside his door, and he sensed more in either direction down the hall. Their presences were consistently oppressive in one direction or another. One sharply white, the next defiantly black, each kind complemented by a nearby guard who was their polar opposite. Together, these guardians would have been trained to cultivate their aptitudes in order to directly counter the push, pull, and flow of another Force-wielder. A dubious skill on the battlefield, as it required total concentration and thereby left a Jedi inexcusably defenseless. Quite useful, however, when managing Force-sensitive prisoners.

Though three shifts had come and gone, the Ronin had not yet given his guards reason to act. He maintained stillness, as he had for the long hours since he returned to himself. He had by that point already been sequestered in this room. The lapse required thought.

It seems to me you haven't thought in a while, let alone now, the voice said.

He inhaled slowly, as if he could summon her closer. She refused. Of course she did. She did not look on his infirmity with kindness.

To begin: How had he come to be here?

It had been a very long while since he so badly lost himself to the chronic disorder of his mind. He had dismissed every warning sign after his first perilous lurch in the *Crow*'s cargo hold, when Chie so expertly unseated his balance within and without. How many more signs had he overlooked?

The fugues had taken him more commonly in the years directly following the fall of the rebellion. They had come upon him most virulently when he bore witness to the shadows of his sin—and what else could he call those two young demons who had collapsed the cavern?

Two Jedi guardians, retrieved from death and moved by an intent other than their own. Seeing the bandit hadn't hurt the same way. She was Sith. She was cruel. She had tried to kill him as well. But two blank-eyed young Jedi—these had struck him. They gave him reason to fear.

"Is it true?" he asked her. "Have you taken others?"

Do you doubt me? she said.

He supposed that was fair. She was obviously up to something. He had met three more demons in the space of the past week than he had in twenty years.

The question remained: Why now? She had resigned herself to obscurity, had seemed almost content to devote herself to spiting him. What had enticed her to act?

Or: What had set her free?

There was a noise at the door. The guard shifting in their seat, coughing slightly. Then the guard spoke, and his clear voice was tentative. "Sir?"

The Ronin frowned. "Do you mean me?"

For a stretch, the guard lacked the courage to answer. "You said something."

"Don't take it personally."

This baffled the guard into silence. The Ronin made out his silhouette through the shadow of the door. A straight-postured Twi'lek boy, who canted his head toward the door more and more with every moment. "Sir . . ."

"That seems an inappropriate thing for you to call me."

"I don't know your name." The guard hesitated. "No one knows your name."

"But you know something." He heard the recognition in the boy's tone. The voice did as well, and her attention fixed on the guard with the idle curiosity she might spare for a daring fool.

"Your face," the guard admitted at last. "From when you were young. I saw you. I think I did. On an old roster."

Clever child, the voice said. *And a liar.*

An uncharitable assessment, if true in fact. If the guard had actually seen the Ronin's decades-younger face on a ship roster, then he had also seen the name the Ronin carried at the time. That meant he recognized exactly whom his lord had seen fit to imprison on the *Reverent*—but he was afraid to admit it. Neither could he stop himself from telling the Ronin that he knew.

How unfortunate. Inquisitive children never did make it far with the Jedi. If they could make themselves useful enough in the practice of strategy or spywork, perhaps they would keep their place in the guardianship. If they ever proved too willing to question their lords, on the other hand . . .

"You should be more careful with yourself," said the Ronin. He knew not how else to warn the boy.

"I just want to know," the guard pressed. "If your people are taking ours again—why?"

The Ronin grimaced. "I don't know."

"Why not?"

"If I am who you think I am, why do you think I would?"

The voice's laughter rang in his ears.

The guard, who couldn't hear the laughter, grew silent. "Is it true, then?" he asked. "Did you betray them too? . . . But then, what *are* you doing here?"

"You'd have to ask your master."

Footsteps interrupted the guard's thought. The boy straightened again, facing forward. When the door slid open, he remained dutifully silent.

Chie stepped through. She looked worse for wear, sagging on one side. One arm was wrapped in a surgical brace and the other held a medical cane. Why anyone would sport such injuries on a vessel equipped with bacta facilities robust enough to repair an army was beyond the Ronin's immediate ability to understand. To his mild frustration, he found he wished her uncomfortable—perhaps even in pain. It had also been a long while since he last wished such ill on another person.

I suppose you still think it unlucky, she said. *Superstitious to the last.*

"There you are," said Chie, as if the Ronin had not been confined to this room for at least a day. He was not by any means difficult to find for anyone in league with the Jedi. "Come on, up you get. Stretch those old legs of yours."

The Twi'lek apprentice's eyes remained firmly down as the Ronin crossed the threshold in Chie's wake. The boy glanced up once after Chie had turned to go down the hall. The Ronin nodded to him. The guard stiffened but continued staring at him even as he left, his mouth troubled with a stubborn curiosity.

The hall outside was built of the same lavish organic materials as the Ronin's cell: wood and paper. It led to a garden. Young trees sprouted at every corner, the source of the scent that had found him even in his prison. A shallow brook wove pleasingly down the center, and vibrantly colored fish squirmed in the clear water. Even the ceiling was dressed in light and hologram to evoke the boundless autumn sky, though the Ronin's innate sensibility for the dimension of mechanical structure told him it was the standard height of any Dreadnought hangar.

He had seen luxury on the flagships of other lords. Gilt throne rooms, dining halls constructed entirely of fragrant woods, luxuriant silks in spacious bedrooms. This conjuration of plain planetary normalcy outstripped them all.

Yet Chie drew most of his attention. She wore robes reminiscent of any Jedi guardian, brown layered over white. Try as he might, he sensed no difference in her. She was the same as she had ever been since they met on the *Poor Crow*. No Jedi. No Sith. Only a person, sure of herself and content to be so.

"Speak up," she said. "That glare will bore a hole in my back if you don't let some of the pressure out."

The Ronin's temple pinched. "For a woman who spoke so ill of the Jedi, you seem quite comfortable among them."

Chie smiled grimly over her shoulder. "You got on well enough with that apprentice. We all have facets."

She stopped when they reached the source of the shouting he had heard from his cell. In an open-air hall lined with sleek wooden flooring, dozens of plain-robed apprentices practiced forms in a wave of synchronous thrusts and sweeps. They came to a stop when their master, a Jedi knight with lightsaber hilt at his waist, called out. Two apprentices came forward at the master's command and took position across from each other to spar with wooden practice blades.

"There *is* a war coming, you realize. The princes and lords all want what they want, and they have no pity for the rest of us. And I'm quite old." Chie gestured wryly at her cane with her injured arm. "When I considered what benefit I could bring the galaxy with my remaining body . . . it wasn't on the Outer Rim. Not anymore." Here, she smiled. "Lord Hanrai has me teaching the children all manner of heresies."

The Ronin couldn't summon a smile in turn.

Chie sighed. "You're still sour about the bridge."

"You could have just thrown yourself off."

"I got the worse of it, believe me." She clucked her tongue at his glower. "I think you'll find we have more in common than you imagine."

He suspected he had killed more friends than she had. Then again, she'd proven willing to injure her comrades too. Either way, he said nothing and sent another surreptitious glance at his wrist.

It blinked briefly at him, there and gone, so swiftly vanished that he might have imagined it. But he wasn't given to optimism, so he had to assume it was real.

Nevertheless, a single blink did not communication make. All he could be certain of was that B5 had managed by some trickery to sneak aboard the *Reverent*, and the droid wanted him to know it.

He crossed his arms in order to conceal his response. He meant to depress the cuff and give the droid affirmation, but his thumb froze over the circle.

He was alive. To what end? He hadn't let himself wonder that in long, long years, just as he hadn't let himself wonder about his goals or the actions he took in their name. He had but the one purpose: the end of the Sith. So when presented with the witch who had refused him any further deaths, the game had changed. Of course he had dedicated himself to pursuing her, just as he had pursued every Sith before her. But he hadn't let himself stop to think what the end of her might mean for him. He knew the thought would threaten to consume and overwhelm him—as, indeed, it had in Seikara.

He had to drop his hand from his wrist before he could be certain he had in fact sent B5 any message. Chie had called for his attention.

Rising from his daze, the Ronin saw that she had led him past the practice hall to a covered walkway that made a border between the courtyard and a second garden. This in turn led to a small wooden building with a dark sloped roof, comely in its sparseness. A fat old tooka-cat lounged before an open door, and beyond it the Ronin could just make out a broad-shouldered figure seated at a low table, waiting for him.

The Ronin didn't wish to join the figure, but more than that, he didn't wish to remain alone with himself.

The Ronin crossed the walkway unaccompanied. The cat opened a single eye at his arrival, shifted its creaking limbs, and returned to a restless slumber. The man inside the building had a pot of tea and a shogi board at the ready on his table. The Ronin had last met him on the other end of the narrow stone bridge flying high over Seikara's black lake.

Lord Hanrai gestured the Ronin to take the seat across from him. "It's good to see you well. How about round two?"

CHAPTER
TWENTY-ONE

THEY BEGAN THE game in silence. Hanrai studied his opponent's strategy with interest. The Sith demonstrated a skill born of practice. His opening moves recalled those Hanrai had learned in his youth, though the Sith broke into daring new stratagems at the first opportunity. He remained expressionless until Hanrai deployed one of his own new maneuvers. The Sith's hand hovered over his pieces just long enough to suggest hesitation.

"You recognize the tactic?" asked Hanrai.

The Sith's frown indicated that he did.

"You played with my old apprentice, then. If you can call that playing. I assume they still cheat."

The Sith smoothed his face expressionless once more. "I don't believe you brought me here for such answers."

"We're playing, sir." Hanrai removed his hands from the board to drink tea and study the landscape outside his teahouse. A dry stone wall separated this patch of garden from the hall where the apprentices sparred, though their shouts were dampened more by a keen little device hidden in the wall itself. Hanrai had often thought of deactivating it. But he pulled himself away from these distractions and back to the table, the game, and the man seated across from him, who was still frowning.

"A game is far more than a matter of victory," said Hanrai. "To play is to uncover a corner of a grander puzzle—that which comprises the entirety of the game itself, its history and its potential. I've brought you not because I wish to win but because I seek to understand a greater whole."

The Sith's eyes remained on the board. "I've never been much for philosophy."

"Then I'll begin with something simpler: the truth."

The Sith snorted. Hanrai smiled. Not one for philosophy, was it? Yet here he objected to what other men might think an obvious thing.

"Not long ago, there was a certain Jedi," said Hanrai as he resumed play. "A knight, who rose from the ranks of the children welcomed into one of our esteemed clans. He was blessed, you could say. Favored by the gods, if you'd rather. Or simply very good at following orders as his masters imagined he should. Yet this was the very man who so famously turned on the Jedi. I've often wondered why."

The Sith neither paused nor twitched nor tensed, though Hanrai knew he recognized the story. Then again, who in this far-reaching galaxy didn't?

"Would you like to hear my suspicion?" Hanrai asked.

"Would I?"

"I have a unique point of view." Hanrai leaned back from the board, his eyes closed. The black current brought images to him as he spoke, alongside scents and sounds. The heavy parchment on which reports to the Emperor were by tradition written; the low whisper of a citizen official afraid to speak frankly; the fragrant soup he shared with his favorite information broker every time they met. "I examined the records, as many as I could find. They differed by their teller. All together, they showed me a man of tremendous talent. Ambitious. Protective. Loyal, deeply so, both to his lord and to his brethren—by which I mean those clansmen adopted beside him. When he was named knight, they became his guardians, and he guarded their lives as fiercely as they guarded his.

"But the galaxy rarely favors such purity of spirit. He was made to choose. A day came on a battlefield when he alone stood between his lord and death. He left the lord to die. Cowardice, some thought. Worse, said others. For the knight lived, as did his guardians. And a Jedi ought never outlive their lord in such a way. For the sake of honor, natural order, and the Empire, it could not be permitted.

"Yet the man refused his sentence. Rather infuriated everyone but his kin when he did. You can see why, I expect. In defying his role, he threatened the very foundation of the Empire. So they declared him rebel, him and his guardians. Dangerous folk, deserving death by any means."

At last, the Sith looked to Hanrai, his gaze implacable. "Do your peers know you're so seditious?"

Hanrai laughed. "They know I'm a Jedi. So tell me, sir. Why do you think this man did what he did?"

The Sith sank into thought. His attention drifted toward the wall and the shouting of the apprentices beyond it. "I think you see the game he played."

"Ah, thank you. I appreciate knowing I don't sound entirely mad. Though I'll tell you what still puzzles me. The reason for the rebellion's dissolution is a matter of debate, certainly, but I've reason to suspect that those who hypothesize the dark lord himself was the root of its demise are in the right. Even so, I must ask: Why would a man who went to such lengths to protect his own later turn on them? How might you explain that?"

He received no response but for more play. Each man moved his pieces, and Hanrai poured more tea. Twice, the Sith seemed on the verge of speaking. Only on the third time did he commit.

"Did you ever see the mirror of Shinsui Temple?" he asked.

"On Rei'izu? Never had the privilege," said Hanrai. "I wasn't named lord until after the entire planet disappeared."

"A splendid thing," said the Sith. "A terrifying one. Tall as ten men and perfectly circular. Immaculately flat and shining. A single glimpse and you could understand why they called it holy."

"It did grant visions, you know. Kyber and all."

"Yes. Visions of possibility. Reasons to fight for the future of one's desire, and the means to do so." The Sith brought a hand to his jaw; Hanrai had noted his tendency to touch the prosthetic when harrowed by darker thoughts. "The Sith took Rei'izu because they sought just such a path. To victory."

"Didn't work out for them very well, I suppose."

"No. Some visions aren't worth seeing."

"But visions terrible enough to turn a man on his own kind?"

The Sith grew silent again. "Perhaps we should be glad the mirror was lost with its home."

Hanrai regarded him for a long moment. The black current of the Force wouldn't tell him the difference between a truth and a falsehood—he relied on his own mind to discern as much. In the Sith, he detected a vested disinterest in playacting. He said what he thought, or he didn't speak. That would prove crucial, in the next few minutes.

"Lost, perhaps," said Hanrai, "but not wholly."

The Sith said nothing, and neither did he touch the board, nor drink his tea, nor look anywhere but for down toward the edge of the table. Thinking.

"The Seikara Caverns. Until some ten years ago, they housed a sliver of the mirror. Can't imagine how it got there."

"I can't imagine how you found it," said the Sith, cool as old frost.

Hanrai tapped his forehead. "I told you, didn't I? I have a unique point of view. I'd say the Force was with us, but I think we both know it's no more with the Jedi than it is with anyone else. To the point, we were searching for a way to return to Rei'izu."

This knit the Sith's brow. He had, after all, gone to the caves for the same reason.

"We recovered the shard," said Hanrai. "I entrusted it to my cleverest student. At the time, it seemed a fitting match."

This summoned an open frown. Hanrai wondered whether it was his own words or ones his student had spoken that gave the Sith such cause for concern.

"They set off soon after, accompanied by their most trusted guardians," said Hanrai. "They did not come back. We heard nothing. *I* heard nothing . . . Yet now they reappear, and in the company of, well. A man such as yourself."

The Sith returned the piece he had just picked up to the place he had taken it from and withdrew his hands from the board. "I would prefer you be more honest."

"In what way?"

"How long was Chie your spy?"

"Not long. Idzuna recruited her first. But when I reached out, she found we shared a sentiment." Hanrai stopped himself there. The Sith frowned still, but the set of the concern had grown more complicated. "Ah. Did you not know their name?"

"They eschew it."

"I think I understand why. They've abandoned nearly as much as you have." Hanrai placed his hands on the table, open and beseeching. "I would have them return, you know."

"Then you shouldn't have had Chie throw them off a bridge." The Sith spoke with humor and an edge. Anger. Some honest, some misplaced.

"Well, how else was I supposed to corner you?" Hanrai asked. The Sith continued to grow ever more taut, as if he expected they would soon each draw their weapons. Hanrai kept his hands on the table, in plain sight. "Let me be more direct."

The Sith had run out of patience. He merely stared, balefully silent. Hanrai suspected that, unless given extraordinary reason, he would say nothing more.

"I assume you've heard war is imminent," said Hanrai. "But once the people say as much, war is already upon us. The Emperor will leave us soon, and when he does, neither prince will yield to the other. Half a dozen lords think this moment more opportunity than threat. Every man on the field yearns to make the galaxy more akin to how he believes it ought to be. Not unlike you did, all those years ago. And now the rest of us must find our place in their game."

The Sith's lip twitched down and his brow creased. When he spoke, it was as if he didn't wish to. "You envision a place for me . . . beside you."

"Indeed. As leader of men—of Jedi. You wished to make a different world. You failed. You needn't fail again. And I have severe need of those who understand *our* failures—the clans.'" Hanrai spread his hands to encompass the teahouse, the garden, the courtyard beyond, and the enormous space within which it was all housed. "The Empire is willing to reward those who play by its rules. Follow in my footsteps. Show yourself worthy of their trust . . . and when they have once more named you one of their own, take their power to make of it what you will."

"I don't believe you understand how many people I've killed," said the Sith. "Or how many of them trusted me when I did."

He was incredulous. Hanrai thought this fair. "I'm aware your convictions have come into conflict with your actions. But consider this— *I've* considered you a great deal. And I see a man worth believing in. A man whose choices could lead us to a victory we haven't dared imagine."

This troubled the Sith to hear. He frowned openly and deeply.

"You'd like a pettier motive? I have one of those too." Hanrai slid a datapad across the table, beside the shogi board. "I can only see so much on my own."

The images on the datapad were of two dead guardians who had, for various reasons, not yet been laid to rest. Their faces absorbed the Sith's attention more wholly than anything Hanrai had yet said. He should have predicted this. After all, it had been the presence of these demons in the caverns that had rendered the Sith immobile for arrest. Hanrai filed this away in his mind—that the Sith's fragilities were reliably triggered—and laid it out plain.

"That witch of yours has been taking our people for months now. If we're to do something about it, I'll need your help understanding just what it is she's up to."

CHAPTER
TWENTY-TWO

Two Jedi sat in their respective cells, unaccompanied and meditative. The Ronin studied them from his position overhead. The observation deck was layered above the cells, and the one-way mirror allowed guards to look straight down onto their prisoners without being seen in turn. This artificial barrier separated him from small, spare rooms that looked much like the one he had been held in, hours ago. The demons under his feet sat much like he had as well.

The Ronin was alone now but for a single guard. Lord Hanrai had escorted him here, and they had spoken together as they went.

He spoke, yes, said the voice. *I don't think you could claim to have done the same.*

As they walked, Hanrai had said, "Of course we seek your expertise on the witch. I understand she was one of the dark lord's guardians when he was a knight—before he betrayed his lord."

"I don't care for pretense," said the Ronin.

"Well, what did you call her?"

The Ronin hesitated to say. He felt as though he lacked permission to name her.

Hanrai took his silence for resistance. "Don't let me push you. To the

point, the skills she cultivated—I would go so far as to say your rebellion would have ended far sooner without them. Not to diminish the
other warriors you trained. You Sith seized on a notion the Jedi have
long since forsaken. You prized individual talent, nurtured it, brought it
to the battlefield—and you trounced us, often."

Trounced, he said. Not killed.

"I never did sort out who designed those lightsaber auxiliaries. Masterful devices. I've collected every one I ever came across. Straight to
the vaults on my estate. One day . . ." Hanrai smiled self-deprecatingly,
or at least affected humility. "My peers still say there was no honor in
Sith tactics. Perhaps there wasn't. But you were brilliant."

Hanrai clearly considered this a compliment. It was, in all likelihood,
why he had allowed the Ronin to keep both of his weapons.

"Your mastery of yourselves drove me to better understand my own
skills. My master—my father—he saw it in me from a young age, that I
had a sensitivity for focus and insight. He rejoiced. Thought it a gift for
the blade. I might never have imagined it could be more, had you not
compelled me to. And ever since I've striven to bring that same understanding to my students."

And what exactly had this lord taught the student the Ronin knew
best?

"But the witch, the things she could do . . . it still defies belief. Even
now."

Even now, because the evidence of her skills sat starkly before them,
but it was nevertheless a trial to truly accept what she had done. Two
young Jedi. A young Sith warrior. More, who Hanrai had told the Ronin
of as they went, confirming the tales he'd heard on the road to Osou
spaceport on Genbara, and among the socialites of Dekien. These
guardians were only the first demons the Jedi had managed to capture.

When Hanrai departed, he also left the datapad, which detailed the
other disappearances. The Ronin had yet to look at it. He expected the
lord believed he didn't care for what he saw any more than any Jedi
did—that these breathing ghosts would be all the argument he required
to make his case. Abandon this heresy, Hanrai said. Rejoin the Jedi and
remake them in your image.

Is it working? she asked. *Is that what you want?*

"I don't know."

"Sir?" said the guard, hesitant.

"They didn't reassign you?" the Ronin asked. It was the same guard who had dared to speak with him in his holding cell. The Twi'lek boy's shift had started only a few hours before; the Ronin supposed it wasn't finished.

"I expect they think I might sway your opinion," said the guard.

"Your master is canny."

From the corner of his eye, he saw the guard bow his head in thought. He heard the insult for what it was. "I think you should know that what we say is likely being listened to."

Of course. It was what he would have done. "I can't fault your lord for that."

What is it you fault him for, then?

The Ronin wished, for the first time in a long while, that she wouldn't do that. He had stopped wishing for this some time ago, when he decided it a pointless, frivolous thing to want things to be other than they were. He couldn't stop her. He suspected he didn't want to, in the same way he still couldn't easily imagine killing her.

He found it difficult to look away from the demons at rest in their cells, so still. They breathed minutely. And to what end?

"Did you know them?" he asked the guard.

"Yes, sir. Ogara led my cohort in our third year. Tsuden led meditations."

"What do you think should be done with them now?"

"I don't know." The Ronin heard doubt in the boy's voice, and reprimand—self-directed. "They seem like themselves. But . . ."

"They're dead. And for no good *reason*."

The voice chuckled. *What reason ever satisfied you?*

You, he thought. Once, you were all the reason I needed.

She recoiled. She didn't believe him. As well she shouldn't. He had betrayed her too terribly in the end.

Here lay the rot: these two ghosts, for all other words were laid incorrectly upon them, had died at the hands of another—one who pursued him, for he had dared to pursue her first. He had for so long committed himself to the only action he could honor. He hunted Sith and killed them, and for twenty years that had been enough. It couldn't be anymore. Not if the witch had at last decided to retaliate. Not if the *Jedi* had to have their say. And didn't all that together make this mess such a hideous reflection of what had driven his hand so long ago?

The Ronin looked to the guard at last. The boy stood his ground, eyes wide, chin raised. He yearned to hear some worthwhile lesson from his prisoner.

"Your master thinks I don't believe in truth," the Ronin said. "Tell him he's a fool. I know truth."

As he spoke, his mind filled with a titanic mirror, a divinity tall as ten men that reflected darkness upon light upon darkness. Even the recollection of it dizzied him to illness.

"Truth is suffering. It is violence without justice. It is the inevitable pain of a wrong that cannot be undone, an evil that cannot be unmade. It is man and Empire. It is the dead. *They* are truth." He looked down on the ghosts, her demons, who had each raised their heads to stare back at him, unflinching. "I am truth."

He snorted then, at himself—at everything. "Here is another honesty," he said to the guard. "I will not serve your lord."

Hanrai had proved far too willing to declare his right to change the world even as he decried those who shared his ambitions. All such men were monsters. The Ronin knew this because he had been one. Was one. And she was one too, now that she had chosen to feed these ghosts to the burgeoning pyre of war.

So, the Ronin would relegate himself to the one thing he could do and know just: kill Sith.

He put out his hand into the space before him and wrenched it as if he had grasped fabric to tear apart. The movement was unnecessary, but it satisfied.

The *Reverent* screamed beneath his feet. The Ronin watched through the thick clear super-tempered glass that separated him from the cells below as the floor on which the ghosts knelt trembled, then split and burst. It fell away beneath them, braided metal giving way to black space and to the brilliance of Dekien below. The ghosts vanished through the rent-open ship-wound, into the void and the light, where they would be no good to anyone.

The Ronin turned to the boy who was his guard. The boy stared down through the transparent sheet of material that was all that protected them from yawning void, mouth just open in startled wonder that hadn't yet had time to become fear.

"I had a pouch," the Ronin said to him. "It was taken. Do you know where?"

The guard turned his wide gaze to the Sith he had failed to contain and asked, "Why?"

"I need it to remind me."

That pouch, his stolen kyber stolen again, was his memory of what he had done and why he would continue to do it. He couldn't afford to waver or to forget. That was the root of the frailty that had led him to Hanrai's prison. He could commit to nothing but the deaths he already owed the worlds, and he *had* to commit, or what purpose had he?

The boy told the Ronin what he knew. In exchange, he told the boy to run. The boy proved wise, and he did.

B5-56 was still hiding, waiting for his master's word on what he should do next. The droid cultivated such faith, both in him and in the worlds and the Force, and many times over the past twenty years the Ronin had found that heartening.

It became a difficulty now. When he told B5 where he meant to go, and why, the droid guessed how he meant to do it and objected. Not for long, because the Ronin promised him that he intended to live, then asked his friend to ensure that he did.

It was the right thing to say, because B5 did worry. The Ronin hadn't lied either. He did mean to leave the *Reverent* a breathing man. If he didn't, who could he trust to end the witch?

CHAPTER
TWENTY-THREE

EKIYA FIGURED SHE had a good chance of losing her mind at any moment in the next, oh, however many hours it took them to retrieve her cargo and escape the *actual* Dreadnought. Assuming any of those ambitions panned out and they didn't end up nicely crisped on the end of a dutiful Jedi lightsaber.

Not that she had much of a choice, given what she'd allowed to be taken. She had asked for the burden of Rei'izu's ghosts. They were hers to recover.

At least Fox and Kouru had come to an accord of sorts. Neither had the silence of someone who felt like they'd won the argument, but they'd remained shut up even as they touched down in the *Reverent*'s yawning shuttle bay. They'd need to talk soon, though, because hell if Ekiya was skipping into a Jedi playpen without some kind of plan.

"I'd like us somewhere a little more out of the way first," said Fox when she tried to bring it up.

Apparently that didn't mean "in the safety of the *Poor Crow*'s cargo hold." The second the authorized crew started filing down the ramp, Fox ushered Ekiya and Kouru right on after them.

Ekiya had just noted that the crew's Jedi knight was missing—and hadn't that been the guy Fox recognized?—when the *Reverent*'s shuttle bay went dark.

Dark-dark. Nothing visible but for the winking stars through the still-open shuttle bay doors. For a moment, Ekiya thought she might be dissociating. Then emergency lights gasped on at low angles across the bay. Anemic red strips picked out the clean-lined underbellies of the fighters that had escorted them from Dekien, and all over, people-shaped silhouettes moved as if in slow motion, calling to one another.

Kouru, grand idiot, pulled out one of her lightsabers. Ekiya smacked the Sith's hand before she could ignite it and produced a miniature glow rod from her vest. When she turned it on, Kouru scowled, but she kept her mouth blessedly shut.

Ekiya's radius of light also carved out Fox's frown, deep enough to show beneath their shadowed mask, which gave the lie to their breezy tone. "Someone's having another tantrum, I expect."

"This is the old man?" Kouru asked.

As if in response, the gravity generators shut off. Just for a breath. Ekiya learned it had happened from a heady second of total weightlessness, followed by a rude, full-body jolt as her heels hit the deck. She staggered to keep her balance, and by the sound of the yelps and curses echoing through the bay, she got off easy.

"Let's consider ourselves fortunate the *Reverent* seems a bit too large for him to really upend." Fox motioned Ekiya and Kouru with them. "Main cargo hold will be this way."

They joined the pack of personnel scattering out of the shuttle bay to the relative safety of the *Reverent*'s inner corridors. Ekiya half expected Kouru to rebel and split off, but the Sith kept close, brow creased, mouth thin.

They'd talked about this. That no matter how much Kouru probably wanted to skive off on her own, without the influence of Fox's magic mind-whatever, she'd be caught in about five seconds.

That being said . . . Ekiya exchanged a look with Kouru as they hurried down a corridor whose lights flared on–off–on. The Sith's mouth twisted even more so than it usually did. She'd noticed too.

The *Reverent*'s personnel glanced their way every so often. Never for long—you know, emergency. But every time they did, the glances stuck *just* a second longer than they had down on Dekien, on the way into the high lords' shipyard.

Fox's influence held for now. They'd have to stop banking on it soon.

One of the Jedi in the middle of the pack they were running with, a guardian who'd flown in on one of the fighters, fell back a little. He cupped a comm to his ear and spoke rapidly into it. Fox lagged to match his pace, getting close enough to lay a hand on the man's shoulder. "What's the word?"

"The Sith, master," the guardian said. "He's escaped. And the demons—"

He cut off when something exploded. No telling what it was or where it'd broken, but Ekiya recognized the percussive thump and echo that traveled up through the *Reverent*'s metal decking and into her feet.

In their corridor, sirens burst out whooping, and lights flashed then guttered, alive then not. Another explosion juddered the deck.

Fox squeezed the guardian's shoulder. "Go, help."

The guardian nodded. He called out and a handful of personnel swerved with him at the next intersection, racing down the branching corridor. Fox beckoned Ekiya and Kouru, and they hung back as the rest of the personnel plowed on ahead.

In seconds it was just them and the half-assed dark.

Fox pointed to a panel in the wall, beside which an understated key lock was affixed. "Janitorial station," they explained. "They ought to have a terminal, one through which we can confirm the location of any recent changes to the cargo manifest, and, if we're lucky, also whatever it is our glowering friend is up to—the big one, I mean."

Kouru bared her teeth.

"Well?" Ekiya gestured at the key lock.

"Well?" Fox turned to her. ". . . No?"

"Do I look like a slicer?" Ekiya said at the same moment Kouru ignited her red lightsaber and drove it through the door.

"We're in a hurry, aren't we?" Kouru said, and she kicked in the panel she had carved out.

Cleaning supplies lined either side of the janitorial station, and thankfully the terminal at the other end woke up as soon as Fox prodded it.

Less thankfully, they pecked at the keys for a sweat-inducing half minute before Ekiya said, "You locked out?"

"No, no—the interface is . . . new."

"You're so old!" Ekiya pushed them aside. "Tell me what to search for."

Ekiya directed Kouru to stand guard by the door for fear that the Sith would try solving this problem with lightsabers too. Fox hovered over Ekiya's shoulder, feeding her keywords as they sifted through data.

The work was painstaking and erratic. Now and again the lights blinked out and so did the console. Once, the whole thing rebooted and they waited a nerve-racking stretch in pitch black before anything came back online.

Another detonation rattled the floor—closer?—as Ekiya dismissed another manifest. She couldn't find sign of her relics in the *Reverent*'s main hold, the sub-hold, or the sub-sub-holds, and she was wrestling her way through permissions to look at records for crew storage when Kouru swore, hopping back into the room.

Ekiya whipped around as a familiar waist-high shape in a hat skidded to a stop before the janitorial station and cooed inquisitively at the char marks on the ruined door.

"Wait—Bee, is that you?" Ekiya shouted from the console. "Where the hell have you been? Get in here—"

B5-56 apologized profusely.

"What do you mean 'busy'?" To B5's innocuous whistle, "Destroying what? Why!"

"A distraction," said Fox. "I see. What's our friend after, then?"

B5 began to slide away as he apologized again but Kouru whipped out a hand and lifted the astromech a good half meter off the ground.

"Rude!" said Fox.

"No," Kouru snapped. "The old man—where is he?"

B5's response made Ekiya snort. "Who's rude now?"

Not the point, she thought as she cursed herself. The point was they were all stuck on this Imperial Dreadnought now, whatever was happening to it—whatever Bee and Grim were *doing* to it—and that was at least partly Ekiya's fault.

She could've let it be and told Fox and Kouru to wait it out on Dekien, at least until one of a dozen less deadly opportunities to rescue her relics—and maybe their errant Sith—arose. But no, Ekiya had to put her foot down. And damned if she wasn't going to put the other down after it.

"Bee," she said, earnest as she could, "please."

His blue eye blinked rapidly once and twice, and for a moment, as the *Reverent* shuddered again, it was the only bright thing in the world.

Then he sighed and blatted at Kouru. At Ekiya's direction, Kouru let him down and B5 projected a flickering map of the *Reverent*'s schematics. He indicated which blinking dot was their current location versus the dot that was Grim's destination.

"Private storage?" said Ekiya. "They take his lightsaber too?"

"Perhaps," said Fox, like they meant *probably not.* "Well, that simplifies things a bit. Given the value of your cargo, Ekiya, I'd warrant the good lord Hanrai consolidated his prizes in the same place. Beefive, would you let Master Ronin know we'd like to rendezvous—"

Their request was drowned out; the ship screamed beneath their feet. The lights went out and did not come back on. In the corridor, yellow emergency strips flared. The only sound for a dark minute was the precipitous creak of distant metal.

"He's doing it again," said Kouru. For the first time since Ekiya had met her, she didn't sound some kind of angry.

"He's what?" Ekiya asked, even as a creeping fear of the answer threatened to choke her.

In the dim amber glow, Kouru's look was all dazed wonder spread thin over dread. "He's tearing the ship apart."

CHAPTER
TWENTY-FOUR

Kouru heard Ekiya curse and Fox say something simi-larly vile. ("Tearing the *ship*—the ship apart?") Yet in moments their anger and panic faded into the practical language of strategy and sur-vival. ("Your ghosts, Ekiya—" "My ghosts, my ass—it's people, Fox. People first, *always*.")

Kouru wanted her say. Her silence shamed her. But the mechanism of her thoughts had slurred into some barely ticking state, and when she at last spoke, it was in a mortifying burst of sound that had less to do with language than surprise.

Fox had laid their hand on her arm. She thought that she probably didn't like them touching her. Yet just as she had said nothing for an achingly silent stretch, she did nothing to make them let go.

"Classic Sith tactic, isn't it?" said Fox. Their tone was neither mock-ing nor cajoling, and Kouru decided this was why she wasn't mad at them specifically. "Endanger as many innocent citizens as possible to keep the morally fussy Jedi busy so only the especially valorous ones come after you. Well, I suppose there's a reason it's a classic. How fortu-nate we know better."

"What?" said Kouru, and she was too proud of her tongue for work-ing to feel foolish about it.

"Our diligent Ekiya intends to return to the shuttle bay to aid the evacuation effort—"

"Don't weasel out of this, you're coming too," Ekiya snapped at Fox.

Fox's hand on Kouru's elbow tightened ever so slightly. "And she has convinced me that my particular skills would be beneficial in this regard."

Kouru's mouth screwed in distaste. She understood the gist, that Fox's command of the black current lent itself to shepherding panicked people in safer directions, but every time she thought of those black tendrils curling into unsuspecting minds—

Focus.

The witch's voice was a cold jolt of lightning to Kouru's core. She stiffened under Fox's touch, and they finally released her. "It's not you," she muttered.

At once, she regretted it. "I'm sorry," said Fox, of all the galling things. "But if she's so insistent on minding your business . . . perhaps you'll find it freeing to do something she'd rather you didn't? She wants you to kill our friend. I'm not saying you don't really want that yourself, only that she very much does as well—but maybe you could make her wait for it."

"You want me to fetch him for you."

"And for him to be alive when you bring him back. Think of it as an experiment in self-determination."

Kouru shook them off before she could think more deeply on it. "Where do we meet?"

"Back at the shuttle bay, if you can. If not . . ." Fox touched B5's hat. A compartment opened on the droid's side, within which lay a wrist cuff resembling the old man's. "We'll find you."

Kouru fitted the cuff around her wrist before anyone could tell her to. Fox translated for B5 as she did—the cuff's blue light blinked slowly; it shared a link with the old man's, and the speed of the blinks would increase as she drew nearer to him. Though she would have to leave soon if she wanted the ship in any navigable shape. Ekiya chimed in to suggest sticking to the main thoroughfares even with the likelihood of running into foot traffic. Most people would be too consumed with thoughts of escape to bother with a strange woman running the wrong way.

The witch remained silent, which was good, as Kouru otherwise might have tried to bore her voice out of her skull through her ears.

The thought gave her pause. Before she could think better of it, she reached to her sash and tossed Fox's lightsaber back to them. They were so surprised that they fumbled the catch, though once they grasped the leather-wrapped hilt, they held it tightly. Kouru fled commentary, exiting the janitorial station through the carved-open door.

She entered a world defined by eerie stretches of creaking near-silence and rips of savage sound. The corridors were strikingly empty, until at junctures they filled with throngs of fleeing people—uniformed personnel, off-duty crew in civilian dress, Jedi too. Kouru cleaved to the sides as these shouting masses pushed past her. A lone officer once tried to make her turn around. Kouru shoved them away and kept running.

Her first obstacle came with a crushing rupture when the deck directly above her collapsed into the one she stood on. There were screams, and these echoed in the back of Kouru's skull, companions to ragged memory of another ship breaking. She gritted her teeth past the shiver in her limbs and pushed herself forward, forward.

The deck had torn so that it slanted down to meet hers. Some people had tumbled with it. Some were caught by fallen supports, others struggled to free their groaning comrades. Kouru scrambled past them all, checking her cuff as she climbed. It blinked very slightly faster than it had before. She continued straight.

That only lasted for so long. At the end of a flickering corridor, she ran into shut blast doors. They would not open, and the light over the keypad beside them glared warning red. She heard nothing through the thick layers of durasteel and had no way to know what lay beyond them. A stretch of rubble and bodies or nothing at all? Carnage, she could navigate. A fresh stretch of vacuum . . . Kouru shuddered.

The cuff's blinking, only nominally useful, grew less so the more paths she lost. She couldn't reliably navigate a disintegrating Imperial Dreadnought. Too many little branches, corridors, and offshoots, and she'd never know which was right until she ran into a damn dead end.

Return to the last intersection and turn right. There is a maintenance corridor that leads to a reinforced transportation shaft.

Kouru's very being bucked with distaste. "Shut up," she snarled at the witch.

At the same time, she stared at her cuff, which blinked still, but whether faster or slower than it had a minute before, she couldn't begin to say. "Fine," she growled.

The witch said nothing as Kouru turned back, but under Kouru's awareness, the pressure of her seemed to loosen just a touch, like a spring allowed to uncoil. Was the witch relieved? Kouru grimaced. She didn't like that either.

Regardless: forward. She turned right at the appointed intersection; she followed it until she ran into another locked door—this one a malfunction, it seemed—and the witch directed her again. It led her on, ever onward, and whenever Kouru checked her cuff, she found the light pulsing ever more steadily.

She passed fewer and fewer people as she went, and the sounds grew less frequent also. When they came now, their immensity left her stunned and stole her breath for precious seconds.

Forward.

She found herself at last on a sheltered bridge, the viewports of which overlooked a bay that housed an armada of land vehicles. A dozen or so four-legged walkers shaped in the fashion of oxen, boars, and other towering beasts. The rest of the war vessels were dressed in classic Imperial regalia—sacred ropes and tassels, blessed streamers, the likes of which Kouru had last seen during the great muster on Rei'izu.

Midway across the bridge, Kouru saw a glimmer in the bay. Her eyes were drawn toward its deck. A crack had lanced through it.

The bay buckled in an instant. Vacuum devoured every iota of equipment that had not been secured. It all spiraled and flailed into the dark as that which had been lashed down strained to be free, the deck to which it had been attached torn and shredded. The bulkheads gasped spurts of formless fire, absent gravity.

Kouru stared, eyes wide to the point of pain. She heard only her breath. Her vision narrowed, fixing on one hulking equine transport hurtling into the black, then on a bulky maintenance cart wavering like a kite on its tether.

The sight pulled at a nightmare within her—memories of panicked faces disappearing into dark corridors, of awful inorganic shrieks, of her master, guiding her forward, and the fear that had already saturated her entirety, because it must have, because otherwise she would have realized that they weren't hunting a saboteur, they were fleeing his work—but now there was nothing.

She should have felt much more than that. Horror and dread. Some variety of pain. She had seen this destruction before, and it had been the gruesome end of everything that had been her life, her *self*.

Kouru hated the ever-lurking volume of space, its unfeeling hunger. More than that, she feared it. Yet now, still, even *knowing* that she had lived that fear ever since the end of the Sith . . . nothing. She felt nothing.

Had that wretched witch stolen this, too?

"But *why*?" Kouru hissed into the dark empty, because if she couldn't have her fear, she'd be greedy with the rage, so long as she could call it her own. "Do you wish me more useful? Compliant?"

Let go, the witch was always telling her. Let go. Now there was hesitation.

My only wish is for you to have what you're owed, said the witch. *If I ask you to let go, it's so that I might give it to you.*

Kouru rounded on her as if she were there to snarl at—but there was no witch; there never was. Kouru was, nevertheless, not alone. The cuff light at her wrist flickered and flared.

The old man had entered the corridor in which Kouru stood. She hadn't heard him approach, as she only became aware of him as he passed her. The corridor was wide enough that they weren't touching, and she would have to lunge to reach him. She was ready to.

He wasn't looking at her.

In that instant, she forgot everything about Fox's request—that she defy the witch by saving the old man. In its place, she had a vicious desire to kill him. She had no hostages, no advantage, but she wanted with every part of herself for him to be dead—and for her own hand to have done the deed.

But she stilled as the seconds dragged on, her hand clenched around the hilt of the lightsaber she had stolen from him and otherwise unmoving.

Kouru knew this man's strengths. He was judicious in his movements, sly and attentive. He had anticipated her in both their fights, watched her every movement with absolute attention even when he seemed to be focused elsewhere.

As he passed her now, he had not slowed and he had not turned, and he looked nowhere but forward. Kouru didn't take any of this as a sign that she had the upper hand. She knew better than to underestimate him, seeing as he had killed her.

Yet she felt bizarrely unheeded. Not dismissed. Unseen. As if she truly were a ghost in any meaningful sense of the word.

The hesitation cost her. The old man stepped off the bridge onto the next section of the *Reverent,* and the bridge's metal girding creaked ominously in his wake.

Up!

Kouru only had time to obey. Above her ran a ventilation shaft. She cut into it with jagged haste, and she leapt through the red-hot hole she had carved with such reckless speed that she burned her palms on the edge as she levered herself up.

Forward, the witch said, hot with urgency.

Kouru scrambled. Below her, metal screamed. She could in her mind picture the collapse of the bridge. It would resemble the deadly distortions of the vehicle bay minutes ago. Screaming necessity forced her to struggle forward, forward, to the point where the ventilation shaft met the rest of the ship's network.

A warning light blinked fretfully over the juncture, her only illumination—her star.

Faster, the witch hissed, *the emergency protocols have been triggered. It's going to close off the point of breach.*

Kouru couldn't waste the breath on a curse. She lunged, slid across the deck, propelled by every ripple of black current she could so flailingly grasp—

And skidded to a halt two meters past the point where the emergency door slammed shut behind her.

Kouru shuddered with deep breaths as she sat up, hunched over her knees in the closed-in dark. The pulsing breeze of the ventilation system froze the sweat on her neck, and cold coagulated in her gut. She wanted her mind blank, empty of anything but the white flare that lived within her.

She couldn't banish the image of the old man walking past her, insensate to her presence. She had seen only a fraction of his face. What had he been feeling that had made him look so hollow? Like a puppet drawn on a string, or a proper demon of the witch's making.

He went forward. Only forward. Just like Kouru had. Like she was still doing now, chasing the witch's wants no matter how she had railed against her least manipulations. What moved him? What did he *want*?

Kouru understood, somewhat, but only because Fox had bothered to tell her. She had never once stopped to wonder about it herself, after the moment on Genbara when she had first understood that the old man wanted to kill her. Then he *had* killed her. And after that?

After that, she chased him, never thinking nor imagining anything other than his death by her hand. Even now knowing what he sought, she had every reason to want him dead. If he was after that which had brought her back to herself, she ought to protect it from him. Self-preservation, plain and simple.

Less simple: that she hated the thing whispering to her bones and moving her without her will. Was it worth persisting if she could only be *permitted* to persist?

Kouru snorted quietly to herself in that cramped smudge of darkness that was the smallest corner of a disintegrating ship. She had precious few delusions about her place in the galaxy. She had been born to parents who wanted her, but they had not been allowed to keep her, because the Force had meant she belonged to the Jedi, and the Jedi belonged to the lords.

Only when the Sith decided they might like to belong to themselves had Kouru tasted the first drop of freedom, and that taste had always been tainted by blood and sweat and the death of those who couldn't bear to see her breathing for her own sake. And it had not lasted.

She had wanted to belong to herself after, and she had tried. But from the clarity of perspective that death granted, she could say that she had more truly belonged to grief and fury. And now? Kouru clenched her fists to feel herself-in-herself. Now?

Now Fox, who she hated, had asked her to save a man she loathed to defy a witch she despised. She had no answer. No worthy want. No way out.

Thus dazed by this circling reverie, it was Kouru's own fault when the shaft beneath her tilted at a severe angle, and she fell with it.

She seized at the black current to slow her slide and she did fractionally decelerate—before she lost hold on herself when she collided with a grate and her breath was knocked from her chest.

Kouru wheezed, momentarily ungrateful for the fact that she was still present in a body that had to endure such pointless, frustrating pain.

The white flare was in her frustration as she heaved herself up, twisted, and struck the grate with her palm. The metal warped under her blow, and when she struck it again the grate clattered to the floor.

Or, the wall. When Kouru swung herself out of the ventilation shaft, she entered near the bottom of a precariously listing section of corridor. She could at least traverse up the precipitous ramp to where the corridor continued toward her ostensible destination. At her end, the hallway had broken with the rest of its floor and hung on to itself by a collection of fraying cables. Kouru dropped down to the floor cautiously, and it swayed slightly.

As she found her footing, she realized she was not alone. She had seen no one but the old man for some time now, but this person looked straight at her, so obviously it wasn't him. All the same, Kouru recognized them, just as they recognized her.

At the top of the ramp of broken corridor stood the old woman Kouru had thrown off the shrine platform in the Seikara Caverns—Chie, she remembered. Chie's arm hung in a sling, and when she settled into a battle-ready stance, Kouru saw a shiver in her back leg. Even so, in her good arm Chie held a staff that sparked at the end. A replacement for the one Fox had halved in Seikara.

Kouru's lip twitched. Chie would pose no challenge, but she would take precious *time.*

"Aunty, *no.*" An interruption—a Twi'lek boy in Jedi apprentice robes, who dodged up from behind Chie. The boy kept a vigilant eye on Kouru, and there was conviction in his posture. To her irritation, she liked it. "Please, take the others back—"

Chie clucked. "Yuehiro."

Yuehiro the apprentice shook his head, attention still fixed on Kouru. "No, Aunty."

"No what?" Chie knocked her staff against Yuehiro's ankle and stepped up beside him. She didn't bother to hide her limp and she met Kouru's look with a casual steel. "Your quarrel isn't with us, Sith. Let's pass without wasting each other's time."

There were more apprentices, Kouru realized. Five or so, all young—younger than Yuehiro, at least. Not that even that stalwart boy was old. Infants, all. Yet more than one looked willing to fight Kouru, if it came to it. She saw the desperation—and ferocity—glinting in their eyes as they stared down at her.

And she *recognized* it, recognized it like she did the horrendous gash of sound echoing all around them that was another chunk of the *Reverent* gutting itself in the vacuum over Dekien. Recognized it like she did the hard angle of Chie's posture as she put herself between the children and what she thought might kill them. Knew it in her heart, because Kouru recalled with ugly dissonance the last she had seen of her master before their ship split at its seams, destroyed by the man who had betrayed the Sith.

So, no. Her quarrel wasn't with Chie and a gang of children. But perhaps it was *about* them.

Kouru turned. She nodded up to the corridor above her. "This way."

Yuehiro glanced at Chie, who didn't move, so neither did the boy. The apprentices behind them tensed.

"If I wanted you dead, I would be more efficient," snapped Kouru. "Come on. I know the way."

Chie's head bent with thought. Then she gestured the children forward. They looked to her with varying degrees of terror and trust, but every last one obeyed.

Yuehiro led the way and stationed himself at the point of the corridor directly across from Kouru. To Kouru's surprise, more than one of the apprentices needed help down the slope—as well as up to the level overhead. Yuehiro boosted these stragglers up onto it or caught their stumbles down the ramp with the black current, guiding them slowly toward him.

Chie worked her way down on her own, one hand on the wall. "This is an interesting development," she said as she stopped by Kouru.

"What's wrong with them?" Kouru asked. "Are they injured?"

Chie flicked her hand scoldingly. "Not every child can run. Help me up."

This, Kouru recognized. A child could have a facility with the Force and lack the physical gifts the lords required of their knights. Any child so afflicted was doomed to guardianship, if they survived that far. Kouru had known many such apprentices as her peers—the children rescued by the Sith.

She bared her teeth at the memory, but she put out her hands to leverage Chie up onto the next level. Then it was just her and Yuehiro, who stared at Kouru with his chin bravely raised.

"You're Sith," he said. "Are you like *him*?"

"Don't insult me," Kouru snapped.

Strangely, a tension bled from the boy's shoulders. He nodded and hopped up onto the level, letting Kouru bring up the rear.

Chie and the other children were already halfway down the corridor to the next intersection. Kouru threw one last look over her shoulder, down the path from which they had come—toward the heart of the Jedi quarters, where B5 claimed the old man was headed.

The witch said nothing, but Kouru felt her desire. She wanted Kouru to chase him.

Kouru turned away.

She had more than one way to revenge herself upon them all—the traitor, the witch, and the rest. It would be one thing to kill the old man, and maybe she still would, if he didn't get himself killed with this fit of madness. It would be another thing to deny him—and *her*—the fuel that fed their fires.

These children would live. No more ghosts for him. No more demons for her.

If Fox took issue with her choice, well, then they should have gone to rescue the execrable man themselves.

CHAPTER
TWENTY-FIVE

THE *REVERENT* WAS doomed, and Hanrai couldn't save more than a portion of it. But knowledge was his vice, his flailing grasp at control, so even as he plunged into the depths of his crumbling ship, he let his attention span multitudes.

He watched the evacuation that spanned the Dreadnought. Personnel rescued their fellows, accounting for the missing and searching for them too. He burned with pride to know the lengths they took in order to treasure each life.

He had sent his knights and guardians to aid where they could. Fetching stragglers, or if they were so gifted, expending every last drop of themselves to hold sections of the ship together long enough for others to escape to safer ground. They worked tirelessly and selflessly in the name of their people, and it gave him peace.

It justified the lie he had told to send them away. He had let them think him safely stowed in a shuttle on its way to Dekien. "You forget yourself, my lord," a guardian had scolded when he first tried to stay. "You must leave. You must *survive.*"

Hanrai couldn't leave. It had been his error that brought the Sith onto the *Reverent,* and thus every last one of these endangered lives was his responsibility. He couldn't send anyone else to face the man, not until he sent himself.

In doing so, Hanrai expected he would die. There was a peace to be had in the understanding. It was a Jedi's sacred duty to die in service to his lord. Now that Hanrai was himself the man others died for, where did he find his honor? His lordly peers might have said: the Empire. Hanrai might have nodded and laughed and agreed for the sake of agreeing, but he would not have agreed in truth. There was no greater purpose left to Hanrai but to die for his own sake.

The Jedi he had once been would have called him an egoist. But that man hadn't yet understood just how different a name became when it belonged to the man to whom others swore themselves. *Hanrai* now stood for so much more than the body he occupied. It would mean something to the galaxy if he died for it.

It was the same sort of name that the Sith—dark lord, rebel, traitor, meditative and tormented man—had railed against when he refused to save his lord for the sake of his guardians. Had he realized what he was doing then? Or had he allowed his protective instinct to overtake his sense of consequence?

What was he thinking now, as he gutted the *Reverent*?

The time for such questions had passed. Hanrai had made his mistake. The Sith was too broken to build upon, and Hanrai would have to kill him. If he didn't—well, it didn't warrant thinking about. He would kill the Sith, and he would die for it, and despite his self-admonishments, it would be headily sweet.

It nevertheless would have been better to have a reason to live.

The moment he thought that, the galaxy complied. It was more generous than many realized. Hanrai saw that he did not hunt alone.

As he proceeded into the depths of the *Reverent,* he saw another figure separate themself from the frantic work of rescue. They hesitated first, their labor interrupted by some unspoken thought that tugged their attention away. Then, they gave in to whatever silence had called them.

They slipped away from the shuttle bay, into the breaking ship. They went unfollowed, in no small part because they were so incomparably good at going where they weren't supposed to and being ignored while they did it. Hanrai felt pride at this too. After all, he had trained them in this subtlety.

They wove all through the *Reverent*'s failing corridors, a wraith fluttering at the edge of his attention until they were, at last, on trajectory to cross his path. This was not his intent or his design; they merely shared a destination. Nevertheless, Hanrai desired the reunion, and he couldn't discount the possibility that his wanting feet drew them closer too. He had hoped to see them again for such a long time now, after all. Ever since he learned they still lived.

He arrived just after them. They had reached the highest garden terrace in the imposing eight-story rotunda of the officer quarters. Each terrace, of which there were also eight, was a circle, and each shone artificial sunlight upon the circle below it. Presently the gardens were styled to evoke a sense of autumn, which was the current season in the territory on Watoru where Hanrai's home estate was located.

A bridge from the highest terrace led straight to a courtyard, which sprawled before the wood-and-paper house that was the lord's domicile on the *Reverent*. It was on this bridge that Hanrai met his student. The artificial lights wavered there as they did everywhere, casting bridge, house, and garden in intermittent sterile shadow. He came upon them in a rare stretch of stable illumination.

Idzuna had paused. They knelt, arms outstretched. A small rotund shape tore out of the house, across the courtyard, and down the bridge, before it threw itself into Idzuna's arms. They cradled the cat to their chest, where it burrowed with miserable purrs.

"Kyuu, you awful little fool," they murmured as they stood. "What are you doing here?"

"I've kept him in fish and crickets," said Hanrai, approaching from the garden. "And I haven't forgotten you either."

Idzuna kept their back turned, and the tension in their shoulders was quite slight. They had retained their impeccable control. "Chie's betrayal made your interest rather clear."

"I'm sorry." Hanrai stopped by the reddened maple overhanging the terrace's shallow pond, which rippled excitedly at the *Reverent*'s every vibration. "You were so intent on hiding. From me, specifically. As if you thought me a threat."

Now Idzuna turned to him. "Well, I do."

"I confess I'm afraid to ask why . . . When you disappeared, Idzuna—I had to tell your parents I'd lost you."

What Idzuna thought of this—what they felt—they kept contained behind that theatrical mask. They held Kyuu carefully, but Hanrai saw the strain in their posture.

The deck shuddered beneath them. The garden itself moaned as its power threatened to sputter entirely.

"I'm afraid I don't really have the time to catch up," said Idzuna, and they started down the bridge.

"No, you're right." Hanrai followed. "But I might as well speak my piece while we make for the same goal."

Hanrai kept a diligent step behind his student as they crossed the bridge and the courtyard. The personal garden, which had been designed for his lordly relaxation, had taken on another life as a meeting place for his students. They had often come here to debate one another beneath the seasonal trees or to best one another in acrobatic competition. The foliage, craftily pruned to evoke the sense that this was but one sheltered copse in the midst of far more vegetation, shivered. The bulkhead to their right had split a finger's width; blue sparks crackled in the rift. It was only a matter of time before the whole garden caught flame.

Idzuna's pace was unhurried, even when a sickly burning fragrance signaled that some mechanism beneath, behind, or within Hanrai's quarters had broken. Their cat let out a low, upset growl, and Idzuna stroked its cheek.

"Would you tell me what it is you want?" they asked without prompting.

"I'd like to," said Hanrai. "I want you home. Serving the Empire—the galaxy—as you once did."

This struck a chord. Idzuna slowed, just a step. Or perhaps they had nearly stopped and recovered their pace. Their silence was answer enough: No.

"I won't ask what happened to you," said Hanrai. "I don't want you to tell me, if you don't care to. If you can't yet, or can't ever. But we lost so much when we lost you, my student. The galaxy was poorer. So was I. You had so much to give. You still do."

Idzuna climbed silently up the shallow steps to the entry hall of Hanrai's personal quarters. This time, they didn't slow.

Hanrai persisted. He saw his student walking a narrow road to a precipice. Once they reached it, they would jump, or they would fall, and he feared either outcome. "There's a young one now—Yuehiro. Inquisitive, philosophical. Gifted with the current. Nosy. Reminds me of you. Imagine what he could become if *you* taught him."

At last, they were brought up short. Idzuna stood on the veranda and waited for Hanrai to join them. They studied their old master as if they hadn't yet quite seen him, and they even deigned to remove their mask. Their face was more gentle than Hanrai expected, because it was as he recalled it. For all that age had crept into the lines of their eyes and mouth, they still looked so very young. Perhaps it was only that he had become so old.

"The things you say are always so kind," they said. "Yet the things you asked me to do . . ."

"I don't regret them. Do you?"

"*Yes.*"

"That, I regret." Hanrai bowed his head, hands clasped behind his back. "You were always admirable, Idzuna. Loyal and resolute. I hated to think I had asked the wrong thing of you."

They laughed without humor. "That's what you'd call it?"

Hanrai rarely found himself speechless. He could on occasion be silent as he considered which words he thought best, most kind or most useful. Even here, he had so many dozens of things to say that he wished for Idzuna to hear. In this moment, an eerily perfect quiet consumed them, his house, and the garden beyond. It was as if time had stilled to allow him the opportunity to select the response that would give his student peace, that would unite them as they once had been united.

Yet no answer summoned from within himself would do. He had words that might satisfy his guilt, his sorrow, or his frustration, but these were all secondary to his aim. "What would you ask of me?" he said at last. "The children need you. The Empire needs you. I'll give what I must to see you come back."

Idzuna smiled. It seemed real. "You don't want me to do that."

"I do. You were a vital part of a future we lost. If you returned—"

"You don't want that," they spat. This seemed real too, and it hurt.
"Why not?"

They turned from him. "It wasn't what you made me for."

The strike came from behind. It cut Hanrai from his shoulder to his midsection, a clean bright line that he understood would kill him swiftly.

He collapsed to the veranda without much pain—thanks to shock, or to where his spinal cord had been cut, or to the fact that he was dying. This allowed him to think, in a narrowing way, on how he still hadn't seen what killed him. He could only see Idzuna, looking down at him, unmoving, cat still cradled in their arms. He thought perhaps there was a sort of grief in the fragile set of their mouth, but that might have only been a self-indulgent shred of hope. It was, either way, shortly extinguished.

CHAPTER
TWENTY-SIX

THE LAST TIME the Ronin had killed with his own two hands, he had struck down a young woman in a forgotten temple in the shadow of a torrent pursuing its natural course. He had prayed after, alone.

His newest victim was an old man, who lay dead upon the floor of a shrine to his own arrogance; the Ronin had sundered it with fire, which still burned beneath his feet. The time for prayer had long since passed.

The Traveler seemed unlikely to pray as well. They stood across from the Ronin, cat held to their chest as they stared down at the body sprawled at their feet. Then they met his eye and smiled that glass smile. Though their wooden mask hung loosely from their fingers, their opinion was as obscured as ever. "Did you get what you came for?"

The Ronin inclined his head. A familiar weight lay nestled in his robes. It brought him no comfort.

He had found his pouch in a puzzle box, hidden in a trunk in the Lord Hanrai's humble bedchamber. The trunk was simple and un-locked, the box neither of these. Dozens of repeating geometric shapes disguised the outlines of the box's moving panels. It would only open if these panels were moved in precise consecutive order. An artisan's mas-terpiece in itself, but the Ronin detected an additional layer of security embedded in the box's sides. A single wrong move would trigger the detonation device within, destroying the box, its contents, and whatever hands had foolishly attempted to break in.

So, he took it.

And with that, he stalled—his limbs slowed, his mind fogged. He couldn't say for how long he stood unmoving in the belly of that breaking beast, sodden with unspeakable feeling that disgusted his every instinct.

Instead, his awareness fled, dispersed through the anatomy of the ship he had rent open, all fire and leakage and crying metal. He wanted with selfish ferocity to be anywhere but within his own body, which had achieved its temporal goal and knew not what else to do.

He wished to kill the witch.

He did. He was sure of it.

But if he was so sure, why couldn't he move?

He returned with a jolt when two voices cut through the stagnant air of the courtyard. Both familiar: the Traveler and Lord Hanrai. Neither sensed his presence. It puzzled.

Then the voice said: *Do you think that's how it is?*

"No."

She had not spoken to him in quite some time. Or she had, and he had chosen not to hear her. Nevertheless, he realized she was right. He was concealed, but not by his own design. One of his visitors had hidden him from the other.

As if it's such a mystery, she said.

Here too, she was right. Lord Hanrai was many things—manipulative, sly, and presuming. But he didn't lie, not quite, not to those whose loyalty he wished to court. He deceived by other means.

The Traveler, meanwhile, was both a liar and an adept of the black current, which could be used to enshroud all manner of things.

The question, now that the Lord Hanrai lay dead at the Ronin's feet and at the Traveler's: Had they drawn a veil over their old master's eyes in order to let the Ronin escape or because they had wished, instead, for this? They must have understood murder was a possibility. Had they bet on it?

The Traveler didn't look shocked. They hadn't at the moment of

Hanrai's death either. They did seem upset. Their features were too brittle for contentment, their fingers deeply sunk in the cat's fur.

But then, they had also looked upset when the Lord Hanrai was alive, their face contorted with the pang of old scars unkindly touched.

And yet. It would have been a comfort to know he had killed the lord for someone else's need. Even if the Traveler had also desired it, he didn't think he had done it for them. Trapped in himself, he had hungered for a point of action and intent, and the death of a man who wanted everything he didn't had seemed the way to get it. It had not worked. He felt no more clarity of purpose than he had before.

The Traveler adjusted the cat in their arms. "Well, that's that. Let's be on our way."

The Ronin remained where he stood. The hilt of his lightsaber hung in his hand, unlit. Inexorably present. "Why did you come for me?"

The Traveler smiled again. It looked no more honest than before. "The last time I left you alone, you got yourself kidnapped. Arrested. Whatever you'd like to call it. I did send someone to come fetch you . . ." They frowned for a moment, as if remembering another chore. "Well, it seems she was distracted. So here I am, and off we go. Back to the safety of a ship that will ferry us away from all this mess."

They were most certainly lying. What about, the Ronin had yet to pinpoint. Every one of their words left three more unsaid. They wanted him to kill a lord, a witch—and what else? And why? No matter how or when he had asked, they had never properly explained themself. He thought it unlikely they ever would. Not unless he pressed the point.

The Ronin couldn't continue in this way, not knowing what he walked toward—not knowing whether it mattered. He ignited his lightsaber. Its tip extended to hover a breath away from the Traveler's throat. It was the most certain light in the darkening ship.

"I'm holding a cat," said the Traveler.

"The cat can go. Tell me why I should trust you."

"I thought you liked me."

"That doesn't matter."

The Traveler did not withdraw from the burning blade. "I suppose your history speaks for itself."

The Ronin expected the voice to have her say, but she held her tongue. She didn't need to speak for him to remember what she would have reminded him of. He had liked her too—loved her—when he destroyed their world.

Ever since, he had been devoted to his penance, though even now he struggled to articulate the entirety of his sin. It was too immense to be succinctly defined. Yet he knew the features of his great error: camaraderie and ambition, also called hope.

That was what stilled him now, and what had frozen him moments before. To want the witch dead—it was so grand a want, and thus it was dangerous, unbearably so. He had thought himself recovered from the temptation of ideals. A cowardly notion, and it fractured under the least scrutiny. It mattered not how he hid and ran from desire and belief. So long as he lived, the world would ripple in his wake, as it did for every being. Each ripple fed into the next until they were as waves, and became a drowning tide.

For a mad moment long ago he had thought he could calm the waters, or even burn them dry. Foolish. Whatever respite he had won was too fleeting to be called true peace. And the price . . .

His hand trembled minutely. The red blade slid a hairsbreadth toward the Traveler's throat. They inhaled, slight and sharp. They were afraid.

Not of him.

On the floor, the body of Lord Hanrai shifted. First in the shoulders, then in the elbows, as Hanrai pushed himself up. "Ah," said Hanrai in a voice so wetly present he might never have been dead, "very clever."

CHAPTER
TWENTY-SEVEN

E KIYA WAS ALONE; the realization hit her like a sucker punch, and from the base of the emptied *Crow,* she stared bewildered around the *Reverent*'s likewise emptied hangar, absent of vessels and personnel and most reliable pieces of tech that hadn't been welded down.

"Alone" wasn't entirely fair—she had B5-56. But she didn't have Fox. Neither did she have the least idea when they'd left.

Sure, it could have happened at just about any point during the mess of trying to direct people onto any ship with room to hold them, but Ekiya had the sneaking feeling that Fox hadn't just slipped away under cover of chaos. She knew with cheerless certainty that they'd reached into her brain and messed with the wires. It felt wretched. Like a betrayal. Worst of all, she didn't know *why*.

B5 nudged her leg with a contrite warble. The droid knew what she was looking for, and he confessed: I saw them leave.

"Why didn't I know about this?"

B5 let out a contrite coo. He feared for his master. He wanted Grim to have any help he could get. And, well . . .

Fox hadn't looked entirely like themself when they slipped away into the dark.

"Oh, great, love that." Ekiya groaned. How was she supposed to be properly mad at someone being led around by their own worm-ridden brain?

Not that sympathy would fix the fundamental problem wherein Ekiya had recovered her ship, yes, but she had nothing of value to put in it besides herself and B5. Would it even be worth leaving, if that was all she could rescue?

The *Reverent* shrieked under her feet and the breaking of it lanced up through her boots into her spine. If she didn't choose now, the *Reverent* would choose for her.

"Ekiya!"

The call came frantic from a mouth she'd never thought would say her name so gladly. Chie came limping into the darkened hangar with a cadre of Jedi apprentices ahead of her, eyes wide in the red emergency lights. Bringing up the rear, inexplicably, was Kouru. The Sith looked over her shoulder once, then urged the kids and Chie forward, nearly sweeping the older woman up into her arms as they closed the distance to the *Poor Crow*.

"Off with us, then," Chie said as she directed the kids toward the *Crow*'s ramp, as if she had already arranged their transport with Ekiya.

Not like Ekiya could argue. What other vessel remained to haul this many off the *Reverent*? And all things given, ferrying Chie and a passel of kids was—well, it wouldn't get Ekiya any closer to Rei'izu, but she wouldn't lose sleep over it.

That thought still didn't fill the hollowing space in her chest when she realized Kouru had come back with no prize but for people. It felt cruel to be disappointed, especially as they'd sent her off to rescue Grim, not relics. Ekiya made sure to get a head count of the kids as they ran up into the *Crow* to make sure none went missing, but the knowledge of all the things Kouru hadn't brought back tarnished her ability to feel anything like relief.

Kouru, positioned on the opposite side of the ramp, met her eyes and held the look. Her jaw clenched. She said something that got swallowed by the dark of the hangar and the screams of the *Reverent*. Ekiya thought it might've been, "I'm sorry."

So as they scrambled up the ramp, an anxious B5 on their heels, she glanced at Kouru and said, "Thanks."

An apology for prioritizing the living over the dead? Ekiya couldn't really countenance the thought, but she appreciated it—especially as they'd be leaving more dead in their wake.

CHAPTER
TWENTY-EIGHT

Hanrai sat upright, cross-legged, and held his arms before him to be duly considered.

The Traveler was fixed on their old master. Horror tightened the corners of their mouth and eyes.

The Ronin wished he felt similarly. He would have preferred it to the frantic rage that flashed under his sternum—that ignited all through his limbs so that he moved before he bid himself to do so.

The crimson blade of his lightsaber swept down from the Traveler's throat toward the hated ghost of a man he had also despised.

Despised, yes. Loathed. He recognized it now, the crystallization of fury—a lodestar by which to guide the maelstrom within him. The Ronin hated Hanrai, him and every lord there had ever been, who styled themselves great to justify the deaths they demanded. For that, he would kill the man. And kill him again, if need be. It would not feel good, in that it would not satisfy, but it would be worth doing.

And it would be safer to kill him than to think of—

Of course, Hanrai refused to die readily. The lordly demon threw himself back and away from his seat on the veranda with velocity and finesse. He skidded and righted himself in the trembling stones of his courtyard. There he stood straight, hands out and open. "Come, sir. I want to talk."

"We've talked enough."

"Not like this."

The Ronin dived toward him from the veranda. Hanrai relented. When they clashed in a spray of stone and physical force, he met the Ronin's blade with his own, sharply blue and shining.

Hanrai's lightsaber gave way. He had dodged back again, away from the courtyard and toward the bridge that led to the terraces. The Ronin didn't stop to wonder why. It wouldn't matter, if he killed the man with due speed.

He wanted to. Needed to. Could not stand for the man to be alive any longer—talking, incessantly, as if that would change the course of his fate.

"We don't have much time, so I'll be frank." Hanrai deflected the Ronin's first strike on the bridge. "She's shown me multitudes. More than I could have ever managed to see on my own."

The Ronin whipped back around to cut into the lord from behind. This sweep Hanrai met and held. Their blades hissed against each other.

"She extends an invitation." Hanrai strove to catch the Ronin's eye. "To Rei'izu."

The fury in the Ronin burst. He shoved the lord back with the power in his body and the power that was *of* his body, the white flare of the Force screaming heat and intensity. It blew Hanrai back to the terrace end of the bridge. The lord regained his footing as if he had leapt on purpose. When he raised his head, he frowned in some admonishment.

Resentment hammered in the Ronin's chest as he steadied his stance. *She* invited him, did she? And to do it, she spoke through a stolen mouth? She could just as well tell him within his own mind. Why do it like this? Spite? Cruelty?

He couldn't know. She wouldn't tell him. He barely felt her now. Could only detect a skimming hint of her weighing against his chest. He was so accustomed to her being more and heavier, a pressure on his lungs and being, that he might well have been imagining she was still there, constricting, making it ever harder to breathe.

He strained to hear her voice. Some whisper, some snicker, anything. Instead, she said nothing. Nothing, nothing, nothing.

He would rather have said nothing also, but the words twisted from his mouth, ripely bitter. "Does she extend a path as well?"

"You have what you need, don't you?" Hanrai asked in the same idle tone he had used over tea. "The mirror shard."

Asinine. The Ronin answered with a flick of his wrist. A battery of fist-sized stones lifted from the terrace pond and screeched through the air toward Hanrai. The lord slashed them away with his lightsaber, and as he did, the Ronin unholstered his blaster and fired twice under the light trail of Hanrai's deflection.

Hanrai avoided both bolts by leaping up and forward. As he came down, the Ronin barely managed to meet his overhead blow. But though Hanrai had been the aggressor, his gaze over the blue of his blade was troubled and directed elsewhere, over the Ronin's shoulder—toward the bridge.

"Ah," Hanrai said, "but I gave it to you. Didn't I, Idzuna?"

It would have been so foolish, base, to take his eyes off Hanrai. That the Ronin even wanted to should have shamed him. Instead, he yearned to turn. In equal measure, he wished the impulse burned from his body.

If he turned—if he looked—he would see the damning truth in the Traveler's face.

The problem was thus: He still suspected Hanrai had not lied.

So, the Ronin wouldn't turn. He couldn't afford the doubt. The only price he was willing to pay today was the second end of a Jedi whose death he had already chosen.

Maddening, then, that Hanrai was untouchable, the wave through which a blade uselessly cut. The Ronin felt the surety of his own strikes and still none hit. No matter his precision, nothing touched Hanrai that the lord didn't choose to touch. The Jedi's expression, unwavering, pitied any who dared try.

Until with a horrendous metal scream, the terrace floor rent open beneath Hanrai, and the Jedi lord dropped like a stone down a well.

The Ronin halted mid-swing. He remained at the ready even as his chest heaved for breath he had not been aware was coming labored.

The sound of feet dashing forward. The Traveler, at his side—that fat, ancient cat still cradled in their arm and latched onto their chest. The creature stared with wide-eyed trepidation toward the crevice in the garden terrace that their dear owner had just torn; the Traveler didn't even bother to look at it as they grasped the Ronin's elbow.

"Off we go, then," they said.

"He's not dead yet," said the Ronin.

"He *is*."

The strange urgency of this insistence perturbed the Ronin. He pushed the disquiet aside. The warring impulses in the Traveler's tone—guilt and spite, hope and dread—they cut too close. The Ronin yearned for the purity of clear direction, even as he knew the want a childish one. But without clarity, he would freeze and fracture as he had before, and this time—

In a way, he got what he wanted. The terrace gave way under them too. It tilted and they tipped off it, scrambling to catch onto the pavement or to each other, the Traveler one-handed as they clutched their screeching cat, the Ronin also hampered as he twisted to keep his blade away from any vulnerable flesh.

He saw what had happened as they fell toward the terrace below. Hanrai had fallen, yes, but he had caught himself on the supports below the split terrace, or he had leapt and climbed his way back up to it from where he fell. Then he had cut through the mechanical gut that kept the repulsorlifts in working order, but only on one side—thus imbalancing the terrace, off which they now plummeted.

Hanrai plunged after them, lightsaber drawn. A tactical advantage, to be sure. Gravity was certainly in his favor.

The Ronin exchanged one brief glance with the Traveler. He nodded toward Hanrai. Their look called him rather an idiot, but their wrist swept up.

They landed together with terrible quickness, their impact barely tempered by the Traveler's command of the black current—and the Ronin leapt back up into the air, thrust forward by that same power.

Hanrai expected to bear down with gravity, and he did, hitting the pavement of the seventh terrace where the Ronin had stood a breath before. He twisted away as the Ronin spun back down upon him, directed by white flare. Not fast enough. The Ronin's reach had increased as he extended the stave of his lightsaber auxiliary, and the ignited blade at the end of his makeshift spear caught Hanrai's arm, singeing robe and muscle.

A demon's burnt flesh smelled like any other man's. But then, the Ronin had learned that long ago.

Hanrai dodged away and shook the injured arm as the Ronin took position across from him, holding the staff at the ready. He would have to take care in his next deployment of it; the longer hilt gave him reach, but it was a larger target for a lightsaber. But between the staff and the blaster, the Ronin had the edge.

Perhaps having realized this, Hanrai frowned and sighed. His next movement brought him so swiftly into the Traveler's range that they could only duck away from their master's slashing blade. They tried and failed to gain more distance; Hanrai was relentless, even as with the black current, the Traveler tore up a flat stone of ornamental rock and hurled it into his side.

Only the Ronin stopped him, and then only for a moment. Hanrai deflected the blaster bolt fired his way as easily as anything, and he didn't wait for the next. Where before he had been the lake untouched, now he was the rapids unyielding.

Still, the Ronin saw no malice in Hanrai. No anger, no heat, no sign of what had changed—except that his student had dared raise a hand against him. Yet where the Traveler's evasions grew increasingly frenetic, Hanrai studied them with a tenderness that belied the ferocity of his bladework.

"You're afraid, aren't you?" Hanrai said as his blade bore down on the Traveler's head, shoved aside at the last second by the Ronin's lunge. "What did you think you would end with my death? What made you want to kill me?"

The Traveler refused to answer. They only flitted away, up onto a boulder in a pond meant to evoke a mountain in a sea, where they stayed, uneasy and unarmed. They needed to let go of that damn cat. They needed to *fight*.

"I don't ask to be cruel," Hanrai called after them. "I want to understand. You owe me as much, don't you?"

"You're owed nothing but death," the Ronin snarled as his blade once more ground against Hanrai's. "For every death *you* demanded."

Something in Hanrai changed. He was resigned as he retracted his blue blade, and as he dodged back, away. He escaped bisection barely, and nearly tipped himself off the terrace. Then he stood still. He waited.

The Ronin advanced. "You Jedi, you lords—hungry for every war, so ready to reap each other's children as eagerly as you send your own to be reaped. Never daring to dream of a world where we didn't bleed for you. Kill for you. Die for you."

He was aware, faintly, of the Traveler holding terribly still on their boulder, where they stood and they watched and did *nothing*.

"And for this you kill me?" Hanrai asked. His lightsaber remained unlit in his hands. "Ironic."

"You earned it."

"And my ship? I am a commander. I deserve the responsibility you lay at my feet. But my crew? My apprentices? You've killed them too."

Yes, some part of the Ronin wished to say. Yes, I've killed them. I've killed others also. Do you think I dare regret it?

No matter that he had never fallen to his knees and sworn his blade to Hanrai, he was as much Hanrai's creature as any child carved in the image of a Jedi. A murderer, and a self-serving one at that. The best the Ronin had ever done was run from the blood he spilled. But he had not run far or fast enough to escape it.

The Ronin let out a shaking, cowardly breath and readied his stance a final time. How foolish he was to want clarity. The clearest vision he had ever known had shown him his own true image, and he had hated that so much he had done everything in his power to destroy it. He faced that image again now. So, he would cut it down as he had before, even as his fingers twitched on his blade grip, furious and afraid.

He would kill Hanrai, or he would not. If he failed, he would die. After that, he would have no burdens left to bear. Unless she took him for her own as well.

Perhaps that was the thought that unmoored him. Or perhaps he should never have imagined his death at all. Or perhaps it was simply error, that old costly friend—and it cost him dear, this time.

The Ronin swung and Hanrai did not. The Jedi lord ducked down and to the side and spun—and skewered. The Jedi's blade was unerringly precise and needed to strike only once. It punctured one of the Ronin's hands, then the next, as well as the hilt held between them. The Ronin's red blade sputtered and died as the blue burned through his flesh.

Rather than tear his lightsaber through the Ronin's palms—it was what a Sith would have done—Hanrai retracted the blade. The Ronin was left with two black holes in his hands that felt like fire and like nothing at all. They trembled as the hilt of his broken lightsaber slipped from between them.

He needed to move. Perversely, he didn't want to. From the corner of his eye he saw Hanrai frowning, brow furrowed. As if he hadn't thought he would get away with this maneuver. Nevertheless, he swung again, a killing chop. His blade cut into the Ronin's side.

It didn't get quite far enough.

There was, as there had been in that dank temple beneath the waterfall, a third lightsaber, unaccounted for. This one proved winter-white and volatile. The blade protruded from Hanrai's chest, much as the Ronin's had when he killed the Sith bandit.

Hanrai, though, was already dead. Nevertheless, when the lightsaber retracted, he fell to his knees. The Traveler stood behind him, the hilt of their blade clutched in a rigid hand.

The Ronin remained upright, somehow. His breath came ever more truncated. His knees shook. But, oh, he still wanted to see Hanrai die. He couldn't let himself go until he had.

"Admirable as ever," Hanrai croaked as the Traveler came around his side.

"Oh, you'll get over it." They stooped to take their old master's lightsaber, which had clattered to the lord's side. "Aren't you supposed to let us go? If *she's* calling for us."

Hanrai's expression, taut with varied pains, defied interpretation. "You would know."

STAR WARS: VISIONS: RONIN

The Traveler balked as they straightened. Their face was also drawn—conflicted, confused.

Hanrai looked far too kindly on them. "You're right. You should leave."

The Traveler couldn't look at him straight. "I didn't want this for you."

"That you wanted anything for me . . ."

They turned from their teacher and said nothing more. Instead, they went to the Ronin, who wavered as they touched his arm, his side. Their distress was plain. It anchored him. Even as it shamed him, he wanted it to. So he relented to the touch and to the aid they provided as they pulled one of his arms about their narrow shoulders.

Cat on their heels, the Traveler led the Ronin away, free arm looped around his waist, gingerly below where he had been cut. Their eyes were fixed forward. Only the Ronin turned back.

Hanrai stared forward also, following their escape off the terrace and into the snarling, shaking halls. He remained on his knees, his fists clenched over them. The hole in his chest was so fine and precise that with each stumbling step, it grew more possible to imagine its absence.

CHAPTER
TWENTY-NINE

T HE REVERENT NO longer needed help in order to die. No lone entity could reverse the disaster. The Ronin had designed it to transcend the singular, so it did. Now he, singular within it, couldn't even envision the entirety of the failure.

Not even his companion's unique facility with the black current could do much but save them time. As they passed through each new chamber, the Traveler felt along the *Reverent*'s trembling hull and urged it to hold, just until they had left—until they could find somewhere else to breathe.

The Ronin knew this because they murmured each request, plea, and gratitude aloud as they dragged a half-dead man down groaning corridors and begged a frightened cat to follow.

They were headed starboard, the Ronin suspected. Toward one of the *Reverent*'s private shuttle bays, perhaps. An escape pod, more likely, if any remained. Either way, toward something the Traveler expected to be there. They knew this ship—or if not this one, then another like it. Another model, another time.

"Where were you, during the war?" the Ronin rasped.

The Traveler looked up at him but briefly. They obscured their feelings with their demeanor and with the black current, in which they were still that glancing fish in clouded night. But they had lost their mask at some point between the moment when the Ronin first killed Hanrai and the moment when they finished the job. More significantly, they could no longer hide from the Ronin very well. He had seen too much of them, both in the days they had spent playing at camaraderie, and now, as together they stumbled through the wreckage of the life the Traveler had left behind. They couldn't conceal the line of exhaustion in their frown or the urgent fear in their silence.

"Shouldn't you keep me engaged?" the Ronin wheezed. "I'm an ailing patient."

"We could play shogi. Fourth foot soldier one forward."

"Boring."

"Brat." The Traveler persuaded a door to open and hauled him through, beckoning the cat after. "Which war? The lords never really laid down arms, you realize—they just kill each other rather more subtly these days."

"The war that mattered."

"To *you*."

"I'm greedy."

The Traveler was silent for a while longer as they brought the Ronin to a bulkhead and urged him to lean against it. He was soon compelled to slide down and sit on the floor. He felt pain, somewhat, in the moments where his body moved, but so long as he could be still, he was only tired—tired, and fading.

It was indeed greedy to want their attention. The Traveler was expending so much on ensuring the *Reverent*'s hull didn't collapse in upon them both, which would end their escape attempt with alarming alacrity.

The problem was that the Ronin had become quite dizzy. And the voice, she was still silent.

"Derelict in my duties," the Traveler said, a light in a fog. "That's where I was."

"You?" he mused.

They clucked. "I got over it, clearly."

"Did you kill any of us? Any Sith."

A silence. He was so nervous that he ached.

"No," they said.

"Why not?"

"You sound offended."

He couldn't keep track of what they were doing. They stood beside him, the slow-blinking cat at their heels, their attention on some manner of console; they swallowed their anxiety. They didn't want him frightened. As if he was a man who knew fear, outside fear of himself.

He welcomed death. At least, he had when he thought all that awaited him was an oblivion of self and consequence. Now he had to wonder whether she would let him rest. She had leashed so many already. Would she make him a demon as well? Or did she only want him dead? It was all too easy to imagine that she would want nothing to do with his ghost.

Still the voice did not respond. He was left alone with the world, which was just him, his frayed and fraying body, and somehow, for some reason, someone else. One who refused to abandon him. A fellow traveler on the road.

He wished he could simply be grateful for their persistence. But an unwelcome thought throbbed in his temples alongside the pain—a thought that had been planted by Hanrai as they played in his garden, and that the Ronin had hoped to tear out and burn.

If indeed all those years ago the lord had given the kyber shard he found on Dekien to his student, and if indeed they had taken it and vanished in their pursuit of Rei'izu . . . Well. Perhaps the Traveler no longer had it. Perhaps the shard had been lost, or discarded. But it had been theirs, once, to carry and use, and they had known its provenance.

Why, then, had the Traveler said nothing of this history? Why had they pretended the lot—Dekien, Seikara, the shard itself—that any of it was some remarkable revelation the Ronin had led them to?

The shape of the answer was not a mystery, yet it was loathsome, and worse, it was familiar. They were a liar, yes. He'd known this. He did not yet know why. He dreaded to. But he needed to.

"You're doing a great deal to keep me alive," he said, his blackened and useless hands heavy in his lap. "I no longer understand your motive."

"Whatever does that mean?"

"You know how to kill."

It was likely cruel to say. He had seen them shy from every violence. Had at the same time seen them deftly wield the black current of the Force and turn it on bodies or turn bodies with it. But he had also seen their fear of ripping flesh and breaking bodies—a fear that had apparently come from knowing they could do it.

Hanrai had called them close. Trusted. Perhaps he had taught them to tell stories. He had not taught them the flute. What else he had taught the Traveler was evident in the clean speed of Hanrai's death, once they had committed to it.

So, murder. For the Traveler, it had never been a matter of whether they could but whether they would—and until minutes ago, they wouldn't. Now they would and had. Hanrai was dead by their own blade. What need had they, then, of a regrettable old man with ruined hands?

"It can't be so hard to fathom," said the Traveler. "I asked for a death. That doesn't mean I want to get my own hands dirty with it."

"Don't." The Ronin realized he had asked the question incorrectly. He hadn't quite realized what he wanted from them. Now he understood.

He needed *to* be needed. Need had once cut through every complication that haunted him. The need of his fellows to be protected, his need to serve them—these had distilled a world too wretchedly large and complex to be understood in any meaningful amount. They had made living bearable, and they had made his life a worthy one.

"Tell me," he said. "Why me?" Why did they mean to keep him? Why was he still alive?

"I'm sorry," they said without looking at him, and then they said more, each confession a stone falling down a hill. "I'm sorry. I tried to finish her. I couldn't. I wish I could have. It's hateful to ask this of you instead. But—it must be you. You have to face her. You."

The Ronin held himself painfully upright, each breath a sharpness as he strove to listen. He wished to catch these stones, and for one to feel rightly weighty. But each fell past him—through him—tumbling away.

Faintly he heard the sound of a door sliding open, and he thought he was picked up again, dragged through the door, and set down upon a bench seat. He might have imagined it. He was too fixed on a problem to pay proper attention.

He had begged for an answer, and the Traveler had at last given him one, even as it pained them to be so honest. They had declared him imperative.

Yet it didn't satisfy. He was required. Why wasn't that enough?

A hand brushed his forehead, palm too soft for bladework, fingers callused with bad flutework. It didn't keep him from falling into a deep, dark, well of unbeing.

CHAPTER
THIRTY

THE RONIN WOKE first in a clouded half-light. He lay limp, as if he had been broken on a desolate, forever field of other shattered things. Impossible shapes hovered over and beside him, impossible because they were whole and familiar, and because if they were who he thought, they could not be whole, and because they would never look down on him without also killing him. He did not yet feel dead.

He woke again in the prickling light of a room he was sure he should have recognized. It had the look of a sick room and smelled like one too—antiseptic layered over blood and sweat. The bacta patch taped to his side itched. The respirator affixed to his prosthetic covered his face from his nose down to his jaw. The bandages wound about both his hands left him at a remove from the world.

He tentatively pressed his palms together. They seemed whole. He could move his fingers, though they were by turns stiff and numb. When he tried to lift himself from the bed, his muscles shook as if untested and new.

He had been healed, but only to an extent. His saviors were pressed for resources. Or they had reason to keep him weak.

Either way, no reason to wait. He forced himself to standing with a hand on the wall—ignoring the twinge in his side and the tightness in his chest. The touch anchored him to the ship, and the ship would tell him all that was worth knowing.

His mind remained stubbornly fogged. No matter how he tried to sort the sensation of pulsing ship from his gasping body, he could not delineate them, so he could not *understand*. He required focus, insight—

The door slid open. A figure stood on the other side, slender and tall, accentuated by her booted heels and the black cloak slung about her shoulders. The Sith bandit looked much as she had the day they met, her eyes flint-sharp and her mouth twisted even more sharply—as if in invitation.

The Ronin moved first; it was the only way he could expect to live. He threw himself at her. Even weak, he was the larger between them, and at times bulk accomplished what finesse never could.

She did as he expected, maneuvered to the side and swept his legs out from under him. In this narrow space there was no avoiding her. Neither could she avoid him.

His hand flashed forward. With a twist of black current, the lightsaber hilt she had stolen from him on Genbara, which she had bound to her waist, was jerked away and clapped into his palm. His grip trembled, but he clutched the leather-bound hilt tight to his chest as he hit the deck and rolled back up behind her, lunging through the door into the corridor beyond.

She lunged after, grasping. Not down for the lightsaber, which he protected. Up. Toward his face. Her fingers latched under the edge of the respirator before she tore it off, prosthetic and all. She got skin in the process, but the stinging tear hurt no more than any other part of his body.

No matter. He still stood, and he breathed—long and rattling, but certain he could—and got three steps into the dim corridor before he staggered.

The bandit followed, prosthetic in hand. He eyed her warily over his shoulder, lightsaber clutched in numb fingers. He would not escape by running.

No sooner did the thought occur than he wavered in place—oxygen deprivation impeded rational thought, he recalled—and sank against the bulkhead, gasping deeper, the shuddering now in his chest. Still she came forward. He ignited his lightsaber and the point wavered between them.

His vision had too far clouded to properly see her face. He knew only that the crooked slant of her mouth was not fear. He recognized the expression—had seen it before, on those whose ire he had earned with murder. Disgust.

An electronic snarl cut short the thought. His vision swam as a familiar shape skidded around the corner and banked toward them. The bandit jerked aside as B5-56 shoved past her, and she hissed as the droid tore the prosthetic from her hand.

Saved, thought the Ronin—until B5 zapped his palm and his lightsaber tumbled from his twitching fingers. B5 caught it with an articulated arm and snarled again. Injured, the droid called him, and an idiot.

The Ronin opened his mouth to snarl back. So he was injured. What of it? He had to—

He coughed, racking, and slid farther down the wall as he wheezed.

B5 shoved the prosthetic into his hand. The Ronin groped it and attached the respirator onto his face. The prosthetic was new, he realized through a bleary haze. It fit more rightly to his jaw. He couldn't imagine where it had come from.

The too-short breaths continued for an unbearable minute as the bandit came to stand over him. She looked about to snatch his lightsaber from B5 until the droid disappeared the elegant hilt into an interior compartment, blatting irritably at her. She had done good work on the repair, he realized as the blade vanished from view. It looked just like it had.

"And they thought *I* would be the problem," the bandit muttered.

"Are you not?" the Ronin rasped, still clasping the respirator to his face.

B5 prodded his knee and murmured a scold.

"What children?"

Too late. The corridor had other doors; two were already half open.

Young people stood nearly out of them—young, but too old to want to be "children" in anyone's eyes. The Ronin recognized them not by their robes, for they had changed into borrowed clothing, but by the way they held themselves. Watchful and edged, ever ready to become sword or shield. Jedi apprentices.

The bandit turned to the lot. "You're not useful here," she said. "Go to sleep."

"We're not sleeping," said one—a Twi'lek boy. The Ronin knew him. His guard from the *Reverent*. When the boy met the Ronin's eye, he held an arm in front of the other children.

"Then go run laps in the cargo bay." The bandit gestured the boy away. "I don't care!"

Two of the Jedi apprentices peeled out of the bunks and flitted away. The rest clustered together in the Twi'lek boy's room and watched warily as the bandit hauled the Ronin upright.

Instinct told him to shed her, but his body disagreed, and he was brought to standing without true resistance.

"So you aren't going to kill me," said the Ronin.

The bandit scoffed. "I will. When you're worth killing."

B5 had found the escape pod. Even now, Ekiya couldn't rightly explain why she'd agreed to rescue it with the *Poor Crow*.

No, she could explain. She just didn't like it. As much as she might've been able to live with Grim bleeding out in the cold of space, she couldn't forsake Fox—not even after they'd crawled through her head and rearranged the furniture to their liking.

When she welcomed them aboard, they'd had the audacity to look relieved.

"Please," she'd said, "*you're* helping *me*—I need you to make sure Chie isn't whipping those Jedi kids up into a mutiny."

The apprentices had had every reason to mistrust the denizens of the *Poor Crow* even before Ekiya invited the man who'd destroyed the *Reverent* onto it. Sure, they knew Kouru as their savior, but it was plainly apparent that they also recognized her from Jedi reports on the catastrophe in the Seikara Caverns. Also, Chie was a snitch, and she answered every question they thought to ask, no matter how it damned the ship's other passengers.

Chie additionally swore up and down that she'd told the kids they shouldn't let the Empire know about Kouru being on the *Crow*—let alone about Grim, now that he was on it too. But Chie had sworn all sorts of things before she threw herself and Fox off that bridge in Seikara. Ekiya couldn't blithely take her word on anything, not anymore.

Frankly, she couldn't take Fox at their word either. But the second Fox stepped off the escape pod, that whining old tooka-cat hefted in one arm, they'd extended their other hand to offer her a box.

It was a little thing. Fit in her palm, all polished geometric slats intricately joined together. It was also extremely locked, and Fox warned her to leave it that way. Grim would open it, they said, when he came around. Until then, they thought it should be hers, for safekeeping.

She hadn't needed to ask what was in it. The box held her ghosts. She just *knew* it. Maybe she remembered the kyber from all that time she'd spent sheltering it in her cargo hold, or maybe it remembered her. As for the houses that had protected the shards, those lovely lanterns, combs, and charms within which they'd been nestled . . . Gone.

Of course the Jedi had never meant to return the relics to Rei'izu's refugees. Ekiya had been foolish to think they'd let precious kyber slip from their grasp. They'd broken down her ghosts into the parts they cared about, and now the remains of the relics were as scattered and lost as the rest of the *Reverent*.

Ekiya stared queasily out the *Crow*'s cockpit window at the debris of Lord Hanrai's great flagship. Scout vessels and other small craft darted through the *Reverent*'s ruins. The ships searched for survivors and for salvage. Glinting flies on a shining corpse.

The box weighed so very little as Ekiya clutched it to her chest. She had to be happy that anything at all had been saved. She had to.

No matter what remained to be rescued from the *Reverent*, over the past hour, the number of scavengers had steadily decreased. Fewer prizes to be won, yes, but also, the dead giant's still-living siblings would soon descend. More Dreadnoughts, and lords, and Jedi.

Every HoloNet channel promised the same threat in a different dress. Reports melted into each other as Chie combed through them from her seat in front of the communications console.

"Moments ago, the Crown Prince issued a proclamation through the prime Imperial channel denouncing—"

"A competing missive from the Second Prince, declaring the incident a horrendous attack perpetrated by none other than—"

"A joint statement released by the lords representing the Mid-Rim Alliance, pledging to send a full contingent of Jedi to Dekien and eliminate this threat once and—"

On and on. Both princes, half a dozen lords, all delivering grave pronouncements on the clear act of Sith aggression that had sealed the fate of Lord Hanrai.

None of it mattered. All they'd ever needed was an excuse to mobilize. The only question was whether it would be days or hours before they started shooting one another under the guise of rooting out the Sith.

"Do you have to?" Ekiya asked. "What are we going to learn on the news that we didn't figure out firsthand?"

"The news isn't for facts, dear," said Chie. "It's for feelings. It's to our benefit to know how the people feel—and how they've been told to."

"Pretty not great, by my guess."

Chie gave her a look that was probably supposed to be reassuring. "You're angry with me."

"Aunty, please. I can't be mad at you! If I were mad at you, I'd want you off my ship, and if you were off my ship, you'd go rat us out to the Jedi, which would nix our very last chance to solve this witchy demon problem—which is, if you remember, *also* on my ship now—and that would just ruin my otherwise wonderful day."

Chie had a new look, exasperation, and the beginning of what might have been an apology. Frankly, Ekiya didn't think she could take it.

Thankfully, before Chie could say anything, Kouru pinged them on the internal comms from Grim's bunk.

"The old man's awake," she said. "What do I . . . *do* with him?"

Ekiya opened her mouth and balked, hands once more clasped

tightly around the puzzle box. She knew the plan as far as she had to. Hand the box to Grim, let him open the damn thing and find the crystal they'd dragged themselves all the way to Dekien to find—a crystal that Fox was really, terribly certain was inside it—and then, presumably, get the hell out of the Dekien system.

All Ekiya had to do was hand over the puzzle box . . . and forget that she'd just watched Grim shred an Imperial Dreadnought from the inside out while it was still packed to the brim with living, breathing beings. Not all of whom had escaped.

Chie took the lead. "I'll be right there," she told Kouru. To Ekiya she said, "Let's ensure he's truly awake and not simply lucid for the next half hour or so. If that box is as tricky as our Fox implies, we'll want him actually alert for it."

Despite herself, Ekiya was grateful as Chie left. She understood Chie was trying to give her time to come to terms. This was very Chie of her, and she had Ekiya's respect for it. Chie was also right about Grim. They needed him properly online if they were going to get their hands on his relic. That was at least part of why Ekiya had let him on the *Crow*. Why she'd helped Fox get him sorted into clothes that didn't have blood on them. Why she'd handed off the new prosthetic, even though he didn't deserve it—because it would have been awful of her to have it and hold it over his head.

It still sucked.

It *sucked,* but it was fine. It had to be. She had to be fine. Or she was going to fly the *Crow* straight into the scintillating Dekien sun and never look back.

Ekiya sat very still in the cockpit, staring at space, trying not to get too worked up about every little noise. Behind her, Chie passed through the galley. Fox spoke up; their cat yowled a complaint. A couple of the apprentices had joined them. Ekiya tried to tune it all out. Her mind kept latching onto words, but every one she heard made her heart beat faster with some sick, nameless fear.

Footsteps broke her focus. Ekiya rubbed the tension from her face and turned in her seat.

It was one of the apprentices. The Twi'lek kid—the ringleader, she'd surmised. Yuehiro. He looked cautious but determined, and he had a bowl with soup.

"Wash is that way," Ekiya said with a nod in the opposite direction.

"Okay." Yuehiro sat in the copilot's seat. "You should eat."

"I'll get to it."

Yuehiro didn't leave. Ekiya sighed under her breath and tucked the box away, then put her hands out for the bowl. The soup was simple—miso paste melted in dashi with rehydrated vegetables—but it was all right. Yuehiro remained, his eyes on the destruction of the grand vessel that had belonged to his lord, his brow increasingly furrowed.

"You kids freaked out?" Ekiya asked. "Don't be . . . Chie's got you."

"I don't think we're 'kids' anymore."

He sounded like one, though. "Just because you have to deal with this—" Ekiya caught herself short of what she really wanted to say and winced. "None of this means you're not a kid."

"Doesn't it?" Yuehiro studied the lights flickering over Dekien with a sense of focus that Ekiya couldn't fathom. His eyes darted from one point to the next, following the course of one ship, then another. His attention fixed on a rare point of blank space. Between one breath and the next, a sleek white Imperial frigate appeared, sliding into place like a knife between ribs as it dropped out of hyperspace. The first of many stabs to come. "Master Idzuna said the Sith made you fight, in the last war."

"*Master Idzuna's* being real free with my personal information."

Yuehiro didn't apologize, though he couldn't bring himself to look straight at her. "What do you think we should do?"

Ekiya snorted. "I seem qualified to answer that? I'm the least Jedi-adjacent person on this ship. Even Bee's more"—she gestured vaguely over her head—"than me."

Yuehiro's hands fisted over his knees and he looked, of all things, guilty. "That's why I'm asking. I think I understand what you're trying to do here. No one's said outright, but I saw the demons from Seikara. I read about more, in Lord—in Hanrai's private library." He steeled himself and bowed his head in her direction. "We want to help, all of us. We aren't the best. None of us were ever going to be knights. Didn't have the strength. Or the . . . temperament. But we're here. What can we do?"

"You what? Don't ask me that. What are you, twelve?"

"Fourteen," said Yuehiro, like that was any better. "How old were you when the Sith took you?"

"Shut up," said Ekiya, because she had also been fourteen. Yuehiro seemed to think this meant he had won, because he brightened. She clucked her tongue. "Don't start. Just—be alive, first and foremost. No one can guarantee your safety right now, all right? The *Crow*'s crawling with weirdos and I barely trust them to look out for themselves, let alone a bevy of infants."

Yuehiro looked no less pleased. Ekiya wanted briefly to shake him. Then her gaze settled on the bowl he'd brought her. It'd been a long time since anyone brought her food rather than the other way around. It shouldn't have been his responsibility.

"You *are* kids." She put a hand on Yuehiro's shoulder and met his eye. "That's not bad. You can still help. You think I can keep an eye on all the aforementioned weirdos all on my own? But I need you to put a little value on the fact that you're not the adults here, okay?"

His brow creased again, but he nodded.

Ekiya handed off the bowl and sent Yuehiro back to his peers. She told him where to find the *Crow*'s med supplies, on the off chance any of them needed something—she'd seen the way one of the shorter kids wheezed, and the way another favored his right leg, and when he asked hesitantly about hormones, she had one of Shogo's emergency stashes to share.

Then Ekiya pinged B5-56 on the comms. She was tired of being the only adult in the room.

CHAPTER
THIRTY-ONE

THE RONIN ATE the food put in front of him under the eye of the bandit and Chie. They likely meant to ensure he kept his hands to himself and the rice porridge. He couldn't begrudge them the suspicion, and he endeavored to ignore that of the two, he found Chie's presence more perturbing. He shouldn't have. And yet. She held herself with unusual confidence, given how many of the *Crow*'s other passengers she had recently attempted to kill or otherwise betray. The bandit, at least, maintained an edge.

Just as he finished, B5-56 swung by to announce that the lot of them were needed in the cockpit. The Ronin was hurried in that direction as quickly as his breathing would allow. They found Ekiya waiting and the Traveler already present, their cat anxiously twitching its tail at their feet.

At Ekiya's gesture, B5-56 closed the door and locked it. The Ronin frowned until Ekiya pushed the puzzle box into his hands. "You know what we need from this, right?" she asked.

He had been told. The *Crow* wanted for fuel, and the growing Imperial presence had made clear that they were tracking every vessel that dared to leave the Dekien system. Their crew had limited opportunities to flee; they would want to do so only once they could be certain of their escape. His relic—the kyber shard of Shinsui Temple—would, they hoped, win that for them. If anyone managed to tail the *Crow* to Rei'izu, they would ideally be too astonished to have stumbled upon the long-lost Imperial homeworld to pay much mind to their original quarry.

The Ronin said none of this, only nodded, as speaking so soon after walking seemed suddenly quite difficult.

"Good. Keep yourself busy. I don't really want to hear anything you have to say right now."

"That seems fair," he wheezed. The evidence of why she had every right to dismiss his opinion lay sprawled in space outside the *Crow*'s viewport: the wreckage of the *Reverent,* strewn across the Dekien system, and the growing fleet of Imperial vessels gathering around it.

Ekiya scowled. "Stop being reasonable. I don't like it when you're reasonable." To the others she said, "I *hate* it when he's more reasonable than the rest of you. We have to talk."

There were only two other seats. Chie took the one beside Ekiya's as if it was her right, and the Traveler took the last remaining because the bandit refused to.

Not "the bandit," he corrected himself. Kouru, the others called her. No matter what she had been—a warrior, a thief, a demon—he'd had no small part in shaping the woman she had become. Moreover, he had killed her and not enjoyed it. At the end of all things, he owed her the dignity of a name.

Kouru scowled at him from her place by the door, as if she could hear his thoughts. Her glare told him to stuff his opinions away somewhere she'd not have to suspect they existed.

"What's happened?" asked the Traveler. They spoke lightly as ever, but the black pool that was their presence in the Force rippled uncontrollably, even when their cat slunk up from the floor to settle in their lap. What could anyone expect? They had just killed their master.

They glanced at him for a moment, and there was an urge in the Ronin's chest to speak. He didn't know what words to offer, and in any case had been asked to keep them to himself. He returned to the puzzle box.

"That's the problem, isn't it?" Ekiya waved out the window. "*Everything's* happened. Are we even on the same page anymore? I feel like we aren't."

Kouru's look was oddly troubled, for someone who had never been their ally. The Ronin admittedly struggled to understand her presence on the *Crow*, outside of the fact that she likely also didn't wish to be caught by the Jedi.

Conversely, Chie tilted her head, intrigued.

"My intentions haven't changed," said the Traveler.

"Have yours, Ekiya?" asked Chie.

Ekiya raised her chin. "You first."

Chie unhurriedly sipped tea from a thermos. "I don't know that I'd say anything's *changed*. More that my opinions have been made more clear. But if you're suggesting I have an opportunity to sway *yours* . . ."

"Chie, really?" the Traveler asked. "I thought we discussed this."

"I think you'll find I thought the discussion tabled while we were prioritizing survival. But if we're questioning our commitment to running to Rei'izu . . ."

"Why*ever* would we do that?"

She looked at them with the sympathetic air of an aunty addressing an underemployed young person. "It puts you in the position of relying on those who you might not otherwise wish to."

"That sounds nearly accusatory."

"Oh, it is. I wouldn't go so far as to blame *you* for the initiation of open aggression, but I wouldn't say your choice in allies helped us avoid it."

Her implication was clear. The Traveler might not have rent apart the *Reverent*, but it would have been in fewer pieces if they'd left the Ronin to his misbegotten devices in a far corner of the galaxy.

"Don't be a fool," Kouru snapped. She waved her hand at the glittering carcass floating outside the viewport. "Your lords wanted war either way. This is an excuse, not a cause."

"I wouldn't delineate so cleanly," said Chie.

"You blame easily enough."

"Well, I'd like us to take some responsibility."

"Take responsibility?" Ekiya snorted. "Is that what you thought you were doing when you threw in with the Jedi? You know what we're dealing with. You've seen the demons. And still you helped them track us down."

Chie met her glare with unflappable equanimity. "Are you so sure I chose wrongly?"

"Yes," said Ekiya. But she descended into an icy silence that complicated her claim. She questioned herself, and likely more than that. It would be hard not to doubt, with the consequence of her allegiances scattered in the space between her and Dekien.

The Traveler let out a sound that might have been a laugh, in brighter contexts. "If you had doubts, Chie, I wish you'd told them to me."

"I didn't doubt you." Chie raised a hand at their chiding frown. "Ekiya's right. I've seen what I've seen. More than any of you have, I expect. Hanrai showed me his reports. Jedi dead and missing. Your Sith witch is hard at work, reaping her puppets. And to what end?"

"Yet you prioritized politics?" The Traveler could no longer keep the strain from their voice. "Chie, what do you imagine happens to the galaxy once Jedi start killing one another in earnest? When the witch has her pick of their ghosts?"

Chie reached over to touch the Traveler's knee, more gently than they seemed to expect. For his part, the Ronin tensed in his seat, yet unwilling to trust her intent. But Chie spoke gently as well. "I understand your fear, Idzuna. I feel it too. But in all my life, I've never heard of a war stopped by a single action, no matter how large."

"No?" said the Ronin.

Every eye turned to him, and he returned to the puzzle box. It was a brazen thing, to remind them of what he had done to stop the last war. It was, from a certain point of view, ironic that he had started the next in much the same way.

"I suppose we shouldn't be surprised if the dark lord still thinks in such simplistic terms," said Chie.

"Don't flatter him with a title," Kouru snapped. "He's no lord of mine."

"He's what?" said Ekiya. She sounded oddly flat. The Ronin would have expected more anger. Perhaps she couldn't summon any more of that, given the depth of loathing she already harbored for him. Her searching eye had shifted to the Traveler. "Did you know?"

Their wince gave the lie to their words. "I don't know that I'd claim I was sure. I suspected. There were indications. Suggestions—"

They broke off because it seemed Ekiya was about to shout at them. Instead, she sank back into her seat, hand to her brow.

The Ronin found himself frowning as well. It had occurred to him that the Traveler might know him for who he had been; they knew so many stories, for one, and they were Hanrai's pupil, for another. But something of their expression now, the disquiet of it, aroused an unnameable suspicion within him.

"Idzuna," said Chie. Did she see how they flinched whenever she said that name? A twitch in their hand was echoed in the flicker of white flare hidden beneath their current. "I won't ask you to abandon those you pity. This man, this woman. We'll tend them as we must—not least to ensure they don't hurt anyone else. But you must see you're chasing a fantasy. The princes won't lay down arms in exchange for a dead Sith's head, no matter how she frightened them. Our work is *here*."

"It isn't," the Traveler insisted. "This isn't princes and lords, Chie, it's more—it's worse."

Kouru scoffed. "Nothing's worse than princes."

"Jedi," suggested the Ronin.

"Sith," said Chie.

"Stop it," Ekiya barked. "None of you *helped*."

The Traveler winced. "Ekiya—"

"No, shut up. You're the worst one." Ekiya stood, hands pressed down hard on the console, refusing to look at them. "Damnit, this is why we had to talk. You've had us hunting the witch ever since we met—not that you ever said a word about how you knew she was around to be hunted. I figured, whatever, you're a Jedi or something. Have to be. But you don't want to talk about it because you don't like Jedi any more than we do. Fine."

Ekiya's hands curled into fists. "But you never said anything about the Jedi lord breathing down your neck. Never warned us. Not a word.

No wonder Chie threw in with him the second he offered her a gram of truth—not that I'm letting you off the hook, Aunty, I'm just saying that I get it!" Finally she turned, only to gesture at the Ronin. "And after you picked up the murder-happy *dark lord himself*—offense intended, Grim—"

"Offense warranted," he agreed.

She made a face, then remembered she now despised him and looked quite sick of him and of herself. She looked away. "Fox, listen to me. I put everything on the line for this. For you. But how am I supposed to trust you? How am I supposed to think you're right?"

"I confess I hoped the air of mysticism would allay some of these concerns," said the Traveler.

"No," said the Ronin, and as he did, he opened the box.

The crew was for a second time silent as they stared at the bounty he unveiled. The box fit within his palm, but it brimmed with crystals. They shone with refracting light that swam in many colors across their faces and the glass. The reds he had long been collecting, accompanied by blues and greens he didn't recognize, and a colorless multitude that had once been lodged in the artifacts Ekiya ferried in the *Crow*.

The Ronin selected a clear crystal from the lot and turned it between his fingers before replacing it and choosing another. The others watched him in a state caught between wonder and terror. He placed the second crystal back into the box as well.

"You never said what happened to the shard you found on Dekien," he said, and he looked the Traveler in the eye. They shifted warily under his gaze, as if they expected a skewering thrust. "In any case, it isn't here. We're unlikely to solve your problem unless you give us a little more truth."

They drew back in their seat. If they meant to run, the Ronin couldn't stop them. He was too weak, and no matter how the crew mistrusted the Traveler, they would never choose helping him over protecting them. So he did all he could. He begged. "Please. I need an answer too."

The Traveler's mouth opened, closed. When they smiled, he feared he had lost. But at last they spoke, and their confession chilled. "Well. The trouble is, I don't recall."

* * *

What do I remember? Oh, you know. The important things. My favorite tea. How to pray. Arithmetic, sort of. Everything else, well. It comes and goes.

The kyber shard, that's stayed with me. A sliver, winter sky—clear but for where it was split down the middle by a hairline fracture that clouded its center. Lovely little thing. Entrusted to me so that it would guide the way to some dire Sith threat.

That's where it gets a bit, how shall I put it? Imprecise. I remember the shard. I remember the need. And I remember Rei'izu.

I did try to kill her—the witch. I know I did. I feel it in my fingers and my chest. Because I failed. Faltered. I can't tell you why now. I had killed before, even when it hurt to.

To wit: I didn't. So what next for the lacking Jedi? I don't know. But I didn't leave. For years, I think. Can you imagine? I wonder if I knew the way out. I wonder if I ignored it.

The things that stick, you see, they're sweet, in part. Firelight. A scene out a window of a courtyard hung in winter chill. A kind of desolation in the silence. Yet it broke, now and again, and I was glad for the sound. Laughter, I think, or a song. Some speck of hope, buried under frost.

The rest, though . . . Fear. My own, I think? Perhaps in part. An anger, pained and grieving. Loss and sorrow, coalescing, calcifying. It hurt to be near. Still I didn't leave. It makes me think I couldn't.

How did I, then? Oh, who knows. I'd like to think it was something I did. That I found the key, or decided it was time, or that perhaps I asked to. But I don't expect that's the case.

I remember a fight. Drawing blood and bleeding. And I remember the world breaking until it changed—and then I was free. Maybe.

I believe she thought me dead. I can't imagine why else she would release me. I was back in the world, but no longer of it. By which I mean I no longer fit into the hole I'd left behind. I feared returning to that life because I had failed, and because . . .

No, there's nothing else I can say that I'm sure is the truth. And if it's truth you want from me, we'll have to end it here.

CHAPTER
THIRTY-TWO

"BUT CAN YOU really take me seriously?" asked Fox as they stroked their cat's twitching ear. "Who can say why I know what I do and why I've forgotten what I don't? Perhaps I'm riddled with holes rent by the black current. Or perhaps I'm merely traumatized. Either way, hardly the reliable sort."

They sounded sickeningly calm. Kouru searched them for some sign of distress, even discomfort. Nothing. She couldn't tear her eyes away, even as she dearly wished to be looking at anything else.

For all she loathed their willingness to poke holes in others' minds, they had been cored in the same way. They were architect and edifice of the same rotten art. It made them eerie and pitiful.

Again, she heard the echo of the witch: Let go, let go. What had the witch made Fox relinquish as she scraped them clean?

Kouru needed to know. She thought, likely foolishly, that knowing would enable her to protect herself. She could more ably protect that which she knew had to be defended.

Doubt tugged at her chest as she crossed her arms in front of it. How could she be sure she hadn't already lost whatever it was the witch wished to take? The voice had been so terribly silent of late.

"But why didn't you *say* anything?" Ekiya demanded. She was all sympathy now, her fury diluted by another's suffering.

Fox looked contemplatively upward. "Shame? Paranoia? Some other offshoot of a mind derailed? None of the above. I don't know. I think it never occurred." They laughed. "That's a little horrifying, isn't it? You should probably throw *me* in the gunner pit."

"We should what in the what?" said Ekiya.

Kouru cursed and turned on her heel, secretly thankful for the distraction.

At first, Kouru intended to kill the Jedi and be done with it. Ekiya wouldn't hear of it.

"You think I want another demon on my ship?" she said. "One of you's bad enough."

"He doesn't have to stay on your ship," said Kouru.

She was misinterpreted. Kouru would have as soon stabbed the man and sent him tumbling out the *Crow*'s air lock. Instead, the crew went through the assiduous process of dragging the old man into the escape pod still affixed to the *Crow*'s abdomen so he could rewire its comms and navigation. He would ensure that the Jedi would land safely on Dekien but be unable to communicate until he did—by which point they would need to be out of the system anyway, or they would already have lost.

In the meantime, Kouru and Ekiya went to stand watch over the gunner pit as Chie made for the cargo bay.

"I expect the children know about him already," Chie said with a sigh. "We'll want to convince them he isn't worth saving."

How that negotiation went, Kouru couldn't imagine. Jedi spawn were by turns proud and fearful. She could see why either variety might think a true Jedi their savior when in the company of Sith and traitors.

But she and Ekiya weren't far from the cargo bay, and they'd heard less than a peep from it, so either the children had killed Chie quietly, or the old woman had miraculously brought them to order.

Or she had promised them an alternative murder. If so, she hadn't yet struck any of the most likely targets—namely Kouru, the old man, and Fox. Kouru still sensed both the old man's simmering flare on one side of the ship and Fox's silvery shadow on the other.

She found herself eyeing Fox especially, nearly to the point of losing focus on the gunner pit's soldered hatch. They remained in the galley where they had been left with the puzzle box and the kyber when everyone else went to be useful.

"I thought you said the shard wasn't in here," they had said as the old man dropped the box in their hands.

"Your master said he gave it to you," the old man had replied. "Did he lie?"

There. That had been when Kouru saw the first and only crack in their demeanor. The question split Fox's smile for a single breath, as if they had been cut then forgotten the injury. "He wasn't in the habit," they said, and surrendered.

Kouru had detected no disruption in them since. Granted, she had limited facility in reading such things. A weakness, if her masters were to be believed, though she had always preferred to judge those she faced by their words and posture over the subtleties of their presence in the Force. Fox gave her little to work with either way, yet she studied them with an obsession she wished herself rid of.

If only she could name what it was she saw in them—and what she wanted to see. She knew in part that she was haunted by the offer they'd extended, and the questions they had asked. At the time, she had thought them a busybody and a sophist, driven by guilt or some other sickness. Now she understood the legitimacy with which they could claim familiarity with her condition.

In all that time they'd spent on Rei'izu, trapped with the witch, they must have seen someone like Kouru. Dozens, even. Must have . . .

Ekiya nudged Kouru's side. Pompous little B5-56 had arrived to tell them the escape pod was ready.

They extracted the Jedi with only a little difficulty—he was still unconscious, but Ekiya insisted on doing most of the extracting herself. "You'd just drop him again. Like he needs another head injury."

"I was going to break his legs," said Kouru.

More accurately, one arm and one leg. If you for some reason wanted a Jedi alive, you did your best to debilitate them physically, or to keep them in enough pain to ruin their focus.

"You're thinking something awful," said Ekiya as they hoisted the man down the corridor.

Kouru snorted. "I'm thinking you worry too much."

"About the Jedi knight who's been stewing in my ship without me knowing about it? Sure. Too much worrying, that's my problem."

"It is. Or you would have let me solve it already."

Ekiya glowered.

Kouru scowled back. "You're never satisfied. We're doing it your way. What more do you want?"

To her surprise, Ekiya sighed heavily as if in apology. "I don't know. For Fox to be an actual creep. For Grim to be more hateful. For Chie to be wrong. For you to not be here. For me to have not been such an idiot with other people's dead . . . For none of this to have happened the way it did."

Kouru gave her a thoughtful look. "Those are some very pointless wishes."

"You're a real jerk, you know that?"

The old man dragged himself up from the floor as they approached the hatch where the escape pod was attached to the *Crow*.

"We could've gotten you a stool, Grim," Ekiya scolded.

The old man nodded as he left; Kouru suspected he wasn't listening. Sulking about his frailties, or about the half-truths of his supposed ally—or about the witch he didn't know how to reach and therefore couldn't kill. Kouru didn't know. She didn't want to. She wished it gave her more pleasure to see him so miserable. It simply didn't satisfy.

Ekiya lowered the Jedi onto the bench in the pod with a caution Kouru didn't share. "Hypocrite."

It took Kouru a moment to realize she'd been addressed. "What are you talking about?"

"Pointless wishes?" Ekiya tilted her head out the hatch in the direction the old man had gone. "I see the way you grimace at him. You don't even know if you want him dead. You're just mad."

The accusation struck Kouru in the sternum. It made real a thought she had until then known only as the sensation of dragging weight. Her lips peeled back. She meant to spit: Of course I want him dead. But so does the witch, and I'll deny her all that I can.

But other words vied for space in her mouth: Have you seen him? Pathetic. What's the point of killing a worm?

She would have been more pleased to see the old man roll over and simply *be* dead—for him to be a thing she no longer needed to know of.

Kouru bit her tongue and turned away. Pointless wishing, was it? If only she could be sure that any of her wishes were her own.

"Sorry," Ekiya said to her back.

This took Kouru by surprise as well. Neither could she understand. "For what?"

"Chie told me. She and the kids wouldn't have made it out without you. So—I don't know. You're clearly not the worst person I've ever met. I can't even say I think Grim dead is worse than Grim not-dead, galactically speaking. So can I really get on your case for that?"

Ekiya flopped onto the seat beside the unconscious Jedi and pulled the medkit out from under the bench, checking its contents. Most of it had been harvested to treat their own injured. She nevertheless surrendered two precious bacta patches out of her vest into the kit before tucking it away and meeting Kouru's apprehensive eye. She rubbed the back of her neck and looked away. "I just mean—I get that's not all you are. I don't want to be one thing either. I'm figuring it out."

Kouru could summon no response. She waited for Ekiya on the other side of the hatch, expecting a rejoinder—or an epiphany, wherein Ekiya realized she'd spoken nonsense to a dead woman. Neither came.

Kouru was forced to watch in silence as Ekiya keyed the launch sequence and sent the pod spiraling into Dekien's orbit.

Not all she was? Kouru couldn't name what else she might be, other than the frustration and the fury and the forward, forward, forward. She could barely suggest that any of that was *hers*. What else could she dream of as a demon—one whose existence hung on the whim of a witch whose will she dared to defy again and again?

Fox had put the question to her, as they flew down the *Reverent*'s throat: Who are you trying to be? Who *for*?

For all the witch had taken from Fox, they knew who and what they wanted to be. Kouru, though, had even less of an answer now than she'd had then.

Ekiya grimaced at the blinking comlink on her wrist. "Shogo's calling. Can't be good. Can I get you to keep an eye out from the gunner pit while I figure out what's about to come make itself our problem?"

Kouru agreed without argument, both because the task would give her time to think and because she far preferred the thought of doing something for Ekiya than the thought of doing it for anyone else, let alone her own untrustworthy self.

The Ronin knew it impolite to eavesdrop—that it was a thing not done among those with whom one shared scant space. Living in such quarters, one learned to hear and not listen, to let a certain portion of the things one knew remain ever unsaid.

He made an exception now because he wasn't about to bring up any of what he'd heard to Ekiya, to say nothing of Kouru. Instead, he took their words with him to the galley table where the Traveler worked. Their cat lay draped half on their lap, and it opened one yellow eye to watch the Ronin ease forward. The Traveler didn't look up and neither did they pour him a cup of tea. Their own sat untouched, their hands preoccupied by the cat and by the kyber.

"You're looming," said the Traveler. "Are you going to threaten me again?"

"I wouldn't like to."

"That isn't a no."

The Ronin creaked to the floor. "Why do you always have to make things difficult?"

"Would you believe it's chronic?"

As the Ronin poured himself tea—lukewarm, over-steeped—the Traveler continued the pretense of their work. They picked a crystal, dawn-blue, turned it over, ran their thumb along its length, and placed it on a patterned square of wrapping cloth before taking the next. One after another, each hue distinct, sun-red beside spring-green and cloud-white and so on.

The construction of a lightsaber was a project of patience, skill, and willingness to allow kyber to define its own purpose. A crystal could not be made to function outside its impulse—not to its most perfect ability. The blades crafted by the masters of old had been forged to suit not a single Jedi but a lineage, and to be exquisite unto themselves.

Small wonder the Jedi clans called the red of the Sith's stolen crystals a curse. The rebels had taken Jedi kyber to power their own blades, and in doing so perverted the crystals' purpose to serve their bloody ends.

The Ronin couldn't say if this was true. He had built tens of blades and never thought the kyber he used defiant, or terrified, or particularly much of anything—not until it fell into Sith hands and became the conduit of their need. This, so far as he had seen, was the moment it reddened—when the kyber attuned itself to a Sith wielder and chose to serve not lineage but a person, acutely singular. Blood indeed, but not a curse.

The next shard the Traveler took up was just such a red, deeply so, near to purple. One of those crystals stolen from a Jedi by the Sith in the years of their rebellion, until it had again been taken. The Ronin remembered it by the saber of the man he'd killed for it—a Sith who'd retreated to searing desert sands. The hilt had been a handsome artifact, for all the times it had been repaired and refashioned with horn and dyed leather.

"Do you know why I collected them?" the Ronin asked.

"I wouldn't presume to." The Traveler laid the crystal down with the rest. "You never said."

"I told you I went to Dekien to die."

They paused. "You didn't put it like that."

The Ronin inclined his head; they wouldn't meet his eye.

"You lived, though," they said.

"Yes. I found . . . direction."

"Not purpose?"

"Nothing so grand." The acridity of the tea flattened on his tongue. "I only knew myself wrong. I doubted that I'd ever done right."

The Traveler's hand closed, their mouth just open. He could almost hear their objection. That he had done some right, at some time—say, when he had forsaken his lord to protect his guardians, or when he had given a new home to Jedi children taken from their kin to be remade in the Empire's image. They wanted to call his intentions honorable, despite the consequences.

How had they, Jedi, come by such sympathy for the Sith? How much of their life had the witch taken, and how to interpret their kindness? How much of it was truly theirs?

No, that care couldn't have come from the witch. Nor was it some gift she had thought to send him. No matter that he had been her sword and shield for all the years she had in turn been his, nor that they had loved each other as much as either of them were capable, she had never been gentle, not with him. Whatever about the Traveler he doubted, he could trust this tender impulse was their own.

That was what made it possible to sit across from them now, even as it made him uneasy. He had known precious little kindness, often because he had eschewed it. It had rarely been afforded to him in his youth, and after that, he had not believed it his due. Even now, he felt a thief as he received it. It would have been easier to be angry with them, as he had been on the *Reverent* when he realized their deceptions. But what anger he felt now was nothing new, and it remained hot only in the deepest core of his being, where it had burned since his boyhood, and where it would continue to roar until he had rendered the last of himself to ash.

"When the witch took Rei'izu," said the Ronin, "I suspect that she did it in haste. To stop me from tearing the heart out of what I'd made, no matter what it cost her to do so. I can't say how she did it. I wonder if she knows herself. All I had left was the shard . . . and hate. I hated her for it. Hated that she made me question what I'd chosen."

He considered the remaining crystals in the box, over which the Traveler's hand hovered. "I think the shard could have taken me back at any time, if I'd wished it to."

"But you didn't," said the Traveler, hand frozen. Did they mean to protect the crystals from him, or was it the other way around?

"I didn't. That's why I left it on Dekien. I knew it was . . . an opportunity. Her invitation. And that if I took it, we would kill each other." The Ronin thought he wanted to smile wryly, but he couldn't. "Yet I continued to kill the rest. I couldn't undo what I had done. I decided it would only add to my regrets to let the Sith linger on. So I committed to the hunt."

"Did you think they deserved to be hunted?"

"Perhaps not all. I never asked myself that at the beginning. By the time I did . . . I suppose I only had space to think it because they had grown more difficult to find. That was when she reached me. When she began to lead me to those she thought might be able to kill me before I killed them."

For a time, the Traveler didn't move. The understanding creeping through their mind remained invisible until their hand settled over the box. As it did, they studied the Ronin with renewed intensity. They had grasped the implication of his words—that although the witch was isolated in whatever faraway place she had taken Rei'izu, somehow, she had still spoken to him, the lord she had banished from it.

He wondered: Had she spoken to them as well? Did she still?

She had abandoned him after she lashed Hanrai's ghost to her yoke. But then, she had only ever crept into the Ronin's ear to better lure him into her traps. Now he suspected she saw more use in murmuring to her latest lure.

"That seems . . . rude of her," said the Traveler.

"I couldn't begrudge her attempts. I still can't. It never did work. Or should I say, it hasn't yet."

"Ah. Is that it?" The Traveler seemed to want to laugh, and when they looked down at the shards, they smiled. "You think she led you to me for the same purpose. Or that I was nudged toward you? That she thought, if all those Sith failed to do him in, why not send a Jedi?"

"It occurred. But if you've been trying to kill me, you haven't done it very well."

"Perhaps I find you too charming." They didn't argue with the possibility that they had indeed been sent. The Ronin marked this alongside their attempt to conceal their dismay.

"Or perhaps," he said, "she sent you for another reason."

Their brow creased. "How ominous."

"Must it be?" The Ronin bowed his head in consideration. "Your master—Hanrai." He corrected himself when they steeled against some poisonous memory.

"I remember," the Traveler said, that steel sharpening their tone; they were unwilling to have the man evoked unless they controlled the way in which he was. They waved at the crystals spread before them. "He said I had the shard once. Implied that we had it still. I'm sure he believed himself. He always did. But it isn't here."

"I believe you," the Ronin said, and the Traveler softened a mote. Before that softness could sour into guilt, he went on: "We have more kyber than what we got from him."

The Ronin put his hand out on the table, palm up. He had done away with the bandages around his hands in order to work on the escape pod, and the flesh in the center of his palms was freshly pale, softer than it had been since his infancy. The Traveler regarded the hand in silence; they didn't ask what he wanted and didn't need to. In that moment, the two of them shared an understanding, one born of shared purpose. A resonance of desire, carried by the Force in black current and reflected in its white flare.

The Traveler retrieved their lightsaber from the folds of their robes. Their grip lent the weight of history to the blade. No matter how they disliked wielding the weapon, or how complex their relationship with their inheritance of it, they carried the burden as a gift. They held it out with a solemnity.

The Ronin nodded to them. The corners of their mouth twitched down, but they let their hand fall away. The hilt lingered, held aloft over the table on the tide of the black current.

"I've no facility with such things," said the Traveler. "They don't ask you to build your own, when you're the heir."

They slowed as they spoke, frowning. The Ronin understood their reason. If they were about to find what they hoped to, then at some point, the Traveler had opened the hilt. Or, someone else had.

The Ronin inclined his head; it was a promise, that he would fill the gaps in their skill and memory with his own expertise. They accepted the offer with an upturned hand. Thus they began their work in tandem, each guiding the other in turn.

They took it apart piece by piece. Unwound the dark leather strip and the metal shards of ornamentation; released the wooden pegs that kept the sides of the hilt secured together; twisted, flicked, and parted the durasteel core with care for the blade's age and artistry.

It would have been so much easier to simply break the thing, to burn it as the Ronin had burned so many others. But it was beautiful, a true relic of the age when the Jedi clans first swore themselves to serve none but the will of their lords, who were themselves the will of all people—an age when they served more than Empire. Though the Ronin thought the Empire deserved far less than all the Jedi had dedicated to it, he thought the blade deserved to be honored for the hopes that had shaped it.

In the end, it floated in pieces between them, much like the shattered *Reverent* just outside the *Crow.* At the heart of the unmade lightsaber hung a crystal: small, colorless, and winter-clear but for a cloud at its middle, defined by the crack that ran down its length.

The Traveler didn't breathe. Neither did the Ronin. He had searched for the shard too feverishly to know what to do when he had found it. So he reached up and took it in hand, between his thumb and forefinger, without much thought in his head but for that he had to.

As he did, the mirror shard consumed him, just as its greater iteration had those many long years ago.

CHAPTER
THIRTY-THREE

Before all else, the Ronin became aware of *her*. A face he hadn't seen since he last left Rei'izu. She, the witch. She sat on her knees across from him, alone in a vast nothing.

Next, in the way that one knew of sun and sky, he became aware that all around them, white flare shone dark and black current burned bright, until each became the other and in so doing were obliterated. A maddening collapse of substance and truth, and one that sparked an old fear within him.

So, he fixed desperately on the one stillness in sight, the witch's face and bearing. As he did, he discovered that she looked not a day older than the day he had left her. A handsome woman, length and angles, her long hair tied back and wisping from the bun, clad in the unpatterned dark kimono and trousers she preferred.

For a moment, he thought he might wish to reach out and touch her. In the same instant, he understood in his bones that he would not be allowed to. There was aught else to lay hands on. This world she occupied, that the Ronin intruded upon, did not strike him as a world per se.

"Oh, it's much more than that," she said.

"You know riddles are beyond me," he said.

"Impatient as ever, I see." He thought for a moment that she wanted to smile, as she once had when she teased him over their games. It wouldn't come. She raised her chin as she took him in, his age and en-feeblements. Weighed him. "What is it you're after?"

He opened his mouth and words failed him. Why did she ask? She had guided him here; she knew all too well what he wanted. Did she need to hear him say it?

He found in the next moment that the world spoke for him. It gained shape before his eyes and beneath his feet, and soon he stood upon the famously wide wooden veranda that jutted out from the main hall of the snowcapped Shinsui Temple complex. Ancient wood, varnished and well tended, elaborately interconnected to rise from the mountain-side. As he stepped forward, he spied in the distance a chasm and the hallowed city beyond—Yojou, the old Imperial capital on Rei'izu. The naked eye showed him orderly leagues interrupted only sparsely by smoke.

He realized, then, that he looked not upon Rei'izu as it might be now, but Rei'izu as it once had been. As if he needed to confirm, he turned his gaze upward. In the cloudless white sky, a motley fleet hovered in disarray. He remembered this day.

The Sith had taken Rei'izu as they took everything else—with the ravening fire of devotion. They had taken it because they had to; their lord and their witch had told them so, and they trusted both to think always first of them. If Rei'izu had to fall, they knew it was for their sake, so they ensured its surrender. To that end, they had lost many ships and more lives, more in a single battle than the rest of their rebel-lion combined.

"We thought it worth it, though, didn't we?" said the witch. She stood beside the Ronin, as she had that day. Her eyes were on the horizon, the city, the mountains, and sky. She saw far more than that, farther and deeper, to the ends of the tethers that bound all worlds together. "It had to be worth it."

He inhaled of frost undercut by fear sweat, blood tang, and dissipat-ing incense. "Yes."

He frowned at her. She looked so like the woman for whom he had conquered Rei'izu—who had in turn conquered Rei'izu for him, weaving ghosts to turn on their still-living comrades, or to rise up and kill again in her name. But though she had been that witch, she was no longer, just as he was no longer the man she had killed for. That young, young man, arrogant enough to believe victory on the scale of worlds and stars was a possible thing, as well as one he wanted.

The witch's lips curved indecipherably as she studied him. Did she see in him more the man he had been or the man he was? Which did she prefer? Whose answer did she most desire?

"That depends on which of you wants to come back," she said.

"I don't want to. I have to."

"You've never *had* to do anything." The witch's look hardened and she turned away, toward the rest of the complex.

As she did, their world in the white-black void of Force grew to encompass not only the veranda and its view of Rei'izu but the Shinsui Temple grounds, now emptied. Their warriors had sent the monks and nuns to shelter in the city below. No being remained on the mountainside but for lord, witch, and their own—the outlawed and heretical.

That was why the skies would soon darken with more ships, formidably pristine, the Imperial blades that halved lives and stars alike. For until this day, in Imperial eyes, the Sith had been nothing but mud and filth. Now they had dared to seize the Imperial heart and homeworld, that which had to be kept immaculate because it was beloved. Now the Sith were poison, and if the Empire didn't excise them in their entirety, they would be its end—because they were proof an Empire could be anything but itself. That it could sicken. That it could die.

"But then, why would we have tempted that anger, if we didn't have to?" she asked, though he thought she didn't want his reply. At least, not until she glanced over her shoulder at him, and her lips curled like a beckoning finger. "I suppose we liked it. Knowing we were the measure by which the Empire found itself wanting. That it saw in us the question it dared not ask—what right have you to own us? What right have you to *be*?"

He ached. "That wasn't why we did it."

The witch turned to the temple. "No. It wasn't."

She looked toward the last thing they had both wanted—that they had *needed*. The temple, and what lay within.

He wished there were a way to see instead his own face as it had been, so that he might search it for a glint of doubt. The fear, that though he and his guardians had fought and fought and fought again—that even as their ranks swelled with more warriors fleeing the clans, and others who seethed or flinched or grimaced at the dream of *Empire*—they were dying, and that all too soon the day would come when the last of them guttered out.

So, Rei'izu. He had come for an answer, and for faith, just as she had. Even to this day, he couldn't say whether it had been his idea to take Rei'izu or hers. They had gone everywhere in sympathetic step, shared every triumph and pain, every hope and fear. Just as now, they walked off the veranda and into the darkened hall together. Their steps echoed in uncanny syncopation with the steps they had taken twenty years before.

They breached the depths of Shinsui Temple's main hall and were alone but for each other. They had removed all those who would allow themselves to be shepherded; the inevitable resistance had been seen to as necessary, and the blood smeared on the varnished wooden floors was so stark in his memory, though he thought that at the time, he had dismissed it.

"What did you feel, when you saw it?" she asked.

She didn't mean the blood. As he lifted his gaze from the floor, to the mirror, he found himself forgetting it too. "Hope," he said, because he couldn't bear a lie.

The kyber mirror rose from the stained wooden dais that was also its altar. They had heard stories of its creation—that it had been found, or fashioned, or given by gods, or that it was itself one of divinity. These all vanished from his mind as he drank in the sight.

So tremendous that it exceeded the mind's ability to hold it in all at once, it was rendered a vertical lake of darkness by the shadows of the hall. The monolithic patterned lanterns that hung from the rafters to make the mirror brilliant had been extinguished. The only light gleamed shallowly from twin candles on slender posts on either side of the dais, and they lit the witch's face as she approached.

The stories spoke of more than the mirror's origin. It was said it had given dominion to so many others—lords, and emperors, and Jedi. But he and she, they dreamed first of safety, true peace for their people, who had thus far known only hard-won moments of respite. They dared to wish for an end to all this struggle, and they thought themselves willing to pay for it, if only they could be shown what it was they reached for.

Her face, reflected in the mirror's consuming well—that was what had made it seem possible to him.

"I'd be flattered, if I didn't know you better," she said. She meant: If I didn't know what came next.

He wanted to turn away, but he couldn't. She knelt before the dais, on boards worn smooth with other supplications, and she began to pray, just as she had those twenty years ago. It was as if her obeisance to their past trapped him within it as well. He stood just behind, her watchful guard. And he waited . . .

For hours, she prayed. Then through the night and into the next day. Then another.

Their fellows came to him, silent in their veneration. They believed wholeheartedly not in the mirror and its secrets but in those who had led them to it. He ate and drank what they brought, and he fed on their conviction because his own threatened to flag.

Still, she did not eat. Did not sleep, did not move. She was in a trance, and he had never seen her fall so far.

Their people needed him. The Empire loomed. Scout ships and drones were spied at the edge of the system, encroaching ever closer. Rumors came from their own scouts and far-flung allies of a fleet amassing, readying to descend—a newfound alliance of lords. He told their lieutenants to muster again, to be ready to fight for their right to breathe. He wavered on his feet, into dreams where he was compelled to bloody the temple boards once more to keep her eyes clear until she at last found their truth.

But her eyes remained closed, her breathing even. He began to fear she would die this way.

"When did you lose patience?" she asked. She never looked away from the mirror. He couldn't rightly say her mouth had moved.

"Is that how it works?" he asked through gritted teeth. He wanted to move, to leave—but she forced him still. "A stark and obvious moment when one breaks?"

"It was for you."

"Not here. I—I was only afraid, here. Afraid of the Empire. Afraid for you. Afraid of what you had seen. Or that you wouldn't see anything."

"You didn't trust me."

"I did," he insists. "I knew you wanted an answer, too, as much as I did, or more." He trembled. His body still wanted to move. He now feared that it would. "But want isn't ever enough."

He took the first step forward. His muscles and joints were sore from the standing, ever standing, but he left his post behind her and walked toward the dais, up the stairs and to the mirror, as offhandedly as he would have approached any familiar artifact of his daily life. In the same idle way, he placed his hand flat upon the kyber.

He was engulfed. So thoroughly did the mirror consume him that for a time he ceased to be.

He wanted an end, an answer, he received—

"What did you see?" she asked.

He could no longer see her. He could no longer see himself. He struggled to answer, to have voice, clinging to words as to buoyant wood in a thundering torrent. "Didn't you see it too? Isn't that why you sat there, silent, keeping it from me? Because you needed another answer— something better than the truth."

Because she had thought the truth would destroy him.

It came to him again as it had then, the entirety of what they had both beheld: Rise and fall, conflict unending, every struggle marked by the birth of the next within itself, no end, only consequence upon consequence, violence upon violence. Eons of it, worlds of it, the pain and the want. Their people had won freedom at the cost of others', and they protected their own with killing.

This they knew, and it had been so worth it when they had been only themselves unto themselves, two once-Jedi now-Sith, who dared to believe that they could resist the tide that sought their drowning by keeping each other afloat.

But in the mirror, oneself disintegrated, and in its place, there was *vision.*

He had carried suddenly the burden of every loss, pain, and sin he had accumulated by the decisions of he-in-himself. Kith and kin rent from hearth and home, and what had been home now a sundered shadow, only a bitter memory to every wailing, weeping soul.

He sought to think: I want none of this, I want it done, I want the silence of sweet night and warm arms, and the right to die only because my bones can no longer hold me—I want it for them, too, because I have sworn myself to them and forsworn all else because of it. I want, I want, I want—

"Want," she murmured, "yes, I think that's where we went wrong. We wanted too much, and all of it wrongly."

He broke away, as if from choking depths to frigid air, one cold cutting another. The witch had seized him around the arms to drag him back from the mirror, and she yanked because he resisted.

The mirror reveals, the stories said. It is clarity unyielding. By its light you may see the path to uncompromising victory.

What it had shown him was not success; it was death, suffering, and woe. He would not tolerate it. He couldn't.

He ripped free of her grasp and lunged toward the mirror. He struck it bare-fisted, incandescent with fury and flare, surging with ruthless current.

The fracture shrieked up from the point of impact, then lanced down. It wasn't enough. He wished with frantic horror for every image, every pain that the mirror had poured into him to disappear back into the channel from which it had come.

With his wish, the fracture widened. Gasped. Fanned. A web of finer cracks spanned outward from the center of the injury until they clouded the mirror with their sheer multitude. The kyber quivered and seemed to sigh before it shattered.

The mirror fell to pieces, a thousand-thousand splinters; one caught in his knuckles. He would remove it only much later, when he was far away from here.

At that moment, he could only stare, as did she. He beheld the absence of divinity until he turned, before he could grasp what he had done—not to the mirror, but to her. Her eyes were still fixed on that which he had destroyed, the riven brilliance across the floor.

The Ronin knew what came next. He left the temple, unspeaking. He half expected that his feet would be driven across the floor. But whatever spell had captured him within the man he had been had since dissolved, as had the memory of the world around them. Fractured and faded, until he was left alone with her and with himself, just them in the midst of everything and nothing.

The witch forced him to meet her unflinching gaze as she asked, "When did you know you would kill us?"

He wanted to look away and couldn't. There was nothing else to see. "Not then," he confessed.

"When?"

"When I did it. I . . . I was not a thinking creature. I was breaking. Broken. I thought, somehow, that I was doing right by cutting out the sickness I'd seeded."

Her hand was on her stomach, as if he had struck her there instead of the mirror. "You killed us."

"Should I justify it?"

"You can't."

"Then *what*?" He felt suddenly, brutally old and wounded, short of breath. He tore the respirator away from his face. "Would you have me dead?"

Her eyes on him were dark and unmoved. "What would that fix?"

He was breathless for a moment, then wheezed and pushed the respirator back to his face. He coughed once and again and wanted to speak but couldn't. It was miserable. Humiliating. He received no further epiphanies. If he were clever, he would have known that for a blessing. He only needed to look as far as what had happened when he received his last.

"Why did you ask me to come back?" he rasped at last.

"I didn't."

His brow creased; that wasn't true. She had invited him. She had sent the Traveler with that shard—the very one he had dug from his hand when he was so far from her and what he'd done, that he had hidden away on Dekien. And now she had made some *choice,* was doing something with this resurgence of demons, something he didn't understand but dreaded.

Yet when the pads of her fingers skimmed his cheek, resting on the edge where his prosthetic lined his jaw, and she turned him to look at her, he saw just truth in her mild frown. That was the mirror in its essence, as it had always been, even as it was now in pieces: truth.

"I never wanted you back," she said softly. "I couldn't stand the thought. But if you must . . ."

He lost sight of her. Her absence was a hole inside him, consuming, and he was too keenly aware of his creaking bones. When he heard her again, it was a balm, even as her voice encircled, gripped, and shredded through what he was. For so long, he hadn't wanted to be a living thing that to be torn asunder was respite. So he thought, at least, until she laid her last curse.

If you must return, then you do it in my name, she said—and there was something new, something changed in this voice—something he had never heard before. *Honor mine as you never have yours.*

It was all nothing for a while after that, then white, then black, then both and neither, until she allowed him again to see.

CHAPTER
THIRTY-FOUR

T HE RONIN MOVED unthinking, his body a vessel of desire sans intent. He had no sense of time—how much had passed, or how much now was passing—he only held his side with one hand, the mirror shard clutched to his chest in the other, as he staggered out of the galley. The Traveler called out to him as they stood, but he had already left. He became aware that his destination was the cockpit as he stepped into it.

Ekiya was already there, and though at first she looked like she wanted to chase him out, she remained at her tense seat before the controls. "Really hope you've got a solution, Grim. We're on the verge of a situation."

A glance at the consoles and out the window painted the problem: the Imperial fleet had done well for itself, clearing the field of all potential concerns. The *Poor Crow* was one of the last few questions remaining, and they had begun to close in on it.

In the interest of efficacy, he held out his palm. The shard shone dully within it. "I know the way. To Rei'izu."

Ekiya looked from his face to the shard, her expression initially contorted with a pity usually reserved for unintelligent children. Then it was the look of a woman who in theory liked what she had heard but despised who she had heard it from. She raised her hands and nodded to permit him to take the copilot's seat. "Fine. Okay. Not like we have time to argue. You tell me what you think you know, and we'll figure it out from there."

They tried this once, twice—him feeding her the calculations, her feeding them into the navicomputer. The navicomputer refused to hold any information he provided. Ekiya grew more troubled by the second, sending wary looks at the communications array and at the expanse of empty space outside the viewport. When the navicomputer blinked and growled and declared the third attempt an error as well, she cursed and threw up her hands.

By then, the rest of the crew had gathered as well. A pair of Jedi apprentices craned their necks over Chie's shoulders, trying to snatch their own glimpse of whatever strangeness was unfolding. Thus far, they'd seen nothing but an old man providing useless information to an increasingly agitated young woman.

B5-56 warbled protest—he was better equipped to speak with the navicomputer, was he not?

"No." The Ronin gripped the shard so hard it threatened to cut into his palm. "It won't work. You need me to do it. She gave me permission."

At this, the Traveler's eyes widened and Kouru's narrowed. Chie half turned to the apprentices as if she were readying to defend them.

Ekiya seemed about to protest again when the communications array flared. Outside the viewport, the object of their dread lanced abruptly into view. The head of a great white spear soared inexorably forward, directly overhead, blocking the light of the Dekien sun. Another Jedi Dreadnought. Ekiya's fist clenched over the *Poor Crow*'s controls. "One chance," she said over her shoulder, "that's all we get, Grim."

If they didn't run soon, fast, correctly, they wouldn't get another chance to run at all.

She let the Ronin have direct access to the navicomputer. This time, he didn't need to translate the mirror shard's murmuring intent into words—he only had to *know*. The coordinates flew from his fingers into the ship. Ekiya's brow furrowed ever deeper as she watched, doubting what she saw. The feed she received in her pilot's seat still declared the Ronin's coordinates were in error, and she shook her head as if trying to free it of a troublesome insect.

Finally, the navicomputer didn't reject the numbers wholesale. Just in time. A contingent of small fighters detached from the Dreadnought overhead as, simultaneously, the lights indicating the activation of its tractor beam illuminated on its undercarriage.

"Hold on!" Ekiya warned, and they were away.

Hyperspace unfolded blue and white and liquid around them until, suddenly, it didn't. It was too soon for them to have appeared back in the cold black reality of space, yet there they were, and there was no sign of the Dreadnought that had loomed over them, or of Dekien, or indeed of anything but for the new immensity that stretched before them.

The *Poor Crow* floated under a gold-limned blue sphere. A planet. Not Dekien. Rei'izu. It bore down on them with its obviousness, a looming impossibility.

CHAPTER
THIRTY-FIVE

THE RONIN SAGGED in his seat. Beside him, Ekiya stared breathless at Rei'izu until the *Crow*'s consoles blazed to life all at once in a cacophony of erratic contradictions.

The ship's systems couldn't agree with one another. One declared they were indeed looking up at Rei'izu as simultaneously another insisted they weren't. Another warned that they were in orbit while another vehemently disagreed that there was anything to orbit *around*.

And where, in all this, was that light coming from? It shone from somewhere, bathing Rei'izu as surely as it did their fingers—the Ronin's glued to his ribs, Ekiya's to the navigation console. Yet they couldn't see its source.

A paradox. How fitting. They had been brought here by an impossible thing and couldn't possibly hope to make sense of it. All the Ronin could say with certainty was that the voice—the witch—had allowed them to come.

She had, hadn't she?

She extends an invitation, Hanrai had said. Yet in the dizzying depths of the mirror shard, she denied having done so. Had said she couldn't stand the thought of the Ronin's return—that she had never even imagined it.

Nevertheless, she had let him through. Why?

That question had to wait. They had too many more urgent problems to answer. Ekiya read them from the *Crow*'s outputs as the Ronin felt them in his bones and follicles. The vessel ached, its innards frayed by the strain of being thrown from the end of the galaxy that existed to the end that didn't.

Ekiya gripped the controls. "This might get bad," she warned the others. "Whatever that jump did, the *Crow* hated it. Oh, hell—"

The *Poor Crow* cried under their feet. Every eye was wide and untrusting. They had just suffered a collapsing ship, and they couldn't help but suspect they might be about to suffer another. Ekiya threw a suspicious look at the Ronin; he had earned it, for the part he'd played in planting this fear.

To her, he raised a cajoling hand. To the Traveler, he said, "We may be in need of the skills you deployed on the *Reverent*."

"The *Crow*'s a bit more complicated, as a project," they warned.

"You have help," said Chie. She turned to the apprentices. "Master Idzuna needs you—let them direct your focus."

Kouru brought up the rear of that effort, following the rest out and throwing one last dubious look over her shoulder.

As she left, Ekiya turned to the Ronin. "I've never—where am I headed?"

Never what? He knew as soon as he thought it. Never flown home. Had likely not ever even seen Rei'izu from its sky, until he'd ordered her taken to a distant front line alongside the other drafted children.

The Ronin knew Rei'izu's skies because he had once flown down into them himself—a selfish maneuver for which he had been scolded, not least of all by B5. But he had always liked to be first to see a world, and to do it alone, in order to judge what dangers it might pose to his people before they were subjected to them.

So, he knew where to point her, and he brought up the coordinates on the nav. "There."

Ekiya had the ship moving as the red lights of imminent danger sparked on one after another. The *Crow* eased handily into the atmosphere, the hull jolted by new gravity.

The Ronin's attention caught on the *Crow*'s innards as they sputtered. It was as if the ship had sickened. Enfeebled as he was, he could do little to contribute to the effort to hold it together. Instead he poured himself into monitoring the *Crow*'s condition as its individual parts tried one by one to darken and drift. If he sensed any of them went untended, he alerted Chie via the internal coms, and she passed the warning on.

For a nauseating moment, the *Poor Crow* crested a mountain range and drifted, all silence. Then it dropped. They were weightless as they dropped with it.

Time elongated. The Ronin was allowed to see the city that stretched out in the basin before them—hazy white with winter twilight, and marked by hundreds upon hundreds of delicate pointed roofs rising over all the others. The shrines and temples of Yojou, the old capital, storied heart of the first Empire and home of a thousand gods. Beyond it lay the chasm and mountains where Shinsui Temple awaited.

It was good to see it and a curse—to be so close, only to fall.

By luck or by prayer, the engine wailed back alight. Ekiya's hands moved frantically across her consoles, taking that last breath of life to send the *Crow* lurching forward, away from the mountainside toward the expansive landing field the Ronin had directed her to.

They lived. By that standard, the landing went well. Moreover, the *Crow* was still recognizably itself, even at the end of its blackened trail of broken-off parts. However, it was probably not safe to be on. They were all outside it within minutes.

The world that awaited them could not be easily reconciled. It was real enough to be uncomfortably cold and unreal enough to require gaping.

They had landed at the port adjacent to the pilgrims' ward, which boasted Yojou's densest collection of religious sites and which had long been preserved by Imperial edict. Its walls were all dark wood and white paint, its roofs tiled and long. To reach the ward, they would cross one of many bridges across the winter-sluggish Moga River that separated it from the rest of Yojou. It was how the pilgrims and tourists would have done it, years ago, and why visitors had favored this port in particular. Many Sith had chosen to land there for similar reasons.

Dozens of ships were still scattered across the landing field, all of different makes and models. Mostly small or of unusual pedigree. The larger vessels had been commandeered by the Sith invaders, and when Rei'izu vanished, no like ships had ever come to replace them.

They saw the shapes as they escaped the *Crow*. Never directly. They appeared from angles and disappeared the second one turned toward them. A man in mechanic's gear crouched over a tool kit below the cruiser to their left. A large-eyed face looked darkly out of a neighboring cockpit. A collection of pilgrims in yellow robes huddled around one another as they glanced nervously toward the ward they could no longer safely travel to. More figures, everywhere they turned, there in one breath and gone in the next.

Chie snorted. Her eyes had been on the horizon where the sun sat nestled between two peaks. She turned to the rest of them and nodded toward it. "The witch stopped far more than seems possible. It hasn't moved."

"It never does," said the Traveler. They regarded the mountains with an odd tranquility.

"Well, that's all tremendously creepy," said Ekiya.

B5-56 chirred a scold at her knees. The droid had been sluggish since the unkind landing; an assessment was in order.

"Sure, miraculous, whatever," said Ekiya to B5. "I want to know what we're eating tonight—let alone where we're sleeping. Then I want to know—" She broke off and crossed her arms against the chill. "What are we *doing*?"

"What you came here to do, I presume," said Kouru. Her voice was familiar and not. The sound correct, the cadence all wrong. She stepped forward from the group, toward the pilgrims' ward, and it seemed as though she left her shadow behind. When she looked over her shoulder, she had no care for any of them but the Ronin. "You're here to kill me, of course."

The Ronin didn't move, though every part of him wanted to. He knew what danger he faced, and he knew he would do better to keep his stillness and reserve his strength. The being facing him wasn't Kouru, because Kouru no longer thought him worth killing—and the eyes fixed on him now fully desired his death.

Wrong. Something of this rang foul, discrepant, something he could not name. For of course it was wrong to see a soul he knew made other than what it was. So many times, he had seen the witch turn the recently dead upon their allies, and to stunning effect. Betrayal bought victory more swiftly than any blade. Perhaps it was only that this was the first time she had turned her work on him.

But no. Some other wrongness haunted him. She, the witch, was not as he remembered.

He couldn't justify this suspicion, no more than he could banish it. It had grown from a kernel this past hour, ever since the kyber shard consumed him with its vision-upon-visions. The witch he met within that storm was one he had known in the resonant core of himself, the part of his being that echoed again in hers.

The witch standing before him here, who wore Kouru as a cloak and urged him to meet her with his blade drawn—he knew her too, from her whispers, but . . .

She smiled, a challenge that made an unsettling curve on Kouru's sullen mouth. "I won't make it easy," she said. She didn't imagine he doubted her. "I couldn't now, could I? I need you to prove you're worth my effort."

She, the witch, if he could still call her that, pointed toward the pilgrims' ward and past it with Kouru's muscled arm. "I'm waiting there, where you left me. Past the ward and the chasm. You'll walk the true pilgrim's path. And if you reach the end, then we'll meet again."

"And if I don't?" He had to ask.

She frowned at him as if it hadn't occurred to her that he wouldn't. "You'll want to, and with all speed. Unless you'd rather Rei'izu take you too."

Then she was gone, as suddenly as she had arrived. Kouru sagged without the witch to hold her up, and the Ronin knelt by her. He didn't believe he could have remained standing if he hadn't.

CHAPTER
THIRTY-SIX

"WHAT EXACTLY DID she mean by 'taken by Rei'izu'?" Chie asked Fox in the immediate aftermath. Her interest seemed practically academic.

Fox had been as transfixed as the rest of them when the witch sashayed past them wearing her Kouru-skin. They'd been stuck with a face Ekiya wanted to call "constipated" because she was afraid it was really "anguished." Now they pretended they'd never known an emotion more intense than "miffed" and smiled ruefully. "I'm not entirely sure. But I know I didn't come here alone the first time. And . . . I think that changed quite quickly."

Ekiya groaned. "All right. How are we getting Grim up the mountain?"

Fortunately, it wasn't a debate. Even Kouru just nodded, once she stood of her own free will, hand pressed to her forehead and a familiar scowl carved into her face. The time for quibbles had apparently passed when Grim pulled his absolute Force garbage nonsense and dumped them on—on—

Ekiya could barely think it. Rei'izu. Real under her feet, but her mind wouldn't catch.

She knew the Yojou skyline better from Imperial propaganda posters than from her own memory. The lost history—Rei'izu! Oh, how it had pained the Empire to be deprived of that precious jewel. Ekiya had been born in a southern district nearer to rice fields than to the pilgrims' ward. She'd never even seen Shinsui Temple until she and the other drafted kids were flying over it as they were shipped out.

It made the next hour feel that much more vague and strange. She had mechanical purpose and was grateful for that, especially after Chie asked her the best route by which to get Grim from the landing field to the chasm and she had to shrug. Luckily, Fox still had a mental map of pilgrims' ward, but it stung Ekiya to admit how little she knew about her own home.

Instead she directed the apprentices to the *Crow*'s food stores and emergency travel satchels—she always had both in case she picked up somebody in dire need of some kind of supply—and argued with Grim over how to move B5-56.

"His processors are on the fritz," Ekiya said, "and his ventilation is barely doing its job. You make him come with us, and he'll burn up before we're even over the first bridge."

"He's coming," Grim insisted.

"You'll break him," Ekiya insisted right back.

B5 blatted unhelpfully.

"You don't feel fine," she snapped. "You're lucky you made it this far. We push you any farther and you're going to be a glorified bucket in a hat."

At that point, Chie pulled Ekiya away, ostensibly to help her rewire a defunct speeder some of the kids had found on the other side of a nearby tourist transport.

Ekiya kept muttering as she was herded. "I'm right, aren't I? Whatever was done to this place just up and ruins anything more technologically complex than a chronometer. That was what downed the *Crow*. That's what's wrong with Bee. We can't drag him any further into this mess or he'll—"

"I suspect you aren't wrong," said Chie. "Otherwise we would have seen one or two curious droids by now."

But they hadn't. They were as absent as the people.

"I doubt our little friend has missed that," Chie went on. "He's still set on accompanying us. So I think we should let him. He'd rather burn out with us than alone. I expect he wishes to be useful before he does."

"Bleak."

Chie nodded to concede the point. Ekiya sighed and didn't harp. She wanted to be kind—to B5, and to everybody, a little bit. Even Grim. At least for now. Especially as Grim put in the effort to apologize. When she brought the speeder back over and gave him her estimate for how long it had—by which she obliquely meant to imply B5 had about as long and no longer—he surprised her by handing over the puzzle box.

"Yours are still in it," she said dumbly. The glinting red splinters were intermingled with all the others.

"They're better off in your keeping," he said. Then paused, and seemed regretful. "If you'd rather not pray for them, leave them where you will."

She clutched the whole thing to her chest and tucked it away in her coat. "I'm not that rude."

She decided then that she could be mad at him later, when she had the time to be. When she didn't have to worry about what the witch might be trying to do to them for the crime of intruding on her sanctuary.

The apprentices had some ideas about that.

"Look, there's another," one of them whispered to his friend.

"It doesn't make *sense*. It has to be an illusion."

They had crossed the bridge into the pilgrims' ward by then. The speeder whirred unpleasantly as it went; for as long as it worked, it carried Chie in the front—Fox's nervous cat crouched by her feet in the footwell—with Grim and B5 in the back. Everybody else moved around it on foot. They tried to get Kouru into the speeder too, until she about bit Fox's hand straight off. Now the Sith demon trailed at their rear, sharp eyes flicking every which way, the ornate hilt that had belonged to Fox's dead Jedi master gripped tight at her side. She'd looked frankly disgusted to take the lightsaber, and Fox had looked all too ready to be rid of it, but none of them could be choosy about their gear in the face of whatever the hell Rei'izu had in store.

Case in point, the thing they all found themselves staring at on the other side of the river, awaiting them in the pilgrims' ward.

A cloud-deer, or what looked like one. Long in the leg and neck, white-flecked fur of variegated purple-gray and horns that branched in beautiful filigree patterns over its head. It stood at the lip of an alley in the pilgrims' ward and stared at them unblinking with a wet black eye. Another trotted up behind it, ears twitching with curiosity.

Ekiya remembered the cloud-deer. They had lived in the hundreds on the grounds of one of Rei'izu's largest and oldest shrines. It was located in the northern stretch of the pilgrims' ward. Their party was coming from the southwest.

More and more cloud-deer wandered across their path the farther they pressed down dusty avenues. There were other signs of intermittent life as well. Sprawling vined plants cracking up through alleyways to unfold into the streets, threatening to trip them up at every turn. Nests built inside open-doored shops and clutches of brilliantly colored little songbirds that followed them from corner to corner, unafraid of the interlopers. One of the apprentices lured an intrepid yellow nub of a bird into their hands in exchange for a thumb of rice.

"See, they're domesticated," the apprentice said to their peers.

"Or it was born after all the people got flattened."

They were still seeing the here-and-gone-again shades. Now they also passed the occasional slumped figure of a defunct droid.

"It still doesn't make sense," one of the apprentices insisted. "She's stopped people, but not animals, stopped the sun—"

"She hasn't stopped the sun, she's stopped the planet—"

"No, she can't have done that either, because if she had, then gravity—"

"Stop trying to make sense of it, it's the Force—"

"Don't 'it's the Force' me—"

Ekiya yearned to complain with them, but they swallowed their bickering the second any adult trailed too close. Fox sensed her agony. They beckoned her toward the front of their little contingent.

Two apprentices passed her as she jogged up. Fox was sending all six out in varying pairs to search storefronts whenever they spotted a likely apothecary or grocer. Whatever the kids scrounged got dumped in the speeder's front seat next to Chie for the cat to guard—medkits and rations, a collection of components for Grim, and so forth. In the back, Grim had B5's chassis open, presumably so he could be neurotic about it.

Could she call him that? There he hunched, dark lord of dark lords, vainly trying to convince a droid that his circuitry wasn't mysteriously sputtering to death.

But what else did she want him doing right now? The man was half dead. Unless they tripped over a portable vat of bacta to dump him into, there'd be no improvement to his lungs before they got him to Shinsui.

Ekiya signaled Yuehiro before he dashed off and told him to look for some kind of face guard—something that would fit over that respirator. Yuehiro looked altogether far too pleased to be trusted. Somewhere, he'd picked up a kitchen knife. It wasn't that Ekiya didn't want him armed, she just didn't like to see it.

Fox had an odd look when Ekiya drew up next to them. Amazed that she still cared enough to look out for Grim? Maybe. In her defense, it just made sense. She didn't want to die. And who else could they hope to pit against the witch?

"How are you?" they asked.

Ekiya's mouth fell open. "What? Why? I'm—weird, obviously."

"You're home. I imagine it's a lot."

It was a lot for them to ask. A dozen awful feelings converged in her all at once. Ekiya stared up at Fox in bewildered upset until she turned away with a purpose.

They had reached an intersection of two streets between the dark wooden structures of the pilgrims' ward. At the end of one street stood the rimed gray walls of a shrine complex. At the end of the other, a square opened up, lined with long abandoned stalls and colored banners. Each way she looked, she for an instant saw one shade (yawning) or another (running).

She recognized none of it. Or she did and she didn't. She could call the colors familiar, and the smells, sort of. Everything she remembered sat too near or too far from her mind, abstracted by a warped layer of nostalgia and alienation.

It wasn't just that she hadn't grown up this far into the city, let alone in the pilgrims' ward. Nor was it that Imperial edict had stripped the ward of the metal and grime of life as anyone truly lived it. It wasn't even that the buildings were here and the people weren't, history absent texture, or that the natural world underlying that history had seen fit to burst through tenderly preserved structures without any kind of regard for what the Empire thought beautiful and worthy of preserving.

It was maybe, a little, that she'd spent twenty years stomping around the rest of the galaxy dreaming of Rei'izu because it was gone, just gone, a fantasy she changed with every recollection, and to be faced with its tangibility, no matter how warped by aforementioned absolute Force garbage nonsense, was to confront a gap between memory and reality. She remembered *a* Rei'izu. Not this one.

It was, on top of all this, that to be *here* meant they weren't *there,* the world where a rent-open Imperial Dreadnought over Dekien meant princes declaring it time to put aside every pretension of peace in favor of sending their Jedi to cut one another open—to say nothing of the pitiful souls who would inevitably get in their way.

And it was that she wouldn't have been here at all, walking these paths and passing these shrines and shadows on her way to sending her own ghosts where they belonged, if not for Fox—and Grim. If she hadn't helped them.

She had what she wanted. The price hadn't even been hers to pay. By any measure it was worth it, even if she couldn't feel that it was.

Fox had the audacity to look sad for once. A small expression, because for them honest meant slight. As she fiercely missed their mask, they laid a hand on her shoulder, all sympathy.

"Thanks," she squawked, and fell back as far as she could without making a problem of herself.

It hurt, was the thing, to see Fox walk these streets like they knew them. It made her feel all the more unreal.

Ekiya ended up dragging her heels by Kouru, who grew wary at her approach but eased ever so slightly when Ekiya neglected to engage her in anything resembling conversation.

Kouru eyed their surroundings with a suspicion Ekiya appreciated. She didn't expect familiarity, just problems. And she clearly wanted very badly for there to be some variety of problem.

The pilgrims' ward insisted on disappointing her. Every time they passed another alley empty of anything but those spectral shades, Kouru wound a little tighter. Ekiya nearly wanted to pat her shoulder. It had felt too awful when Fox patted hers to really entertain the impulse.

A few hours in—by Chie's guess, as every one of their chronometers disagreed with the others—the speeder stopped working in the middle of a square a few orderly blocks from the chasm end of the pilgrims' ward. That meant figuring what they could afford to carry and what to abandon, and also arguing with Grim about B5.

Ekiya didn't want anything to do with any of that, so she stuck with Kouru on patrol. Kouru gave her a long side eye about it but lacked the patience to ask.

They paused at a corner of the square from where they could see Shinsui. The temple complex was from this angle obscured by the trees on the mountainside across the chasm. Its roofs, laden with snow, blazed in the unmoving rays of the unsetting sun. Kouru glared at it like she thought it would flinch.

Abruptly she looked elsewhere—down the street they were standing on the lip of. The angle of the sun meant the entire street was cast in shadow. Bordered by two straight-edged wooden structures, it sloped upward at its end until it became stone steps lined with snow-bitten foliage.

A figure stood on the steps, darkly clothed. Kouru couldn't tear her eyes away. Neither could Ekiya. It looked like any other one of the shades, but still she stared, breath held.

It vanished.

Ekiya swallowed her breath. Of course it poofed, she told herself. The shades didn't stick. They popped in and out of existence at even the slightest movement. She'd shifted her gaze just so, or inhaled too deeply, or—

Then she could see it again. This time, the figure stood at the bottom of the stone stairs.

Ekiya cursed and grabbed at Kouru's arm. Kouru wouldn't move. Not like a statue wouldn't move, but like the rock over a volcanic fissure was horribly still until it burst.

And because she wouldn't, couldn't go, neither could Ekiya. She just stood there, fear winding up from her soles into her skull as the figure advanced. Down the slope. Onto the street. Closer. It flickered into view just before a break between the structures lining the street, where gold twilight streamed through. The next time the shade appeared, they'd be fully illuminated, and their shadow would stretch long as a sword.

Kouru's foot slid back and Ekiya jerked again at her arm. "Hey, no, come on," she whispered urgently, telling herself all the while that she needed to shout, get help, because why else were they traveling in a group if not to make sure they didn't have to face this kind of terror alone? "Kouru, *come on.*"

Kouru growled and threw her off. There was a fury in her face that made Ekiya back up a startled step. Instinct had her hand at her waist, on the blaster she hated using but always carried because a kid didn't cut her teeth on assassinating a Sith warrior without learning how to defend herself.

They were caught like that, staring hard at each other. Seconds passed, stretching into a minute. The street remained empty but for the two of them. The figure did not appear again.

Ekiya didn't know what to call the look on Kouru's face, the moment she realized the shade wasn't coming back. All twisted up with anger—and also, Ekiya thought with dawning sympathy, loss.

"Sorry," she said. "Guess I spooked it."

"You did no such thing," Kouru spat. "That was no ordinary shade. It was a warrior. A Sith."

"What gave it away, the melodramatic flouncing around the shadows?"

Kouru's white-knuckled hands gripped the dead lord's lightsaber like a bone she wanted to break. "It was a vessel of the witch. A demon."

Past the bluster and snarl, Ekiya heard a tremor of fear. It made her feel a terrible heel. She allowed Kouru the grace of silence for a minute as she contacted Chie—to warn her to keep an eye out for any shades that proved particularly persistent, or that, much more problematically, started to move.

The whole time, Kouru's gaze remained fixed on the stairs and the street. Ekiya should have focused on the same things. They needed to stay on guard until the rest of the crew was ready to move out. Instead, Ekiya kept glancing at Kouru. The rigidity of her attention, and the fragility.

She thought: Don't say anything. Her mouth, forever a chump for the hurt and mad about it, declined to obey. "So . . ." said Ekiya. "You clearly didn't love getting puppeted around like that, back on the landing field. I'm guessing you don't want to talk about it."

The very suggestion gave Kouru a look of true horror.

Ekiya raised her hands. "I get it. I know you think Grim's the worst. I don't think you're definitely wrong about him either. But I'm also sure that the witch doesn't feel like the best alternative. So I guess I'm saying—sorry. It's awful."

Kouru stared down at the empty street as if she *wanted* the shade to return. It made Ekiya drop her hand back to the blaster at her waist. Just in case. "I saw the witch's work once before," said Kouru. "When the Sith gathered here for the great muster."

The invasion, thought Ekiya, though she didn't say it. Kouru also paused, mouth twisted with conflict. It probably shamed her to feel anything that complicated her anger.

"We fought," she said at last. "We bled. Died. And she raised us up. Our fellows once more beside us. Enemies turned to allies. I was . . . breathless. Invigorated. All awe and delight. *Hope.*"

She looked up, toward the chasm and the temple, both now hidden by buildings. "When they had served their purpose, she released them. We prayed to speed them on." Then she was looking at her hands like she couldn't understand that they were indeed hers. "And I . . . am not serving the purpose she set for me."

The unspoken conundrum: If the witch had raised Kouru to kill Grim and Kouru had failed to do so, then why did she still have any hands to speak of? Why was she not once more dead and formless, a memory in the cosmic unquantity of the Force?

Ekiya had nothing like an answer. She knew what happened to her people's ghosts. She only half understood what the Jedi did with theirs. She had not the faintest idea what stories Kouru's people told about their own dead. She had no comfort to offer, let alone answers. Then again, no one had answers except for the witch, and the witch didn't seem likely to help anyone but herself anytime soon.

"All right," Ekiya said. "Well. You're still here. So maybe that means you being here has less to do with what she wants than you thought it did."

"Don't be a fool. I died. She returned me by her will. I am her creature." Kouru grimaced at the stone steps. They remained empty. Inviting. "I am evidently her creature still."

"Are you? She got you when we landed, sure, but she's not wearing you now."

"Is she not?"

"Don't play mind games with yourself. You're never going to win."

Kouru finally looked away toward the square, where the rest of their shabby crew had finally emptied the speeder of everything worth carrying. Ekiya was compelled to turn her attention back to the steps. Out of the corner of her eye, a shade flickered in a door halfway down the street. She held her breath. It didn't move.

"I . . . don't know why I'm helping you," said Kouru.

"Do you want to?"

Kouru bared her teeth like a pouting dog.

Ekiya rubbed the back of her own neck. "Sorry. Wrong question. Too big. I barely know what I want and we're stomping all over the biggest want I've ever had. I got home." She put her hand to her side, where she'd tucked away the puzzle box full of the ghosts that belonged both to her and to other people. "But . . . I can't stop thinking, why am *I* here? I thought I was coming for other people. I didn't think I cared for my sake. But I do. I must. Because when I got off the *Crow* and I saw Rei'izu, I felt . . . nothing. And I hated that."

"What do you feel now?"

It seemed very important to Kouru to know, so Ekiya thought hard before she answered. She didn't have the time she would have wanted.

The comlink on her wrist blinked—Chie's signal to join back up. So, as they ducked out of the alley, and into the light of the square, she said all she could think to say: "I feel like I'm not done yet. I never feel done. Is that my problem?"

Kouru seemed to want to scowl, but her face wouldn't let her get that mean. When she spoke, it was a bit like she thought Ekiya couldn't hear her, though she wasn't truly quiet, just distracted. "You said you want to be more than one thing. The you I've known has always wanted things outside herself. Perhaps you should identify what you want within yourself as well."

Ekiya put her hands together in mock prayer. "How very Jedi of you."

"Hold your tongue or I'll eat it."

"Oh, *my*."

Kouru didn't smile, but she scoffed, and Ekiya laughed because she thought, maybe, that she deserved to. In any case, she doubted they'd get many more chances, and if she had to name her own wants, laughing was probably one of them.

CHAPTER
THIRTY-SEVEN

THEIR PACE SLOWED considerably as they neared the chasm. The old man wouldn't leave his droid, and said droid was badly waning. Soon enough, B5-56 would go the way of the speeder. Kouru found her hand on the lord's lightsaber, thinking of severing B5's legs. But the shadows grew thicker the closer they drew to the park at the north end of the pilgrims' ward, and she concluded it would be better for all of them if the droid could shoot at least one demon before he expired.

At last, only a frosted park separated them from the chasm edge. Pairs of cloud-deer watched their advance from between fruit trees rendered barren black by cold. The inanimate shades had lessened. By the day the witch took Rei'izu, the Sith had already banned any pilgrims from the path to Shinsui Temple. So, there had been no people to leave behind their vestiges.

Only the Sith remained, and they came swiftly and from wicked angles. They appeared in bursts of black current spliced with white flare that cut so violently into the world they felt like a wound even before they had severed flesh.

Kouru met the first head-on. Their party had chosen to take the wide pale path of gravel and sand that led through the park to the first bridge.

The demon whirled out from behind the thick trunk of a tree that sheltered the way. They were as shadowed and fast as the one Kouru had seen just an hour before, and in their hands was a long, thick staff, at the head of which a bright red blade shone sharply. They swung for the old man's head.

Kouru's heart caught in her throat as she, white flare lining every fiber of her musculature, threw herself past him and tackled the demon to the ground, blue-white blade jabbing into the demon's midsection.

The demon dissipated before they hit the frozen dirt, so Kouru tumbled over root-riddled ground alone. She sprang back to her feet as the demon once more manifested. It hurtled past her, back toward the path. The old man was ready by then.

He had armed himself when they left the speeder. His lightsaber, recovered from her on the *Crow*, had been hung at his waist beside that ancient blaster. Kouru suspected the latter would be more useful as a bludgeoning device under Rei'izu's strange strictures, but his lightsaber thrummed redly as he awaited the demon.

He struck clean through the shade and it melted into the air like ashen cobwebs. Not even its weapon remained. The old man's blade reflected in the blackened lacquer of the half-mask that guarded his face—a proper Sith piece of armor, its molded scowl long-toothed and fearsome. It looked much like the one he had cut off Kouru's jaw not so long ago. He met her eyes over it and nodded. Her lip curled and she didn't linger. She hadn't done it for him.

That was the last moment of calm. From then, the Sith demons emerged from every dark corner, and all was chaos, cunning, and blood.

Kouru spun around a demon with two fiery short swords and plunged her blue blade into his back. He convulsed and vanished soundlessly. It hurt to see him disperse.

Even as she slashed and skewered, she dreamed of fighting with, not against these echoes; she coveted their red radiance. But they belonged to the witch, and every one of their stolen kyber blades was an artifact of the old man's power. She hated both witch and traitor-lord, she told herself, and the hate was tidily uncomplicated.

The shades nevertheless harrowed her heart. She wished them free unto themselves just as she wished herself her own again. What self she still had left.

Every hesitation had a price. Another demon emerged from the lee of a twisted old cherry tree and surged past, near through her. Kouru was at the last second shoved aside by one of the apprentices—the one who looked after the others, Yuehiro. The boy grunted, and the sweetness of burnt flesh tickled Kouru's nose.

Fury shot through her, hot and blinding. She lunged toward the demon. It escaped her thrust and made a beeline for the old man. He was already engaged with another figure, their red blades snarling against each other.

An ambush. Kouru saw in flashes at the corner of her eyes: Fox throwing another demon aside, B5 firing two quick shots, Ekiya—

No. Focus. She didn't control the battlefield and couldn't hope to. Even had she been keener to the subtleties of presence, the Sith demons were too brief and unstable to properly track. Her only chance to strike lay in the moments they dared to appear.

The one she chased vanished when it was still out of sword's reach from the old man. Kouru thought, quick quick quick: If you were to kill him, what angle would you pick?

The old man halved the demon he had been dueling and staggered. His shoulders heaved and he planted his feet to right himself. Before his bent form, Kouru's target bloomed darkly, its blade already raised overhead to cut him to the ground.

Kouru was the white flare itself as she cleaved it cleanly from head to sacrum. It dissolved into nothing so close to her mouth that she felt as though she inhaled its leavings.

She was left staring at the old man and his hard breathing, his sallow cheeks. He nodded at her again, but this time his gaze dropped as he braced himself on his knees. An unexpected fear gripped her, to see him so frail. They hadn't even made it to the bridges.

A pained grunt drew her attention back around. It had come from Yuehiro, who was now crouched on the ground. A black burn cut deep into the boy's left arm, just below his shoulder. He cradled the arm to his side, but it hung limp in his grip.

"What were you thinking?" Kouru demanded as she stormed toward him.

Yuehiro squared his jaw and shook his head. There was no apology in his eye. Kouru was taken aback by a jolt of recognition. There had been a time, she was certain, when she too had shoved her way forward into danger when she should have let a more experienced warrior take a blow they'd earned.

She had at least possessed the sense not to be nearly dismembered.

So Kouru felt no compunctions—none at all—about snarling into the boy's face. "I didn't save your life to see you waste it."

Yuehiro swallowed hard and looked away.

Chie clucked as she swept between them. She handed her cane to Kouru and knelt to inspect Yuehiro. "It's hardly the children's fault that they went from nearly dying on an Imperial Dreadnought to nearly dying on Rei'izu. They're doing quite well."

"They are, for the circumstances, but perhaps not well enough," said Fox. Their cat was on their heels, tail lashing and ears turned back as it eyed every passing shadow. "I suspect it's time we consider parting ways."

Kouru rounded on Fox and jerked her head at another of the apprentices who was laid out on the ground, clutching her stomach, with two of her fellows leaning over her. "You'd leave them to die?"

"The opposite, I hope. You've noticed by now that our intrusive friends have a rather singular interest, yes?" They inclined their head toward the old man. He was crouched by B5, Ekiya beside them. A wisp of thin smoke curled through the little droid's hat. "They target him first and foremost. The rest of us are but obstacles. So, step kindly out of the way and be kindly left alone."

"They're Sith," Kouru countered. "They *think*. Leave what you value behind, and they'll find a way to make it your weakness."

"They're shades. Barely present. If they *were* still as cunning as you fear, I believe we would be dead by now."

Kouru's argument stuck in her throat. She agreed in terms of pure instinct, though it stung to do so.

Fox drew closer, their feet crunching on frosted ground. "We've come this far only because we did so together," they said, so very considerately soft. "They've given of themselves to ensure it. They have nothing left to offer but their lives."

"Let them pay what they will," said Kouru, though as she said it she wished it back in her mouth. She turned away, toward Yuehiro, who was stoically determined as Chie bound his arm to his body. "They don't want to stay," she said shortly. "They won't."

"Like hell they won't." Ekiya joined them, arms crossed so her hands were entrenched in the folds of her coat. Her furtive eyes flicked from Fox to Kouru. "Bee's down for the count. You could drag him, I guess, but you might as well break your own ankles and save yourself the trouble."

"You make it sound like you're not coming," said Fox.

Kouru eyed Ekiya sharply; she was thinking the same thing. The children she could feasibly justify leaving behind. They were injured, and amateurs, and too determined to help. But Ekiya—

"Well, I'm not," said Ekiya as she retrieved something from the folds of her coat and shoved it into Kouru's hands.

It took Kouru a moment to understand what she now held. It scintillated against her skin, so she *knew* it as keenly as she knew heat or pain, but she couldn't begin to explain why Ekiya would have given it to anyone, let alone to her. The small box of kyber shards hung heavy in her hands. The old man's prizes alongside Ekiya's own treasured ghost hoard. She looked up from it to Ekiya, who met her with an expression both flustered and defiant, then bowed.

"Please."

"Why?" Kouru asked, because she couldn't yet accept that it had happened. She wanted badly for Ekiya to realize she had made a mistake, because she couldn't fathom what she was meant to do with this gift.

"I know where I'm useful, and it's not wrestling with undead Sith." Ekiya nodded over her shoulder toward the apprentices. "Them I can manage. Teen's a teen, whether they can invert your brain or no. And they're good kids. And they're hurt."

Kouru couldn't bring herself to put the kyber away. She tried to catch Ekiya's eye again, but the woman remained stubbornly evasive, bending over to scoop up Fox's cat, which had sensed Fox's intent to leave it behind and begun to whine.

"This isn't what you want," Kouru said. "You said—you came here to put them where they belonged. Not to give them up."

Ekiya lightly kicked Kouru's heel. "You told me I had to want something for myself, not outside myself. Okay. I want help. Do this for me."

"You trust me?"

"Why not? You're stubborn as they come. And you like me. And I asked. Please."

Kouru slid the box inside her cloak, half expecting as she did that it would be taken back. But Ekiya's hands remained wrapped around the cat, and Fox's were occupied with soothing the idiot creature. Kouru was permitted to stow it away, and in the end, all she could say was, "I don't know your prayers."

Ekiya clucked her tongue. "I'm not asking you to *pray*."

No, she was asking Kouru to *be* her prayer. Carry my ghosts, she said, and bring them where they're meant to be. Do it for me, because I have faith that you can.

Ludicrous.

And yet, Kouru wanted to do it. It would be a gift, she realized, to have a reason to go forward that was neither the witch nor the old man.

Let them try and stop her.

CHAPTER
THIRTY-EIGHT

T HEY LEFT THE apprentices and B5-56 with Chie, Ekiya, and the cat at an overlook from where they could see the first bridge. B5 could no longer move independently, but his internal comlink still functioned well enough that the old man's wrist cuff blinked now and again. The old man told the droid to look out for the others. B5 told him that he intended to pray.

A day ago, it might have annoyed Kouru to hear the droid say as much, but as she stepped out onto the bridge with the old man and Fox, she decided she would take Ekiya's lesson and accept any help she could get.

The long bridge to the first shrine was made of ancient roots and branches, grown into intricately knotted rope. It creaked over a chasm that plunged into mists so thick and silent that they swallowed the cry of every darting bird within them. The first shrine stood atop a monumental column of weathered gray stone and rose five stories tall, an eight-ringed dark spire jutting from its peak. There was no path around it. Pilgrims were meant to pay respects at every altar on their way to Shinsui Temple. For all Kouru did little of her own praying, she expected it would feel wrong to simply pass through.

"Each shrine houses the relic of a long-dead monk, or a Jedi, or an emperor—who knows!" said Fox as they drew close. "They're gods and they're not. They reveal the entirety of the universe to be an elaborate pattern of infinitely succeeding elemental particles, or they reveal the folly of clinging to the wisdom of bodily knowledge when the only true path to divinity comes in transcending mean flesh and the obliteration that follows. They're quite holy, either way. And beautiful. Have you ever seen them before?"

"No," said Kouru.

The old man only nodded. He was inscrutable, other than for being tired. It had pained him to leave his droid, but he pushed on with the determined countenance of the dying. This, Kouru grudgingly understood.

It was Fox who concerned her. They were so awed by the shrines, so enchanted by the chasm. All the things they didn't remember about their time on Rei'izu no longer seemed to bother them, as they had on the *Crow*. Had they also forgotten their fear? It made Kouru hold more tightly to every feeling that she could with any certainty call her own.

A figure awaited them before the door to the first shrine, broad and tall. A demon. It stood as they neared.

Fox swept their arm out and upward, and the black current knocked the demon off balance. The demon twisted to regain their bearing, but before they landed, Kouru dived toward them, singeing with white flare. She stabbed her blue-white blade into the demon's shoulder and carved away an arm with momentum enough to send the body whirling past and behind her. They fell in the direction of the old man, and he cut them down in one swift strike. The demon's form bled blackly into the air as had all the shades before them.

Fox clapped their hands free of imaginary dust and ushered their comrades toward the shrine.

"It would have been easier if you used your blade," Kouru muttered as she passed.

"Oh, let's not grow dependent on it. Master Ronin only had so much time to put it back together. And what happens if we have to dig out the shard again?"

Kouru narrowed her eyes, unconvinced.

Meanwhile, the old man frowned. "They've no need of it."

Kouru scoffed.

Regardless, they pressed on. Through the darkened pagoda and past the idol interred within, and on to the next woven bridge. The shrines were built in such a clever way that each successive pillar only became visible once the pilgrim had exited the shrine prior. As they stepped back into the permanent evening light, the second shrine loomed gloomily before them, enshrouded by mist.

On the next bridge, Fox seemed about to start another story. Kouru hissed them quiet and jerked her chin ahead.

Another demon awaited them on the steps of the second shrine. It had a companion, one who crouched upon the third tier of snow-covered eaves.

Meanwhile, behind them, in the entryway of the first shrine, they saw a shadowed silhouette picking itself up off the ground—a silhouette that looked alarmingly like that of the demon they had just felled.

"Well, either that one was hiding, or we have a bit more of a resurrection problem than we thought," said Fox.

The old man cursed and looked agitatedly at his wrist cuff. There was a brief flurry of communication between him and B5. It seemed to cut off before he wanted it to.

"They're rising up in the park as well," said the old man.

Kouru cursed this time, and more savagely.

"We'll just have to pray they're all more interested in their old commander than in harassing the stragglers," said Fox. "Either way, we ought to hurry."

Kouru bristled, but she couldn't argue. Forward was the only direction that would solve the matter. So long as the witch continued to resurrect her demons, there would be no safety on Rei'izu.

It at least confirmed that the witch no longer played by her old rules; Kouru was no exception. The witch did not relinquish the dead she wielded. Until they dealt with her, Kouru would never be free.

They met the two demons waiting at the second shrine before the one from the first could catch up to them. The numbers still lay in their favor. But the old man was already flagging. He staggered once, nearly caught by a strike, and was saved only by Fox yanking him back with the black current.

Kouru swept past both and threw the demon against a painted wall with a burst of white flare. She followed with a kick, her heel digging into their side and sending them to the ground, where she drove her blade into their head.

Just as she did, the demon used the last of their strength to thrust their blade toward her like a spear. She twisted away—but it bit hungrily into her side. The demon evaporated beneath her, her wound the only evidence it had ever existed.

Yet when Kouru lifted her hand away from her ribs, they were unmarred.

"Well, that's certainly an advantage," said Fox as they came up the steps. The old man trailed behind them, hand pressed to his own still-wounded side. "Were you doing that before?"

Kouru's brow creased and her head ached strangely as she tried to recall. She was near certain that since her death she had been hurt, here and there—at Seikara, when Ekiya had blackened her eye, and on the *Reverent*, where she burned her hands, and elsewhere, when she . . . "I didn't *feel* it, then," she said.

Fox glanced behind them. The demon from the first shrine was midway down the bridge and fast advancing. Revived, repaired, and strong as ever—just like Kouru. "I suppose there's something to be said for learning from example. Though I think we ought not to learn from yours."

Kouru's brow remained furrowed as they hurried through the shrine. Fox's words stank. She didn't know what of.

Perhaps it was that they were uninjured as well. But then, they were far more skilled at unseating their opponents at range. She shook her head. If something needed to be done about Fox, the old man would know it before she did.

That was, if she could trust the old man to deploy his mercilessness on Fox. He was undeniably weak when it came to them. Hobbled by an affection—a dependence. She couldn't let her eye wander too far from either of them.

She had her own self to mind as well. Though the witch had been silent since the *Reverent*—outside of when she stole Kouru's body wholesale—a whisper had begun to lick at Kouru's ear every now and then. She refused to entertain it. The witch would not have her again, if she could help it.

They progressed as quickly as they were able, which was nerve-rackingly not quick at all. The old man continued to decline. Fox spent nearly as much time lugging him forward as they did fending off their foes. Much of the violence was left to Kouru. She didn't mind—she couldn't. Violence had always been a natural end for her, and moreover, the witch's power allowed her to fight fearlessly, sure she would emerge unscathed.

Even so, they needed the old man to reach the temple alive, and with every encounter, they lost ground.

They couldn't afford to meet more than the one or two demons they faced at each shrine—or the three they found at the fifth, the last of whom speared Kouru through the middle before the old man threw it bodily off the pillar. It took him a painful half minute to regain his breath after that, and she lifted him upright.

"You're being reckless," he rasped.

"You're jealous," she countered, then caught herself and glowered.

She didn't want his care, but reluctantly she understood it. It came from his guilt, which he deserved, not least of all for the ills he'd done to her twice over. She by no means admired what he had become. Yet, something in her wanted to hold on to the man she remembered knowing of before—the rebel, the commander, the lord.

That was certainly not the man Fox had to near drag along as they made their way across the bridge for the sixth shrine.

"Tell me, Kouru," they said, "how many do we have picking themselves up on the fifth?"

She strained her eyes to see and could only report two.

"Then we're lucky—they rise where they fall. We should have been punting them off the sides this whole time."

The demons in the sixth shrine seemed to know their scheme. They dodged and lunged with uncanny awareness of the precipitous cliffs. They had been warned, either by what they saw when their prey passed through the fifth shrine, or by the witch's whispers in their own ears. Kouru nearly lost an arm ridding herself of the last.

"Send him forward," she grunted as she joined Fox and the old man on the misty stretch to the final shrine. "Fast as you can through the seventh, then to the temple. We cover, and we cut the bridge once he's made it."

The old man balked.

"We'll catch up," Fox assured him. "We can't leave you without care-givers, can we?" To Kouru they added, "Speaking of. Let's let as many of them get on the bridge as possible—send all we can into the abyss. En-sures they'll have to find another way across, unless they'd like to spend a lot of time climbing. And then, well, more of a buffer."

Kouru nodded tentatively. She didn't hate the plan, especially as it was her own. But realizing it would leave her standing side by side with Fox's uncanny calm unnerved her from skin to bone.

The last bridge was as beautiful as the others, intricately grown and hung with lanterns. Kouru noticed its beauty because they planned to destroy it. As they waited on its slats while the old man staggered to the temple cliffs, Fox maintained an elegantly straight posture. They still hadn't touched their blade.

Kouru felt mad for thinking something wrong. But it *was*. The Jedi clans boasted of their warriors' serenity in the face of peril because the Jedi were all too comfortable with their power. Kouru had suffered from this same myopia for well over a decade, when she had been the worst violence in her little world. Now she was all tension and fear. It didn't matter that her body would recover from injury, or that her every pain was but temporary. She was with every iota of her being determined to send these demons to the faraway depths, yes, but after them, she had the interminable witch to reckon with. And she, great wraith, she loomed.

Fox didn't *care*. Kouru had seen them swallow fear, and she had seen it make them cavalier and cruel. This was something else, something defined as much by the gaps eaten into their mind as by their wholly unmarred flesh.

When the first demons appeared on the eaves of the seventh shrine, Kouru could no longer hold it in. "Whatever's going on with you," she bit out, "you need to get it together."

"Is that a smidge of concern I hear? I'm touched."

"It's a damn heap of concern. You're a liability."

"No more so than you."

Kouru balked. She suspected the witch still murmured to Fox, from the hollow spaces in their head that she had carved into them. She had done the same to Kouru—was still trying to do so even now. But Fox had never admitted to hearing any such whispers. It made Kouru afraid that they didn't realize the whispers were there.

Her strange look had made Fox pause, and they lifted a hand to their mouth as if their own words were foreign to them. They were so struck by her stare that when the first demons stepped onto the bridge, Kouru dashed forward to meet them alone.

It wasn't until she was pressed back to where Fox still stood and diverted a slash meant for their neck that they startled back to themself. They inhaled sharply and at last leaned into the fray.

Yet as they did, the black current as ever their sole weapon, the whisper in Kouru's ear sharpened. *Careful,* it said, *careful, careful.*

She was no fool—of course she was careful.

But why would the witch warn her of her own creature?

"Kouru," Fox said as they retreated together toward the temple, luring their foes farther onto the bridge. "Have you sorted out what it is you're here for?"

They didn't mean here on Rei'izu, or on this warpath—they meant her very being. The answer to the questions they had posed not so long ago: Who was she? Who for?

Ekiya's ghost hoard weighed heavily in Kouru's cloak. The Jedi lord's lightsaber sat perfect and unclean in her grip. The witch loomed darkly beneath her feet and at her back, hungry for the traitor Kouru shepherded toward her.

Her answer was none of these. It was something else and other, something *more.* She hadn't yet captured it on her tongue, but—"I'm close. Have you? Were you right?"

Did they mean to fix their mistakes?

"Yes." They said it so quickly, yet a cloud had gathered behind their eyes.

Kouru's heart was wary, but she felt at the same time an unexpected pang of sympathy. "Then tell me," she pushed. "Who are you? And why?"

They had reached the end of the bridge. The witch's demons neared, and they had such little time—but Kouru insisted. Fox's gaze had glazed with distance. They wanted to answer her in good faith, she thought. In a way, they did.

A winter-white flash of light and shriek of sound, and the bridge gave way under Kouru's feet. Fox had done the severing, so they'd known just when to leap back. They landed on the rocky cliffside as Kouru threw herself toward it, falling, falling, grasping blindly for purchase.

She found it where she couldn't have anticipated. A hand latched around her forearm and gripped her with feverish need. The same fingers that had just cut the bridge out from under her dug desperate bruises into her arm. Fox's face was stricken with a dazed understanding, a horror.

Kouru dug the same bruises into their flesh, teeth gritted, eyes bright—if they knew they weren't alone in their own mind, then they could *fight*. It was what she had done, and she'd done it at their behest. If they could together wrench freedom from the witch—

Let go.

Kouru's nails bit into Fox's arm. Their teeth clenched, but they held on. Yes—that was what they needed. The need for self and outside of self—

Let go. Let go, let go.

Kouru gasped and it hurt to do so. Breath didn't belong in her deadness, and she was only shadowing life, but she *would* cling because—

Let go.

Kouru refused to listen. It didn't matter. Fox did.

Their grip slackened. Kouru's arm slid between their fingers, and then she was free. She fell. They had let go.

As she plunged, the wind screaming in her ears, she stared up at the vanishing white figure and thought: They could still catch me.

Then Kouru didn't see them at all, only the white upon white of a devouring mist, and she was at last alone.

CHAPTER
THIRTY-NINE

THE RONIN SAW the bridge fall from the distance of the stone steps that led to Shinsui Temple. He had collapsed upon them, one hand clutched to his aching side, the other balanced so he could check his wrist cuff for any sign of light. It was still dark as the bridge tumbled into the mist, graceful as a broken spiderweb, loosing small black shapes as it tore.

For long minutes after, he was alone. When he wasn't, only the Traveler returned. They held their arm in front of them as if it had been injured, the sleeve fallen away to show an unmarred stretch of flesh from wrist to elbow. Once close enough to speak, they said in the dull tone of shock, "She let go."

The Ronin winced and straightened, his eyes closed. He wasn't sure whether he owed Kouru another prayer. He thought probably he did, but that she wouldn't appreciate it. He held his tongue.

Neither spoke as they made their way up the stairs. The Ronin went slowly, and the Traveler cajoled him to use their shoulder. It took them a long half hour to reach the top of the steps.

No demon followed, nor harried them on the path. The expanse of the temple courtyard was unpeopled. Some birds flitted here and there, and a corner of the courtyard had been uprooted by a tower of a pine tree. But there was no sign of enemy, shade, or witch.

The final stairs were wooden, leading up to the main hall that sat on elaborate stilts so as to best overlook the chasm and the capital beyond. Shinsui's great veranda was also empty. The sun crawled over it through wooden pillars until the light met the painted doors that protected the imposing chamber where the mirror had been held. These were closed. The Ronin looked questioningly to his companion.

"If you're asking me how it went last time . . . well." They didn't remember. And yet . . .

"You seem . . . content."

"So do you."

The Ronin snorted. He didn't know what he felt. They had fought and they had suffered losses, and they didn't yet know just how high that tally ran. Concern shadowed his heart, but he could only harbor so much of that when he needed the strength to face what lay beyond that door.

He was displaced. He had come to these doors only once before, but he had returned to them time and again in his memory. Often, in the early days, when he thought of them relentlessly. Less so later, when he only tripped into the recollection without intention or purpose. Very occasionally, when he dreamed.

He indicated that he wanted to sit. He needed to. His bones creaked against exhaustion and cold, and if the door was closed, then they had been granted the reprieve of time. The Traveler eased him onto the ground and sat too, at his back. They each had one eye on the door and the other on the veranda. They would be ready for attack from either direction.

"I never imagined actually coming back," he confessed. "I don't know what to feel."

"Quite the admission, coming from you. Ah, or are you hoping I'll finally divulge the last of my secrets?"

Their air was coy but brittle. Either way, the Ronin had long since learned that the most effective tactic to take with the Traveler was silence. They seemed faintly annoyed that he remembered this and they rubbed the arm they had cradled on their return from the bridge.

Had they been hurt? No. Not even a bruise.

The Ronin touched his brow to ease a clouding haze. It had been too long since he last slept.

The Traveler was speaking. "Anyway, I can't imagine you want to hear the woeful tale of a substandard heir, o terrible Dark Lord of the Sith, he that rallied the rebellion against the iniquities of the child-thieving Jedi clans."

"Is it wrong to want to better know my ally?"

Their silence was strange again. But then, they both understood that they had reached their last opportunity to share anything at all. There would be truth or there would be nothing.

"Can you really call me that?" they asked. "Who knows what else I'm keeping from you?"

"Not you."

The Traveler stiffened, then laughed. "Well."

"I wouldn't fault a child for their birth."

"You might be better off if you did." The words were cold, but their tone was contemplative. "I don't want you thinking I had some grand moral objection to my duties. I was fearful. Lazy. Perhaps because I thought an indolent child would never be trusted to do anything worth noticing. My parents thought Hanrai would turn me around . . . I suppose he did. It's amazing how grateful you can be for a touch of freedom."

"He taught you to kill."

"Very quietly, too. And I was so good at it!"

"Not here." The witch yet lived. Presumably.

"Everyone hits their limit eventually."

The Ronin frowned over his shoulder. He could just make out the curve of their face, oddly still. "You speak of fear as if you overcame it. But you feared him."

"Did I? I suppose so." Their look was at once pained and amused by their failure to understand themself. "You called me content here. Maybe I am. I don't know who I was when I came the first time. When I stayed. But I don't think I was afraid."

Not until whatever they met had sent them away again. They'd spoken of blood and grief, a catastrophic failure they could not recall. But before that, melancholy. Sweetness, laughter, *a speck of hope.*

And now?

"I was afraid," the Ronin said. "I am."

It felt like a dire mistake to admit it, but the Traveler said nothing, only listened, their back pressed warm to his.

"From the moment the Jedi took me in . . . I don't know that the fear ever left."

He had been afraid of the Jedi, of his place in the galaxy, of the responsibility and the risk. Afraid for himself and his fellows, of what would become of them when they were grown. Of how they could never dream to be more than weapons so easily let to die. Of how he had come into violence so naturally and well, and yet he was still *afraid*. What right had he to be? What reason?

His body coiled with every recollection.

"What are you afraid of now?" asked the Traveler.

"That I shouldn't have come." In the splinter of the mirror, the witch had said she didn't want him to. Had Hanrai lied? If so . . . "I don't think I understand why I have."

"Well, I did ask you to. Though I suppose my word was never the most convincing argument. Even less so now."

"I . . . felt compelled to respond. That doesn't mean I should have."

He had spent so many years thinking he would never seek to return. He had not thought that there was no point in trying because he couldn't; he had thought, rather, that there was a very good reason why he shouldn't. Yet here he was, present and permitted to be.

One way or another, either he or the witch would die in a matter of hours. Minutes. Whenever the door next opened. Was that what he had run from all this time? So long as they were apart, both of them could live.

The Traveler wasn't looking at him as they spoke, but they stood, their arms obscured in front of them. He thought they might be clutching their wrist again. "It seems to me you've spent a long time dreading what you've done wrong. And you haven't spent much of it thinking about what you could do right."

"You suppose I know what right would be."

"I think you would have to choose."

The Ronin frowned, and frowned more deeply when they came

around in front of him to meet his look. He wanted to turn away; that meant, in all likelihood, that he shouldn't. "You choose as wrongly as I have, you lose some right to choose at all."

"Yet here you are, persisting even so."

The Traveler's mouth was wry, their eyes tired but soft. They held out their hands to take his and coaxed him up. The Ronin ached, but some of the ache came from disuse. It would be better to stand for a while, at least to stretch.

"Do you know, for a time, I thought it was enough to simply be alive. That I might not owe anyone anything but for my breath to myself. But now . . ." The Traveler's gaze tracked to the temple door, and it was troubled. "If we are to be alive, we probably ought to be doing something."

It sounded worthy of being true. Simultaneously, the Ronin didn't like that they thought it was. Nor could he imagine allowing it to be true of himself. The Ronin had long since thought himself past the point of doing right, let alone doing good. Not with all the mistakes he had made, and the ones he was still making. But once he had run out of hope for himself, it was so damningly easy to give it up for others too. That, he couldn't abide.

Lit by a half-sunk sun, the Traveler reached up for his face. Their touch on his cheek was as it had been when they fled the shambles of the *Reverent,* by turns smooth and callused. He allowed them to remove his mask, as well as to detach the respirator from his prosthetic. It was unwise, but if they wanted it, then so did he. Foolish though it made him. Selfish though he was.

Bare-faced, the Ronin's breath came short because they were on a mountain, and because he had labored a great deal to get there, and because he was tired, and because he was closer to living intimacy than he had allowed himself to be in many a long, long year.

How strange, then, that his chest eased and his breaths lengthened when he saw what the Traveler held in their other hand: a familiar lightsaber hilt, yet unlit, that was not theirs because it was his. He had neither seen nor felt them take it. But then, he'd never known they were cheating until they had already done it. Nevertheless, it felt more correct to see his blade in their hand than to have felt their unguarded closeness so near his mouth.

He couldn't put a name to the feeling on their face. The uncertainty on their brow was at odds with the confidence in their grip. He had grown so used to their presence in current and flare that he felt the pricking eddies of their disconcertion as if they were his own. They didn't quite understand themself. That didn't mean they wouldn't act. Or that they didn't want to do what they were about to.

Though all things given, it seemed unlikely that they did.

"Is this it?" The Ronin's voice had been made anemic by his injury. "Is this what you think is right?"

For long, unmoving moments, the world didn't move, and the Traveler didn't speak, though their gaze was fixed on his lightsaber in their hand. Their mouth fell open. He thought he would hear an answer. Then they ignited the red length of his blade. Its point hovered at the tip of his bare throat.

CHAPTER FORTY

Kouru fell. Fell and fell. Fell until she hit flat hardness and was shattered by it.

She was at that point too broken to know what had broken her. She had only body, a mess of pain and other frustrations, and she saw nothing she could make sense of. Black. White. One bleeding into the other. One becoming then *being* the other even as it was still itself, as if there had not ever been a division.

Nonsense.

The only clarity she still possessed: a hope that in the next breath, she would die, and in the breath after that, she would be new and whole and ready to—what, exactly?

She had for a fleeting stretch possessed bright purpose. Take the ghosts in the kyber, deliver them to their proper death. Do this not because you desire it but because you are trusted to. Because trust is something outside of who you are, and who you are is vulnerable to every kind of control, so it is better by far to be driven by that which you aren't.

Kouru couldn't trust herself. Her *self* was not her own. But given another's trust, she had clung to it viciously.

It had done her no good in the end. Even with that tether, she had fallen.

Better a tether that couldn't hold her than a leash that squeezed her neck till it snapped.

Kouru snorted, then coughed, and was miserable for it. She let her head fall back against bright-dark hardness—it had to be stone, yes?—and from the corner of her eye, she spied a shining thing.

What breath was left to her caught in her throat. A kyber shard, translucently brilliant, lay just out of reach. Kouru heaved her broken-ness toward it. The crystal must have fallen when she did. When she laid her hand on it and clutched it to her chest, she spied another shining shard, and another. Ekiya's ghosts lay sprawled across the landscape of black-white-black—

Kouru refused to think any more of the world. It hurt her to do so, and she had her obligation. Her body was unready to be upright, but she demanded it, and to her mild wonder, it obeyed. She staggered forward, rescued one crystal after another. She had failed them—failed Ekiya, failed herself—but if she could collect them, she might—

"Let go," said a voice in her ear.

Kouru snarled at it—she had heard more disembodied voices than she ever wished to again—and clutched the kyber all the harder, until it dug its points into her palms.

Yet as she did, she tightened her hands too much, and one of the shards slipped out from between her fingers. Kouru caught at it as it tumbled, but it hit the white-black-white ground, where she lost track of it.

Kouru dropped to her knees, the rest of her treasures held close to her chest. She searched for the ghost crystal that had escaped, but she could find no sign of it. Still she scoured the world for any trace. A translucent sliver would be all too easy to misplace in this impossibly colored-uncolored landscape.

She feared, somehow, that she was wrong. That the crystal had not simply fallen. That it was *gone*.

No sooner did she have the thought than another crystal slid out from her grasp. Then another and another. Kouru tried in vain to catch them too.

"Let go," said the voice again, and for once, a body accompanied it—a body of sorts. A hand jutted out from the strange ground beneath Kouru's knees and seized her forearm. It held Kouru fast as every shard that had slipped from her hands fell and fell until—

She saw what came of them, this time. They tumbled in a glinting rain and where they landed, the ground rippled outward in delicate, intersecting circles. Whether the shards were swallowed by the white-black surface or dissolved into it, they were gone.

Kouru stilled. The hand on her arm remained, but its grip lessened. It no longer needed to keep her in place; understanding did that all on its own.

Kouru had been given the kyber, these ghosts, so that they could go where they were meant to. They had already stayed too long. As their crystals receded into white flare and black current—because of course that was what the world (all worlds) was made of, the color-uncolor of the Force itself—they were unmade, just as they were made more themselves than they had ever been.

Her fingers had clenched for so long that it hurt to unfold them, and it took a while. Kouru flattened her palms as best she could and let the remaining kyber pour down her hands to where it belonged. More and more ripples flooded out from her knees as the ghosts ceased to be what-they-had-been and became what-they-must-be.

She wished it were enough. That it didn't leave her feeling like so much nothing.

"That's why I keep telling you to let go," said the voice, and Kouru realized suddenly that she'd never heard it before. Not like this.

She followed the length of the arm holding her to where it broke through the ground. There, mirrored beneath her knees as if her own reflection stared back at her, crouched another person. She knew the woman, but barely. She had seen that face once, from a distance, and she had loved it instantly and fiercely. Those angled features, the handsome mouth.

The witch awaited her on the other side, holding tight to Kouru's arm and looking for all the world like she thought they shared some sort of secret.

Kouru wished to wrest her hand from the witch's grasp. Yet she didn't. Or couldn't, because she hadn't been allowed. "Let go?" she snapped, because her tongue was still her own. "And let you take me again? I'd rather eat my own eyes."

"You're very set on being difficult." The witch ignored Kouru's affronted glower and shifted her grasp so that she held Kouru's empty upturned hand by the wrist. "You don't even know what it is you're still holding on to."

Kouru wrapped her fingers into a fist. "You can't have me. Not again."

"I never took you to begin with."

It was a lie, yet it didn't sound like one. Kouru searched the witch's impassive face for any sign of deception. If anything, she found annoyance, which only served to annoy her in turn. "What are you talking about?" she snapped.

"Your tether. Your leash."

As the witch spoke these words, her grip became a vise that held Kouru from skin to bone and deeper still. Kouru strained against her and could find no purchase—her feet had begun to sink into the unsolidity of the ground beneath her. Into the witch's realm.

She struggled and writhed. Rescue came suddenly around her waist, when something jerked her in the other direction—a string, no, many strings. Kouru seized at them. She pulled herself upward to safety by their length.

Sprawled on flatness and shuddering for breath, her eyes tracked the strings to their source. This nearly undid her.

Each string led to a memory, one that Kouru inhabited fully and instantaneously. Every one left her more haggard and breathless than the last, until she was left heaving on her back, racked with her own self. The day the Jedi took her, a child—the day they took her mind—the day the Sith set her free—and the day they died—until the day she died as well, and—

A hand caught hers again. The witch's fingers reached up through the rippling surface of the world and clasped Kouru's cold and shaking palm. "Let go," she murmured, and at last it sounded like a promise. "Let go, as I did."

Like the ghosts had, as the crystals that had housed them for these long years had receded into the nothing of the Force. Let go. Be free.

Kouru couldn't stand the thought. "I don't want to be gone," she said, and hated terribly how young she sounded.

"Then don't be," said the witch. "I'm not."

Kouru clenched the witch's fingers in her own. She rolled painstakingly onto her hands and knees so that she could once more see the witch. This time, she was met not with a face but with a vastness—Rei'izu, that frozen landscape, extended in all directions on the other side of the world.

"What are you?" Kouru asked, for once more full of wonder than fire.

"Nothing more than you are. Nothing more than you could be."

The hand still wrapped around Kouru's pulled her gently downward, until her face rested on the surface that divided the world she was in from the world beneath, and through it she saw:

A woman, once, who had been betrayed, and who then was dead in order to serve this, the frozen world. The witch who had taken Rei'izu because in order to protect it, she had *become* it.

You too, she was saying. *This could be yours as well. Not in the form I've chosen, but in a form of your own design.*

Kouru believed her. Trusted the witch's words from her nerves to her soul, because they were in a world where falsehood existed only as farce, and truth resonated cleanly from one heart to the next. She could have just such a magnitude, if only she wanted it.

Yet she hesitated.

"Why?" asked Kouru. "Why would you tell me this?"

Two hands rose this time, and they grasped Kouru's face as a mother would her child's. "I wanted so much more for you—all of you, children twice-stolen. What did we rescue you into? More blood. More war. I gave you so little, before the end. Now I'll give you whatever I can. I must. And . . ."

The witch drew Kouru closer. Kouru did not resist. She no longer wanted to. And so as her face breached the surface between the worlds, she saw what the witch bade her see on Rei'izu—the land that belonged to the witch, for it *was* the witch.

Just before the doors that led into the main hall of Shinsui Temple, two figures stood on the great veranda. One held a lightsaber, ignited and red. The other held nothing at all. Soon, one would kill the other. Kouru knew both figures too well to assume she knew which would leave the victor.

Fox had cunning but too much mercy. The old man always struck before he let himself regret. He would not hesitate. Except for Fox, he might falter, and if he did . . . He was dying. It wouldn't take much.

"Either murder would be a ruin," the witch whispered. "It would ensure a fate I do not wish for, shatter the haven I have striven to be. Bastion. Promise. Peace."

"I don't understand." Kouru grasped the hands that held her face. "You brought us here. You wanted this."

"I don't," the witch promised. "I never did."

It made no sense, but it was true. It had to be, in this place.

Which meant the thing that had fished Kouru out of simple death, that had threaded through her mind and dragged her so far, that wanted still to bind her—that had not been the witch. It never had been. Something *else* dug its fingers through the worlds, wearing the dead as it pleased, and whatever it sought, the witch did not desire. In fact, she feared its fruition. She prayed Kouru did too.

Kouru feared a great many things. She certainly feared an eternity of being summoned again and again, always a puppet, made to pursue an end she had never even been asked to understand.

Yet the alternative offered by the witch who was world . . . Kouru couldn't begin to conceive it.

Quiet and peace. An unfathomable dream. It was too far removed from the world of cruelties, petty and grand alike, that clung to Kouru like her own skin. But some wisp of her, oh, it yearned. If only she could think such an existence possible.

She did know someone who could think such things—someone more capable of hope, whose faith she had recently come to rely on. A person who knew how to think of worlds other than the one she lived in, and who pursued those better worlds, even when she couldn't imagine herself living in them. When Kouru thought on this, she found that it became suddenly far easier to do the same thing herself.

Yes, she thought, I know how to want this. I can want it for her. I can want it for more. And I do.

There was an unfolding, within and without her. Kouru diminished, expanded, and clutched the witch's hands. "If I do this, I can stop them," she said, because she dared not ask it. She couldn't bear a no.

"Please," said the witch, and, "come."

Kouru took a last deep breath and inclined her head. She let the witch's hands guide her forward, away from one world and into the next.

Kouru let go.

CHAPTER
FORTY-ONE

THERE WAS NO sound on the veranda but for the Ronin's own labored breathing. It would take little effort for the Traveler to kill him. They needed only advance; they would extend their arm just so, or slide their step forward, and the lightsaber they'd taken from him would pierce his naked throat. He didn't move. He wondered if he couldn't.

The Ronin didn't believe he wished to die. Not here and not by their hand. He was certain, in a way he rarely had been, that they didn't wish for his death either. They would nevertheless kill him, if he allowed them to. Therefore, for their sake, he couldn't.

He didn't yet know how he would do it. He feared he would have to kill them first. He didn't want that either. His fingers trembled at the thought. He couldn't let that stop him.

Then the red blade fell from the Traveler's hand. They looked to where it tumbled across the ancient wooden floor, expression caught between concern and relief. Then they fell too, toward the Ronin.

He reached for them, and for a fleeting instant his hand met the resistance of cloth and flesh. Then that physicality melted away like mist over water. This was how their shape unspooled as well, white face and hand and robe all coming apart under light, until nothing of the Traveler remained but for a pain in the Ronin's palm.

When he unfurled his hand, he found a winter-clouded splinter of kyber. It threatened to dig into his flesh, just as it had twenty years ago, when he had struck it from the mirror.

It was the first and only remnant any of Rei'izu's shades had left behind. He wanted to believe that meant it had been left for him on purpose. That it was a gift. He would not be able to ask.

Now the only other thing before him was the Traveler's murderer, who stood on the veranda behind where they had been. The blue-white blade with which she had killed them singed the very air. Kouru was oddly lit, as if the sun couldn't touch her but she shone all the same.

The Ronin's breath came low and tight. In anger, partly. In relief as well, though it sickened him to admit. He knew he had been spared having to act himself, but neither was he glad to see the Traveler dead. Still, he stood straight to hold Kouru's gaze. She stared at him differently—not as a man she loathed nor as one for whom she felt any compassion, but as one from whom she expected something more. Some small dark part of him flickered with terror. He did not permit himself to flinch; his body was too frail, and if he let it falter, the whole of him would crumble.

Kouru broke the look to kneel. As she did, he thought there was someone else—beside or behind her, or standing where she had been— someone so familiar that his heart instantly ached. But when Kouru stood again, it was only as herself. Herself . . . and more than herself. She wore Kouru like a memory. Was she fading too? Or would she soon brighten past his eye's ability to hold her?

Kouru held out the Ronin's mask and respirator in one hand, the hilt of his lightsaber in the other. The kyber shard he tucked away. The rest he took from her to fit to his prosthetic and sash with hands that still shook.

Kouru turned her head to the doors. They had opened minutely, parted by a stark dark line. "She's waiting for you."

"You seem better equipped to face her," he said.

"You'd be a coward? Now?" She eyed him sharply. Then her lip curled and she turned away. When she spoke again, she faced the darkness behind the doors straight-backed. "Remember why you first came here. What you hoped to find."

An answer. A reason to live. Something to follow death upon death. The mirror had offered him its vision once already, and he had been a poor steward of its truth. Had fled the horror of it by becoming a horror himself.

Now the terrible truth he had faced was rampant. A sea of ghosts, taken and trapped, wrought into demons and recurring until their last use had been wrung from them. Death was no mercy. If it had ever been, he would have to think himself a good man for having given it to so many, and he knew better.

"Go," she said. "Don't leave them like this."

It was the least he could do: free those he had condemned.

So, he went as he was asked to, forward and through the doors, to meet his calling and to die, if need be.

CHAPTER
FORTY-TWO

THE INNER CHAMBER was as the Ronin remembered it, a largeness defined by its artistic origin. Imposing not by dint of sheer size but because living hands had rendered it grand for the sake of grandiosity, to evoke the enormity of world upon world. It was minimally lit, as it had been the last time he entered it. The intricate metal lanterns hanging from long chains overhead glowed but dimly, and the candles perched on slender metal sticks bloomed as he passed them.

With every step, he remembered the place more freshly. He smelled smoke and blood. Saw it again on the floorboards. Heard distant cries and more distant prayer. The scream of ships in ozone. Haggard breath in his ear.

He slowed—did not stop—and closed his eyes briefly. When they opened, there was no smoke or blood, no crying, no screaming, no breath. And before him stretched the mirror.

It stood where it always had on its low dais, vastly round. Though its surface was fogged with a thousand-thousand fine cracks, it was altogether clear but for a single point in the center, a splinter-shaped gap that welled with gathered candlelight.

As he neared and walked up the steps to be close to it, he took the last kyber shard he still carried from within his robes. It caught the light unevenly as he fit it into place.

When he did, the mirror was again a mirror, and it showed him his silhouette. His reflection, refracted until it seemed youthful. He realized then that the figure he saw was, in fact, not him at all, though she bore elements of the man he had been in her eyes and her smile, just as in her nose and bearing she also resembled the woman who had been called his witch.

The Ronin inhaled sharply, though the respirator slowed the gasp and made it painful. He knew what, who, he beheld without having to be told, because yes, he had loved the witch, and she had loved him too, before he betrayed everything they had done together. Everything they had made. Everything, like the person he now faced, a young woman dressed in plain and practical dark robe and trousers so like her mother's, though she had cropped her hair pleasingly short to her chin.

At her gesture, he and she sat as one across from each other. He was helpless to resist her request. There was a low table between them, and it did not occur to him to question how it existed simultaneously within the mirror and outside of it, because questioning would have been a foolish thing to do in the presence of a mirror that was divine. On the table lay a board drawn with squares, and on the board were familiar wooden tokens carved like arrowheads with characters inked upon their backs; it looked much like the board he had taken to playing on with her mother. She took the first move. He followed suit.

"Aren't you curious?" she said. "Ask me who I am."

When she spoke, her voice struck him like a wrongly sung chord. He realized it was not the first time they had spoken. They had conversed before, many times, most often when she was an echo in his ear, trying to lead him to his death at the hands of another Sith.

"I would not presume to know," he said.

Her smile was vinegar sharp. Liar, she seemed to say. He called himself one too. He did presume. And, oh, he wanted to ask, to know—

*   *   *

—that once she was a child, and she was alone—

The understanding ran all through him like a chilling shock, and his hand shook midway through laying down a knight.

Across from him, she shrugged. "I've nothing to hide. Not now."

His weakness meant that he succumbed to knowing—because he did still want that knowledge, even if he didn't deserve it.

So, he saw—

A child, alone. Not at first, because for a time there is mother, a warmth who ensures she is fed and clean and made safe. But mother has promised to give herself up to Rei'izu, to ensure that the world is safe for the child and for the rest—the Sith who are yet with them. So, after a time, mother is gone, in that she *was* person and flesh but she *becomes* world and time, and she persists, but not in the way a child most needs.

The child is still not quite alone, so long as there are mother's friends and comrades. Her warriors, her shades, and her Sith. They care for the child too, as they can, but all too soon, they fade. Bit by bit. Less and less. At length, over time, they too are shadow and memory. They leave the girl with a meager understanding of herself, and only a sliver of the teaching she should have enjoyed.

Only the mirror endures. Though it lies in shattered pieces across the temple floorboards, from the time she can crawl, she is drawn to its shards. She collects and pieces them together before she even knows words. It shows her more than she can make sense of, but a child makes sense of very little at first, and she is always absorbing, learning, growing.

One day, once she is properly alone but for the mirror, it tells her that someone is coming—

*   *   *

"I thought it would be you," his daughter said as she moved a chariot.

It was an ache that it hadn't been. "Why did you think that?" he asked.

She smiled, and he found himself thinking of how the Traveler smiled no matter what feeling truly stirred behind their eyes. "I didn't yet know what you were."

The figure who arrives is solitary and cuttingly familiar, though they are younger than when the Ronin met them on the Genbara country road. They are bare-faced and white-haired, and he learns that they eschewed Jedi garb even before they forswore the clans entirely, preferring long-sleeved robes and colored tassels.

He understands the moment with a bone-scraping suddenness. They, Idzuna, stand at the mouth of the great temple's main hall. Before them is his daughter, a child, not half their size and staring inquisitively up at them. Their hand rests on the hilt of their scion's blade. The child's eyes slide from Idzuna's face down to the hilt, and she squints in wonder at its graceful shape. Their fingers curl more tightly around it, as if to shield it from her view.

Idzuna has come to Rei'izu because their lord sent them to kill what remnants of the Sith lurk upon it. But the only living thing worth killing is this, her, a young girl abandoned. Their hand falls from their side, blade abjured. They kneel and they speak, and they beckon the girl closer. She takes their empty, upturned palm.

This is the way of it, for long years after. They take it upon themself to raise her, to protect and teach her, because the thought that she might have earned death is beyond their ability to reconcile—

"They pitied me," said his daughter. She was amused and bitter, compassionate as well, a mix that even a monk would envy. "They pitied themself. And they abhorred our imprisonment."

The Ronin inhaled slowly; the air sharpened in his chest. "What happened?"

"You ask so easily now." She carried a bitterness for him too, but she didn't hide the truth.

Idzuna seeks to be a real tutor, a worthy master, as the Jedi once were at their most noble. They teach her as they weren't taught, of history and her place in it—unique, both bound and unfettered. They nurture her relationship with her mirror, help her to pick through and understand that which she sees through it.

As she comes to know the world, she finds herself chasing the ghosts of the shades who raised her first, and all their pain from before their rebellion, and during it, and the terrible moment when it all ended. Always she circles that final hinge, the turn—when he, the man who was her father, chose to become the man who betrayed her mother—

"I did want to know," she said as if this were a passing interest, obscure and academic. "I feared to learn it, but I needed the answer."

"I disappointed." He must have.

Her mouth curved with knowing pity. "You think I expected better?"

She is nearly what she has now become—tall and angled from her face to her limbs, frowning deeply with sweat beading her brow as she sits on the dais before her grand and painstaking project, the resurrection of the mirror. She lifts and orients slivers into place with black current and white flare coursing through her in equal and balanced measure, her master less and less able to enjoin her to eat and sleep. She is so close to revelation. So close to more satisfying truth. Some miracle that will inspire realization, that will give sweet meaning to all she has suffered, and all the suffering of those who came before her.

She is learning to reach through the kyber, to seek its resonance elsewhere in the worlds beyond Rei'izu, and at last to direct it. She sees Jedi in their multitude, Sith in their dwindling vestige, and she searches, searches—until she at last finds him.

It is a curse, and it is instantaneous. Her first brush with his miserable longing only magnifies the need and questions in her own heart. She sees in cruel and bracing fullness all that he had seen when he first threw himself into the mirror.

The interminable and implacable cycle, and the horror of it all. The desolation and regret. The futility. The anguish. It tears into her. She is made asunder.

"It haunts me still," she said, and tenderly. He heard in her such sympathy for who he had been made to be by fate and Jedi, lord and Sith. "What choice had you but to rebel? And what choice was that, in the end?"

"No worthy one," he said. He could think only of the pain he'd wrought.

"I don't condemn you."

What was he to do with that? She of all people deserved to—and should have.

"By that logic, are you in any position to tell me what I *should* do, Father?"

The word settled on him wrongly, a prickling fit. She inclined her head with a wry half smile, as if to suggest the discomfort was his due. If that was so, then he relented. He hadn't earned fatherhood; she gave it to him not as reward but as a blade through a hand.

She took a token and moved it forward to capture one of his own. "Here's what I say. You weren't wrong. How could you be? Princes and the Jedi who make much of them, they worship honor until it exceeds the lives that should define it. Their ways are selfish and cruel. Unjust. I think you were right to defy them. I think it's a pity you failed."

Her hand rested by the board as she raised her attention to the rim of her mirror, the faraway-ness of it, and as he followed her gaze, some sneaking sliver of him began to sink.

"I can't condemn you for failure either," she said. "It's overwhelming, my mirror. It is the world—every world. To realize that entirety while still trapped in a small and wounded body? I couldn't have imagined it, if I hadn't lived it through you."

* * *

She knows the mirror more intimately than she knows any other part of herself, and even then, when she learned what he learned in the way that he learned it, through the memory of his own frail flesh . . .

It ruins her, this young girl, just as she said it did. She crumples and is found, so she isn't forced to endure it alone, because she has a master, and a world, and both would love and shelter her through any pain they could, but oh, it is a vile immensity to suffer, and it takes her days to sleep, days more to speak. She does little of either, caught as she is in the throes of monstrous revelation.

Until the day she wakes and feels at last anew. Refreshed. She rises with epiphany in her mind and resolution in her heart.

"I'll end it," says the girl, yet sweat-damp from the trial she has barely recovered from. "I'll end it for you. For them. For everyone."

The Ronin, speechless, formless, witnessing through the girl's own eyes, can barely comprehend the words. Neither can the person to whom the memory of the girl is in fact speaking—her master, Idzuna, looking much more akin in age to the point at which he met them. This expression, though, he has only recently come to know: confusion, concern, a hint of fear.

"Princes, Jedi," the girl spits. "I can unseat them. Unmake them."

They speak gently to this, softly, though the words run muddy together in her mind. They urge her to sit back, to rest, so that they might talk more about just what it is she wishes to do, what *they* can do, together—

They wish to pacify her, she thinks. To ameliorate. There can be none of that. She hears: Do you exaggerate? Do you overstep?

She does not. She *cannot.* She has seen what she's seen through the mirror, that sublime vessel that holds the entirety of all worlds. Have they not told her that she alone has ever had such intimacy with it? She, daughter of the dark lord and the witch, she *sees* as no other can, and she—she, in all the history of existence—is most uniquely positioned to take the galaxy in her hands and tear it apart, shape it anew.

She tells them so again, tries to, with more correct and impassioned words.

"No," they say, and it is like they've struck her. "No. You have power, a gift—you *are* a gift—but you're a child. You've never killed."

"I haven't?" she snarls, for she is the mirror, and her master's words are laughably small and wrong. "I've killed. I've *been* killed. I've had that pain, that agony. A thousand times I've lived it—even yours. I reached you too. I know what you've done. I've seen."

Their face is pale and hollowed.

"Even if I hadn't, why would that be reason not to? To spare my little soul? I've seen everything you have, *been* everything you have—and more." She takes their limp hands to beg. She wants them to see her. "I understand why you chose to do it. Why others have too. You killed to protect. To save. To take away power ill used. How is that not right?"

Even as the girl pleads with her teacher, the Ronin feels a tug in his heart—an awareness not his own that understands this moment differently from the distance of time.

His daughter knows, now, that her master wished to protect her. She understands as well that they were too ridden by their own old griefs to accept that she might protect them in turn.

This is why they let go of her hands. It's why as they do, they flick their wrist and summon an eddy of black current to break her mirror.

She lashes out. How can she not?

They are thrown back with wrenching violence, a shock wave of her pure frustration and fear. When they land, it's not well. They crack, they bleed, they die.

"Funny how little it takes, if a body doesn't expect it," she said quietly, her hands folded unmoving before her, the board and pieces untouched. "Ironic, perhaps, how well they understood that."

The Ronin wished to speak. To say: It isn't a tidy comparison. She didn't kill them on purpose.

The smile didn't quite make it to her lips. "I didn't mean to bring them back either."

*   *   *

In a way, it's proof of her argument—that she and the mirror are so closely intertwined that she can do as she pleases no matter the pleasure. When she regrets and wants, her heart responds with full knowledge, and the world is hers to change. This time, it is her mother's understanding that filters into hers.

She captures Idzuna's ghost and binds it to new purpose as if she's done so a thousand-thousand times.

They are the first of many. Every fallen Jedi since, every dead Sith, every soul killed for someone else's demands that she can through flare and current reach—she has caught and held them tight to her chest, and will until she has collected so many that their return will spell doom for every Jedi, prince, and emperor who has ever dared to stand over a world and declare they know how it should be. And when they have burned out the poison—then at last the galaxy can rest, and heal, and bear new fruit for sweeter mouths.

The Ronin felt petty in his body. He was so shoddy a phantom against her radiance. He had begun to cry. He asked, though he wondered if he deserved to, "Why?" He meant: Why am I here? Why send them to bring me? Did you not mean to kill me too?

She met his eye across the table, hers alive with need, and she bowed, beseeching. "I didn't wish you dead, Father. I wished you stronger. Better. More alike to the man you were—as close as you could be—honed by battle, survival, and choice. And then . . . I would have your strength be mine."

Hers, as knight, as warrior, as lord of demons. She showed him what it would mean—what they could together be. A raging torrent, a roaring blaze, that would at last wreak justice upon the Empire, until it became wet ash on blackened ground.

"Do this for me," she pleaded. "Let me be your end."

CHAPTER
FORTY-THREE

I't's as if he's dreaming, or praying. He has an indeterminate dilation of time and thought to ask: Is she right? Even if he didn't think she was, would he have the right to say so? He had his chance and ruined it. How dare he hinder hers?

A familiar scoff by his ear: "She isn't wrong. I might do the same, if I had her power."

Kouru stands by his right, arms crossed and scowling up at the towering pool of black and white and color. Her brow creases.

"Oh?" says the Ronin. "Then why do you hesitate?"

She turns her sneer on him, as if annoyed to find herself wanting to respond. But he hears a need in her voice—a need for him to hear. "All I've ever wanted is to be my own . . . She isn't hers. She belongs to this. To you. That's no more free than I am. Maybe she can't be, until it all burns."

Then it should burn, shouldn't it? For her sake. And for the sake of everyone for whom the world has been nothing but shackle.

To his left, he hears a thoughtful hum. A man he knew but briefly waits there for his chance to speak, which isn't very lordly of him. Hanrai tilts his head at the Ronin in knowing humor. "You could say that's my concern as well. She's never had a chance to know anything else."

"Is that not for the better?" asks the Ronin.

"I suppose the alternative never did you any favors." Hanrai frowns, and as he gazes up at the devouring pool of the mirror, his profile hardens. "I can't help wondering how many more of you she'll create, before she's finished. The lost, the wanting. How will she know when to stop burning? Will she? Can she? How many die for her satisfaction?"

As many as it takes, the Ronin thinks—then turns away, ashamed of the thought. It sounds so much like the man he was, from whom he has spent twenty long years running.

But then, the sin from which he fled is not the sin she pins to him. He thought he had burned too much. She says: You did not burn enough.

"This is a pretty mess I've left you with, isn't it?" The Traveler speaks from behind his back. They are seated, as they were not an hour before, their spine warm against his. "The silent treatment again? Well, I'm sorry."

"You have nothing to apologize for," he says, very quiet. He has just seen them die, and then he saw them die again.

"Well, someone should . . . And I cheated you enough times to have earned the pleasure."

He huffs, and a smile creeps to the corner of his mouth. They straighten against his back; they wanted to hear him sound so near pleased, and that knowledge curls around his heart. "Aren't you supposed to be advising me?" he asks.

"I think I've proven pretty awful at that."

He would protest, but it's too absurd to deserve acknowledgment. They know better. *He* knows better. They devoted their years to her, his daughter, his heir, granted counsel, companionship, and care; for some shred of time, they gave the same to him. If they have words, he wants them. They make him wait so long that he would fear them gone, if not for the warmth still pooled against his back.

At last they say, "Not to be fatalistic, but I don't know that I have a stake in this anymore, beyond what stake you decide you have. I want her to . . . live. By her own terms. I'm only sorry I couldn't help her more." The slightest touch grazes his knuckles. "I wouldn't mind if you made it too. But that's rather up to you."

They recede, all three of them. He pays utmost attention to the withdrawal of the one he can't see, because he is ready to expect it will be the last of the Traveler that he ever receives. The traces of each ghost become ever more difficult to attend as they are replaced by an intensity that he cannot help but perceive in full and vital detail.

She is sublime, his witch.

"And what of you?" he asks. "You didn't want me to see her—to know her. You protected her from me. Did you let me through because she asked it of you?"

She says: *I told you the terms.*

He inhales the memory, sharp as a knife against the roof of his mouth.

If you must return, then you do it in my name. Honor mine as you never have yours.

Honor who she is and what she stood for—stands for, as she is now. Witch and mother and world.

He failed her so terribly, and for that, what did they become? A dead woman and a dead man walking. He cannot persist as this. He must honor her. What she now is, what they made, and what they might yet be—

The Ronin stood and put out his hand to his daughter. In it lay the hilt of his lightsaber, the one he had fashioned to represent blood and clan, to be his, yes, but to be hers as well—to belong to all who had ever chosen to own their own souls. A legacy reforged.

She accepted the weapon with her head still bowed, but when she raised her face to meet his, her eyes were alight with gratitude.

She ignited the blade and he spread his arms before him. When she lunged, she struck true, hot and cold and driving into his gut—and he wrapped shivering arms around her hard shoulders to draw her into a deep and binding embrace. Her nose drove into his shoulder and she gasped in aborted surprise as he lurched backward, bringing her with him.

They went like that, together, out of the mirror and into the world. As they did, the great mirror, so recently healed, shattered behind her, raining down around them in brilliant splinters. And then it was gone, a broken thing, and they were alone with each other in a world left yet unburnt.

CHAPTER
FORTY-FOUR

THE TEAHOUSE SAT on a mild hill at the southeastern edge of the pilgrims' ward, which gave it a decent view of its immediate neighborhood, though it was difficult to see any of the truly enviable sights Yojou had to offer. For this reason, it had always been favored more by locals than pilgrims and tourists, and now the three old men sitting around inside it were largely left to their own devices.

One, the owner of this teashop, was sorting through his inventory on the veranda. Some of his teas had been left remarkably unravaged by the vagaries of time, and some even tasted quite good. His friend was nursing tired bones after having spent the day helping to clean out a neighbor's eatery, which had fared poorly all around. The men talked through the events of the day and caught up with one another's lives, although as far as either could truly remember, it had been only a week or so since their last meeting, rather than a week and twenty years.

Inevitably, the gossip turned to those very missing decades. How strange to think they had passed without anyone on Rei'izu around to notice. Stranger still that as far as anyone remembered, the Sith had only just cut a bloody swath through the city, and now those dark warriors were all gone, vanished like ghosts under sunlight.

"I suppose the Jedi these days are better than the ones we had," said the owner of the teashop.

"What makes you say that?" asked the third man in the shop.

Neither of the other two recognized him. He hadn't fared well during the Sith invasion; his injuries were still fresh and in need of recuperation. Despite the wounds, he was so imposing that they might have mistaken him for a Jedi himself, had he not been so tattered, and had he not introduced himself by asking if they had any droids in need of a technician.

At present, he was seated inside, in front of the teashop's power droid. He had contributed little of anything to their conversation since his arrival, perhaps due to whatever injuries demanded he wear that prosthetic and respirator. Nevertheless, his hands were deft, and the power droid had whirred to life within minutes after he'd first begun to work on it. The teashop owner was therefore inclined to like the man, and had supplied him with a steady stream of tea since his arrival.

"Well, I don't know if you recall, but when the Sith came . . ." This was turning into a bit of a neighborhood joke. As if anyone could forget that which had, by their reckoning, happened barely a week ago. ". . . they killed every Jedi on Rei'izu. Now a gaggle of Jedi apprentices break a decades-long Sith curse?"

The third man looked contemplative as he took a pull of tea. "Perhaps they were less afraid to try."

"Suppose I'm thankful either way. Oh—you're finished already? You've a gift, sir."

"It's the best thing I know how to do," said the third man.

His own droid, an eccentric little astromech in a hat, blinked at him from the veranda. A lean old woman had come to fetch the third man; one of her arms hung in a sling and she walked with a staff. As the third man sighed under his breath and went to join her, the teashop owner and his friend waved him off and bid him come back soon, to enjoy a cup without the labor he had done to earn his first.

The Ronin thought he might not mind doing so, but the tightness underlying Chie's idle expression suggested he wouldn't have the luxury.

"I thought you'd run off," she said.

B5-56 warbled confirmation. The droid would have preferred the Ronin still in bed, as he had forgone any more bacta than was strictly necessary to ensure he didn't die. Rei'izu was too sorely in need of every resource it could get, between the ones taken by the Sith and the ones ruined by time. Chie had refrained from the same help, hence the limp that still haunted her step.

"Well, he didn't run fast enough," she told B5.

"If you want me hobbled, just say so," he said.

Chie raised a brow. Their rapport had remained brittle for most of the past week. The Ronin was admittedly somewhat bewildered to hear himself bantering with her. But as they walked down the hill to an intersection with a street busy with people returning from this or that business of recovery to the safety and light of their own homes, he found it difficult to be wary.

"The children wouldn't care to see you chained," said Chie. "They think you frail, Uncle Grim."

Having stayed behind as decoys when the crew rescued the Ronin from the temple, the apprentices had been saddled with the credit of saving Rei'izu. They were busy enough being so lauded that if Chie really wanted him bound in a forgotten mountain storehouse—or, more likely, at the bottom of a river—they wouldn't have known about it until it was too late. No, his truce with Chie was real, as was evidenced by her next words.

"There's exciting news. An Imperial ship is due to arrive in, oh, the next hour or so. They haven't made clear just who's coming to visit the old homeworld, but if they've gone to the trouble to announce that someone *is* . . ."

It was no doubt someone rather important, very possibly someone who might just be able to identify the battered technician navigating the pilgrims' ward beside Chie. But if she was giving him a warning, she didn't intend to turn him in. Probably.

"You still think so little of me," she said to his frown.

"I'd say it's the opposite."

Not just anyone could put a Sith on edge as soon as look at them, let alone walk beside one seemingly without a care. Chie only smiled.

They met a brief roadblock. A small flock of rogue cloud-deer were doing their damnedest to intrude on a grocer's, and a determined flock of citizens was doing their damnedest to shoo them away. The Ronin and Chie slowed, inclined to offer assistance, though B5 sighed a complaint, urging them to keep pace.

Lucky for B5, help arrived. A voice called out to them from down an alley that ran to a parallel avenue. Ekiya was there, driving the speeder she'd restored in the landing field on their arrival. The ban on advanced technologies in the pilgrims' ward had been temporarily lifted in light of, well, everything.

"I can't believe you—were you really going to walk the whole way?" she scolded once they were all piled into the speeder. "First of all, you're all very old. Second of all, you're dying—not you, Bee, you're fine. Third, we're on a schedule!"

"Where are the children?" Chie asked.

"I'm not their babysitter."

Yet Ekiya rattled off where each was, and in rapid succession. Yuehiro in particular had apparently wanted to ensure the Ronin "didn't get shanked"—Ekiya's words. "I told him he'd already visited you at the clinic way too conspicuously—last thing we need is any more rumors about some weird old guy the saviors of Rei'izu are hanging out with."

The Ronin had indeed heard the whispers that a full-fledged Jedi knight was lurking somewhere in the pilgrims' ward. He had heard just as many answering snorts, largely along the lines of, "Oh, yes, as if Jedi *hide*."

Some brief sound murmured by his ear, like the laughter of a passerby.

Ekiya had moved on to talking through a supply list. She was reluctant to take much from Rei'izu, given how exhausted their limited stores already were, so she expected that it would be best to stop at a nearby system to stock up on any additional necessities. The way she put it made the Ronin frown.

"You're leaving?"

"Were you going to fly yourself out?"

"I could."

"With that gut wound? I don't think so."

His frown deepened. Ekiya had only just returned to her home. She deserved to remain. She rolled her eyes as if she thought him not especially bright.

"Let's say you hear Rei'izu's back on the map—are you really going to take that at face value? Now? Propaganda! At best." Ekiya's hands tightened on the controls. "Lots of people are going to have to hear about it firsthand before they let themselves believe it. So I'm going to tell them. Bring them, if they need it . . . Starting with everyone whose ghosts came home first."

An odd pressure pushed against the Ronin's heart at this last; it felt, strangely, as though it came from outside himself. Someone else's feeling weighing on his own.

"She did bring them," he said. "Like you asked."

"Of course she did," said Ekiya. "Stubborn jerk."

Once he had parted ways with her and Chie—the former into the *Poor Crow* to prep for takeoff, Chie away with the speeder, leaving him with only a nod—the Ronin took his own last look at the pilgrims' ward, and at Shinsui Temple beyond. He could just see its roofs, newly cleared of snow, catching evening light from a sinking sun.

"You could talk to her yourself, you know," he said.

"Don't patronize me," said Kouru.

It wasn't at all like speaking to the voice—to his daughter. Kouru made herself visible, for one, though she didn't look like she had while alive, or like she had as a ghost under thrall. Standing under the light projected down the *Crow*'s walkway, she seemed to refract and concentrate it within herself. Where he had been interested in his last look at Rei'izu, her gaze was directed firmly up the ramp, into the *Crow*. Priorities.

"You can't possibly enjoy being confined to my company," he said as he walked up into the ship, B5 at his heels.

"I'm not," Kouru muttered. "I go where I please."

"She just likes to whine," said the Traveler.

They were already in the *Crow*, crouched on the floor at the end of the walkway, where their cat had rolled onto its belly to receive attention. Their fingers dragged through the cat's fur and it purred. Like the witch's effect on Rei'izu, their interactions with the world were unpredictably conditional, running on a logic the Ronin had yet to decipher. He had some doubts about whether he ever would.

He had a strange sense that, if he suggested it, they could play a round of shogi together. He hadn't yet asked.

"You have a look," said the Traveler. "He has a look," they said to Kouru.

She made a face of her own. "Don't involve me in this."

"Are you coming, then?" the Ronin asked.

They each frowned at him in seeming surprise. Kouru's was genuine, the Traveler's affected.

Because Kouru's was honest, she made some true effort to respond. Though she wore sincerity like an ill-fitting shoe, she spoke with confidence. "Don't make it sound like I'm going anywhere with you in particular."

"For what it's worth, I think I am," said the Traveler. Their shape had the same refracting quality as Kouru's, and in that moment they seemed to intensify, thrumming with current and flare, like the witch when she was the world. They had been a ghost, once. Now . . .

Now here before him were two beings; they were the only two of the dead who had remained. The Ronin had thought it a mercy, that the rest were now free. But it seemed to him that neither Kouru nor the Traveler regretted their fate.

"You're the only one who can really explain what in all the worlds has happened to you, Kouru," the Traveler went on, "but it seems to me that you won't rest until all those worlds have stopped making more children in your image."

Kouru slowly wrapped her fingers into a fist, studying her grip. Looking at her was for a moment like staring into a sun comprising a thousand-thousand futures—a promise of the Empire aflame, or shattered, or remade entire—but coalesced into a single, quintessentially personal need. She sniffed. "I suppose I'd like to see the Jedi no longer aspiring to be such disappointments."

"As for myself, well . . ." The Traveler paused where the hallway met the galley. "Perhaps I'll find my peace once the two of you have died more natural deaths."

This was how the Ronin learned his daughter was already on the *Crow*. He had expected as much, but it still came as a surprise to see her seated there at the low table in the center of the galley, dressed in the mundanity of flesh and life.

Her name was Mirahi. She had offered it to him only belatedly, like an afterthought, the day after he woke from the injuries he had sustained when she stabbed him.

He discovered, suddenly, that he couldn't move. Neither could he speak. He suspected Mirahi had noticed; her eyes remained on the book in her hands—stolen, he believed, from the temple—but her fingers had tensed just so.

The Ronin's hand was lifted. The Traveler had taken it in theirs. "Look at it this way," they said lowly, "you've already done the brave thing. You chose not to die. Go on, now. Live."

"You say that as if it's easy," he muttered.

"Of course it isn't. It might not ever be." They turned over his hand and raised his palm to their lips. "How lucky that you needn't live alone."

He let his palm rest on their cheek. It was damnably easier to breathe than it had been a second before. They nodded him along, and he stepped forward into the galley.

Mirahi's head rose from the book as he did. She nodded stiffly at her master, then exchanged a somewhat stiffer, warier look with Kouru. Her stiffest look was for her father, who was certain his joints creaked audibly as he sat opposite her at the table.

By the time the Ronin was on the floor, it was just them, alone but for B5; the droid whistled all too innocently as he made his way off toward the cockpit to help Ekiya's preparations.

"Wherever have you been?" asked Mirahi as she put down her book.

"You didn't know?"

"You broke my mirror, Father."

The Ronin nodded in concession, though he had to wonder: Did she still think it hers? He had been less than fully aware of the situation as they left the great temple, but he knew that he would have died had Mirahi chosen to kill him. Instead, the mirror shattered, Rei'izu burst back into sudden life, and Mirahi cooperated with Chie, Ekiya, and the children to ensure they were all safely away from the temple before anyone could ask any inconvenient questions about the large dying man and his suspiciously colored lightsaber.

It was altogether difficult to understand her motive. She hadn't yet tried to finish the job and slit his throat in his sleep. Nor had she done much of anything but keep to herself in the belly of the *Crow* and read.

"If it took me over a decade to fix, I can't imagine they'll be any faster," Mirahi said. Then she exhaled through her nose, as if she'd been caught out. She produced from within her robes a splinter of crystal— winter-clouded at the center, and clear all over. "I suppose I kept a piece."

"Bold."

"It's mine. Though it doesn't do nearly as much when it's just this." Mirahi cradled the sliver in her palm and hesitated. "It might make a good lightsaber, if the blade were more expertly constructed."

She was, he realized, asking him to teach her how to do so. This was no less difficult to grasp. He had landed himself in the most troubling of circumstances. He had little enough idea of how to speak to her as a fellow person in the flesh, let alone as . . . a father.

"You expect to need a blade?" he asked.

"I'm not about to sit back and let the Jedi go about their business, am I? Are *you*?"

The Ronin was struck silent, though neither was he without interest.

Mirahi took the kyber splinter between her fingers and examined it idly. "You brought me back to the world. I'm not very pleased with you about it, not least because I haven't yet sorted out how you managed it."

He couldn't have explained it to her if he tried. Whatever insights Kouru or the Traveler had to share, they had not yet seen fit to do so, if they even could. All he could be certain of was that the mirror hadn't seen fit to protect itself. He had a sense that it could have, had it wished to.

"All in all," his daughter said, "you've made this whole mess far more difficult to wrestle with. But the Empire, Jedi, all their nasty business . . . They can't very well go unattended. And you still owe me, don't you?"

She was, in a way, asking of him what she had when they sat across from each other at the base of her great mirror. The only difference was that she was no longer asking for his death but for his life.

He did want to give it to her. He could no longer justify the man he had been before her, no more than he could justify the man he had been before that, or before that.

Briefly, there was a whisper in his ear. It lacked the elegance of words, because the one from whom it came was losing her grasp on what it meant to convey oneself in the language of the living. Instead, his witch spoke to him through memory and want: *Honor my name as you never have your own.*

Honor the life that was their daughter, and what she might grow to do. Honor the world as it could and should be, and the life of every child, ghost, and god that sought to make it that way. Honor it with his presence. With his life. By entering the world and walking its length with purpose.

The Ronin laid the battered hilt of his lightsaber on the table. "I offer what I have," he said, and he began to take it apart as she watched.

ACKNOWLEDGMENTS

Like many young people, I was left changed by my first contact with *Star Wars*. It captivated my seven-year-old attention and refused to let go, and from that point on, I've chased its joys with a passion. My relationship with my Japanese heritage is somewhat more fraught. I had the luck to grow up in Hawaii, where Japanese culture saturates the local landscape, but the trauma of war and internment shadowed the generations before me. I learned to speak Japanese not at home but in school, and my family's history is riddled with unspoken memories.

It was therefore a gift to be offered the opportunity to devise this book. I find myself continually stepping back to admire the recursive beauty of it—that as a fourth-generation Japanese-American, I've had the chance to iterate on an American saga that is itself an iteration on Japanese narratives. I am unbearably grateful.

To Tom Hoeler, Gabriella Muñoz, the editorial team at Del Rey, and the fine folks at Lucasfilm: I couldn't have dreamed this story up without the prompt you provided. It didn't seem possible until you told me it was. Thank you for opening doors, and for encouraging me to pursue every flourish.

To Caitlin McDonald, my agent and friend: Your keen eye has helped me hone my prose for so many years. It's through your faith and encouragement that I have been able to pursue this work. I would be less human without it and without you.

To Suzanne, my accountability buddy: My IRL Jedi by whom I am consistently inspired, and with whom I strive to keep up—you help me across every finish line, and this one even more so than usual. I can't wait to cheer on your next dashing venture.

To every writer I've met in pubs and treehouses, or with whom I've otherwise wailed as we try desperately to pilot the mecha that are our stories: Your friendship, your camaraderie, and your words are my hope and indulgence. Please continue to feed me. I hunger so.

To my family: I owe this book to you. Your support has ensured I'm still here, no matter how my body may have rebelled against the idea. I am alive because of you. I hope to be alive *for* you.

And to my wife, with whom I broke up for nine hours in college until we had remedied the absence of the original trilogy in your life: You have always given so much of yourself to helping me, whether it be by providing my disorderly body rest and ease, or by insisting that I honor my right to happiness, or by listening intently as I keen, or by keeping my *Star Wars* secret, or by letting me be a wild nerd about *Star Wars* to you, or by going to every *Star Wars* movie with me on premier or as close to it as possible. I am writing, always, for you.

(And I did not put a dilithium crystal in the Star War, you troll.)

ABOUT THE AUTHOR

EMMA MIEKO CANDON is a queer author and escaped academic drawn to tales of devouring ghosts, cursed linguistics, and mediocre robots. Her work includes *Star Wars: Visions: Ronin*, a Japanese reimagining of the *Star Wars* mythos, and *The Archive Undying* (2023), an original speculative novel about sad giant robots and fraught queer romance. As an actual cyborg whose blood has been taken for science, Emma's grateful to be stationed at home in Hawaii, where they were born and raised as a fourth-generation Japanese settler. By day, they edit anime nonsense for Seven Seas Entertainment, and by night they remain academically haunted by identity, ideology, and imperialism. At all hours of the day, they are beholden to the whims of two lopsided cats and relieved by the support of an enviably handsome wife.

emcandon.com
Twitter: @EmmaCandon

ABOUT THE TYPE

This book was set in Minion, a 1990 Adobe Originals typeface by Robert Slimbach (b. 1956). Minion is inspired by classical, old-style typefaces of the late Renaissance, a period of elegant, beautiful, and highly readable type designs. Created primarily for text setting, Minion combines the aesthetic and functional qualities that make text type highly readable with the versatility of digital technology.